Morgana Vargas Llosa

MARIO VARGAS LLOSA was awarded the Nobel Prize in Literature in 2010, "for his cartography of structures of power and his trenchant images of the individual's resistance, revolt, and defeat." He has also been awarded the Cervantes Prize, the Spanish-speaking world's most distinguished literary honor. His many works include *The Feast of the Goat*, *The Bad Girl*, and *Aunt Julia and the Scriptwriter*.

EDITH GROSSMAN, one of our most celebrated translators of literature in Spanish, has translated the works of Nobel laureates Mario Vargas Llosa and Gabriel García Márquez, among others. Her version of Miguel de Cervantes's *Don Quixote* is considered the finest translation of the Spanish masterpiece in the English language.

ALSO BY MARIO VARGAS LLOSA

THE DISCREET HERO

THE DISCREET HERO

MARIO VARGAS LLOSA

TRANSLATED FROM THE SPANISH BY

EDITH GROSSMAN

PICADOR   FARRAR, STRAUS AND GIROUX . NEW YORK

THE DISCREET HERO. Copyright © 2013 by Mario Vargas Llosa. Translation copyright © 2015 by Edith Grossman. All rights reserved. Printed in the United States of America. For information, address Picador, 175 Fifth Avenue, New York, N.Y. 10010.

picadorusa.com • picadorbookroom.tumblr.com
twitter.com/picadorusa • facebook.com/picadorusa

Picador® is a U.S. registered trademark and is used by Farrar, Straus and Giroux under license from Pan Books Limited.

For book club information, please visit facebook.com/picadorbookclub or e-mail marketing@picadorusa.com.

Designed by Jonathan D. Lippincott

The Library of Congress has cataloged the Farrar, Straus and Giroux edition as follows:

Vargas Llosa, Mario, 1936–
    [Héroe discreto. English]
    The discreet hero / Mario Vargas Llosa ; translated from the Spanish by Edith Grossman. — First U.S. edition.
        p.   cm.
    ISBN 978-0-374-14674-0 (hardcover)
    ISBN 978-0-374-71157-3 (e-book)
    I. Grossman, Edith, 1936– translator.   II. Title.
PQ8498.32.A65 H4713 2015
863'.64—dc23

2014031209

Picador Paperback ISBN 978-1-250-08162-9

Our books may be purchased in bulk for promotional, educational, or business use. Please contact your local bookseller or the Macmillan Corporate and Premium Sales Department at 1-800-221-7945, extension 5442, or by e-mail at MacmillanSpecialMarkets@macmillan.com.

Originally published in Spain as *El héroe discreto* by Alfaguara Ediciones

First published in the United States by Farrar, Straus and Giroux

First Picador Edition: March 2016

10 9 8 7 6 5 4 3 2

To the memory of my friend
Javier Silva Ruete

Our beautiful task is to imagine there is a labyrinth and a thread.

—Jorge Luis Borges, "The Fable's Thread"

THE
DISCREET
HERO

I

Felícito Yanaqué, the owner of the Narihualá Transport Company, left his house that morning, as he did every morning Monday to Saturday, at exactly seven thirty, after doing half an hour of qigong, taking a cold shower, and preparing his usual breakfast: coffee with goat's milk and toast with butter and a few drops of raw chancaca honey. He lived in the center of Piura, and on Calle Arequipa the noise of the city had already erupted, the high sidewalks filled with people going to the office or the market, or taking their children to school. Some devout old women were on their way to the cathedral for eight o'clock Mass. Peddlers hawked their wares: molasses candies, lollipops, plantain chips, empanadas, and all kinds of snacks; and Lucindo the blind man, with the alms can at his feet, had already settled in at the corner under the eaves of the colonial house. Everything just as it had been every day from time immemorial.

With one exception: This morning someone had attached to the old studded wooden door of his house, at the height of the bronze knocker, a blue envelope on which the name of the owner, DON FELÍCITO YANAQUÉ, was clearly written in capital letters. As far as he could recall, it was the first time anyone had left him a letter hanging this way, like a judicial notice or a fine. Normally the mailman would slide a letter through the slot in the door. He took down the letter, opened the envelope, and began to read, moving his lips as he did so.

Señor Yanaqué:
The fact that your Narihualá Transport Company is doing so well is a source of pride for Piura and Piurans. But

also a risk, since every successful business is at risk of being ravaged and vandalized by resentful, envious people and other undesirable types, and as you know very well, we have plenty of them here. But don't worry. Our organization will take care of protecting Narihualá Transport, along with you and your worthy family, against any accident, unpleasantness, or threat from criminal elements. Our compensation for this work is $500 a month (a modest sum to protect your inheritance, as you can see). We'll contact you soon regarding forms of payment.

There's no need for us to emphasize the importance of your utmost discretion with regard to this matter. Everything should be kept strictly between us.

May God keep you.

Instead of a signature, the letter had a rough drawing of what seemed to be a spider.

Don Felícito read it a few more times. The letter, covered in ink-blots, was written in an irregular hand. He was surprised, amused, and had the vague feeling it was a joke in bad taste. He crumpled the letter and envelope and was about to toss them into the trash basket at Lucindo the blind man's corner. But then he changed his mind, smoothed it out, and put it in his pocket.

There were a dozen blocks between his house on Calle Arequipa and his office on Avenida Sánchez Cerro. He usually used this time to prepare for the day's appointments as he walked, but today he also turned over in his mind the letter with the spider. Should he take it seriously? Go to the police and file a complaint? The blackmailers said they'd get in touch regarding "forms of payment." Would it be better to wait until they did before going to the police? Maybe it was nothing but an idle joke intended to harass him. It was certainly true that for some time now crime had been on the rise in Piura: break-ins, muggings, and even kidnappings, people said, settled quietly by the families of white children in El Chipe and Los Ejidos. He felt unsettled and indecisive, but he was sure about at least one thing: Under no circumstances and not for any reason would he give a cent to those gangsters. And once again, as he had so many times in his life, Felícito recalled his father's dying words: "Never let anybody walk all over you, son. This advice is the only inheritance you'll have." He'd paid attention and never let anybody walk all over him. And with more than fifty years behind him, he was too old now to change his ways. He was so caught up in these thoughts that he barely nodded a greeting to Joaquín Ramos, the reciter of poetry, and walked even faster; on other occasions he would stop to exchange a few words with that unrepentant bohemian, who had probably spent the night in some dive and was only now going home, his eyes glassy, wearing his usual monocle and tugging at the young she-goat he called his gazelle.

When he reached the offices of the Narihualá Transport Company, the buses to Sullana, Talara, Tumbes, Chulucanas, Morropón, Catacaos, La Unión, Sechura, and Bayóvar had already left, on schedule, all with a good number of passengers, as had the jitneys to Chiclayo and the vans to Paita. There was a handful of people dispatching packages or verifying the schedules of the afternoon buses and jitneys. His secretary, Josefita of the broad hips, flirtatious eyes, and low-cut blouses, had already placed the list of the day's appointments and commitments on his desk, along with the thermos of coffee he'd drink throughout the morning until it was time for lunch.

"What's wrong, Boss?" she greeted him. "Why that face? Did you have bad dreams last night?"

"Minor problems," he replied as he took off his hat and jacket, hung them on the rack, and sat down. But he stood up immediately and put them on again, as if he'd remembered something very urgent.

"I'll be back soon," he said to his secretary on his way to the door. "I'm going to the police station to file a complaint."

"Did thieves break in?" Josefita's large, lively, protruding eyes opened wide. "It happens all the time in Piura nowadays."

"No, no, I'll tell you about it later."

With resolute steps, Felícito headed for the police station a few blocks from his office, right on Avenida Sánchez Cerro. It was still early and the heat was tolerable, but he knew that in less than an hour these sidewalks lined with travel agencies and transport companies would begin to swelter, and he'd go back to the office in a sweat. Miguel and Tiburcio, his sons, had often told him he was crazy to always wear a jacket, vest, and hat in a city where everyone, rich or poor, spent the entire year in shirtsleeves or a guayabera. But since he had founded Narihualá Transport, the pride of his life, he had never abandoned those items meant to preserve propriety; winter or summer he always wore a hat, jacket, vest, and tie with its miniature knot. He was a small, very thin man, frugal and hardworking, who, in Yapatera, where he was born, and in Chulucanas, where he attended elementary school, had never worn shoes. He began to only when his father brought him to Piura. He was fifty-five years old and had maintained his health, industriousness, and agility. He thought his good physical condition was due to the morning qigong exercises his late friend, the storekeeper Lau, had taught him. It was the only sport he'd ever engaged in besides walking, if those slow-motion movements that were, more than an exercise for the muscles, a distinctive, scientific way of breathing, could be called a sport. By the time he reached the police station he was furious. Joke or no joke, whoever wrote that letter was making him waste his morning.

The interior of the station was an oven, and since all the windows were closed, the light was very dim. There was a fan at the entrance, but it wasn't working. The police officer at the reception desk, a beardless young man, asked how he could help him.

"I'd like to speak to the chief, please," said Felícito, handing him his card.

"He's on vacation for a few days," the officer explained. "If you like, Sergeant Lituma can take care of you. He's in charge of the station for now."

"I'll talk to him, then. Thank you."

He had to wait a quarter of an hour before the sergeant deigned to see him. By the time the officer had him go into the small cubicle, Felícito's handkerchief was soaked from wiping his forehead so often. The sergeant didn't stand to greet him. He extended a plump, damp hand and indicated the empty chair across from him. He was a stocky man, tending toward fat, with narrow, affable eyes and the beginnings of a double chin that he rubbed from time to time with affection. The khaki shirt of his uniform was unbuttoned and had circles of perspiration under the arms. On the small desk was a fan that did work. Felícito was grateful for the gust of cool air that caressed his face.

"How can I help you, Señor Yanaqué?"

"I just found this letter. It was stuck to my front door."

He watched Sergeant Lituma put on a pair of glasses that made him look like a shyster lawyer and, with a tranquil expression, read the letter.

"Well, well," he said finally, making a face that Felícito couldn't interpret. "This is the result of progress, sir."

When he saw the trucker's confusion, he shook the letter in his hand and explained. "When Piura was a poor city, these things didn't happen. Who would have thought back then to demand money from a businessman? Now that there's money around, the smart guys play rough and try to make hay while the sun shines. The Ecuadorans are to blame. They distrust their government and bring their capital here to invest it. They're using us Piurans to stuff their pockets."

"That's no consolation, Sergeant. Besides, listening to you, it would seem like a problem that things are going well now in Piura—"

"I didn't say that," the sergeant interrupted him quickly. "It's just that everything has its price in this life. This is the price of progress."

The sergeant shook the letter with the spider in the air again, and it seemed to Felícito Yanaqué that his dark, plump face was mocking him. A yellow-green light, like the one in the eyes of iguanas, flashed in the sergeant's eyes. At the back of the station he could hear a voice shouting, "The best asses in Peru are here in Piura! I'll swear to that, damn it!" The sergeant smiled and raised his finger to his temple. A very serious Felícito felt claustrophobic. There was barely room for the two of them between the grimy wooden partitions covered with announcements, memos, photos, and newspaper clippings. The office smelled of sweat and age.

"The son of a bitch who wrote this is a good speller," the sergeant declared, looking at the letter again. "At least I don't see any grammatical mistakes."

Felícito felt his blood boil.

"I'm not good at grammar and I don't think that matters very much," he muttered with a certain tone of protest. "What do you think's going to happen now?"

"For the moment, nothing," the sergeant replied, not changing his expression. "I'll take your information, just in case. Maybe things won't go beyond this letter. Somebody has a grudge and wants to give you a hard time. Or maybe they're serious. It says they'll contact you about payments. If they do, come back and we'll see."

"You don't seem to think it's very serious," Felícito protested.

"For the moment it isn't," the sergeant admitted with a shrug. "This is only a crumpled piece of paper, Señor Yanaqué. It might be nothing but bullshit. But if it becomes serious, the police will act, I assure you. Well, let's get down to business."

It took a while for Felícito to recite his personal and business information. Sergeant Lituma wrote everything down in a green notebook, using a pencil stub he kept wetting in his mouth. The trucker answered the questions, which seemed useless to him, growing increasingly disheartened. Coming here to file a complaint had been a waste of time. This cop wouldn't do anything. Besides, didn't everybody say the police were the most corrupt of the public institutions? The letter with the spider had probably come from this foul-smelling cave. When Lituma said the letter had to remain in the police station as proof of the charge, Felícito made a gesture of annoyance.

"I'll want to make a photocopy first."

"We don't have a photocopier here," the sergeant said, indicating with his eyes the Franciscan austerity of the station. "Lots of places on the avenue make copies. Just go and come right back, sir. I'll wait for you here."

Felícito went out to Avenida Sánchez Cerro and found what he was looking for near the General Market. He had to wait while some engineers made copies of a pile of blueprints, and he decided he would not submit to more of the sergeant's questions. He handed the copy of the letter to the young officer at the reception desk, and instead of returning to his office plunged again into the center of the city filled with people, horns, heat, loudspeakers, mototaxis, cars, and noisy trolleys. He crossed Avenida Grau, walked in the shade of the tamarinds on the Plaza de Armas, resisted the temptation to have a frozen fruit drink at El Chalán, and headed for La Gallinacera, the old slaughterhouse district along the river where he'd spent his adolescence. He prayed that Adelaida would be in her little shop. It would do him good to talk to her. She'd raise his spirits and, who knows, the holy woman might even give him some good advice. The heat was at its height and it wasn't even ten o'clock. He felt the dampness on his forehead and a spot that was burning hot on the back of his neck. He walked quickly, taking short, fast steps, bumping into the people who crowded the narrow sidewalks that smelled of piss and fried food. A radio at top volume blared the salsa number "Merecumbé."

Felícito sometimes told himself—and had even said so on occasion to his wife, Gertrudis, and to his children—that God, to reward his lifelong efforts and sacrifices, had placed two people in his path, the grocer Lau and the holy woman Adelaida. Without them, things wouldn't have gone well for him in business, his transport company wouldn't have moved forward, he wouldn't have created a respectable family or enjoyed his robust good health. He'd never had many friends. Ever since poor Lau had been carried off to the next world by an intestinal infection, he had only Adelaida. Fortunately, she was there, at the counter of her small shop that sold herbs, figures of saints, notions, and odds and ends, looking at photographs in a magazine.

"Hello, Adelaida," he said, extending his hand. "Gimme five. I'm glad to see you."

She was an ageless mulatta, short, fat-bottomed, big-breasted, who walked barefoot on the dirt floor of her shop; her long, curly hair hung loose to her shoulders, and she was wearing her usual coarse, clay-colored tunic or habit that fell to her ankles. She had enormous eyes and a gaze that seemed to bore into rather than look at you, softened by an amiable expression that gave people confidence.

"If you've come to visit me, something bad's happened or's gonna happen to you." Adelaida laughed and patted his back. "So what's your problem, Felícito?"

He handed her the letter.

"They left it on my front door this morning. I don't know what to do. I filed a complaint at the police station, but I think it was a waste of time. The cop I talked to didn't pay much attention to me."

Adelaida touched the letter and smelled it, inhaling deeply as if it were perfume. Then she raised it to her mouth and Felícito thought she actually tasted an edge of the paper.

"Read it to me, Felícito," she said, giving it back to him. "I can see it's not a love letter, hey waddya think."

She listened very seriously as he read her the letter. When he finished, she made a mocking pout and spread her arms. "Waddya want me to say, baby?"

"Tell me if this thing is serious, Adelaida. If I ought to worry or not. Or if it's just a lousy trick. Clear this up for me, please."

The holy woman gave a laugh that shook her entire hefty body hidden beneath the wide mud-colored tunic.

"I'm not God—I don't know those things," she exclaimed, raising and lowering her shoulders and fluttering her hands.

"Your inspiration doesn't tell you anything, Adelaida? In the twenty-five years I know you, you never gave me bad advice. It's always useful. I don't know what my life would've been without you, comadre. Can't you tell me something now?"

"No, baby, nothing," Adelaida said, pretending to be sad. "No inspiration comes to me. I'm sorry, Felícito."

"Well, what can you do," the businessman said, taking out his wallet. "When it's not there, it's not there."

"Waddya giving me money for if I couldn't give you advice?" Adelaida protested. But in the end she slipped the twenty-sol bill that Felícito insisted she accept into her pocket.

"Can I sit here for a while in the shade? I'm worn out with so much running around, Adelaida."

"Sit down and rest, baby. I'll bring you a glass of nice cool water fresh from the filtering stone. Just make yourself comfortable."

While Adelaida went to the rear of the store and then came back, Felícito examined in the half-light the silvery cobwebs hanging from the ceiling, the ancient shelves with packets of parsley, rosemary, coriander, and mint, and boxes of nails, screws, seeds, eyelets, and buttons, the prints and images of the Virgin, of Christ, of male and female saints and holy men and women cut from magazines and newspapers, some with lit candles in front of them and others with adornments—rosaries, amulets, and wax or paper flowers. It was because of those images that in Piura she was called a holy woman, but in the quarter century he'd known her, Adelaida had never seemed very religious to Felícito. He'd never seen her at Mass, for example. And people said the parish priests considered her a witch. Sometimes the street kids shouted at her: Witch! Witch! It wasn't true, she didn't do witchcraft like so many sharp-witted *cholas* in Catacaos and La Legua who sold potions for falling in love, falling out of love, or bringing bad luck, or the medicine men from Huancabamba who passed a guinea pig over the infirm, or the ones in Las Huaringas who thrust their hands into the afflicted, who paid them to be free of their ailments. Adelaida wasn't even a professional fortune-teller. She did that work only occasionally and only with friends and acquaintances, not charging them a cent. Though if they insisted, she'd keep the little gifts they were moved to give her. Felícito's wife and sons (as well as Mabel) mocked him for the blind faith he had in Adelaida's inspirations and advice. He not only believed her; he'd become fond of her. He regretted her solitude and her poverty. She had no husband or family he knew of; she was always alone but seemed content with her hermit's life.

He'd seen her for the first time a quarter of a century earlier, when he was an interprovincial truck driver and didn't have his transport company yet, though he dreamed night and day about owning one. It happened at kilometer 50 on the Pan-American Highway, in one of those settlements where bus drivers, truck drivers, and jitney drivers always stopped to have chicken soup, coffee, a shot of chicha, and a sandwich before facing the long, burning-hot run through the Olmos desert filled with dust and stones, devoid of towns, without a single gas station or repair shop in the event of an accident. Adelaida, who already wore the mud-colored tunic that would always be her only article of clothing, had one of the stands that sold dried meat and soft drinks. Felícito was driving a truck loaded with bales of cotton from Casa Romero to Trujillo, traveling alone because his helper had backed out of the run at the last minute when Hospital Obrero informed him that his mother had fallen very ill and might pass at any moment. He was eating a tamale, sitting at Adelaida's counter, when he noticed her giving him a strange look with her deep-set, piercing eyes. Hey waddya think, what was the matter with the woman? Her face was contorted. She looked frightened.

"What's wrong, Señora Adelaida? Why are you looking at me like that, like you suspected something?"

She didn't say anything. She continued to stare at him with her large, dark eyes and made a face that showed repugnance or fear, sucking in her cheeks and wrinkling her brow.

"Do you feel sick?" an uncomfortable Felícito asked.

"Better if you don't get in that truck," she said finally in a hoarse voice, as if making a great effort to control her tongue and throat. She gestured with her hand toward the red truck Felícito had parked at the side of the road.

"Don't get in my truck?" he repeated, disconcerted. "And why not, if you don't mind my asking?"

Adelaida moved her eyes away from him for a moment to look to either side, as if she were afraid that the other drivers, customers, or owners of the shops and bars in the vicinity, might hear her.

"I have an inspiration," she said, lowering her voice, her face still upset. "I can't explain it to you. Just believe what I'm telling you, please. Better if you don't get in that truck."

"I appreciate your advice, señora, and I'm sure you mean well. But I have to earn my bread. I'm a driver, I make my living with trucks, Doña Adelaida. How would I feed my wife and two little boys if I didn't?"

"Then at least be very careful," the woman begged, lowering her eyes. "Listen to me."

"I'll do that, señora. I promise. I always am."

An hour and a half later, at a curve on the unpaved road, the bus from La Cruz de Chalpón came skidding and screeching out of a thick, grayish-yellow cloud of dust and hit his truck with a great clamor of metal, brakes, shouts, and squealing tires. Felícito had good reflexes and managed to swerve, turning the front part of the truck out of the way, so that the bus crashed into the chute and cargo, which saved his life. But until the bones in his back, shoulder, and right leg healed, he was immobilized in a sheath of plaster that not only hurt but also caused a maddening itch. When he was finally able to drive again, the first thing he did was go to kilometer 50. Señora Adelaida recognized him right away.

"Well, well, I'm glad you're better now. The usual tamale and a soda?"

"I beg you, Señora Adelaida, for the sake of what you love best, tell me how you knew the bus from La Cruz de Chalpón would run into me. It's all I think about ever since it happened. Are you a witch, a saint, or what?"

He saw her turn pale, and she didn't know what to do with her hands. She lowered her head in confusion.

"I didn't know anything about that," she stammered, not looking at him, as if she'd been accused of something very serious. "I just had an inspiration, that's all. It happens sometimes, I never know why. And hey waddya think, I don't want it to happen, I swear. It's a curse that's fallen on me. I don't like it that Almighty God made me like this. I pray every day for Him to take back this gift He gave me. It's something terrible, believe me. It makes me feel like I'm to blame for all the bad things that happen to people."

"But what did you see, señora? Why did you tell me that morning it would be better not to get into my truck?"

"I didn't see anything, I never see the things that are going to happen. Didn't I tell you that? I just had an inspiration that if you got into that truck, something could happen to you. I didn't know what. I never know what it is that's going to happen. Just that there are things it's better not to do because they'll turn out bad. Are you going to eat that tamale and drink your Inca Kola?"

They'd been friends since then and soon began to use familiar address with each other. When Señora Adelaida left the settlement at kilometer 50 and opened her little shop selling herbs, notions, odds and ends, and religious images in the area near the old slaughterhouse, Felícito came by at least once a week to say hello and chat for a while. He almost always brought a little present— some candy, a cake, sandals—and when he left he placed a bill in her hands, as hard and callused as a man's. He'd consulted her about all the important decisions he'd made in those twenty-some years, especially since the establishment of Narihualá Transport: the debts he assumed, the trucks, buses, and cars he bought, the places he rented, the drivers, mechanics, and clerks he hired or fired. Most of the time, Adelaida laughed at his questions. "Hey waddya think, Felícito, what do I know about that? How can I tell you if a Chevrolet or a Ford is better, how can I tell you about the makes of cars if I've never had one and never will?" But from time to time, though she didn't know what it was about, she'd have an inspiration and give him some advice: "Yes, get into that, Felícito, it'll be good for you, I think." Or "No, Felícito, that's not a good idea. I don't know what it is but something about it smells bad." For him the words of the holy woman were revealed truths, and he obeyed them to the letter, no matter how incomprehensible or absurd they might seem.

"You fell asleep, baby," he heard her say.

It was true, he'd dozed off after drinking the glass of cool water Adelaida had brought him. How long had he been nodding in the hard rocking chair that gave him a cramp in his rear end? He looked at his watch. Good, just a few minutes.

"It was all the tension this morning, the running around," he said, getting to his feet. "See you soon, Adelaida. Your shop is so peaceful. It always does me good to visit you, even if you don't have an inspiration."

And at the very instant he said the key word "inspiration," which Adelaida used to define the mysterious faculty she'd been given, foretelling the good or bad things that were going to happen to some people, Felícito noticed that the holy woman's expression had changed since she'd said hello, listened to him read the spider letter, and assured him it inspired no reaction at all in her. She was very serious now: Her expression was somber, she was frowning and biting a fingernail. One might say she was controlling an anguish that had begun to paralyze her. She kept her large eyes fastened on him. Felícito felt his heart beat faster.

"What is it, Adelaida?" he asked in alarm. "Don't tell me that now . . ."

Her callused hand took him by the arm and her fingers dug into him.

"Give them what they ask for, Felícito," she murmured. "It's better if you give it to them."

"Give five hundred dollars a month to extortionists so they won't do me any harm?" He was scandalized. "Is that what your inspiration is telling you, Adelaida?"

The holy woman released his arm and patted it affectionately.

"I know it's wrong, I know it's a lot of dough," she agreed. "But after all, what difference does money make, right? Your health is more important, your peace of mind, your work, your family, your little girlfriend in Castilla. Well, I know you don't like me telling you that. I don't like it either, you're a good friend, baby. Besides, I'm probably wrong, I'm probably giving you bad advice. You have no reason to believe me, Felícito."

"It isn't the dough, Adelaida," he said firmly. "A man shouldn't let anybody walk all over him in this life. That's what it's about, that's all, comadrita."

II

When Don Ismael Carrera, the owner of the insurance company, stopped by his office and suggested having lunch together, Rigoberto thought, "He's going to ask me again to change my mind," because Ismael, along with all his colleagues and subordinates, had been startled by Rigoberto's unexpected announcement that he'd take his retirement three years early. Why retire at the age of sixty-two, they all said, when he could stay three more years in the manager's position that he filled with the unanimous respect of the firm's almost three hundred employees.

"And really, why, why?" he thought. He wasn't even sure. But the truth was that his determination was immovable. He wouldn't take a step backward, even though by retiring before the age of sixty-five, he wouldn't keep his full salary or have any right to all the indemnities and privileges of those who retired when they reached the upper age limit.

He tried to cheer himself by thinking of the free time he'd have. Spending hours in his small space of civilization, protected against barbarism, looking at his beloved etchings and the art books that crowded his library, listening to good music, taking a trip to Europe once a year with Lucrecia in the spring or fall, attending festivals, art fairs, visiting museums, foundations, galleries, seeing again his best-loved paintings and sculptures and discovering others that he would bring into his secret art gallery. He'd made calculations, and he was good at math. By spending judiciously and prudently administering his almost million dollars of savings, as well as his pension, he and Lucrecia would have a very comfortable old age and be able to secure Fonchito's future.

"Yes, yes," he thought, "a long, cultured, and happy old age." Why then, in spite of this promising future, did he feel so uneasy? Was it Edilberto Torres or anticipatory melancholy? Especially when, as now, he looked over the portraits and diplomas hanging on the walls in his office, the books lined up on two shelves, his desk meticulously arranged with its notebooks, pencils and pencil holders, calculator, reports, turned-on computer, and the television set always tuned to Bloomberg with the stock market quotations. How could he feel anticipatory nostalgia for this? The only important things in his office were the pictures of Lucrecia and Fonchito—newborn, child, adolescent—which he would take with him on the day of the move. As for the rest, soon this old building on Jirón Carabaya, in the center of Lima, would no longer be the insurance company's headquarters. The new location, in San Isidro, on the edge of the Zanjón, was almost finished. This ugly edifice, where he'd worked for thirty years of his life, would probably be torn down.

He thought Ismael would take him, as always when he invited him to lunch, to the Club Nacional and he, once again, would be incapable of resisting the temptation of that enormous steak breaded with *tacu-tacu* they called "a sheet," or of drinking a couple of glasses of wine—so that for the rest of the afternoon he'd feel bloated and dyspeptic, and lack all desire to work. To his surprise, when they got into the Mercedes-Benz in the building's garage, his boss told the driver, "To Miraflores, Narciso, La Rosa Náutica." Turning to Rigoberto, he explained, "It will do us good to breathe a little sea air and listen to the gulls screeching."

"If you think you're going to bribe me with a lunch, Ismael, you're crazy," he warned him. "I'm retiring no matter what, even if you put a pistol to my head."

"I won't do that," said Ismael with a mocking gesture. "I know you're as stubborn as a mule. And I also know you'll be sorry, feeling useless and bored at home, getting on Lucrecia's nerves all day. Soon you'll show up on bended knee asking me to put you back in the manager's office. I'll do it, of course I will. But first I'll make you suffer for a good long time, I'm warning you."

He tried to remember how long he'd known Ismael. A lot of

years. Ismael had been very good-looking as a young man. Elegant, distinguished, sociable. And, until he married Clotilde, a seducer. He made women, single and married, old and young, sigh for him. Now he'd lost most of his hair and had just a few white tufts on his bald head; he'd become wrinkled and fat and dragged his feet when he walked. His denture, fitted by a dentist in Miami, was unmistakable. The years, and especially the twins, had ruined him physically. They'd met the first day Rigoberto came to work at the insurance company in the legal department. Thirty long years! Damn, a lifetime ago. He recalled Ismael's father, Don Alejandro Carrera, the founder of the company. Severe, tireless, a difficult but upright man whose mere presence imposed order and communicated certainty. Ismael respected him though he never loved him. Because Don Alejandro forced his only son, recently returned from England, where he'd studied economics at the University of London and completed a year's training at Lloyd's, to work in every division of the firm, which was just beginning to be prominent. Ismael was close to forty and felt humiliated by an apprenticeship that even had him sorting the mail, running the cafeteria, and tending to the machinery in the electrical plant and to the security and cleanliness of the company. Don Alejandro could be somewhat despotic, but Rigoberto recalled him with admiration: a captain of industry. He'd made this company out of nothing, starting out with almost no capital and loans that he repaid down to the last cent. And the truth was that Ismael had carried on his father's work in excellent fashion. He too was tireless and knew how to exercise his gift for command when necessary. But with the twins at its head, the Carrera line would end up in the garbage. Neither one had inherited the entrepreneurial virtues of their father and grandfather. When Ismael died, pity the insurance company! Fortunately, he would no longer be there as manager to witness the catastrophe. Why had his boss invited him to lunch if not to talk to him about his upcoming retirement?

La Rosa Náutica was filled with people, many of them tourists speaking English or French; Don Ismael had reserved a table next to the window. They drank a Campari and watched some surfers riding the waves in their rubber suits. It was a gray winter morning, with low leaden clouds that hid the cliffs and the flocks of screeching seagulls. A squadron of pelicans glided past, just grazing the ocean's surface. The rhythmic sound of the waves and the undertow was pleasant. "Winter is melancholy in Lima, though a thousand times preferable to the summer," Rigoberto thought. He ordered grilled corvina and a salad and told his boss he wouldn't have even a drop of wine; he had work to do in the office and didn't want to spend the afternoon yawning like a crocodile and feeling like a zombie. It seemed to him that a self-absorbed Ismael didn't even hear him. What was troubling him?

"You and I are good friends, aren't we?" his boss said suddenly, as if just waking up.

"I suppose we are, Ismael," Rigoberto replied, "if friendship can really exist between an employer and his employee. The class struggle is real, you know."

"We've had our battles at times," Ismael continued very seriously. "But even so, I think we've gotten along pretty well these thirty years. Don't you agree?"

"All this sentimental beating around the bush just to ask me not to retire?" Rigoberto teased. "Are you going to tell me that if I leave, the company will go under?"

Ismael wasn't in the mood for jokes. He eyed the scallops à la parmigiana that had just been brought to him as if they might be poisoned. He moved his mouth, making his denture click. There was disquiet in his half-closed eyes. His prostate? Cancer? What was wrong with him?

"I want to ask you for a favor," he murmured, very quietly, not looking at him. When he raised his eyes, Rigoberto saw them filled with perplexity. "Not a favor, no. A huge favor, Rigoberto."

"If I can, of course," he agreed, intrigued. "What's wrong, Ismael? You look so strange."

"I want you to be my witness," said Ismael, lowering his eyes again to the scallops. "I'm getting married."

The fork with a mouthful of corvina stayed in the air for a moment and then, instead of carrying it to his mouth, Rigoberto returned it to his plate. "How old is he?" he thought. "No younger than seventy-five or seventy-eight—maybe even eighty." He didn't know what to say. He was dumbstruck with surprise.

"I need two witnesses," Ismael added, looking at him now, more calmly. "I've gone over all my friends and acquaintances. And I've reached the conclusion that the most loyal people, the ones I trust most, are Narciso and you. My driver has accepted. Do you?"

Still incapable of saying a word or making a joke, Rigoberto managed only to nod his agreement.

"Of course I do, Ismael," he finally stammered. "But tell me that this is serious and not the first symptom of senile dementia."

This time Ismael smiled, though without a shred of joy, opening his mouth and displaying the explosive white of his false teeth. There were well-preserved septuagenarians and octogenarians, Rigoberto told himself, but his boss was not one of them, of course. On his oblong skull, under the white tufts, there were plenty of dark spots, his forehead and neck were furrowed with wrinkles, and there was something defeated in his appearance. He dressed with his usual elegance: a blue suit, a shirt that looked recently ironed, a tie held with a gold clip, a handkerchief in the breast pocket.

"Have you lost your mind, Ismael?" Rigoberto exclaimed suddenly in a delayed reaction to the news. "Are you really getting married? At your age?"

"It's a perfectly rational decision," he heard him say firmly. "I've made it knowing very well that things will come down around my ears. No need to tell you that if you're my witness at the wedding, you'll have problems too. Well, what's the point of talking about what you already know."

"Do they know?"

"Don't ask stupid questions, please," his boss said impatiently. "The twins will go through the roof, move heaven and earth to annul the marriage, have me declared incompetent, put me in a mental hospital, a thousand other things. Even have me killed by a hired assassin, if they can. Certainly you and Narciso will also be targeted. You know all this and even so you've said yes. I wasn't wrong. You're the sincere, generous, noble fellow I always thought you were. Thanks, old man."

He extended his hand, grasped Rigoberto by the arm, and kept his hand there for a moment with an affectionate pressure.

"At least tell me who the lucky bride is," asked Rigoberto, trying to swallow a mouthful of corvina. He'd lost his appetite.

This time Ismael really smiled and looked at him mockingly. A malicious light glinted in his eyes as he said, "Have a drink first, Rigoberto. If my telling you I was getting married made you turn pale, when I tell you who she is you might have a heart attack."

"Is the gold digger so ugly?" he murmured. With a prologue like this, his curiosity was boundless.

"It's Armida," said Ismael, spelling out the name. He waited for Rigoberto's reaction, like an entomologist with an insect.

Armida? Armida? Rigoberto went over all the women he knew, but none had that name.

"Do I know her?" he finally asked.

"Armida," Ismael repeated, scrutinizing and measuring him with a little smile. "You know her very well. You've seen her a thousand times in my house. It's just that you never noticed-her. Because nobody ever notices domestic servants."

Rigoberto's fork, holding another mouthful of corvina, slipped from his fingers and fell to the floor. As he bent over to pick it up he felt his heart begin to pound. He heard his boss laughing. Was it possible? Was he going to marry his servant? Didn't these things happen only in soap operas? Was Ismael serious or was he kidding? He imagined the rumors, the inventions, the conjectures, the jokes that would inflame the gossips of Lima: This diversion would last a long time.

"Somebody here is crazy," he mumbled. "You or me. Or are we both crazy, Ismael?"

"She's a good woman and we love each other," his boss said, without the slightest sign of discomfort. "I've known her a long time. She'll be an excellent companion in my old age, you'll see."

Now Rigoberto could see her, re-create her, invent her. A good-looking brunette, very black hair, lively eyes. A typical woman from the coast with an easy manner, slim, not very short. A fairly presentable *chola*. "He must be forty years older than her, maybe more," he thought. "Ismael has lost his mind."

"If your intention in your old age is to be part of the most sensational scandal in the history of Lima, you'll succeed," he said with a sigh. "You'll be fodder for the gossips for God only knows how many years. Centuries, perhaps."

Ismael laughed openly, with good humor this time, agreeing.

"At last I've told you, Rigoberto," he exclaimed with relief. "The truth is I found it very difficult. I confess I had endless doubts. I was dying of embarrassment. When I told Narciso, that black man's eyes opened as wide as saucers, and he almost swallowed his tongue. Well, now you know. There'll be a huge scandal and I don't give a damn. Do you still agree to be my witness?"

Rigoberto nodded his head: Yes, yes, Ismael, if he asked how would he not agree. But, but . . . Damn, he didn't know what the hell to say.

"Is this wedding absolutely necessary?" he finally found the courage to say. "I mean, to risk facing everything that you'll suffer. I'm not thinking only of the scandal, Ismael. You can imagine where I'm going with this. Is it worth the monumental trouble this will unleash with your sons? A marriage has legal and economic effects. Well, I imagine you've thought about all this and that I'm talking to you like a fool. Am I right, Ismael?"

He saw his boss drink half a glass of white wine in a single swallow. He saw him shrug and agree.

"They'll try to have me declared incompetent," he said sarcastically, making a scornful face. "Of course a lot of palms will have to be greased, what with judges and shyster lawyers. I have more money than they do, so they won't win the suit, if they decide to bring it."

He spoke without looking at Rigoberto, without raising his voice so people at nearby tables couldn't hear him, with his eyes fixed on the ocean. But he clearly wasn't seeing the surfers, or the gulls, or the waves rushing to the shore and throwing off white foam, or the double line of cars driving along the Costa Verde. His voice was filling with rage.

"Is it all worth it, Ismael?" Rigoberto repeated. "Lawyers, notaries, judges, court appearances, the indecency of reporters digging into your private life ad nauseam. All that trouble, besides the fortune that this kind of whim will cost you, the headaches and quarrels. Is it worth it?"

Instead of responding, Ismael surprised him with another question.

"Do you remember when I had my heart attack in September?"

Rigoberto remembered very well. Everyone had thought Ismael would die. It had taken him by surprise in his car, driving back to Lima from a lunch in Ancón. He'd passed out and Narciso took him to the Clínica San Felipe. They kept him in intensive care for several days, on oxygen, so weak he couldn't speak.

"We thought you were done for, what a scare you gave us. Why do you bring that up now?"

"That was when I decided to marry Armida." Ismael's face had become sour and his voice filled with bitterness. At that moment he looked older. "I was close to death, of course I was. I could see it up close, touch it, smell it. I was too weak to speak, that's true. But I could hear. That pair of contemptible sons I have didn't know that, Rigoberto. I can tell you. Only you. You'll never tell anyone about it, not even Lucrecia. Swear you won't, please."

"Dr. Gamio has been crystal clear," Miki said enthusiastically. "He kicks the bucket tonight, brother. A massive heart attack. A devastating heart attack, he said. And slim chances of recovery."

"Not so loud," Escobita reproached him. He spoke very softly in the half-light that deformed silhouettes, in the strange room that smelled of formaldehyde. "From your lips, compadre. Couldn't you find out anything about the will in Dr. Arnillas's office? Because if he wants to fuck us, we're fucked. That old bastard knows all the tricks."

"Arnillas keeps his mouth shut because he's been paid off," said Miki, lowering his voice. "I went to see him this afternoon and tried to get something out of him but there was no way. I asked around anyway. Even if he wanted to fuck us, he couldn't. The money he gave us when he got us out of the company doesn't count, there are no documents and no solid proof. The law's absolutely clear. We're compulsory heirs. That's what it's called: compulsory. He can't do anything, brother."

"Don't be so sure, compadre. He knows all the tricks. As long as he can fuck us he's capable of anything."

"Let's hope he doesn't last the day," said Miki. "Because, if nothing else, the old geezer will give us another sleepless night."

"'Old bastard' says one, 'I hope he croaks right now' says the other, less than a meter away from me, happy to know I was dying," Ismael recalled, speaking slowly, his gaze lost in the void. "Do you know something, Rigoberto? They saved me from dying. Yes, those two, I swear it. Because listening to them say those outrageous things gave me an incredible will to live. To deny them the satisfaction, to not die. And I swear my body responded. I decided right there, right in the hospital: If I recover, I'm marrying Armida. I'll fuck them before they can fuck me. They wanted war? They'd have one. And they'll have one, old man. I can see their faces now."

Bitterness, disappointment, anger filled not only his words and voice but also the grimace that twisted his mouth, the hands that crushed his napkin.

"It could have been a hallucination, a nightmare," Rigoberto murmured, not believing what he was saying. "With all the drugs in your body, you could have dreamed the whole thing, Ismael. You were delirious, I saw you."

"I knew very well my sons never loved me," his boss continued, ignoring him. "But not that they hated me so much that they'd wish me dead so they could get their inheritance once and for all. And of course squander in the blink of an eye what my father and I broke our backs to build up over so many years. Well, they won't be able to. Those hyenas will be disappointed."

Hyenas described Ismael's sons pretty well, thought Rigoberto. A couple of scoundrels, one worse than the other. Lazy, too fond of carousing, abusive, a pair of parasites who dishonored the name of their father and grandfather. How had they turned out this way? It certainly wasn't for lack of affection and care from their parents. Just the opposite. Ismael and Clotilde always bent over backward for them, doing the impossible to give them the best upbringing. They dreamed of turning them into two fine gentlemen. How the devil did they turn out so bad? It wasn't all that strange that they'd had their sinister conversation at the foot of their dying father's bed. And they were stupid on top of everything else, not even thinking he could hear them. They were capable of that and worse, of course. Rigoberto knew this very well; over the years he'd often been the shoulder his boss had cried on, Ismael's confidant about his sons' outrageous behavior. How Ismael and Clotilde had suffered because of the scandals the boys had caused from the time they were very young.

They'd attended the best school in Lima, had private tutors for the courses in which they were weak, gone to summer school in the United States and England. They learned English but spoke an illiterate Spanish full of the awful slang and dropped endings of Lima's young people, hadn't read a book or even a newspaper in their entire lives, probably didn't know the capital of half the countries in Latin America, and neither one had been able to pass even the first year at the university. They'd made their debut as villains while still adolescents, raping a girl they picked up at a run-of-the-mill party in Pucusana. Floralisa Roca, that was her name, a name right out of a novel of chivalry. Slim, rather pretty, with terrified, tear-filled eyes, her thin body trembling with fear. Rigoberto remembered her clearly. She was on his conscience, and he still felt remorse for the ugly role he'd had to play in the matter. The whole imbroglio came back to him: lawyers, doctors, police reports, desperate measures to keep the names of the twins out of the articles about the incident in *La Prensa* and *El Comercio*. He'd had to speak to the girl's parents, an Ican couple already along in years, and it cost close to $50,000, a fortune at the time, to placate and silence them. He remembered very clearly the conversation he had one day with Ismael. His boss pressed his hands to his head, held back his tears while his voice broke: "How have we failed, Rigoberto? What did Clotilde and I do to have God punish us like this? How can we have these thugs for sons! They're not even sorry for the outrage they committed. Can you imagine? They blame the poor girl. They not only raped her, they hit and abused her." "Thugs," that was the word exactly. Perhaps Clotilde and Ismael had spoiled them too much, perhaps they hadn't been strict enough. They shouldn't have always excused their escapades, not so quickly, at any rate. The twins' escapades! Car crashes caused by driving drunk and drugged, debts incurred using their father's name, forged receipts at the office when Ismael had the bad idea of placing them in the company to toughen them up. They'd been a nightmare for Rigoberto. He had to go in person to inform his boss about the brothers' exploits. They even emptied the petty cash box in his office. That was the last straw, fortunately. Ismael let them go, preferring to give them an allowance to finance their idleness. Their record was endless. For example, they enrolled at Boston University and their parents were ecstatic. Months later, Ismael discovered they'd never set foot in BU, had pocketed their tuition and allowance, and forged their grades and attendance reports. One of them—Miki or Escobita?—ran over a pedestrian in Miami and was a fugitive because he fled to Lima while out on bail. If he ever returned to the United States, he'd go to prison.

After Clotilde's death, Ismael gave up. Let them do whatever they wanted. He'd advanced them part of their inheritance so they could increase it if they chose or squander it, which naturally is what they did, traveling through Europe and living the high life. By now they were grown men, close to forty. His boss wanted no more headaches with his incorrigible sons. And now this! Of course they would try to annul the marriage, if it actually happened. They'd never allow an inheritance they'd waited for, with the voraciousness of cannibals, to be snatched away from them. He imagined their paroxysms of rage. Their father married to Armida! A servant! A *chola*! He laughed to himself: Yes, what faces they'd make. The scandal would be tremendous. He could already hear, see, smell the river of slander, conjecture, jokes, falsehoods that would spread like wildfire along the telephone lines in Lima. He could hardly wait to tell Lucrecia the news.

"Do you get along with Fonchito?" His boss's voice pulled him out of his thoughts. "How old is your son now? He must be fourteen or fifteen, isn't he?"

Rigoberto shuddered as he imagined Fonchito turning into someone like Ismael's sons. Happily, his son didn't go in for carousing.

"I get along pretty well with him," he replied. "And Lucrecia even better than I do. Fonchito loves her just as if she were his mother."

"You've been lucky: A child's relationship with a stepmother isn't always easy."

"He's a good boy," Don Rigoberto acknowledged. "Studious, well-behaved. But very solitary. He's in that difficult period of adolescence. He withdraws too much. I'd like to see him with more friends, going out, falling in love with girls, going to parties."

"That's what the hyenas did at his age," Don Ismael lamented. "Go to parties, have a good time. He's better off the way he is, old man. It was bad company that ruined my sons."

Rigoberto was about to tell Ismael the nonsense about Fonchito and the appearances of one Edilberto Torres, whom he and Doña Lucrecia called the devil, but he restrained himself. To what end—who knew how he would take it. At first he and Lucrecia had been amused by the supposed appearances of that asshole and had celebrated the boy's luminous imagination, convinced it was another of the tricks he liked to spring on them from time to time. But now they were concerned and considered taking him to a psychologist. Really, he had to reread that chapter on the devil in Thomas Mann's *Doktor Faustus*.

"I still can't believe all of this, Ismael," he exclaimed again, blowing on his demitasse. "Are you really sure you want to do it—get married?"

"As sure as I am that the world is round," his boss declared. "It's not only to teach those two a lesson. I'm very fond of Armida. I don't know what would have happened to me without her. Since Clotilde's death, her help has been invaluable."

"If memory serves, Armida's very young," murmured Rigoberto. "How many years older are you, if you don't mind my asking?"

"Thirty-eight, that's all," Ismael said with a laugh. "Yes, she's young, and I hope she reinvigorates me, like the young girl did with Solomon in the Bible. The Shulamite, wasn't it?"

"All right, all right, it's your business, your life," Rigoberto said, resigned. "I'm not good at giving advice. Marry Armida and let the world end, what difference does it make, old man."

"If you're interested, we're very compatible in bed," Ismael boasted, laughing, while he gestured to the waiter to bring the check. "To be even more precise, I rarely use Viagra because I hardly need it. And don't ask me where we'll spend our honeymoon because I won't tell you."

III

Felícito Yanaqué received the second letter signed with a spider a few days after the first, on a Friday afternoon, the day he always visited Mabel. Eight years ago, when he set her up in the small house in Castilla, not far from the Puente Viejo, a bridge that had since fallen victim to El Niño's devastation, he'd see her two, even three times a week; but over the years the fire of passion had subsided, and for some time now he saw her only on Fridays after he left the office. He'd spend a few hours with her, and they almost always ate together, in a nearby Chinese restaurant or in a Peruvian restaurant in the center of the city. Sometimes Mabel cooked him a dried-beef stew, her specialty, which Felícito dispatched happily with a nice cold beer from Cusco.

Mabel took good care of herself. In these eight years she hadn't gotten fat: She still had her gymnast's figure, her narrow waist, pert breasts, and round, high ass that she still shook joyfully when she walked. She was dark, with straight hair, a full mouth, very white teeth, a radiant smile, and laughter that infected everyone around her with joy. Felícito thought she was as pretty and attractive as she'd been the first time he saw her.

That was in the old stadium in the Buenos Aires district during a historic match: Atlético Grau, which hadn't been in the first division for thirty years, took on and defeated none other than Alianza Lima. For him it was love at first sight. "You're in a daze, compadre," joked Colorado Vignolo, his friend, colleague, and competitor—he owned La Perla del Chira Transport—with whom he would go to soccer games when the teams from Lima and other departments came to Piura to play. "You're staring at that little brunette so hard you're missing all the goals." "I've never seen anything so beautiful," Felícito murmured, clicking his tongue. "She's absolutely fantastic!" She was a few meters away, accompanied by a young man who put his arm across her shoulders and from time to time caressed her hair. After a while, Colorado Vignolo whispered in his ear, "I know her. Her name's Mabel. You're primed and loaded, compadre. That one fucks." Felícito gave a start: "Are you telling me, compadre, that this delicious girl is a whore?"

"Not exactly," Colorado corrected himself, nudging him with his elbow. "I said she fucks, not that she whores around. Fucking and whoring are two different things, my friend. Mabel is a call girl, or something like that. Only with certain privileged men, and only in her own house. Charging an arm and a leg, I imagine. Do you want me to get you her phone number?"

He did, and, half dead with embarrassment—for, unlike Colorado Vignolo, who had been living high and whoring since he was a kid, Felícito had always led a very austere life, dedicated to his work and his family—he called her, and after beating around the bush, arranged a meeting with the pretty woman from the stadium. She met him for the first time at the Balalaika, a café on Avenida Grau near the benches where the old gossips, founders of CILOP (Center for the Investigation of the Lives of Other People), would gather to enjoy the cool breeze at nightfall. They had lunch and talked for a long time. He felt intimidated by so pretty and young a girl, wondering from time to time what he would do if Gertrudis or Tiburcio and Miguelito suddenly appeared in the café. How would he introduce Mabel to them? She played with him like a cat with a mouse: "You're pretty old and worn out to fool around with a woman like me. Besides, you're really a runt, with you I'd always have to wear flats." She flirted with him all she wanted, bringing her smiling face close to his, her eyes flashing, grasping his hand or arm, a contact that made Felícito shiver from head to toe. He had to go out with Mabel for close to three months—taking her to the movies, inviting her to lunch or dinner, taking a ride to the beach at Yacila and the chicha bars in Catacaos, giving her a good many presents, from lockets and bracelets to shoes and dresses that she picked out herself—before she would allow him to visit her in her little house north of the city, near the old San Teodoro cemetery, on a corner in the labyrinth of alleyways, stray dogs, and sand that was the last remnant of La Mangachería. The day he went to bed with her, Felícito Yanaqué cried for the second time in his life (the first had been the day his father died).

"Why are you crying, old man? Didn't you like it?"

"I've never been so happy in my life," Felícito confessed, kneeling and kissing her hands. "Until now I didn't know what it meant to feel pleasure, I swear. You've taught me happiness, Mabelita."

A short while afterward, without further ado, he offered to set her up in what Piurans called a *casa chica*, a permanent love nest, and give her a monthly allowance so she could live without worries or concerns about money, in an area better than this one filled with streetwalkers and Mangache pimps and bums. Surprised, all she could find to say was: "Swear you'll never ask me about my past or make a single jealous scene for the rest of your life." "I swear it, Mabel." She found the little house in Castilla, near the Salesian fathers' Don Juan Bosco Academy, and furnished it as she pleased. Felícito signed the lease and paid all the bills without once arguing about the price. He paid her monthly allowance punctually, in cash, on the last day of the month, just as he did with the clerks and workers at Narihualá Transport. He always consulted her about the days he'd come to see her. In eight years he'd never shown up unexpectedly at the little house in Castilla. He didn't want the bad experience of finding a pair of trousers in his lover's bedroom. He also didn't check on what she did on the days of the week they didn't see each other. True, he sensed that she stepped out on him and silently thanked her for doing it discreetly, without humiliating him. How could he have objected? Mabel was young and high-spirited; she had a right to have a good time. She'd already done a great deal by agreeing to be the mistress of an old man as short and ugly as he was. It wasn't that he didn't care, not at all. When he occasionally saw Mabel in the distance, coming out of a shop or a movie theater with a man, his stomach twisted with jealousy. Sometimes he had nightmares in which Mabel announced, very seriously, "I'm getting married, this will be the last time we see each other, old man." If he could, Felícito would have married her. But he couldn't. Not only because he already was married but because he didn't want to abandon Gertrudis the way his mother, that cruel woman he'd never known, had abandoned him and his father, in Yapatera, when Felícito was still on the breast. Mabel was the only woman he'd ever really loved. He'd never loved Gertrudis; he married her out of obligation, due to that youthful mistake and, maybe, maybe, because she and the Boss Lady set a good trap for him. (He tried not to think about this because it embittered him, but it was always running through his mind like a broken record.) Even so, he'd been a good husband. He gave his wife and children more than could have been expected from the poor man he'd been when he married. That was why he'd spent his life working like a slave, never taking a vacation. That had been his whole life until he met Mabel: working, working, working, breaking his back day and night to make something of his small capital until he could open the transport company he'd dreamed of. The girl had revealed to him that sleeping with a woman could be something beautiful, intense, moving, something he never imagined the few times he'd gone to bed with the whores in the brothels on the road to Sullana or with a woman he'd meet—once in a blue moon, as it turned out—at a party, but that never lasted more than a night. Making love with Gertrudis had always been something convenient, a physical necessity, a way to calm anxiety. They stopped sleeping together after Tiburcio was born, more than twenty years ago. When he heard Colorado Vignolo tell stories about all the women he'd bedded, Felícito was stupefied. Compared to his compadre, he'd lived like a monk.

Mabel greeted him in her robe, affectionate and chatty as usual. She'd just watched an episode of the Friday soap opera and talked about it as she led him by the hand to the bedroom. The blinds were already closed and the fan turned on. She'd put the red cloth over the lamp because Felícito liked looking at her naked body in the reddish light. She helped him undress and fall back on the bed. But unlike other times—all the other times—this time Felícito Yanaqué's sex did not give the slightest indication of getting hard. It lay there, small and chagrined, encased in its folds, indifferent to the affectionate caresses lavished on it by Mabel's warm fingers.

"So what's wrong with him today, old man?" she asked in surprise, giving her lover's flaccid sex a squeeze.

"It must be because I don't feel very well," an uncomfortable Felícito apologized. "Maybe I'm getting a cold. I've had a headache all day and I keep getting the shivers."

"I'll fix you a nice hot cup of tea with lemon and then I'll give you some loving and see if we can wake up this sleepyhead." Mabel jumped out of bed and put on her robe again. "Don't you fall asleep on me too, old man."

But when she came back from the kitchen holding a steaming cup of tea and a Panadol, Felícito had dressed. He was waiting for her in the living room with its crimson flowered furniture, withdrawn and serious beneath the illuminated image of the Sacred Heart of Jesus.

"You have something more than a cold," said Mabel, curling up beside him and scrutinizing him in an exaggerated way. "Maybe you don't like me anymore. Maybe you've fallen in love with some cute little Piuran out there."

Felícito shook his head, took her hand, and kissed it.

"I love you more than anybody in the world, Mabelita," he said tenderly. "I'll never fall in love with anyone else, I know I'd never find another woman like you anywhere."

He sighed and took the letter with the spider out of his pocket.

"I received this letter and I'm very worried," he said, handing it to her. "I trust you, Mabel. Read it and see what you think."

Mabel read it and reread it, very slowly. The little smile that always fluttered around her lips was fading. Her eyes filled with uneasiness.

"You'll have to go to the police, right?" she said at last, hesitatingly. She seemed disconcerted. "This is a shakedown and I guess you have to file a complaint."

"I already went to the police station. But they didn't take it very seriously. The truth is, sweetheart, I don't know what to do. The

police sergeant I talked to said something that's true all of a
sudden. Since there's so much progress now in Piura, crime is in-
creasing too. Gangs are demanding money from merchants and
businesses. I'd heard about it but never thought it could touch me.
I confess I'm a little nervous, Mabelita. I don't know what to do."

"You're not going to give them the money they're asking for,
are you, old man?"

"Not a cent, absolutely not. I don't let anybody walk all over
me, you can be sure about that."

He told her that Adelaida had advised him to give in to the
extortionists.

"I think this is the first time in my life I'm not going to follow
the inspiration of my friend the holy woman."

"You're so naïve, Felícito," was Mabel's irritated response.
"Talking about something so important with that witch. I don't
know how you can swallow all the fairy tales that hustler feeds
you."

"With me she's never been wrong." Felícito regretted having
mentioned Adelaida; he knew Mabel detested her. "Don't worry,
this time I won't follow her advice. I can't. I won't do it. That must
be what's making me upset. It feels like something awful is bearing down on me."

Mabel had become very serious. Felícito saw those pretty red
lips pursing nervously. She raised a hand and slowly smoothed his
hair.

"I wish I could help you, old man, but I don't know how."

Felícito smiled at her, nodding. He stood, indicating that he'd
decided to leave.

"Don't you want me to get dressed so we can go to the movies?
It'll take your mind off this for a while, come on."

"No, sweetheart, I don't feel like the movies. Another day. Forgive me. I'm going to bed instead, because what I said about a cold
is true."

Mabel walked with him to the door and opened it so he could go
out. And then, with a start, Felícito saw the envelope attached
beside the doorbell. It was white, not blue like the first one, and
smaller. He guessed instantly what it was. A few steps away some

boys were spinning tops on the sidewalk. Before opening the envelope, Felícito went to ask them if they'd seen who put it there. The kids looked at one another in surprise and shrugged. Naturally nobody had seen anything. When he went back to the house, Mabel was very pale, and a gleam of distress flickered deep in her eyes.

"Do you think that . . . ?" she murmured, biting her lips. She looked at the unopened white envelope in his hand as if she could make it disappear.

Felícito went inside, turned on the light in the small hallway, and with Mabel hanging from his arm and craning her neck to read what he was reading, he recognized the capital letters in the same blue ink.

Señor Yanaqué:

You made a mistake going to the police station in spite of the recommendation made by the organization. We want this matter to be resolved privately, through dialogue. But you're declaring war on us. You'll have it, if that's what you prefer. And if that's the case, we can promise you'll lose. And you'll be sorry. You'll have proof very soon that we're capable of responding to your provocations. Don't be obstinate, we're telling you this for your own good. Don't risk what you've achieved after so many years of hard work, Señor Yanaqué. And above all, don't bring your complaints to the police again, because you'll regret it. Think of the consequences.

May God keep you.

The drawing of the spider that substituted for a signature was identical to the one in the first letter.

"But why did they put it here, on my house?" Mabel stammered, clutching tightly at his arm. He felt her trembling from head to toe. She'd turned pale.

"To let me know they know about my private life, what else could it be?" Felícito put his arm around her shoulder and hugged her. She shuddered, and it made him sad. He kissed her hair. "You don't know how sorry I am that you've become mixed up in this because of me, Mabelita. Be very careful, sweetheart. Don't open the door without checking the peephole first. Better yet, don't go out alone at night until this is straightened out. Who knows what these guys are capable of?"

He kissed her hair again and whispered in her ear before he left: "I swear on the memory of my father, the holiest thing I have, that nobody will ever hurt you, love."

In the few minutes that had passed since he'd gone out to talk to the boys spinning tops, it had grown dark. The old-fashioned lights in the area barely lit the sidewalks that were filled with large cracks and potholes. He heard barking and obsessive music, the same note over and over again, as if someone were tuning a guitar. Even though he kept tripping, he walked quickly. He almost ran across the narrow Puente Colgante, now a pedestrian walkway, and recalled that when he was a boy, the nocturnal lights reflected in the Piura River frightened him, made him think of a whole world of devils and ghosts in the depths of the water. He didn't respond to the greeting of a couple coming toward him. It took him almost half an hour to reach the police station on Avenida Sánchez Cerro. He was sweating and so agitated he could barely speak.

"We don't usually see the public this late," said the very young police officer at the entrance, "unless it's a very urgent matter, señor."

"It's urgent, extremely urgent," Felícito said in a rush. "Can I speak to Sergeant Lituma?"

"What name shall I give him?"

"Felícito Yanaqué, Narihualá Transport. I was here a few days ago to file a complaint. Tell him something very serious has happened."

He had to wait a long time out on the street, listening to the sound of male voices speaking obscenities inside the station. He saw a waning moon rise over the surrounding roofs. His entire body was burning, as if he were being consumed by fever. He recalled his father's fits of shaking when he suffered attacks of tertian fever back in Chulucanas, and the cure was to sweat it out, wrapped in a heap of burlap. But it was fury, not fever, that made him tremble. At last the very young, beardless policeman returned and had him go in. The light inside the station was as dim and sad as on the streets of Castilla. This time the officer didn't show him to Sergeant Lituma's tiny cubicle but to a larger office. The sergeant was there with a higher-ranking officer—a captain, judging by the three stripes on the epaulets of his shirt—short, fat, and with a mustache. He looked at Felícito without joy. His open mouth revealed yellow teeth. Apparently Felícito had interrupted a game of checkers. He was about to speak, but the captain cut him short with a gesture.

"I'm familiar with your case, Señor Yanaqué, the sergeant brought me up to date. I've already read the letter with spiders that they sent you. You may not remember, but we met at a Rotary Club lunch in the Piuran Center, a while ago now. There were some good carob syrup cocktails, as I recall."

Without saying anything, Felícito deposited the letter on the checkerboard, disturbing the pieces. He felt that his rage had risen to his brain and almost kept him from thinking.

"Sit down before you have a heart attack, Señor Yanaqué," the captain said mockingly, pointing to a chair. He chewed on the ends of his mustache and his tone was arrogant and provocative. "Oh, by the way, you forgot to say good evening. I'm Captain Silva, the chief of police, at your service."

"Good evening," Felícito said, his voice strangled by irritation. "They just sent me another letter. I demand an explanation, officers."

The captain read the paper, bringing it closer to the lamp on his desk. Then he passed it to Sergeant Lituma, muttering, "Well, well, this is heating up."

"I demand an explanation," repeated Felícito, choking. "How did the gangsters know I came to the station to file a complaint about this anonymous letter?"

"In many ways, Señor Yanaqué." Captain Silva shrugged, looking at him with pity. "Because they followed you here, for example. Because they know you and know you're not a man who lets himself be extorted but goes to the police and complains. Or because somebody you told that you'd filed a complaint repeated it to somebody else. Or because, suddenly, we're the ones who wrote the letters, the villains who want to extort you. That's occurred to you, hasn't it? That must be why you go around in such a bad mood, hey waddya think, as your fellow Piurans say."

Felícito repressed his desire to tell him yes. At this moment he was angrier with the two officers than with whoever wrote the letters.

"You found it the same way, attached to your front door?"

His face burned as he replied, hiding his embarrassment.

"They attached it to the front door of a person I visit."

Lituma and Captain Silva exchanged glances.

"This means, then, that they have a thorough knowledge of your life, Señor Yanaqué," Captain Silva commented with malicious slowness. "These bastards even know who you visit. They've done a good job of intelligence, it seems. So we can deduce that they're professionals, not amateurs."

"And now what's going to happen?" the trucker asked. His rage of a moment ago had been replaced by a feeling of sadness and impotence. What was happening to him was unfair, it was cruel. What were they punishing him for up there? Holy God, what crime had he committed?

"Now they'll try to scare you to soften you up," the captain explained as if he were chatting about how mild the night was. "To make you believe they're powerful and untouchable. And pow! That's where they'll make their first mistake. Then we'll begin to track them down. Patience, Señor Yanaqué. Though you may not believe it, things are going well."

"That's easy to say when you're watching from the audience," the trucker philosophized. "Not when you're receiving threats that upset your life and turn it upside down. You want me to be patient while these outlaws plan something bad against me or my family to soften me up?"

"Bring Señor Yanaqué a glass of water, Lituma," Captain Silva ordered the sergeant with his usual sarcasm. "I don't want you to have a fainting fit, because then we'll be accused of violating the human rights of a respectable Piuran businessman."

This cop wasn't joking, thought Felícito. Yes, he could have a heart attack and drop dead right here on this filthy floor covered with cigarette butts. A sad death in a police station, sick with frustration because some faceless, nameless sons of bitches were toying with him, drawing spiders. He recalled his father and was moved as he evoked his hard face: the lines like knife wounds, always serious, very dark, the bristly hair and toothless mouth of his progenitor. "What should I do, Father. I know, not let them walk all over me, not give them a cent of what I've earned honestly. But what other advice would you give if you were alive? Spend my time waiting for the next anonymous letter? This is making me a nervous wreck, Father." Why had he always called him Father and never Papa? Not even in these secret dialogues with him did he dare to use the informal *tú*. Like his sons with him. Tiburcio and Miguel had never used *tú* with him. But they both did with their mother.

"Do you feel better, Señor Yanaqué?"

"Yes, thank you." He took another sip from the glass of water the sergeant had brought him and stood up.

"Let us know about any new developments right away," the captain urged him as a way of saying goodbye. "Trust us. Your case is ours now, Señor Yanaqué."

The officer's words sounded sarcastic to him. He left the station profoundly depressed. For the entire walk along Calle Arequipa to his house he moved slowly, close to the buildings. He had the disagreeable sensation that someone was following him, someone who liked to think he was demolishing Felícito bit by bit, plunging him into insecurity and uncertainty, a real cocksucker so sure that sooner or later he'd defeat him. "You're wrong, motherfucker," he murmured.

At the house, Gertrudis was surprised he'd come home so early. She asked whether the Truckers' Association of Piura board of directors, of which Felícito was a member, had canceled their Friday-night dinner at Club Grau. Did Gertrudis know about Mabel? How could she not know? But in these eight years she'd never given the slightest hint that she did: not one complaint, not one scene, not one innuendo, not one insinuation. How could she not have heard rumors or gossip that he had a girlfriend? Wasn't Piura a pretty small world? Everybody knew everybody's business, especially what they did in bed. Maybe she knew and preferred to hide it to avoid trouble and just get along. But sometimes Felícito told himself no: Given the quiet life his wife led—no relatives, only leaving the house to go to Mass or novenas or rosaries in the cathedral—it really was possible she didn't know a thing.

"I came home early because I don't feel very well. I think I'm getting a cold."

"Then you didn't eat. Do you want me to fix you something? I'll do it, Saturnina's gone home."

"No, I'm not hungry. I'll watch television for a little while and go to bed. Anything new?"

"I had a letter from my sister Armida, in Lima. It seems she's getting married."

"Ah, that's nice, we'll have to send her a present." Felícito didn't even know Gertrudis had a sister in the capital. First he'd heard about it. He tried to remember. Could she be that little barefoot girl, very young, who ran around El Algarrobo boardinghouse where he met his wife? No, that kid was the daughter of a truck driver named Argimiro Trelles who'd lost his wife.

Gertrudis agreed and went off to her room. Ever since Miguel and Tiburcio had left to live on their own, Felícito and his wife had separate rooms. He saw her shapeless bulk disappearing in the small dark courtyard, around which the bedrooms, dining room, living room, and kitchen were located. He'd never loved her the way you love a woman, but he felt affection for her mixed with some pity, because even though she didn't complain, Gertrudis must be very frustrated with a husband who was so cold and unloving. It couldn't be otherwise in a marriage that wasn't the result of falling in love but of a drunken spree and a fuck in the dark. Or, who knows. It was a subject that, in spite of doing everything he could to forget it, came to Felícito's mind from time to time and ruined his day. Gertrudis was the daughter of the owner of El Algarrobo, a cheap boardinghouse on Calle Ramón Castilla in the area that back then was the poorest in El Chipe, where a good number of truck drivers would stay. Felícito had gone to bed with her a couple of times, almost without realizing it, on two nights of carousing and cane liquor. He did it because he could, because she was there and was a woman, not because he wanted the girl. Nobody wanted her. Who'd want a broad who was half cross-eyed, slovenly, and always smelled of garlic and onion? As a result of one of those two fucks without love and almost without desire, Gertrudis became pregnant. That, at least, is what she and her mother told Felícito. The owner of the boardinghouse, Doña Luzmila, whom the drivers called the Boss Lady, filed a complaint against him with the police. He had to go and make a statement and acknowledge before the police chief that he'd gone to bed with a minor. He agreed to marry her because it bothered his conscience that a child of his might be born without a father and because he believed the story. Afterward, when Miguelito was born, the doubts began. Was he really his son? He never got anything out of Gertrudis, of course, and he didn't talk about it with Adelaida or anybody else. But for all these years he'd lived with the suspicion that he wasn't. Because he wasn't the only one who went to bed with the Boss Lady's daughter during those little parties they had on Saturday nights at El Algarrobo. Miguel didn't look anything like him; the boy had white skin and light eyes. Why did Gertrudis and her mother make him the one responsible? Maybe because he was single, a decent guy, hardworking, and because the Boss Lady wanted to marry off her daughter any way she could. Maybe Miguel's real father was some white guy who was married or had a bad reputation. From time to time the question returned and ruined his mood. He never let anyone know about it, beginning with Miguel himself. He always treated him as if he were as much his son as Tiburcio. If he sent him into the army, it was to do him a favor, because the boy was leading a dissipated life. He'd never shown any preference for the younger son who was his spitting image: a Chulucano *cholo* from head to foot, with not a trace of white in his face or body.

Gertrudis had been hardworking and self-sacrificing during the difficult years. And afterward too, when Felícito had opened Narihualá Transport and things got better. Even though they had a nice house, a servant, and dependable income, she still lived with the austerity of the years when they were poor. She never asked for money for anything personal, only food and other daily expenses. From time to time he had to insist that she buy herself shoes or a new dress. But even though she did, she always wore flip-flops and a robe that looked like a cassock. When had she become so religious? She wasn't like that in the beginning. It seemed to him that over the years Gertrudis had turned into a piece of furniture, that she'd stopped being a living person. They spent entire days not exchanging a word except for good morning and good night. His wife had no women friends, she didn't pay visits or receive them, she didn't even go to see her children when they let days go by without coming to see her. Tiburcio and Miguel dropped by the house occasionally, always for birthdays and Christmas, and whenever they did she was affectionate with them, but except for these occasions, she didn't seem to have much interest in her sons either. Once in a while Felícito suggested going to the movies, taking a walk along the seawall, or listening to the Sunday band concert on the Plaza de Armas after noon Mass. She agreed docilely, but these were excursions during which they barely said a word, and Gertrudis seemed impatient to get back to the house, to sit in her rocking chair at the edge of the small courtyard, beside the radio or the television, inevitably tuning in to religious programs. As far as Felícito could recall, he'd never had an argument or a disagreement with this woman who always yielded to his will with total submission.

He stayed in the living room for a while, listening to the news. Crimes, muggings, kidnappings, the usual. One of the news items made his hair stand on end. The announcer said that a new method for stealing cars was becoming popular with thieves in Lima. They took advantage of a red light to throw a live rat inside a car driven by a woman. Overcome by fear and revulsion, she'd let go of the wheel and bolt out of the vehicle, screaming. Then the thieves would take it, very calmly. A live rat on their skirts, how indecent! Television poisoned people with so much blood and filth. Usually, instead of the news, he'd put on a Cecilia Barraza record. But now he anxiously followed the commentary of this newscaster on *24 Horas*, who stated that crime was on the rise all over the country. "You're telling me," he thought.

He went to bed at about eleven, and even though he fell asleep immediately, no doubt because of the intense emotions of the day, he woke at two in the morning. He could barely close his eyes again. He was assaulted by fears, a sensation of catastrophe, and, most of all, the bitterness of feeling useless and impotent in the face of what was happening to him. When he did doze off, his head seethed with images of diseases, accidents, and misfortunes. He had a nightmare about spiders.

He got up at six. Next to his bed, watching himself in the mirror, he did qigong exercises, thinking, as usual, about his teacher, the storekeeper Lau. The posture of the tree that sways forward and back, from left to right and around, moved by the wind. With his feet planted firmly on the floor, trying to empty his mind, he swayed, looking for his center. Looking for his center. Not losing his center. Raising his arms and lowering them very slowly, a very light drizzle that fell from the sky, refreshing his body and his soul, calming his nerves and his muscles. Keeping the sky and the earth in their place and not allowing them to join, with his arms—one raised, stopping the sky, the other lowered, holding down the earth—and then, massaging his arms, his face, his kidneys, his legs to get rid of the tensions stagnating everywhere in his body. Parting the waters with his hands and bringing them together again. Warming the lumbar region with gentle, slow massage. Opening his arms the way a butterfly spreads its wings. At first the extraordinary slowness of the movements, the slow-motion breathing that was meant to keep the air passing to every corner of the organism, made him impatient, but over the years he'd grown accustomed to it. Now he understood that in this slowness lay the benefit brought to his body and spirit by the delicate, deep inhalation and exhalation, the movements with which, by raising one hand and extending the other against the ground, his knees slightly bent, he kept the stars in place in the firmament and averted the apocalypse. When, at the end, he closed his eyes and remained motionless for a few minutes, his hands clasped as if in prayer, half an hour had gone by. Now the clear, white light of a Piuran dawn was coming through the windows.

Some loud knocks at the street door interrupted his qigong. He

IV

The wedding of Ismael and Armida was the shortest, most sparsely attended that Rigoberto and Lucrecia could remember, even though it provided them with quite a few surprises. It took place very early in the morning, in the town hall of Chorrillos, when the streets were still filled with pupils in uniform heading for school and office workers from Barranco, Miraflores, and Chorrillos hurrying to work in jitneys, cars, and buses. Ismael, who'd taken the expected precautions to keep his sons from finding out ahead of time, let Rigoberto know only the night before that at nine sharp he should appear at the office of the mayor of Chorrillos, accompanied by his wife if he so desired, and be sure to bring his identity documents. When they reached the town hall, the bride and groom were there with Narciso, who had on a dark suit, white shirt, and blue tie with little gold stars for the occasion.

Ismael was dressed in gray, with his usual elegance, and Armida wore a tailored suit, new shoes, and was visibly constrained and confused. She called Doña Lucrecia "señora" even after Lucrecia had embraced the bride and asked her to use informal address. "Now you and I are going to be good friends, Armida." But for the ex-maid it was difficult, if not impossible, to comply.

The ceremony was very quick; the mayor stumbled through the obligations and duties of the contracting parties, and as soon as he finished reading, the witnesses signed the register. There were the obligatory embraces and handshakes. But it all seemed cold, thought Rigoberto, false and artificial. The surprise came when Ismael turned to Rigoberto and Lucrecia with a sly little smile as they were leaving the office: "And now, my friends, if you're free,

I'll invite you to the religious ceremony." They were going to be married in a church as well! "This is more serious than it seems," Lucrecia remarked as they went to the old Church of Nuestra Señora del Carmen de la Legua on the outskirts of Callao, where the Catholic wedding took place.

"The only explanation is that your friend Ismael is moonstruck and has really fallen in love," Lucrecia added. "Do you think he's senile? He really doesn't look it. My God, who can make heads or tails of all this? I certainly can't."

Everything was prepared in the church where, in colonial times, they say travelers from Callao to Lima always stopped to pray to the Blessed Virgin del Carmen for protection from the gangs of thieves who swarmed over the open countryside, which in those days separated the port from the capital of the viceroyalty. The priest took no more than twenty minutes to marry the couple and give his blessing to the newlyweds. There was no celebration at all, not even a toast, except, once more, congratulations and hugs from Narciso, Rigoberto, and Lucrecia. Only at that moment did Ismael reveal that he and Armida were leaving for the airport to begin their honeymoon. Their luggage was already in the trunk of the car. "But don't ask me where we're going, because I won't tell you. Ah, and before I forget. Be sure to read the society page in tomorrow's *El Comercio*. You'll see the notice informing Limeñan society of our wedding." He guffawed and gave a mischievous wink. He and Armida left immediately, driven by Narciso, who'd gone from being a witness to resuming his position as Don Ismael Carrera's driver.

"I still don't believe all this is happening," Lucrecia repeated, as she and Rigoberto were returning home to Barranco along the Costanera. "Doesn't it seem like a game, a play, a masquerade? Well, I don't know what, but not something that actually happens in real life."

"Yes, yes, you're right," her husband agreed. "This morning's show seemed unreal to me. Well, now Ismael and Armida are leaving to have a good time. And be free of what's coming, what's going to happen to those of us who stay here, I mean. The best thing would be if we left soon for Europe. Why not move up our trip, Lucrecia?"

"No, we can't, not while we have this problem with Fonchito," said Lucrecia. "Wouldn't you feel bad about going away now, leaving him alone, when his mind's so confused?"

"Of course I would," Don Rigoberto corrected himself. "If it weren't for those damn appearances, I'd have bought our tickets by now. You don't know how I'm looking forward to this trip, Lucrecia. I've studied the itinerary with a magnifying glass down to the smallest detail. You're going to love it, you'll see."

"The twins won't find out until tomorrow, when they see the notice," Lucrecia calculated. "When they learn the lovebirds have flown, the first person they'll ask for an explanation is you, I'm positive."

"Of course they'll ask me," Rigoberto agreed. "But since that won't happen until tomorrow, let's have a day of total peace and tranquility today. Let's not talk about the hyenas again, please."

They tried. They didn't mention Ismael Carrera's sons at all at lunch, or that afternoon, or at dinner. When Fonchito came home from school, they told him about the wedding. The boy, who since his encounters with Edilberto Torres always seemed distracted, absorbed in his own thoughts, didn't seem to think the news was so important. He listened to them, smiled to be polite, and went to his room because, he said, he had a lot of homework to do. But even though Rigoberto and Lucrecia didn't mention the twins for the rest of the day, they both knew that no matter what they did, or what they talked about, that uneasiness at the back of their minds remained: How would the twins react when they found out about their father's wedding? It wouldn't be a civilized, rational reaction, of course, because the brothers weren't civilized or rational; there was a reason they were called hyenas, a perfect nickname given to them in their neighborhood when they were still in short pants.

After dinner, Rigoberto went to his study and prepared, once again, to make one of the comparisons he loved so much because they absorbed his attention and made him forget everything else. This time he listened to two recordings of one of his favorite pieces of music, the Brahms Concerto No. 2 for Piano and Orchestra, op. 83, played by the Berlin Philharmonic, conducted in the first instance by Claudio Abbado, with Maurizio Pollini as soloist, and in the second with Sir Simon Rattle as conductor and Yefim

Bronfman at the piano. Both versions were superb. He'd never been able to decide unequivocally for one or the other; each time he'd find that both, being different, were equally excellent. But tonight something happened to him with Bronfman's interpretation at the beginning of the second movement—Allegro appassionato—that settled it: He felt his eyes fill with tears. He'd rarely wept listening to a concerto: Was it Brahms, or the pianist, or the emotion caused in him by the day's events?

When it was time for bed, he felt as he'd wished to: very tired and totally serene. Ismael, Armida, the hyenas, Edilberto Torres seemed distant, far behind him, banished. Would he fall asleep, then, right away? What a hope. After spending some time tossing and turning in bed, in the room that was almost dark except for the lamp on Lucrecia's night table, he was still wide awake, and then, seized by a sudden inspiration, he asked his wife in a very quiet voice, "Sweetheart, haven't you wondered about Ismael and Armida's affair? When and how it began? Who took the initiative? What little games, coincidences, touches in passing, or jokes precipitated it?"

"Exactly," she murmured, turning over as if remembering something. She came very close to her husband's face and body and whispered in his ear: "I've been thinking about that constantly, darling. From the first moment you told me about it."

"Oh, yes? What were you thinking? What ideas came to you, I mean?" Rigoberto turned toward her and encircled her waist with his hands. "Why don't you tell me?"

Outside the room, on the streets of Barranco, the great silence of night had fallen, interrupted from time to time by the distant murmur of the ocean. Were the stars out? No, they never appeared in the Lima sky at this time of year. But in Europe they'd see them shining and twinkling every night. Lucrecia, in the dense, unhurried voice of their best times, the voice that was music to Rigoberto, said very slowly, as if reciting a poem, "This may sound incredible, but I can reconstruct for you in full detail Ismael and Armida's romance. I know it's robbed you of sleep and filled you with unpleasant thoughts ever since your friend told you in La Rosa Náutica that they were getting married. And how do I know? You'll be flabbergasted: Justiniana. She and Armida have been close friends for a long time. I mean, since Clotilde's attacks began and we sent her over to help Armida in the house for a couple of days. Those were such sad days: The world fell down around poor Ismael whenever he thought that his lifetime companion and the mother of his children might die. Don't you remember?"

"Of course I remember," Rigoberto lied, speaking syllable by syllable into his wife's ear as if it were a shameful secret. "How could I not remember, Lucrecia. And then what happened?"

"Well, the two of them became friends and began to go out together. Armida, it seems, already had the plan in mind that turned out so well for her. From a maid who made beds and mopped floors to nothing less than the legal wife of Don Ismael Carrera, a respected, well-heeled big shot from Lima. And in his seventies to boot, maybe even his eighties."

"Forget about commentary and what we already know," Rigoberto rebuked her, playing now at being distressed. "Let's get to what really matters, my love. You know very well what that is. The facts, the facts."

"I'm getting to that. Armida planned everything very shrewdly. Obviously, if this little girl from Piura didn't have certain physical charms, her intelligence and shrewdness would have done her no good. Justiniana saw her nude, of course. If you ask how and why, I don't know. Certainly they bathed together at some point. Or slept in the same bed one night, who knows. She says we'd be surprised to learn how well-shaped Armida is when you see her naked, something one doesn't notice because of how badly she dresses, always in those baggy outfits for fat women. Justiniana says she isn't fat, her breasts and buttocks are high and solid, her nipples firm, her legs well shaped, and believe it or not, her belly's as taut as a drum. With an almost hairless pubis, like a Japanese girl—"

"Is it possible that Armida and Justiniana got excited when they saw each other naked?" an overheated Rigoberto interrupted. "Is it possible they started to play, touching each other, fondling each other, and ended up making love?"

"Everything's possible in this life, dear boy," Doña Lucrecia suggested with her usual wisdom. Now husband and wife were welded together. "What I can tell you is that Justiniana even felt a tickle you know where when she saw Armida naked. She confessed as much to me, blushing and laughing. She jokes a great deal about those things, you know, but I think it's true that seeing Armida naked excited her. So who knows, anything might have happened between those two. In any case, nobody could have imagined what Armida's body was really like, hidden under the aprons and coarse skirts she wore. Even though you and I didn't notice, Justiniana thinks that when poor Clotilde entered the final stage of her illness and her death seemed inevitable, Armida began to pay more attention to her appearance than she had before—"

"What did she do, for example?" Rigoberto interrupted her again. His voice was slow and thick and his heart was pounding. "Was she provocative with Ismael? Doing what? How?"

"Each morning she'd show up looking much more attractive than before. Her hair arranged, with small flirtatious touches that nobody would notice. And some new movements of her arms, her breasts, her bottom. But old man Ismael noticed. In spite of how he was when Clotilde died—in shock, like a sleepwalker, shattered by grief. He'd lost his compass, he didn't know who or where he was. But he knew something was going on around him. Of course he noticed."

"Again you're moving away from the point, Lucrecia," Rigoberto complained, holding her tight. "This isn't the time to be talking about death, my love."

"Then, oh what a miracle, Armida turned into the most devoted, attentive, and accommodating creature. There she was, always near her employer to prepare a chamomile maté or a cup of tea for him, pour him a whiskey, iron his shirt, sew on a button, put the finishing touches to his suit, give his shoes to the butler to polish, tell Narciso to hurry and get the car right away because Don Ismael was ready to go out and didn't like waiting."

"What does all that matter," Rigoberto said in vexation, nibbling his wife's ear. "I want to know more intimate things, my love."

"At the same time, with an intelligence only we women have, an intelligence that comes to us from Eve herself and is in our souls, our blood, and, I suppose, in our hearts and ovaries too, Armida began to set the trap into which the widower, devastated by his wife's death, would fall like an innocent babe."

"What did she do to him," Rigoberto pleaded urgently. "Tell me everything in lavish detail, my love."

"On winter nights Ismael would shut himself in his study and suddenly start to cry. And as if by magic, Armida would be at his side, devoted, respectful, sympathetic, calling him tender nicknames in that northern singsong that sounds so musical. And shedding a few tears too, standing very close to the master of the house. He could feel and smell her because their bodies were touching. While Armida wiped her employer's forehead and dried his eyes, without realizing it, you would say, in her efforts to console him, calm him, and be loving toward him, her neckline shifted and Ismael's eyes couldn't help but be aware of those plump, dark, young breasts brushing against his chest and face, which, from the perspective of his years, must have seemed like those not of a young woman but of a little girl. Then it must have occurred to him that Armida was not only a pair of tireless hands for making and stripping beds, dusting walls, waxing floors, washing clothes, but also an abundant, tender, palpitating, warm body, a fragrant, moist, exciting closeness. That was when poor Ismael, during his employee's fond displays of loyalty and affection, probably began to feel that the hidden, shrunken thing between his legs, beyond all help from lack of use, was starting to show signs of life, to revive. Of course, Justiniana doesn't know this but can only guess. I don't know either, but I'm sure that's how it all began. Don't you think so too, my love?"

"When Justiniana was telling you all this, were you and she naked, my darling?" As Rigoberto spoke, he just barely nibbled at his wife's neck, ears, and lips, and his hands caressed her back, buttocks, and inner thighs.

"I held her the way you're holding me now," responded Lucrecia, caressing him, biting him, kissing him, speaking inside his mouth. "We could hardly breathe, we were drowning, swallowing each other's saliva. Justiniana thinks Armida made the first move, not him. That she was the one who touched Ismael first. Here, yes. Like that."

"Yes, yes, of course, go on, go on," Rigoberto purred, becoming excited, his voice barely making a sound. "That's how it had to be. That's how it was."

For some time they were silent, embracing each other, kissing each other, but suddenly Rigoberto, making a great effort, restrained himself. And moved gently away from his wife.

"I don't want to finish yet, my love," he whispered. "I'm enjoying this so much. I want you, I love you."

"All right, a parenthesis," Lucrecia said, moving away too. "Let's talk about Armida then. In a sense what she's done and achieved is admirable, don't you agree?"

"In every sense," said her husband. "A real work of art. She's earned my respect and reverence. She's a great woman."

"By the way," said his wife, her voice changing, "if I die before you, it wouldn't bother me at all if you married Justiniana. She already knows all your habits, the good ones and the bad, especially the bad. So keep it in mind."

"And that's enough about death," Rigoberto pleaded. "Let's go back to Armida and don't get so distracted, for God's sake."

Lucrecia sighed, pressed close to her husband, placed her mouth on his ear, and spoke very slowly.

"As I was saying, she was always there, always near Ismael. Sometimes, as she bent over to remove that little stain on the armchair, her skirt would move up and, without her noticing it—but he would notice—out would peek a rounded knee, a smooth, elastic thigh, a slim ankle, a bit of shoulder, arm, neck, the cleft between her breasts. There never was, there couldn't be, the slightest hint of vulgarity in these moments of carelessness. Everything seemed natural, casual, never forced. Chance arranged matters in such a way that through these trivial episodes the widower, the veteran, our friend, the horrified father of his children, discovered he was still a man, that he had a live cock, a very live cock. Like the one I'm touching now, my love. Hard, damp, trembling."

"It moves me to imagine the joy Ismael must have felt when he learned he still had his cock and, though it hadn't done so for a long time, it began to crow again," Rigoberto digressed, moving beneath the sheets. "I'm touched, my love, by how tender, how nice it must have been when, still submerged in the bitterness of his widowhood, he began to have fantasies, desires, ejaculations, thinking about his employee. Who touched whom first? Let's guess."

"Armida never thought matters would go that far. She hoped that Ismael would become fond of having her near, discovering thanks to her that he wasn't the human ruin suggested by how he looked, that beneath his wretched look, his uncertain walk, his loose teeth, his poor eyesight, his sex still flapped its wings. That he was capable of feeling desire and, overcoming his sense of the ridiculous, would finally dare one day to take a bold step. And a secret, intimate complicity would be established between them in the large colonial mansion that Clotilde's death had turned into a limbo. Perhaps she thought that all of this might move Ismael to promote her from servant to lover. Even that he'd set her up in a little house and give her a small allowance. That's what she dreamed about, I'm certain. Nothing else. She never would have imagined the revolution it would cause in our good Ismael, or that circumstances would transform her into an instrument of revenge for a grieving, vindictive father.

"But, what is this? Who is this intruder? What's happening here under these sheets?" Lucrecia interrupted her account, turning back and forth, exaggerating, touching him.

"Go on, go on, my darling, for God's sake," Rigoberto pleaded, choking, growing more and more excited. "Don't stop talking now that everything's going so well."

"So I see," Lucrecia said with a laugh, moving to take off her nightgown, helping her husband remove his pajamas, each of them entwined around the other, rumpling the bed, embracing and kissing each other.

"I need to know how it was the first time they went to bed," Rigoberto demanded. He held his wife very tight against his body and spoke with his lips glued to hers.

"I'll tell you, but at least let me breathe a little," Lucrecia replied calmly, taking some time to put her tongue in her husband's mouth and receive his in hers. "It began with crying."

"Who was crying?" Rigoberto lost his concentration and became tense. "About what? Was Armida a virgin? Is that what you're talking about? Did he deflower her? Did he make her cry?"

"One of the fits of crying that sometimes happened to Ismael at night, silly," Doña Lucrecia admonished him, pinching his buttocks, kneading them, letting her hands run down to his testicles, gently cradling them. "When he thought about Clotilde. Loud crying; his sobs could be heard through the door, the walls."

"Sobs that reached even Armida's room, of course." Rigoberto became excited. He talked as he turned Lucrecia around and settled her beneath him.

"They woke her, got her out of bed, made her rush to console him," she said, slipping easily under her husband's body, spreading her legs, embracing him.

"She didn't have time to put on her robe or slippers," Rigoberto took the words out of her mouth. "Or to comb her hair or anything. And that's how she ran into Ismael's room, half naked. I can see her now, my darling."

"Remember that everything was dark; she kept tripping over furniture, guided by the poor man's crying to his bed. When she reached it she embraced him and—"

"And he embraced her too and ripped off the chemise she was wearing. She pretended to resist, but not for very long. Almost as soon as the struggle began, she embraced him too. She must have been very surprised to discover that Ismael was a unicorn at that moment who pierced her, made her shriek—"

"Who made her shriek," Lucrecia repeated and shrieked in turn, imploring: "Wait, wait, don't come yet, don't be mean, don't do that to me."

"I love you, I love you!" he exploded, kissing his wife on the neck and feeling her become rigid and, a few seconds later, she wailed, her body slackened, and she lay motionless, gasping.

They lay like this, still and silent, recovering, for a few minutes. Then they joked, got up, washed, straightened the sheets, put on pajamas and nightgown again, turned out the light on the night table, and tried to sleep. But Rigoberto remained awake, hearing Lucrecia's breathing becoming gentler and more regular as she sank into sleep and her body stopped moving. Now she was asleep. Was she dreaming?

And then, in a totally unexpected way, he discovered the reason for the association his memory had been weaving in a sporadic, confused way for some time; that is, ever since Fonchito began to tell them about those impossible encounters, those improbable chance meetings with the outlandish Edilberto Torres. He had to reread that chapter from Thomas Mann's *Doktor Faustus* immediately. He'd read the novel many years before, but he clearly remembered the episode, the mouth of the volcano in the story.

He got up silently and, barefoot and in the dark, went to his study, his small space of civilization, feeling his way along the walls. He turned on the lamp at the easy chair where he usually read and listened to music. There was a complicit silence in the Barranco night. The ocean was a very distant sound. He had no trouble finding the volume in the bookcase of novels. There it was. Chapter 25: He'd marked it with a cross and two exclamation marks. The mouth of the volcano, the most personal chapter, the one that changed the nature of the entire story, introducing a supernatural dimension into a realist world. The episode in which for the first time the devil appears and talks to the young composer Adrian Leverkühn in Palestrina, his Italian retreat, and proposes his celebrated pact. As soon as he began to reread it, Rigoberto was taken in by the subtlety of the narrative strategy. The devil appears to Adrian as a normal, ordinary little man; the only unusual thing about him is the cold that emanates from him at first and makes the young musician shudder. He'd have to ask Fonchito, as a somewhat foolish, casual point of curiosity, "Do you feel cold each time this individual appears?" Ah, Adrian also suffers from premonitory migraines and nausea before the encounter that will change his life. "Tell me, Fonchito, do you happen to get headaches, an upset stomach, physical ailments of any kind whenever this person appears?"

According to his son, Edilberto Torres was a normal, ordinary little man too. Rigoberto felt a sudden terror at the description of the little man's sarcastic laugh that exploded unexpectedly in the half shadows of the mansion in the Italian mountains where the disquieting conversation took place. But why had his unconscious connected everything he was reading to Fonchito and Edilberto Torres? It made no sense. The devil in Thomas Mann's novel alludes to syphilis and music as the two manifestations in life of his

V

The notice, paid for out of his own pocket, that Felícito Yanaqué published in *El Tiempo* made him famous overnight throughout Piura. People stopped him on the street to congratulate him, show their solidarity, ask for his autograph, and, above all, warn him to be careful: "What you've done is very rash, Don Felícito. Hey waddya think! Now your life's really in danger."

None of this went to the trucker's head, and none of it frightened him. What affected him most was observing the change the small notice in Piura's principal newspaper caused in Sergeant Lituma and, especially, in Captain Silva. He'd never liked this vulgar police chief who used any pretext to run his mouth about Piuran women's bottoms, and he thought the antipathy was mutual. But now the captain's attitude was less arrogant. On the very afternoon of the day the notice was published, both police officers showed up at his house on Calle Arequipa, affable and ingratiating. They'd come to demonstrate their concern over "what was happening to you, Señor Yanaqué." Not even when the fire set by the spider crooks leveled part of Narihualá Transport had they been so attentive. What pangs of conscience troubled this pair of cops now? They seemed truly sorry about his situation and eager to challenge the extortionists.

Finally, Captain Silva took a clipping of the *El Tiempo* notice out of his pocket.

"You must have been crazy when you published this, Don Felícito," he said, half in jest, half seriously. "Didn't it occur to you that this kind of hotheaded act could get your throat slit or put a bullet in the back of your neck?"

"It wasn't a hotheaded act, I thought about it a lot before I did it," the trucker explained gently. "I wanted those sons of bitches to know once and for all that they won't get a cent out of me. They can burn down this house, all my trucks, buses, and jitneys. Even knock off my wife and children if they want. Not one fuckin' cent!"

Small and steadfast, he said this without exaggeration or anger, his hands quiet, his glance firm, his determination serene.

"I believe you, Don Felícito," the distressed captain agreed. And he got to the point: "The thing is, without wanting to, without realizing it, you've gotten us into one enormous jam. Colonel Rascachucha, our regional chief, called the station this morning about the notice. Do you know why? Tell him, Lituma."

"To tell us to go to hell and call us morons and losers, sir," the sergeant explained sorrowfully.

Felícito Yanaqué laughed. For the first time since he'd begun to receive the spider letters, he was in a good mood.

"That's what the two of you are, Captain," he murmured with a smile. "I'm so glad your boss told you off. Is that word really his name? Cuntscratcher?"

Sergeant Lituma and Captain Silva laughed too, uneasily.

"Of course not, that's his nickname," the chief explained. "His real name is Colonel Asundino Ríos Pardo. I don't know how he got that moniker or who gave it to him. He's a good officer, but he swears a lot. He doesn't put up with any nonsense, he'll curse out anybody for the least little thing."

"You're wrong to think we haven't taken your complaint seriously, Señor Yanaqué," Sergeant Lituma interjected.

"We had to wait until the crooks revealed themselves before we could act," the captain went on with sudden energy. "Now that they have, we're taking care of business."

"That's cold comfort to me," said Felícito Yanaqué, frowning annoyance. "I don't know what you're doing, but as far as I'm concerned, nobody's going to give me back the business they burned down."

"Doesn't your insurance take care of damages?"

"It ought to, but they're giving me a hard time. They claim that only the vehicles were insured, not the premises. Dr. Castro Pozo,

my lawyer, says maybe we'll have to go to court. Which means I
lose either way. And that's that."

"Don't you worry, Don Felícito," the captain said, calming him
with a pat on the shoulder. "We'll catch them. Sooner or later, we'll
catch them. Word of honor. We'll keep you up to date. We'll say
goodbye now. And please give my best to Señora Josefita, that beautiful secretary of yours."

It was true that from that day on, the police began to show signs
of diligence. They questioned all the drivers and clerks at Narihualá
Transport. They kept Miguel and Tiburcio, Felícito's two sons, at
the station for several hours, subjecting them to a barrage of questions the boys couldn't always answer. And they even hounded Lucindo to identify the voice of the person who asked him to tell Don
Felícito his business was on fire. The blind man swore he'd never
heard the voice before. But in spite of all this activity by the police, the trucker felt depressed and skeptical. Deep down he had
the feeling they'd never catch the extortionists. They'd keep after
him, and then it would suddenly end in tragedy. Still, these gloomy
thoughts didn't make him yield an inch in his resolve not to give
in to their threats or attacks.

What depressed him most was the conversation with Colorado
Vignolo, his compadre, colleague, and competitor, who came looking for him one morning at Narihualá Transport, where Felícito
had set up an improvised office—a board on two oil barrels—in a
corner of the garage. From there he could see the shambles of
scorched corrugated iron, walls, and furniture the fire had turned
his old office into. The flames had even destroyed part of the roof.
Through the open space a piece of high, blue sky was visible. Just
as well it rarely rained in Piura, except in El Niño years. Colorado
Vignolo was very troubled.

"You shouldn't have done this, compadre," he said as he embraced him and showed him a clipping from *El Tiempo*. "How could
you risk your life like this? You're always so calm about everything,
Felícito. What got into you this time? What are friends for, hey
waddya think? If you'd consulted me, I wouldn't have let you do
anything so dumb."

"That's why I didn't consult you, compadre. I figured you'd tell me not to place the notice." Felícito pointed at the ruins of his old office. "I had to respond somehow to the people who did this to me."

They went to have coffee in a dive that had recently opened at the corner of Plaza Merino and Calle Tacna, next to a Chinese restaurant. It was dark, and numerous flies circled in the gloom. From there you could see the dusty almond trees in the little square and the weathered façade of the Church of the Virgen del Carmen. There were no other customers, and they could talk openly.

"It's never happened to you, compadre?" Felícito asked. "You never had one of those letters, demanding money?"

He was surprised to see that Colorado Vignolo had a strange expression on his face; he seemed to be in a daze and for a moment didn't know how to answer. There was a guilty gleam in his hooded eyes; he blinked incessantly and avoided looking at his friend.

"Compadre, don't tell me you . . ." Felícito stammered, squeezing his friend's arm.

"I'm no hero and don't want to be one," Colorado Vignolo replied in a quiet voice. "So yes, I am telling you. I pay them a small amount every month. And though I can't prove it, I can tell you that all or almost all the transport companies in Piura make those payments too. It's what you should have done instead of being reckless and confronting them. We all thought you were paying too, Felícito. What a foolish thing you've done. I can't understand it and none of our colleagues can either. Have you lost your mind? My friend, you don't get into fights you can't win."

"It's hard to believe you'd bend over for those sons of bitches," Felícito said sadly. "I swear I can't wrap my mind around it. You always seemed like such a tough guy."

"It's not much, a small sum that's included in general expenses." Colorado shrugged, embarrassed, not knowing what to do with his hands, moving them as if they were in the way. "It's not worth risking your life over something so minor, Felícito. That five hundred they asked for would've been cut in half if you'd just been willing to negotiate with them, I can tell you that. Don't you see what they've done to your business? And on top of that, you put that notice in *El Tiempo*. You're risking your life and your family's life. And even poor Mabel's, don't you realize that? You won't ever be able to stand up to them, as sure as my name's Vignolo. The earth is round, not square. Accept it and don't try to straighten out the crooked world we live in. The gang's very powerful, it's infiltrated everywhere, beginning with the government and the judges. You're really naïve to trust the police. It wouldn't surprise me if the cops were in on it. Don't you know what country we're living in, compadre?"

Felícito Yanaqué barely listened to him. It was true, it was hard for him to believe what he'd heard: Colorado Vignolo making monthly payments to those crooks. He'd known him for twenty years and always thought he was an upstanding guy. Fuck, what a world this was.

"Are you sure all the transport companies are making payments?" he repeated, trying to look into his friend's eyes. "Aren't you exaggerating?"

"If you don't believe me, ask them. As true as my name's Vignolo, if not all, then most. This isn't the time to play the hero, Felícito my friend. The important thing is to be able to work and have your business run smoothly. If the only way is to make payments, you make them and that's the end of it. Do what I do and don't stick your neck out, compadre. You might be sorry. Don't risk what you've built up with so much sacrifice. I wouldn't like to attend your funeral Mass."

After that conversation, Felícito couldn't shake his depression. He felt sorrow, pity, irritation, astonishment. Not even in the nighttime solitude of his living room, when he played the songs of Cecilia Barraza, could he think about anything else. How could his colleagues let themselves be squeezed this way? Didn't they realize that by giving in they were tying their own hands and feet and compromising their own futures? The extortionists would demand more and more money until the businessmen were bankrupt. It seemed that all of Piura was out to get him, that even the people who stopped him on the street to embrace and congratulate him were hypocrites involved in the plot to take what he'd achieved after so many years of hard work. "Whatever happens, don't you worry, Father. Your son won't let those cowards—or anybody else—walk all over him."

The fame the little notice in *El Tiempo* brought him didn't change Felícito Yanaqué's orderly, diligent life, though he never got used to being recognized on the street. He felt embarrassed and didn't know how to respond to the praise and expressions of solidarity from passersby. He always got up very early, did qigong exercises, and arrived at Narihualá Transport before eight o'clock. He was concerned that the number of passengers had gone down but understood it; after the fire at his business, it was to be expected that some clients would be frightened, afraid the crooks would seek reprisals against the vehicles and attack and burn them on the road. The buses to Ayabaca, which had to climb more than two hundred kilometers on a narrow, zigzagging route along the edges of deep Andean precipices, lost something like half their customers. Until the problem with the insurance company was resolved, he couldn't rebuild the offices. But Felícito didn't care that he had to work on a board and barrels in a corner of the depot. He spent hours on end with Señora Josefita, going over the surviving account books, bills, contracts, receipts, and correspondence. Fortunately, they hadn't lost too many important papers. The one who couldn't be consoled was his secretary. Josefita tried to hide it, but Felícito saw how tense and unhappy she was at having to work in the open, in plain view of the drivers and mechanics, the passengers who arrived and departed, the people who lined up to send packages. She confessed as much, her somnolent face pouting like a little girl's.

"Having to work in front of everybody makes me feel, I don't know, like I'm doing a striptease. You don't feel like that, Don Felícito?"

"A lot of those guys would be happy if you did strip for them, Josefita. You've heard all the compliments Captain Silva pays you whenever he sees you."

"I don't like that cop's comments at all." Josefita blushed, delighted. "And even less the way he looks at me you know where, Don Felícito. Do you think he's a pervert? That's what I hear. That the captain only looks at that on women, as if we didn't have anything else on our body, hey waddya think."

On the day the notice came out in *El Tiempo*, Miguel and Tiburcio asked to see him. Both of his sons worked as drivers and
inspectors on the company's buses, trucks, and jitneys. Felícito took
them to the restaurant in the Hotel Oro Verde in El Chipe for shell-
fish ceviche and a Piuran dried-beef stew. A radio was playing and
the music forced them to speak in loud voices. From the table they
could see a family swimming in the pool under the palm trees.
Felícito ordered soft drinks instead of beers. From his sons' faces
he suspected what was on their minds. Miguel, the older one, spoke
first. Strong, athletic, white-skinned, with light eyes and hair, he
always dressed with some care, unlike Tiburcio, who rarely changed
out of jeans, polo shirts, and basketball sneakers. At the moment
Miguel wore loafers, corduroy trousers, and a light blue shirt with
a racing-car print. A hopeless flirt, he had the vocation and manners of a snob. When Felícito had forced him to do his military
service, he thought that in the army Miguel would lose his rich-
kid affectations, but he didn't—he came out of the barracks just
as he'd gone in. As he had more than once in his lifetime, the trucker
thought: "Can he be my son?"

The boy wore a watch with a leather band that he kept strok-
ing as he said, "We've thought about something, Father, and talked
it over with Mama." He was blushing, as he always did whenever
he spoke to his father.

"Oh, so you two are thinking," Felícito joked. "I'm glad to
know it, that's good news. May I ask what brilliant idea you've had?
You're not going to consult the witch doctors of Huancabamba
about the spider extortionists, I hope. Because I already consulted
with Adelaida, and not even she, who can foretell everything, has
any idea who they can be."

"This is serious, Father," Tiburcio interjected. Felícito's blood
ran in this one's veins, no doubt about it. Tiburcio looked like him,
with the brown skin, straight black hair, and thin, slight build of
his progenitor. "Don't kid around, Father, please. Listen to us. It's
for your own good."

"All right, agreed, I'm listening. What's this about, boys?"

"After that notice you published in *El Tiempo*, you're in a lot of
danger," said Miguel.

"I don't know if you realize how much, Father," added Tiburcio. "You might as well have put the noose around your own neck."

"I was in danger before that," Felícito corrected them. "We all are. Gertrudis and you too. Ever since the first letter from those sons of bitches arrived, trying to extort money from me. Don't you know that? This isn't just about me but about the whole family. Or aren't you the ones who'll inherit Narihualá Transport?"

"But now you're more exposed than you were before, Father, because you defied them publicly," Miguel said. "They're going to react, they have to do something in the face of this kind of challenge. They'll try to get back at you because you made them look ridiculous. Everybody in Piura says so—"

"People stop us on the street to warn us," Tiburcio interrupted. "'Take care of your father, boys, they won't forgive his rash act.' That's what they tell us everywhere we go."

"In other words, I'm the one provoking them, poor things," Felícito interjected, indignant. "They threaten me, they burn down my offices, and I'm provoking them because I let them know I won't be extorted like those asshole colleagues of mine."

"We're not criticizing you, Father, just the opposite," Miguel insisted. "We support you, it makes us proud that you placed that notice in *El Tiempo*. You've given the family a very good name."

"But we don't want them to kill you, listen to us, please," Tiburcio added. "It would be a good idea to hire a bodyguard. We've already looked into it, there's a very reliable company. It protects all the big shots in Piura. People in banking, farming, mining. And it's not too expensive, we have the rates here."

"A bodyguard?" Felícito started to laugh, a forced, mocking little laugh. "A guy who follows me around like my shadow with his pistol in his pocket? If I hire protection, I'd be giving those thieves just what they want. Do you have brains in your heads or sawdust? I'd be confessing I'm scared, that I'm spending my dough on that because they scared me. It would be the same as paying them. We won't talk about this anymore. Go on, eat, your stew's getting cold. And let's change the subject."

"But Father, we're doing it for your own good." Miguel still tried to persuade him. "So that nothing happens to you. Listen to us, we're your sons."

"Not another word on this subject," ordered Felícito. "If something happens to me, you'll be in charge of Narihualá Transport and can do whatever you want. Even hire bodyguards, if you feel like it. There's no way I will."

He saw his sons lower their heads and reluctantly begin to eat. Both of them had always been fairly dutiful, even during adolescence, when kids tend to rebel against parental authority. He didn't recall their giving him many headaches, except for a few stunts, nothing very important. Like Miguel's accident, when he killed a donkey on the highway to Catacaos—he was learning to drive and the burro walked in front of the car. They were still pretty obedient, even though they were grown men. Even when he ordered Miguel to join the army as a volunteer for a year to toughen him up, he obeyed without a word. And truth be told, they did their work well. He'd never been especially hard on them, but neither was he one of those indulgent fathers who spoil their children and turn them into bums or faggots. He'd tried to guide them so they'd know how to face adversity and be able to move the company forward when he couldn't anymore. He had them finish school, learn to be mechanics, get licensed to drive buses and trucks. And both had worked every job at Narihualá Transport: guard, sweeper, bookkeeper's assistant, driver's helper, inspector, driver, etcetera, etcetera. He could die at peace, they were both ready to replace him. And they got along with each other, they were very close, thank goodness.

"Me, I'm not afraid of those sons of bitches," he suddenly exclaimed, hitting the table. His sons stopped eating. "The worst they can do is kill me. But I'm not afraid of dying. I've lived fifty-five years and that's plenty. I'm at peace knowing Narihualá Transport will be in good hands when I go to join my father."

He noticed that the boys tried to smile but were upset and nervous.

"We don't want you to die yet, Father," murmured Miguel.

"If those guys hurt you, we'll make them pay," declared Tiburcio.

"I don't think they'll dare to kill me," said Felícito, trying to reassure them. "They're thieves and extortionists, that's all. You need more balls to kill than you do to send letters with drawings of spiders."

"At least buy a revolver and carry it with you, Father," Tiburcio persisted. "So you can defend yourself just in case."

"I'll think about it, we'll see," Felícito conceded. "Now I want you to promise me that when I leave this world and Narihualá Transport is in your hands, you won't give in to extortion by these motherfuckers."

He saw his sons exchange a look that was somewhere between surprise and alarm.

"Swear to God, right now," he demanded. "I want to rest easy on that score in case something happens to me."

They both agreed and crossed themselves as they murmured, "We swear to God, Father."

They spent the rest of lunch talking about other things. Felícito began to think about an old idea. Since they'd left home to live on their own, he knew very little about what Tiburcio and Miguel did when they weren't working. They didn't live together. The older one boarded in a house in the Miraflores district, a white neighborhood, of course, and Tiburcio rented an apartment with a friend in Castilla, near the new stadium. Did they have girlfriends, lovers? Were they carousers, gamblers? Did they get drunk with their friends on Saturday night? Did they go to bars and taverns or patronize whorehouses? What did they do in their spare time? On Sundays when they stopped by to have lunch in the house on Calle Arequipa, they didn't talk much about their private lives, and he and Gertrudis didn't ask questions. Maybe he should talk with them, find out a little more about the boys' personal lives.

The worst thing during this period were all the interviews, the result of the notice in *El Tiempo*, at several local radio stations, with reporters from the newspapers *Correo* and *La República*, and with the correspondent in Piura for RPP Noticias. The journalists' questions made him very tense: His palms got sweaty and chills ran down his spine. His answers were punctuated by long pauses; he searched for words, denying vehemently that he was a civic hero or an example for anybody. Not at all, what an idea, he was simply following the philosophy of his father, who'd left him this piece of advice as an inheritance: "Son, never let anybody walk all over you." They'd smile; some looked at him with an intimidating expression. He didn't care. Screwing up his courage, he went on. He was a workingman, that's all. He'd been born poor, very poor, near Chulucanas, in Yapatera, and everything he had he'd earned by working. He paid his taxes, obeyed the law. Why should he allow a few crooks to take what he had, sending him threats without even showing their faces? If nobody gave in to extortion, extortionists would disappear.

He didn't like to receive awards either; he broke into a cold sweat when he had to give speeches. Of course, deep down, he was proud and thought how happy his father, the sharecropper Aliño Yanaqué, would have been at the Exemplary Citizen medal pinned on his chest at a Rotary Club lunch in the Piuran Center, attended by the regional president and the mayor and the bishop of Piura. But when he had to approach the microphone to express his gratitude, he became tongue-tied and lost his voice. The same thing happened when the Enrique López Albújar Civic-Cultural-Athletic Society declared him Piuran of the Year.

This was when a letter came to his house on Calle Arequipa from the Club Grau, signed by the president, the distinguished chemist-pharmacist Dr. Garabito León Seminario. It stated that the board of directors had unanimously accepted his application for membership in the institution. Felícito couldn't believe his eyes. He'd sent in his application two or three years ago, and since they never responded, he thought they'd voted against him because he wasn't white, which is what they believed they were, those gentlemen who went to the Club Grau to play tennis, Ping-Pong, Sapo, the card game *cacho*, swim in the pool, and dance on Saturday nights to the best orchestras in Piura. He'd found the courage to apply after he saw Cecilia Barraza, the Peruvian artist he admired most, sing at a party in the Club Grau. He'd gone with Mabel and sat at the table of Colorado Vignolo, who was a member. If he'd been asked to name the happiest day of his life, Felícito Yanaqué would have chosen that night.

Cecilia Barraza had been his secret love even before he saw her in photographs or in person. He fell in love with her because of her voice. He didn't tell anyone about it; it was private. He'd been in La Reina, a now-defunct restaurant on the corner of the Eguiguren Seawalk and Avenida Sánchez Cerro, where on the first Saturday of each month the board of directors of the Association of Interprovincial Drivers of Piura, of which he was a member, would meet for lunch. They were toasting with carob syrup cocktails when suddenly he heard someone on the radio singing one of his favorite waltzes, "Soul, Heart, and Life," with more charm, emotion, and candor than he'd ever heard before. No Peruvian singer he knew—not even Jesús Vásquez, or the Morochucos, or Lucha Reyes—interpreted this beautiful waltz with as much feeling, charm, and mischievous wit as this singer he was hearing for the first time. She imbued each word and syllable with so much truth and harmony, so much delicacy and tenderness, that it made you want to dance, even to cry. He asked her name and was told: Cecilia Barraza. As he listened to that girl's voice, he seemed to understand completely, and for the first time, many of the words in Peruvian waltzes that had seemed mysterious and incomprehensible before—"arpeggios," "skylights," "ecstasy," "cadence," "yearning," "celestial"—became clear:

> *Soul to conquer you,*
> *heart to love you,*
> *and life to live it*
> *beside you!*

He felt vanquished, moved, bewitched, loved. From that time on, at night before he went to sleep, or at dawn before he got up, he sometimes imagined himself living among arpeggios, cadences, skylights, and yearnings beside the singer named Cecilia Barraza. Without telling anyone, least of all Mabel, of course, he'd lived platonically in love with that smiling face, those expressive eyes, that seductive smile. He assembled a fine collection of photographs of her that had appeared in newspapers and magazines, which he jealously guarded under lock and key in a desk drawer. The fire had made short work of them, but not of his collection of Cecilia Barraza records, which was divided between his house on Calle Arequipa and Mabel's house in Castilla. He believed he owned every CD made by the artist who, in his modest opinion, had raised Peruvian music—*valses, marineras, tonderos, pregones*—to new heights. He listened to them almost every day—generally at night after supper, when Gertrudis had gone to bed—sitting in the living room, where they kept the television set and stereo. The songs made his imagination soar; sometimes he was so moved his eyes grew wet at the sweet, caressing voice that saturated the night. And so, when it was announced she would come to Piura to sing at the Club Grau, and the event would be open to the public, he was one of the first to buy a ticket. He invited Mabel, and Colorado Vignolo had them sit at his table, where they had a sumptuous meal with both white and red wine before the show. Seeing the singer in person, even if she was at some distance, put Felícito into an ecstatic trance. She seemed prettier, more charming, and more elegant than in photographs. He applauded so enthusiastically after each song that Mabel said to Vignolo, pointing at him, "Look, Colorado, at the state this dirty old man is in."

"Don't be evil-minded, Mabelita," he said, dissembling, "what I'm applauding is Cecilia Barraza's art, just her art."

The third spider letter arrived some time after the second, just when Felícito was wondering whether after the fire, the notice in *El Tiempo*, and the uproar it had caused, the crooks hadn't resigned themselves to leaving him in peace. It had been three weeks since the fire, and the dispute with the insurance company still hadn't been resolved, when one morning, at the improvised desk in the garage, Señora Josefita, who was opening the mail, exclaimed, "How strange, Don Felícito, a letter with no return address."

The trucker snatched it from her hands. It was what he'd feared.

Dear Mr. Yanaqué:

We're glad you're now so popular and well-respected a man in our beloved city of Piura. We hope this popularity is beneficial to Narihualá Transport, especially after the mishap the business suffered because you're so stubborn. It would be better for you to accept the lessons of reality and be pragmatic instead of remaining as obstinate as a mule. We wouldn't want you to suffer another loss even more serious than the last. That's why we invite you to be flexible and attend to our requirements.

Like the rest of Piura, we're aware of the notice you published in *El Tiempo*. We feel no rancor toward you. What is more, we understand your decision to place the notice, giving in to a temperamental fit of rage, in view of the fire that destroyed your offices. We've forgotten it, you forget it too, and we'll start again from zero.

We're giving you two weeks—fourteen days, counting from today—to use your reason and reconsider, so that we can resolve the matter that concerns us. If you don't, you can be certain of the consequences. They'll be more serious than anything you've suffered so far. A word to the wise, as the saying goes, Señor Yanaqué.

May God keep you.

This time the letter was typed, but the signature was the same drawing in blue ink found in the two earlier ones: a spider with five long legs and a dot in the center that represented the head.

"Do you feel sick, Don Felícito? Don't tell me it's another of those letters," his secretary said.

Her boss had lowered his arms and seemed to have collapsed into his chair, very pale, his eyes staring at the piece of paper. Finally he nodded and brought his finger to his mouth, indicating that she should be silent. The people in the garage didn't need to know. He asked for a glass of water and drank it slowly, making an effort to control the anxiety that had overwhelmed him. His heart felt agitated and it was difficult to breathe. Naturally those bastards hadn't stopped, naturally they hadn't changed their tune. But they were wrong if they thought Felícito Yanaqué would give in. He felt rage, hatred, a fury that made him tremble. Perhaps Miguel and Tiburcio were right. Not about the bodyguard, of course, he'd never throw his dough away on something like that. But maybe about the revolver. Nothing in this life would give him as much pleasure as shooting them, if those shits ever came within range. Riddle them with bullets and even spit on their corpses.

When he'd calmed down a little, he walked very quickly to the police station, but Captain Silva and Sergeant Lituma weren't there. They'd gone out to lunch and would be back at about four. He sat in a cafeteria on Avenida Sánchez Cerro and ordered an ice-cold soda. Two women approached to shake his hand. They admired him, he was an example and an inspiration for all Piurans. They said goodbye and gave him their blessing. He thanked them with a smile. "The truth is, right now I don't feel like a hero at all," he thought. "More like a prick. A real asshole, that's what I am. They're playing with me, having their fun, and I can't find my way out of this damn mess."

He was returning to his office, walking slowly along the high sidewalks of the avenue, surrounded by noisy mototaxis, cyclists, and pedestrians, when in the midst of his dejection he felt a sudden, overwhelming desire to see Mabel. See her, talk to her, maybe feel his desire gradually waking, a disturbance that for a few moments would make him dizzy, make him forget about the fire, and Dr. Castro Pozo's ongoing quarrels with the insurance company, and the latest spider letter. And maybe, after taking his pleasure, he might be able to sleep for a while, peacefully and contentedly. As far as he could remember, not once in these years had he dropped in on Mabel unannounced, in the middle of the day; he'd always come after dark and on days decided with her in advance. But these were extraordinary times and he could change the routine. He was tired, it was hot, and instead of walking he took a cab. When he got out in Castilla, he saw Mabel at the door of her house. Was she going out or coming back? She stood looking at him in surprise.

"What are you doing here?" she said in greeting. "Today? At this hour?"

"I didn't mean to bother you," Felícito apologized. "If you have an engagement, I'll go."

"I do, but I can cancel it." Mabel smiled at him, recovering from her surprise. "Come in, come in. Wait for me, I'll take care of it and be right back."

In spite of her friendly words, Felícito noted her irritation. He'd come at a bad time. Maybe she was going shopping. No, no. She was probably meeting a girlfriend for a stroll and then lunch. Or maybe a young man was waiting for her, young like her, one she liked and maybe they were seeing each other in secret. He felt a pang of jealousy imagining that Mabel was going to meet a lover. Some guy who'd undress her and make her cry out. He'd ruined their plans. He felt a current of desire, a tingling in his groin, the beginning of an erection. Well, after how many days. Mabel looked nice this morning in a white dress that left her arms and shoulders bare, spike-heeled sandals, her hair arranged, her eyes and lips made up. Could she have a boyfriend? He'd gone inside, taken off his jacket and tie. When Mabel came back, she found him reading the spider letter again. Her irritation had vanished. Now she was as smiling and affectionate as always.

"It's just that I got another letter this morning," Felícito apologized, handing it to her. "I blew up. And then suddenly I wanted to see you. That's why I'm here, my love. Forgive me for dropping in like this, without letting you know. I hope I haven't ruined any plans."

"This is your home, old man." Mabel smiled at him again. "You can come here whenever you want. You haven't ruined any plans. I was going to the pharmacy to pick up a few things."

She took the letter, sat down next to him, and as she read her expression changed to anger. A cloud seemed to dim her eyes.

"In other words, these damn people won't stop," she exclaimed very seriously. "What will you do now?"

"I went to the police station but the cops weren't there. I'll go back this afternoon. I don't know what for, those assholes don't do a thing. They string me along, that's all they know how to do. String me along with talk."

"So you came to me for a little pampering." Mabel lifted his spirits, smiling at him. "Isn't that right, old man?"

She caressed his face and he grasped her hand and kissed it.

"Let's go to the bedroom, Mabelita," he whispered in her ear. "I want you so much, right now."

"Well, well, I wasn't expecting that." She laughed again, exaggerating her surprise. "At this time of day? I don't recognize you, old man."

"Well, now you see," he said, embracing her and kissing her on the neck, inhaling her. "You smell so good, baby. I must be changing my habits, getting younger, hey waddya think."

They went to the bedroom, undressed, and made love. Felícito was so excited he had an orgasm almost as soon as he entered her. He kept embracing her, caressing her in silence, playing with her hair, kissing her neck and body, biting her nipples, tickling her, touching her.

"How affectionate you are, old man." Mabel grasped his ears, looking into his eyes, very close to his face. "One of these days you'll tell me you love me."

"Haven't I already told you that a lot of times, you foolish girl?"

"You say it when you're excited and so it doesn't mean anything," Mabel grumbled, joking with him. "But you never say it before or after."

"Well I'm telling you now when I'm not so excited. I love you very much, Mabelita. You're the only woman I've ever really loved."

"Do you love me more than Cecilia Barraza?"

"She's only a dream, a fairy tale," Felícito said, laughing. "You're my only love in real life."

"I'll take your word for it, old man." Weak with laughter, she tousled his hair.

They talked for quite a while, lying in bed, and then Felícito got up, washed, and dressed. He went back to Narihualá Transport and attended to matters in the office for a good part of the afternoon. On his way home, he stopped at the police station again. Now the captain and the sergeant were there and received him in the captain's office. Without saying a word, he handed them the third spider letter. Captain Silva read it aloud, sounding out each word before the attentive gaze of Sergeant Lituma, who listened as he handled a notebook with his plump hands.

"Well, everything's following its predictable course," stated Captain Silva when he finished reading. He seemed very satisfied at having foreseen everything that had happened. "They won't give in, which was to be expected. That perseverance will be their ruin, I've already told you that."

"Then should I be very happy?" Felícito asked sarcastically. "Not satisfied with burning my office, they keep sending me anonymous letters, and now they're giving me a two-week ultimatum, threatening me with something worse than the fire. I come here and you say that everything's following its predictable course. The truth is you haven't made a millimeter's progress in your investigation, while these motherfuckers do whatever they damn well feel like doing to me."

"Who says we haven't made any progress?" Captain Silva protested, gesturing and raising his voice. "We've made good progress. For the present we've determined that they're not from any of the three known gangs in Piura that extort money from businessmen. Further, Sergeant Lituma has found something that might be a good clue."

He said this in a way that made Felícito believe him in spite of his skepticism.

"It's still too soon to tell you about it. But something is something. You'll know as soon as we have anything concrete. Believe me, Señor Yanaqué. We're dedicated to your case, body and soul. We spend more time on it than on all the rest. You're our first priority."

Felícito told them his sons were worried and suggested that he hire a bodyguard, and he'd refused. They also suggested he buy a revolver. What did they think?

"I don't advise it," Captain Silva answered immediately. "You should carry a pistol only when you're prepared to use it, and you don't look to me like someone capable of killing anybody. You'd put yourself in danger for no reason, Señor Yanaqué. Well, you'll decide. If, in spite of my advice, you want a gun permit, we'll expedite the application. You should know it takes time. You'll have to pass a psychological test. Well, sleep on it."

Felícito reached home when it was already dark and in the garden crickets were singing and frogs croaking. He had supper right away: chicken broth, a salad, and some gelatin served to him by Saturnina. As he was going to the living room to watch the news on television, he noticed Gertrudis's silent, bovine form approaching him. She held a newspaper in her hand.

"The whole city's talking about the notice you published in *El Tiempo*," said his wife as she sat down in the easy chair next to the one he was in. "Even the priest mentioned it in his sermon at Mass this morning. All of Piura has read it. Except me."

"I didn't want to worry you, that's why I didn't say anything to you," Felícito apologized. "But if you have it there, why haven't you read it?"

He noticed her shifting in the chair, uncomfortable and averting her gaze.

"I've forgotten how," he heard her mumble. "Since I never read because of my eyes, I almost don't understand what I read now. The letters dance around."

"You have to go to the optometrist then and have your eyes tested," he admonished her. "How can you possibly have forgotten how to read? I don't think that happens to anybody, Gertrudis."

"Well it's happening to me," she said. "Yes, I'll go have my eyes tested one of these days. Why don't you read me what you published in *El Tiempo*? I asked Saturnina, but she doesn't know how to read either."

Gertrudis handed him the paper, and after he put on his glasses, Felícito read:

Dear Spider Extortionists:
    Although you've burned the offices of Narihualá Transport, a business I created with the honest effort of a lifetime, I'm publicly informing you that I will never pay the amount you demand to give me protection. I'd rather you kill me. You won't receive one cent from me, because I believe that honest, hardworking, decent people shouldn't be afraid of crooks and thieves like you but should face you with determination until you're sent to prison, which is where you belong.
    Signed,
    Felícito Yanaqué (I don't have a maternal surname)

The female shape was motionless a long while, ruminating on what she'd just heard. Finally, she murmured, "Then what the priest said in his sermon is true. You're a brave man, Felícito. May the Captive Lord have mercy on us. If we get out of this, I'll go to Ayabaca to pray to Him on His feast day, the Twelfth of October."

VI

"There won't be any story tonight, Rigoberto," said Lucrecia when they lay down and turned off the light. His wife's voice was tinged with anxiety.

"I'm not in the mood tonight for fantasies either, my love."

"Did you finally hear from them?"

Rigoberto said he had. Seven days had gone by since Ismael and Armida's marriage, and he and Lucrecia had been worried the entire week, waiting for the hyenas' reaction to what had occurred. But each day passed and brought nothing. Until two days ago, when Ismael's lawyer, Dr. Claudio Arnillas, called Rigoberto to warn him. The twins had learned that the civil ceremony had taken place in the Chorrillos town hall and consequently knew he was one of the witnesses. He should be prepared, they'd be calling him any time now.

They did, after a few hours.

"Miki and Escobita asked to see me and I had to agree, what else could I do," he added. "It'll be tomorrow. I didn't tell you right away so as not to ruin your day, Lucrecia. The problem finally caught up with us. I hope to get out of this with no broken bones, at least."

"Do you know something, Rigoberto? I don't care that much about them, we already knew this was going to happen. We were expecting it, weren't we? We'll just have to swallow the unpleasantness, there's nothing else to do." His wife changed the subject. "For the moment, I don't give a damn about Ismael's marriage and the tantrums of a couple of parasites. What worries me more, what keeps me awake, is Fonchito."

"That little brat again?" Rigoberto said in alarm. "Have the appearances returned?"

"They never went away, baby," Lucrecia reminded him, her voice breaking. "I think what's happening is that the boy doesn't trust us and doesn't talk to us anymore. That's what upsets me most. Don't you see how the poor kid is? Sad, absentminded, withdrawn. He used to tell us everything, but now I'm afraid he keeps things to himself. And maybe that's why misery is eating him alive. Haven't you noticed it? You've been so focused on the hyenas, you haven't even seen how your own son has changed these past few months. If we don't do something soon, anything could happen to him and we'd regret it for the rest of our lives. Can't you see that?"

"I see that very well." Rigoberto turned over beneath the sheets. "It's just that I don't know what else we can do. If you know, tell me and we'll do it. I don't know what's left. We've taken him to the best psychologist in Lima, I've spoken to his teachers, every day I try to talk to him and win back his trust. Tell me what else you want me to do and I'll do it. I'm as worried about Fonchito as you are, Lucrecia. Do you think I don't care about my son?"

"I know, I know," she agreed. "It's occurred to me that maybe, well, I don't know, don't laugh, I'm so confused by what's happening to him that, well, you know, it's an idea, just a foolish idea."

"Tell me what you're thinking and we'll do it, Lucrecia. Whatever it is I'll do it, I swear."

"Why don't you talk to your friend Father O'Donovan? Well, don't laugh, I don't know."

"You want me to go and talk to a priest about this?" Rigoberto was surprised. He gave a little laugh. "Why? So he can exorcise Fonchito? Have you taken the joke about the devil seriously?"

It had all started several months earlier, perhaps a year ago, in the most trivial way. At lunch one weekend, Fonchito, in an offhand manner, as if it weren't at all important, suddenly told his father and stepmother about his first encounter with that individual.

"I know what your name is," the man said, smiling at him affably from the next table. "Your name is Luzbel."

The boy sat looking at him in surprise, not knowing what to say. He was drinking an Inca Kola from the bottle, his school knapsack on his lap, and only now had he noticed the man's presence in the secluded little café in Barranco Park, not far from his house. The man had silvery temples, smiling eyes, and was extremely thin, dressed modestly but very properly. He wore a purple and white argyle pullover under his gray jacket. He was sipping a small cup of coffee.

"I've absolutely forbidden you to talk to strangers, Fonchito," Don Rigoberto reminded him. "Have you forgotten already?"

"My name's Alfonso, not Luzbel," he replied. "My friends call me Foncho."

"Your papa's saying this for your own good, honey," his step-mother intervened. "You never know who could be one of those men who meddle with boys at the school gates."

"They're drug dealers, or kidnappers, or pedophiles. So you just be careful."

"Well you ought to be named Luzbel." The gentleman smiled. His slow, educated voice pronounced each word as precisely as a grammar teacher. His long, bony face looked recently shaved. He had long fingers with trimmed nails.

"I swear he seemed like a very proper person, Papa."

"Do you know what 'Luzbel' means?"

Fonchito shook his head.

"'Luzbel,' that's what he said to you?" Don Rigoberto became concerned. "Did you say 'Luzbel'?"

"The one who carries the light, the bearer of light," the man explained calmly.

"He talked like he was moving in slow motion, Papa."

"It's a way of saying you're a very handsome young man. When you grow up, all the girls in Lima will be crazy about you. Didn't they teach you who Luzbel was in school?"

"I can see it coming, I can imagine very well what he wanted," Rigoberto murmured, giving him his full attention now.

Fonchito shook his head again.

"I knew I had to leave right away. I remember very clearly how often you told me I should never talk to strangers like that man who wanted to teach me what that name meant, Papa," he explained, gesturing. "But . . . but, I tell you, there was something in him, his manners, the way he spoke, that made me think he wasn't a bad man. Besides, he made me curious. At Markham I don't remember them ever telling us about Luzbel."

"He was the most beautiful of the archangels, the favorite of God on high." He wasn't joking, he spoke very seriously, the hint of a benevolent smile on his carefully shaved face; he pointed a finger at the sky. "But Luzbel, since he knew he was so beautiful, became vain and committed the sin of pride. He even felt equal to God. Imagine. Then God punished him, and from being the angel of light, he became the prince of darkness. That's how it all began. History, the appearance of time and evil, human life."

"He didn't seem like a priest, Papa, or one of those Evangelical missionaries who give away religious magazines door to door. I asked him: 'Are you a priest, señor?' 'No, no, me a priest, Fonchito, whatever gave you that idea?' And he started to laugh."

"It was irresponsible of you to talk to him, he probably followed you here," Doña Lucrecia scolded him, caressing his forehead. "Never again, never again. Promise me, honey."

"I have to go, señor," said Fonchito, standing up. "They're expecting me at home."

The gentleman did not attempt to keep him. As a kind of farewell, he smiled at him more openly, nodded slightly, and barely gestured goodbye with his hand.

"You know very well who he was, don't you?" Rigoberto repeated. "You're fifteen now and know about these things, don't you? A pervert. A pedophile. I suppose you understand what that means, I don't need to explain it to you. He was looking you over. Lucrecia's right. It was a mistake to answer him. You should have stopped everything and left as soon as he spoke to you."

"He didn't look like a fag, Papa," Fonchito reassured him. "I swear. I recognize queers on the prowl for boys right away because of how they look at me. Even before they open their mouths, honestly. And because they're always trying to touch me. This man was just the opposite—very educated, very refined. He didn't seem to have evil intentions, really."

"They're the worst kind, Fonchito," Doña Lucrecia declared, frankly alarmed. "Hypocrites, who don't seem to be but are."

"Tell me, Papa," Fonchito said, changing the subject. "What he told me about the archangel Luzbel, is it true?"

"Well, it's what the Bible says." Don Rigoberto vacillated. "It's true for believers, at any rate. It's incredible that at the Markham Academy they don't have you read the Bible, at least for your general education. But let's not get distracted. I'll tell you again, son: It's absolutely forbidden for you to accept anything from strangers. No invitations, no conversations, no nothing. You understand, don't you? Or do you want me to forbid you to go out at all?"

"I'm too old for that now, Papa. Please, I'm fifteen."

"Yes, as old as Methuselah." Doña Lucrecia laughed. But Rigoberto immediately heard her sighing in the dark. "If we'd only known how far this would go. My God, what a nightmare. I think it's gone on for a year."

"A year or even a little more, love."

Rigoberto forgot about the stranger who talked to Fonchito about Luzbel in the café in Barranco Park almost immediately. But he was reminded and became uneasy a week later when, according to his son, as he was coming back from playing soccer at San Agustín Academy, the same gentleman showed up again.

"I had just taken a shower in the San Agustín lockers and was going to meet up with Chato Pezzuolo so we could ride the jitney together to Barranco. And you won't believe it but there he was, Papa. Him, the same man."

"Hello, Luzbel." The gentleman greeted him with the same affectionate smile. "Remember me?"

He was sitting in the hall that separated the soccer field from the exit door of San Agustín Academy. Behind him was the dense serpent of cars, trucks, and buses moving along Avenida Javier Prado. Some vehicles had their headlights on.

"Yes, yes, I remember," said Fonchito, sitting up straight. And, in an unequivocal tone, he confronted him. "Excuse me, but my papa has forbidden me to talk to strangers."

"Rigoberto is absolutely right," the man said, nodding. He was wearing the same gray suit as last time, but the purple sweater was different, without the white diamond pattern. "Lima is filled with bad people. There are perverts and degenerates everywhere. And good-looking boys like you are their favorite targets."

Don Rigoberto opened his eyes very wide.

"He mentioned me by name? Did he say he knew me?"

"Do you know my papa, señor?"

"And I knew Eloísa, your mama, too," the gentleman replied, becoming very serious. "And I also know Lucrecia, your stepmother. I can't say we're friends, because we hardly see one another. But I like both of them very much; since the first time I saw them, they seemed a magnificent couple. I'm glad to know they take good care of you and look out for you. A boy as handsome as you is not at all safe in the Sodom and Gomorrah that Lima is."

"Could you tell me what this Sodom and Gomorrah is, Papa?" Fonchito asked, and Rigoberto noticed a sly gleam in his eyes.

"Two ancient cities, very corrupt, and because they were, God destroyed them," he replied cautiously. "It's what believers believe, at least. You have to read the Bible a little, son. For your general education. At least the New Testament. The world we live in is filled with biblical references, and if you don't understand them, you'll live in total confusion and ignorance. For example, you won't understand anything of classical art or ancient history. Are you sure he said he knew Lucrecia and me?"

"And my mama too," Fonchito specified. "He even said her name: Eloísa. He said it in a way that made it impossible not to believe he was telling the truth, Papa."

"Did he tell you his name?"

"Well, not that," Fonchito said, disconcerted. "I didn't ask him and I didn't even give him time to tell me. Since you ordered me not even to say a word to him, I ran away. But I'm sure he knows you, knows both of you. If not, he wouldn't have told me your name, he wouldn't have known my mother's name, or that my stepmother is named Lucrecia."

"If by any chance you run into him again, be sure to ask what his name is," said Rigoberto, scrutinizing the boy with suspicion. Could what he was telling them be true, or was it another of his inventions? "But don't talk to him, let alone accept a Coca-Cola or anything else. I'm more and more convinced he's one of those depraved people who wander loose through Lima looking for young boys. What else would he be doing at the San Agustín Academy?"

"Do you want me to tell you something, Rigoberto?" said Doña

Lucrecia, pressing her body against his in the dark as if reading his mind. "Sometimes I think he's making all of it up. Typical of Fonchito and his fantasies. He's played that trick on us before, hasn't he? And I tell myself there's nothing to worry about, that this gentleman doesn't exist and can't exist, that Fonchito invented everything to make himself interesting and to make us uneasy and dependent on him. But the problem is that Fonchito is an expert trickster. Because when he tells us about their encounters, it seems impossible that what he's saying isn't true. He speaks so honestly, so innocently, so persuasively—well, I don't know. Don't you react the same way?"

"Of course I do, just like you," Rigoberto confessed, embracing his wife, warming himself with her body and warming her. "A great trickster, of course. I only hope he's invented this whole story, Lucrecia. I hope, I hope. At first I didn't think too much about it, but now these appearances are beginning to obsess me. I start to read and the little brat distracts me, I listen to music and there he is, I look at my prints and what I see is his face, which isn't a face but a question mark."

"Honestly, with Fonchito at least you're never bored," said Doña Lucrecia, attempting to joke. "Let's try to rest a little. I don't want to spend another sleepless night."

A few days went by and the boy didn't mention the stranger to them again. Rigoberto began to think that Lucrecia was right. It had all been a fantasy of their son's to make himself interesting and capture their attention. Until one cold, drizzly winter evening when Lucrecia greeted him with an expression that startled him.

"Why that face?" Rigoberto kissed her. "Because of my early retirement? You think it's a bad idea? Are you terrified at the thought of seeing me here at home all day?"

"Fonchito." Lucrecia pointed to the lower floor, where the boy's bedroom was. "Something happened to him at school and he won't tell me what. I realized it as soon as he came in. He was very pale, trembling. I thought he had a fever. I took his temperature, but no, he didn't have one. He was withdrawn, frightened, he could barely speak. 'No, no, I'm fine, Stepmother.' He had almost no voice. Go see him, Rigoberto, he's in his room. Let him tell you what happened. Maybe we ought to call Medical Alert. I don't like the way he looks."

"Damn it, again," Rigoberto thought. He raced down the stairs to the lower floor of the apartment. In fact, it was the brat again. Fonchito resisted at first. "Why should I tell you if you don't believe me, Papa?" But finally he gave in to his father's loving words. "It's better to get it off your chest and share it with me, my boy. It'll do you good to tell me about it, you'll see." His son was pale and didn't seem himself. He spoke as if the words were being dictated to him or he might burst into tears at any moment. Rigoberto didn't interrupt him once; he listened without moving, totally absorbed in what he was hearing.

It was during the thirty-minute recess they had at midafternoon at Markham Academy, before the final classes of the day. Instead of going to play on the soccer field, where his classmates were kicking the ball or lying on the grass and talking, Fonchito sat in a corner of the empty stands reviewing the last math lesson; that subject gave him the most trouble. He was beginning to immerse himself in a complicated equation with vectors and cube roots when something, "like a sixth sense, Papa," made him feel he was being watched. He looked up and there the man was, sitting very close to him in the empty stands. He was dressed as correctly and simply as always, with a tie and a purple sweater under his gray jacket. He carried a portfolio of documents under his arm.

"Hello, Fonchito," he said, smiling at him casually, as if they were old friends. "While your classmates play, you study. A model student, as I already imagined you were. Just as it should be."

"When had he arrived and climbed into the stands? What was he doing there? The truth is I began to tremble and I don't know why, Papa." His son had grown a little paler and seemed stunned.

"Are you a teacher at the academy, señor?" Fonchito asked, frightened and not knowing what he was frightened of.

"A teacher, no, no I'm not," the man answered, as calm as always and with the urbane manners that never left him. "I help out at Markham Academy from time to time, with practical matters.

I'm an administrative adviser to the director. I like to come here, if the weather's nice, to see you students. You remind me of my youth, and in a way, you rejuvenate me. But what I said about nice weather isn't true anymore. What a shame, it's begun to rain."

"My papa wants to know what your name is, señor," said Fonchito, surprised that it was so difficult for him to speak and that his voice was trembling so much. "Because you know him, don't you? And my stepmother too, don't you?"

"My name is Edilberto Torres, but Rigoberto and Lucrecia probably don't remember me, we met in passing," the gentleman explained, with his usual circumspection. But today, unlike the other times, the man's well-bred smile and friendly, penetrating eyes, instead of soothing him, made Fonchito feel very apprehensive.

Rigoberto noticed that his son's voice was breaking and his teeth were chattering.

"Easy, son, there's no rush. Do you feel sick? Can I bring you a glass of water? Would you rather finish telling me this story later, or tomorrow?"

Fonchito shook his head. He had trouble getting the words out, as if his tongue had fallen asleep.

"I know you won't believe me, I know I'm telling you all this just for the sake of talking, Papa. But . . . but, it's just that then something very strange happened."

He looked away from his father and stared at the floor. He was sitting on the edge of the bed, still in his school uniform, shrinking into himself, a tormented expression on his face. Don Rigoberto felt a wave of tenderness and compassion for the boy. It was evident he was suffering. And he didn't know how to help him.

"If you tell me it's true, I'll believe you," he said, running his hand over the boy's hair in one of his infrequent caresses. "I know very well you've never lied to me and that you're not going to start now, Fonchito."

Don Rigoberto, who'd been standing, sat down on his son's desk chair. He saw the effort Fonchito was making to speak, and how distressed he was, looking at the wall and the books on the shelf to avoid meeting his father's eyes.

"Then, while I was talking to the man, Chato Pezzuolo came running over. My friend, you know him. And he was shouting, 'What's wrong with you, Foncho! Recess is over, everybody's going back to class. Hurry up, man.'"

Fonchito jumped to his feet.

"Excuse me, I have to go, recess is over." He said goodbye to Señor Edilberto Torres and ran to his friend.

"Instead of saying hello, Chato Pezzuolo made faces and touched his head as if I had a screw loose, Papa."

"Are you crazy, compadre, or what, Foncho?" he asked as they ran toward the classroom building. "Who the hell were you saying goodbye to?"

"I don't know who that guy is," Fonchito explained, panting. "His name's Edilberto Torres and he says he helps the school director out with practical things. Have you ever seen him here before?"

"But what guy are you talking about, asshole?" exclaimed Chato Pezzuolo, gasping, not running anymore. He'd turned to look at him. "You weren't with anybody, you were talking to thin air, like a nut who's sick in the head. You haven't gone crazy, have you, compadre?"

They'd reached their classroom, and from there it was impossible to see the stands on the soccer field.

"You didn't see him?" Fonchito grabbed his arm. "A man with gray hair, wearing a suit, a tie, a purple sweater, sitting right next to me. Swear you didn't see him, Chato."

"Don't fuck around," said Chato Pezzuolo, pointing a finger at his temple again. "You were all alone, nobody else was there but you. Either you lost your mind or you're seeing things. Don't be a pain in the ass, Alfonso. You're trying to fuck with me, right? I promise you can't."

"I knew you wouldn't believe me, Papa," Fonchito whispered, sighing. He paused and then declared, "But I know what I see and what I don't see. And I'm sure I'm not a nut case. What I'm telling you is what happened. Exactly what happened."

"All right, all right," Rigoberto said, trying to calm him, "probably it was your friend Pezzuolo who didn't see this Edilberto

Torres. He must have been in a blind spot, something blocked his view. Don't think about it anymore. What other explanation can there be? Your friend Chato couldn't see him and that's that. We're not going to start believing in ghosts at this point in our lives, son, isn't that right? Forget all that, and especially Edilberto Torres. Let's say he doesn't exist and never existed. He's long gone, as you say nowadays."

"Another of the boy's feverish imaginings," Doña Lucrecia would remark later. "He'll never stop surprising us. I mean, a man appears and only he sees him, right there on his school's soccer field. What an extravagant imagination he has, my God!"

But later, she was the one who urged Rigoberto to go to Markham, without telling Fonchito about it, to talk to Mr. McPherson, the director. The conversation caused Don Rigoberto a good deal of grief.

"Naturally, he didn't know and hadn't ever heard of Edilberto Torres," he told Lucrecia that night, when they usually talked. "And then, as was to be expected, the gringo felt free to mock me. It was absolutely impossible for a stranger to have entered the school, let alone the soccer field. Nobody who isn't a teacher or an employee is authorized to set foot there. Mr. McPherson also believes this is one of those fantasies that intelligent, sensitive boys tend to have. He told me there was no reason to give the matter any importance. At my son's age, it's perfectly normal for a child to see a ghost occasionally, unless he's a dolt. We agreed that neither of us would tell Foncho about the interview. I think he's right. What's the point of playing along with something that makes no sense."

"Well, if it turns out that the devil does exist, it seems he's Peruvian and his name is Edilberto Torres." Lucrecia had a sudden fit of laughter. But Rigoberto noticed it was a nervous laugh.

They were lying down, and it was obvious by this time that there would be no stories, no fantasies, and no lovemaking. This had been happening more often recently. Instead of inventing stories that excited them both, they began to talk, and often they enjoyed it so much that time slipped away until they were overcome by sleep.

"I'm afraid it's no laughing matter." A moment later she reversed herself and became serious again. "This has gone too far,

Rigoberto. We have to do something. I don't know what, but something. We can't just look away, as if nothing were going on."

"At least now I'm certain that it's a fantasy, something very typical of him," Rigoberto reflected. "But what's he trying to do with these stories? Things like this aren't unprovoked, they come from somewhere, with roots in the unconscious."

"Sometimes he's so quiet, so closed within himself, that I want to die of sorrow, my love. I feel that the boy is suffering in silence and it breaks my heart. Since he knows we don't believe in his apparitions, he doesn't tell us about them anymore. And that's even worse."

"He might be having visions, hallucinations," Don Rigoberto digressed. "It happens to the most normal people, whether they're clever or stupid. They think they're seeing what they don't see, what's only in their head."

"Sure, of course they're inventions," Doña Lucrecia concluded. "We assume the devil doesn't exist. I believed in him when I met you, Rigoberto. In God and the devil, what every normal Catholic family believes. You convinced me they were superstitions, the foolish beliefs of ignorant people. And now it turns out that the one who doesn't exist has interfered with our family, and what do you have to say to that?" She gave another nervous little laugh and then fell silent. To Rigoberto she seemed quiet and pensive.

"To be honest, I don't know whether he exists or not," he admitted. "The only thing I'm sure about now is what you just said. He might exist, I could get as far as that. But I can't accept that he's a Peruvian named Edilberto Torres, and that he devotes his time to stalking the students at Markham Academy. Please don't fuck with me."

They discussed the matter from every angle and finally decided to take Fonchito for a psychological evaluation. They made inquiries among their friends. Everyone recommended Dr. Augusta Delmira Céspedes. She had studied in France and was a specialist in child psychology, and those who'd placed their sons or daughters with problems in her care had high praise for her skill and good judgment. They were afraid Fonchito might resist and took every precaution to present the matter to him delicately. But to their surprise, the boy didn't raise the slightest objection. He agreed to see her, went to her office several times, took all the tests Dr. Céspedes gave him, and always had the best attitude in the world when he talked to her. When Rigoberto and Lucrecia went to her office, the doctor received them with an encouraging smile. She was close to sixty, rather plump, agile, amiable, and droll.

"Fonchito is the most normal boy in the world," she assured them. "Too bad: He's so charming I would have liked to keep him as a patient for a while. Each session with him has been a delight. He's intelligent, sensitive, and for that very reason sometimes feels distant from his classmates. But this is absolutely normal. If you can be totally sure of anything, it's that Edilberto Torres is no fantasy but a flesh-and-blood person, as real and concrete as the two of you and me. Fonchito hasn't lied to you. Exaggerated things a little, perhaps. That's what his rich imagination is for. He's never taken his encounters with that gentleman as either heavenly or diabolical apparitions. Never! What nonsense. He's a kid with his feet planted very firmly on the ground and his head in the right place. You're the ones who have invented all this, and for that very reason you're the ones who really need a psychologist. Shall I make you an appointment? I see not only children but also adults who suddenly begin to believe the devil exists and wastes his time walking the streets of Lima, Barranco, and Miraflores."

Dr. Augusta Delmira Céspedes continued joking as she accompanied them to the door. When they said goodbye, she asked Don Rigoberto to show her his collection of erotic prints one day. "Fonchito told me it's terrific" was her final joke. Rigoberto and Lucrecia left her office floundering in a sea of confusion.

"I told you that going to a psychologist was very dangerous," Rigoberto reminded Lucrecia. "I don't know why I ever listened to you. A psychologist can be more dangerous than the devil himself, I've known that ever since I read Freud."

"Shame on you if you think we should joke about this the way Dr. Céspedes does," Lucrecia said in self-defense. "I only hope you're not sorry."

"I don't take it as a joke," he replied, serious now. "I was happier thinking that Edilberto Torres didn't exist. If what Dr. Céspedes says is true, and this person does exist and is pursuing Fonchito, tell me what the hell we're supposed to do now."

They did nothing, and for a long time the boy didn't talk to them again about the matter. He continued to go about his normal life, going to school and coming home at the usual times, going to his room for an hour or sometimes two every afternoon to do his homework, and going out some weekends with Chato Pezzuolo. Though he did so reluctantly, pushed by Don Rigoberto and Doña Lucrecia, he also went out occasionally with other boys from the neighborhood, to the movies, to the stadium to play soccer, or to a party. But in their nocturnal conversations, Rigoberto and Lucrecia agreed that even though this seemed normal, Fonchito wasn't the same boy he'd been before.

What was different? It wasn't easy to say, but both were sure he'd changed. And that the transformation was profound. A problem of his age? It was a difficult transition from childhood to adolescence: A boy's voice changes and becomes hoarse, and the fuzz that announces his future beard starts to appear on his face; he begins to feel he's no longer a child but not yet a man, and in the way he dresses, sits, gestures, and talks to his friends and to girls, he tries to become the man he'll be later on. Fonchito seemed more laconic and withdrawn, much more sparing in his answers to their questions at meals about school and his friends.

"I know what's wrong with you, kid," Lucrecia challenged him one day. "You've fallen in love! Is that it, Fonchito? Do you like some girl?"

With no hint of a blush, he shook his head no.

"I don't have time for those things now," he replied seriously, without a shred of humor. "Exams are coming and I'd like to get good grades."

"I like that, Fonchito," Don Rigoberto said approvingly. "You'll have plenty of time for girls later on."

And suddenly his rosy face lit up with a smile, and in Fonchito's eyes the impish mischief of earlier times appeared.

"Besides, you know that the only woman in the world I like is you, Stepmother."

"Oh, my God, let me give you a kiss, my boy," Doña Lucrecia commended him. "But what do those hands mean, my husband?"

"They mean that talking about the devil suddenly sets my imagination and some other things on fire, my love."

And for a long while they took their pleasure, imagining that the joke about the devil and Fonchito had passed on to a better life. But no, it hadn't passed on yet.

VII

It happened one morning when Sergeant Lituma and Captain Silva, the latter distracted for a moment from his obsession with Piuran women in general and Señora Josefita in particular, were working, all five senses focused on the task, trying to find the link that would give focus to the investigation. Colonel Ríos Pardo, alias Rascachucha, the regional police chief, had reprimanded them again the night before, ranting like a madman because news of Felícito Yanaqué's defiance of the crooks in *El Tiempo* had reached Lima. The minister of the interior had called him personally to demand that the business be resolved immediately. The press was following the story, and not only the police but the government itself was being made to look ridiculous in the public eye. The rallying cry from headquarters was: Get your hands on the extortionists and make an example of them!

"We have to justify the police, damn it," the ill-tempered Rascachucha bellowed from behind his enormous mustache, his eyes like red-hot coals. "A couple of hicks can't laugh at us like this. Either you hunt them down ipso facto, or I swear by San Martín de Porres and by God Himself that you'll regret it for the rest of your life!"

Sergeant Lituma and Captain Silva analyzed with a magnifying glass the statements of all the witnesses, made file cards, compared and cross-referenced data, shuffled through hypotheses and rejected them one after the other. From time to time, taking a breather, the captain would burst into praise, charged with sexual fever, of the curves of Señora Josefita, with whom he'd fallen in love. Very seriously, and with salacious gestures, he explained to his subordinate that those gluteals were not only large, round, and symmetrical but also "gave a little jiggle when she walked," something that aroused his heart and his testicles in unison. For that reason, he maintained, "in spite of her age, her moon face, and her slightly bowed legs, Josefita is the goddamnedest woman."

"Hotter than gorgeous Mabel, if I'm forced to make comparisons, Lituma," he went on, his eyes popping as if he had the backsides of the two ladies right in front of him and were hefting them both. "I acknowledge that Don Felícito's girlfriend has a nice figure, aggressive tits, and well-formed, fleshy legs and arms, but her ass, as you must have noticed, leaves much to be desired. It's not very touchable. It didn't finish developing, it didn't blossom, at some point it went into decline. According to my classification system, hers is a timid ass, if you know what I mean."

"Why don't you concentrate on the investigation instead, Captain?" Lituma asked him. "You saw how furious Colonel Ríos Pardo is. At this rate we won't ever get rid of this case or be promoted again."

"I've noticed that you have absolutely no interest in women's asses, Lituma," was the captain's judgment, pretending to commiserate with him and putting on a grief-stricken face. But immediately afterward he smiled and licked his lips like a cat. "A defect in your manly formation, I'm telling you. A good ass is the most divine gift God gave to female bodies for the pleasure of males. I've been told that even the Bible recognizes this."

"Of course I have an interest, Captain. But with all due respect, in you there's not only interest but obsession and depravity too. Let's get back to the spiders now."

They spent many hours reading, rereading, and examining word by word, letter by letter, stroke by stroke the extortionists' letters and drawings. They'd requested a handwriting analysis of the anonymous letters from the central office, but the specialist, in the hospital following hemorrhoid surgery, was on a two-week leave. It was on one of those days, as they were comparing the letters to the signatures and writing samples of criminals on file in the office of the public prosecutor, that a suspicion sprouted in Lituma's mind. A memory, an association. Captain Silva noticed that something had happened to his colleague.

"You look like you're in a trance all of a sudden. What's up, Lituma?"

"Nothing, it's nothing, Captain." The sergeant shrugged. "It's silly. I just remembered a guy I met. He was always drawing spiders, as I recall. Just bullshit, I'm sure."

"I'm sure," the captain repeated, staring at him. He brought his face up close to Lituma's and changed his tone. "But since we don't have anything, bullshit is better than nothing. Who was this guy? Go on, tell me."

"A pretty old story, Captain." The police chief noticed that Lituma's voice and eyes were fraught with discomfort, as if it bothered him to root through those memories, though he couldn't avoid it. "I imagine it doesn't have anything to do with this. But, yes, I remember clearly, that motherfucker was always drawing, scribbling things that could have been spiders. On papers, on newspapers. Sometimes even on the ground in chicha bars, with a stick."

"And who was this so-called motherfucker, Lituma? Tell me right now and don't keep beating around the fucking bush."

"Let's go have some juice and get out of this oven for a while, Captain," the sergeant suggested. "It's a long story, and if you don't get bored, I'll tell it to you. My treat, don't worry."

They went to La Perla del Chira, a little bar on Calle Libertad next to a lot where, Lituma told his boss, in his youth there used to be a cockpit that had pretty heavy betting. He'd gone a few times but didn't like cockfights; it made him sad to see how the poor animals were destroyed by pecking beaks and slashing razors. The place had no air-conditioning, but fans helped to cool it down. It was deserted. They ordered two eggfruit juices with lots of ice, and then lit their cigarettes.

"The motherfucker's name was Josefino Rojas and he was the son of Carlos Rojas, the bargeman who used to carry cattle from the ranches to the slaughterhouse on the river during the flood months," said Lituma. "I met him when I was very young, still wet behind the ears. We had our little gang. We liked binges, guitars, beers, and broads. Somebody nicknamed us 'the Unconquerables,' or maybe we did it ourselves. We wrote our anthem."

And in a low, rasping voice, Lituma sang, in tune and happily:

We're the Unconquerables,
for us working has no class:
only guzzling!
only gambling!
only girls fucked up the ass!

The captain congratulated him, bursting into laughter and applauding. "Nice, Lituma. I mean, at least when you were young you paid attention."

"There were three of us Unconquerables at first," the sergeant continued nostalgically, lost in his memories. "My cousins, the León brothers—José and Mono—and yours truly. Three guys from Mangachería. I don't know how Josefino hooked up with us. He wasn't from Mangachería, he came from Gallinacera, near the old market and slaughterhouse. I don't know why we let him in the group. Back then there was a terrible rivalry between the two neighborhoods. Fistfights and knife fights. A war that made a lot of blood flow in Piura, I can tell you."

"Come on, you're talking about the prehistory of this city," said the captain. "I know where Mangachería was, in the north, from Avenida Sánchez Cerro down, near the old San Teodoro cemetery. But Gallinacera?"

"Right there, close to the Plaza de Armas, beside the river, toward the south," Lituma said, pointing. "It was called Gallinacera because of all the *gallinazos*, the turkey buzzards the slaughterhouse attracted when they were killing cattle. We Mangaches were Sanchezcerristas and the Gallinazos were Apristas. The motherfucker Josefino was a Gallinazo and told us that when he was a kid he'd been a butcher's apprentice."

"So you were gang members."

"Just street kids, Captain. We made mischief, nothing very serious. It never got past fistfights. But then Josefino became a pimp. He'd seduce girls and put them to work as whores in the Green House. That was the name of the brothel as you left Catacaos, when Castilla wasn't named Castilla yet but was still Tacalá. Did you know that whorehouse? It was really fancy."

"No, but I've heard a lot about the famous Green House. A

legend in Piura. But getting back to the pimp. Was he the one who drew the spiders?"

"The same, Captain. I think they were spiders, but maybe my memory's playing tricks on me. I'm not really sure."

"And may I ask why you hate this pimp so much, Lituma?"

"Lots of reasons." The sergeant's heavy face darkened and his eyes grew red with anger; he'd begun to rub his double chin very quickly. "Mainly for what he did to me when I was in jail. You know the story, they ran me in for playing Russian roulette with a local landowner. In the Green House, to be exact. A white guy, a drunk whose last name was Seminario and who blew his brains out during the game. Taking advantage of the fact that I was in jail, Josefino stole my girl. He started her whoring for him in the Green House. Her name was Bonifacia. I brought her here from Alto Marañón, in Santa María de Nieva, in Amazonia. When she started in the life, they called her 'Selvática,' Jungle Girl."

"Ah, well, you had plenty of reason to hate him," the captain admitted, shaking his head. "So you have quite a past, Lituma. Nobody would think so seeing you now, so tame. As if you'd never killed a fly in your life. Really, I can't imagine you playing Russian roulette. I played only once, with a buddy of mine one night when we were drinking. My balls still freeze up when I think about it. And this Josefino, may I ask why you didn't kill him?"

"Not for lack of wanting, but I had no desire to go back to the slammer," the sergeant explained briefly. "But I did give him a beating—he must still be aching from it. I'm talking at least twenty years ago, Captain."

"Are you sure the pimp spent all his time drawing spiders?"

"I don't know whether they were spiders," Lituma corrected him again. "But he definitely was drawing all the time. On napkins, on any piece of paper he had in front of him. It was his mania. Maybe it has nothing to do with what we're looking for."

"Think and try to remember, Lituma. Concentrate, close your eyes, look back. Spiders like the ones on the letters sent to Felícito Yanaqué?"

"My memory's not that good, Captain," Lituma apologized. "I'm talking about something that happened years ago, I told you—

maybe twenty, maybe more. I don't know why I made that connection. We should probably forget it."

"Do you know what happened to Josefino the pimp?" the captain insisted. His expression was grave and he didn't take his eyes off the sergeant.

"I never saw him again, or my cousins, the other two Unconquerables. Since I was readmitted to the force, I've been in the mountains, the jungle, in Lima. Going all around Peru, you might say. I came back to Piura just a little while ago. That's why I said my idea was probably silly. I'm not sure they were spiders. He definitely was drawing something. He did it all the time and the Unconquerables made fun of him."

"If Josefino the pimp is alive, I'd like to meet him," said the chief, hitting the table lightly. "Find out, Lituma. I don't know why, but it smells right to me. Maybe we've bitten into a nice piece of meat. Tender and juicy. I feel it in my spit, my blood, my balls. I'm never wrong about these things. I'm beginning to see light at the end of this tunnel. Good for you, Lituma."

The captain was so happy that the sergeant regretted telling him about his hunch. Was he sure that back when they were all Unconquerables, Josefino never stopped drawing? Now he wasn't so certain. That night, when his shift was over and, as usual, he walked up Avenida Grau to the boardinghouse where he lived in the Buenos Aires district near the Grau Barracks, he struggled with his memory, trying to be certain it wasn't a false one. No, no it wasn't, though now he wasn't as convinced as he had been. Images of his years as a kid on the dusty streets of Mangachería returned in waves: He, Mono, and José would go to the sandy tracts of land just outside the city to set traps for iguanas at the foot of the carob trees, hunt birds with slings they made themselves, or hide in the thickets and sand dunes to spy on the women who washed their clothes in the river near the culvert, in water up to their waists. Sometimes, because of the water, their breasts would show through their clothes and the boys' eyes and crotches would burn with excitement. How did Josefino get into the group? He no longer could remember how, when, or why. In any case, the Gallinazo joined them when they weren't little kids anymore. Because by then they were going to

the chicha bars and spending the few soles they earned doing oc-
casional jobs—like selling bets on horse races—on gambling, carousing, and drunken binges. Maybe they weren't spiders, but they
were definitely drawings, and Josefino made them all the time—he
remembered that very clearly—while he was talking, or singing,
or beginning to brood about his evil deeds, isolating himself from
the others. It wasn't a false memory, but maybe what he drew were
frogs, snakes, pricks. Lituma was assailed by doubts. Suddenly they
were the crosses and circles of tic-tac-toe, or caricatures of the people they saw in La Chunga's bar, one of their haunts. La Chunga,
that slut! Did the bar still exist? Impossible. If she were alive, she'd
be so old by now that she wouldn't be physically able to run it.
Though who knows. She was a tough woman who wasn't afraid
of anybody and could hold her own in confrontations with drunks.
Once she even challenged Josefino when he tried to act smart
with her.

The Unconquerables! La Chunga! Damn, how time flew. The
León brothers, Josefino, and Bonifacia were probably dead and buried by now, nothing left of them but memory. How sad.

He was walking almost in darkness, because after you passed
the Club Grau and entered the residential neighborhood of Buenos Aires, the streetlights were farther apart and dimmer. He walked
slowly, tripping over the cracks in the asphalt, past houses that once
had gardens and two stories and over time had become lower
and poorer. As he approached his boardinghouse the buildings
turned into huts, rough constructions with adobe walls, posts of
carob wood, and corrugated metal roofs on streets without sidewalks and hardly any automobile traffic.

When he returned to Piura after serving for many years in Lima
and in the mountains, he moved into a room on the military base,
where police as well as soldiers could live. But he didn't like that
much intimacy with his associates on the force. It was like still being in the service, seeing the same people and talking about the
same things. That's why, after six months, he moved to the house
of the Calancha family, who had five rooms for boarders. It was
extremely modest and Lituma's bedroom was tiny, but he paid very
little and felt more independent there. The Calanchas were watch-

ing television when he came in. The husband had been a teacher and his wife a municipal employee. They'd been retired for some time. Board included only breakfast, but if the tenant desired, the Calanchas could order in lunch and dinner from a nearby restaurant whose stews were pretty substantial. The sergeant asked if they happened to remember a little bar near the old stadium, run by a fairly masculine woman who was named, or called, La Chunga. They looked at him uneasily, shaking their heads no.

That night he lay awake for a long time and didn't feel very well. Damn, he never should have mentioned Josefino to Captain Silva. Now he was almost certain the pimp hadn't been drawing spiders but something else. Rummaging around in his past wasn't a good idea. It made him sad to remember his youth, to think about how old he was—close to fifty now—how solitary his life was, the misfortunes that had battered him, that idiotic Russian roulette with Seminario, his years in prison, what happened to Bonifacia, which left a bitter taste in his mouth each time he thought about it.

He slept at last, but badly, and had nightmares that left him with a memory of calamitous, terrifying images when he woke. He washed, had breakfast, and was out before seven, on his way to the spot where his memory guessed La Chunga's bar had been. It wasn't easy to orient himself. In his memory, this had been the outskirts of the city, just a few huts of clay and wild reeds built on the sandy tracts. Now there were streets, cement, houses made of reputable materials, streetlights, sidewalks, cars, schools, gas stations, shops. So many changes! The old neighborhood was now a part of the city and bore no resemblance to his memories. His attempts to speak to residents—he asked only older people—led nowhere. Nobody remembered either the bar or La Chunga; a lot of people in the area weren't even Piuran but had moved here from the mountains. He had the unpleasant sensation that his memory was lying to him; none of the things he remembered had existed, they were phantoms and always had been phantoms, pure products of his imagination. Thinking about that frightened him.

At midmorning he called a halt to the search and returned to the center of Piura. It was hot, and before going back to the police station, he had a soda at the corner. The streets were filled with noise, cars, buses, students in uniform. Lottery-ticket sellers and trinket vendors hocking their wares, sweaty people all in a hurry, crowding the sidewalks. And then his memory retrieved the name and number of the street where his cousins, the León brothers, had lived: Calle Morropón 17. In the very heart of Mangachería. Half closing his eyes, he saw the faded façade of the one-story house, grillwork on the windows, pots of wax flowers, the chicha bar over which a white flag on a reed fluttered, a sign that cold chicha was served there.

He took a mototaxi to Avenida Sánchez Cerro and, feeling the drops of sweat streaming down his face and wetting his back, he walked into the ancient labyrinth of streets, alleys, crescents, dead ends, empty lots that had been Mangachería, a neighborhood, people said, that got its name because in colonial times it had been populated by slaves brought over from Madagascar. This had all changed too—in its form, people, texture, and color. The dirt streets were paved in asphalt, the houses were made of brick and cement, there were some office buildings, street lighting, not a single chicha bar or burro left in the streets, only stray dogs. Chaos had turned into order and straight, parallel streets. Nothing here resembled his Mangache memories now. The neighborhood had been made respectable and become colorless, impersonal. But Calle Morropón still existed, and so did number 17. Except that instead of his cousins' little house he found a large auto repair shop, with a sign that read: WE SELL REPLACEMENT PARTS FOR ALL MAKES OF CARS, VANS, TRUCKS, AND BUSES. He went inside, and in the huge, dim place that smelled of oil he saw dismantled car bodies and engines, heard the sound of welding, observed three or four workers in blue overalls leaning over their machines. A radio played music from the jungle, "La Contamanina." He walked into an office where a fan was humming. A very young woman sat in front of a computer.

"Good afternoon," said Lituma, removing his kepi.

"Can I help you?" She was looking at him with the slight uneasiness with which people usually regarded the police.

"I'm looking for a family that used to live here," Lituma explained, indicating the premises. "When this wasn't a repair shop but a house. Their name was León."

"As far as I know, this has always been a repair shop," said the girl.

"You're very young, you can't remember," Lituma replied. "But maybe the owner knows something."

"You can wait for him if you'd like." The girl indicated a chair. And then, suddenly, her face lit up. "Oh, I'm so dumb. Of course! The owner's name is León, Don José León, to be precise. He probably can help you."

Lituma dropped into the chair, his heart pounding. Don José León. Damn. It was him, his cousin José. It had to be the Unconquerable. Who else could it be?

He was on pins and needles as he waited. The minutes seemed endless. When the Unconquerable José León finally appeared in the shop—though he was now a stout, big-bellied man with streaks of gray in his thinning hair, dressed like a white man in a jacket, business shirt, and shoes shined as bright as glass—Lituma recognized him immediately. He stood, filled with emotion, and held out his arms. José, surprised, didn't recognize him and brought his face very close to examine him.

"I see you don't know who I am, cousin," said Lituma. "Have I changed that much?"

José's face broke into a broad smile.

"I don't believe it!" he exclaimed, holding out his arms as well. "Lituma! What a surprise, brother. After so many years, hey waddya think."

They embraced, patted each other's backs under the astonished gazes of the secretary and the workers. They scrutinized each other, smiling and effusive.

"Do you have time for a coffee, cousin?" Lituma asked. "Or would you prefer to get together later or tomorrow?"

"Let me take care of two or three little things and then we'll go and remember the days of the Unconquerables," said José, giving him another pat on the back. "Sit down, Lituma. I'll be free in no time. What a huge pleasure, brother."

Lituma sat down in the chair again and from there he watched León examine papers on the desk, check some large books with the secretary, leave the office and walk around the shop, inspecting the mechanics' work. He noticed how confident he seemed giving orders and greeting his employees, the ease with which he gave instructions or took care of questions. "Man, how you've changed, cousin," he thought. It was difficult for him to reconcile the ragged José of his youth, running barefoot among the goats and burros of Mangachería, with this white owner of a large repair shop, who wore a suit and dress shoes in the middle of the day.

They went out, Lituma holding José's arm, to a cafeteria-restaurant called Piura Linda. His cousin said their meeting called for a celebration and ordered beers. They toasted the old days and spent a long time nostalgically comparing their shared memories. Mono had been his partner in the repair shop when José first opened it. But then they'd had differences, and Mono left the business, though the two brothers were still very close and saw each other frequently. Mono was married and had three children. He'd worked a few years for the city and then opened a brickyard. It was doing well, many of the construction companies in Piura placed orders with him, especially now, when money was flowing in and new neighborhoods were going up. Every Piuran dreamed of owning a house, and it was terrific that good times had come. José couldn't complain. It was difficult at first, there was a lot of competition, but gradually word spread about the quality of his service and now, in all modesty, his shop was one of the best in the city. He had more than enough work, thank God.

"In other words, you and Mono stopped being Unconquerables and Mangaches and turned into rich white men," Lituma joked. "I'm the only one who's still a poor beggar and will be a cop forever."

"How long have you been here, Lituma? Why didn't you look me up earlier?"

The sergeant lied, saying only a short while, and that the inquiries he'd made regarding José's whereabouts had gone nowhere, and then he'd decided to take a walk around the old neighborhoods. That's how he'd come face-to-face with Morropón 17. He never could have imagined that the sandy tracts with those crummy huts had turned into this. And with a first-rate auto repair shop!

"Times have changed, fortunately for the better," José agreed.

"These are good times for Piura and for Peru, cousin. I hope they last, knock wood."

He'd married too, to a woman from Trujillo, but the marriage had been a disaster. They'd fought like cats and dogs and finally divorced. They had two daughters who lived with their mother in Trujillo. José went to see them from time to time, and they spent their vacations with him. They were at the university, the older one studying to be a dentist and the younger one a pharmacist.

"Congratulations, cousin. Both will be professionals, what luck."

And then, when Lituma was getting ready to bring the pimp's name up in conversation, José, as if reading his mind, beat him to it.

"Do you remember Josefino, cousin?"

"How could I forget a son of a bitch like him," Lituma said with a sigh. And after a long pause, as if just making conversation, he asked, "Whatever happened to him?"

José shrugged and made a contemptuous face.

"I haven't heard anything about him for years. He became a crook, you know. He lived off women, had little whores working for him, and went from bad to worse. Mono and I didn't have much to do with him. He'd come by from time to time to put the touch on us, telling us stories about his ailments and the loan sharks who were threatening him. He even got involved in something really ugly—a crime of some kind. They accused him of being an accomplice or an accessory after the fact. I wouldn't be surprised if one day he turns up somewhere murdered by those hoodlums he liked so much. He's probably rotting in some jail, who knows."

"That's true, he was drawn to crime, like a fly to honey," said Lituma. "The fucker was born to be a crook. I don't understand why we hooked up with him, cousin. Besides, he was a Gallinazo and we were Mangaches."

And at that moment Lituma, who'd been looking at without really seeing the movements of one of his cousin's hands on the table, saw that José was drawing lines with his thumbnail on the rough wooden surface covered with carved-in words, burns, and stains. Barely able to breathe, he focused his eyes and repeated to himself that he wasn't crazy and he wasn't obsessed because what his cousin was doing, without realizing it, was tracing spiders with his nail. Yes, spiders, like the ones on the threatening anonymous letters Felícito Yanaqué had received. He wasn't dreaming and he wasn't seeing things, damn it. Spiders, spiders. Fuck, fuck.

"Now we have one hell of a problem," he murmured, hiding his agitation and indicating Avenida Sánchez Cerro. "You must know about it. You must have read the letter in *El Tiempo* from Felícito Yanaqué, the owner of Narihualá Transport to the guys who are trying to extort him."

"The biggest balls in Piura," his cousin exclaimed. His eyes shone with admiration. "I not only read that letter, like every other Piuran, but I cut it out, had it framed, and have it hanging on the wall in my office, cousin. Felícito Yanaqué is an example for all the asshole executives and business owners in Piura who bend over for the gangs and pay them protection money. I've known Don Felícito a long time. In the shop we do the repairs and tune-ups for Narihualá Transport's buses and trucks. I wrote him a few lines congratulating him for his letter in *El Tiempo*."

He poked Lituma with his elbow, pointing to the braid on his epaulets.

"You cops have an obligation to protect that guy, cousin. It would be a tragedy if the gangs sent a killer to take care of Don Felícito. You know they already burned down his place."

The sergeant looked at him, nodding. So much indignation and admiration couldn't be an act; he'd made a mistake, José hadn't been drawing spiders with his nail, only lines. A coincidence, a fluke, like so many others. But at that moment his memory struck another blow; lighting everything so he could see it in the clearest, most obvious way, it reminded him, with a lucidity that made him tremble, that in fact, ever since they were kids, the one who was always drawing stars that looked like spiders, with a pencil, a twig, or a knife, was his cousin José, not Josefino the pimp. Of course, of course. It was José. Long before they even knew Josefino, José was always drawing. He and Mono often teased him about his obsession. Fuck, fuck.

"Let's have lunch or dinner together soon and you'll have a

chance to see Mono, Lituma. What a kick he'll get out of seeing you!"

"Me too, José. My best memories are Piuran, why deny it. When we hung out together, when we were the Unconquerables. The best time of my life, I think. Back then I was happy. The hard times came later. Besides, as far as I know, you and Mono are the only family I have left in the world. Whenever you want, you two tell me the date and I'll be there."

"Then lunch is better than dinner," said José. "Rita, my sister-in-law, is incredibly jealous, she keeps an eye on Mono like you wouldn't believe. She makes big scenes whenever he goes out at night. I even think she hits him."

"Lunch, then, no problem." Lituma felt so agitated that, afraid José might suspect what was whirling around in his head, he looked for an excuse to say goodbye.

He went back to the station distracted, confused, dazed, paying so little attention to where he was stepping that a fruit vendor's tricycle almost knocked him down as he crossed at a corner. When he reached the station, Captain Silva understood his state of mind as soon as he saw him.

"Don't add to the headaches I already have, Lituma," he warned, standing up at his desk so violently that the cubicle shook. "What the hell's wrong with you now? Who died?"

"What's died is the suspicion that it was Josefino Rojas who drew the spiders," Lituma stammered, taking off his kepi and wiping away sweat with his handkerchief. "Now it turns out that the suspect isn't the pimp but my cousin José León. One of the Unconquerables I told you about, Captain."

"Are you kidding me, Lituma?" the disconcerted captain exclaimed. "Just explain to me how I'm supposed to swallow that shit you just said."

The sergeant sat down, trying to make the breeze from the fan blow directly into his face. In complete detail he recounted everything that had happened to him that morning.

"In other words, now it's your cousin José who draws spiders with his fingernails." The captain was angry. "And on top of that, he's so hopelessly dumb he betrays himself in front of a police sergeant, knowing very well that all of Piura is talking about the spiders of Felícito Yanaqué and Narihualá Transport. I can see your brains have been completely fried, Lituma."

"I'm not sure he was drawing spiders with his nails," his subordinate apologized, filled with remorse. "I might be wrong about that too. Please forgive me. I'm not sure about anything anymore, Captain, not even the ground I walk on. Yes, you're right. It's bedlam in my head, like a stewpot full of crickets."

"A stewpot full of spiders, you mean." The captain laughed. "And now, look who's here. The only piece missing. Good morning, Señor Yanaqué. Come in, come in."

Lituma knew right away from the trucker's face that something serious had happened: Another letter from the gang? Felícito was ashen, dark circles under his eyes, his mouth half open in an idiotic expression, his eyes dilated with fear. He'd just removed his hat and his hair was messy, as if he'd forgotten to comb it. He, who was always so elegantly dressed, had buttoned the first button of his vest into the second buttonhole. His appearance was ridiculous, careless, clownish. He couldn't speak. He didn't respond to the greeting but took an envelope from his pocket and handed it to the captain, his hand trembling. He looked smaller and more fragile than ever, almost like a midget.

"Fuck," muttered the chief, taking the letter and beginning to read aloud:

Dear Señor Yanaqué:
    We told you your obstinacy and your challenge in *El Tiempo* would have unpleasant consequences. We told you you'd regret your refusal to be reasonable and reach an understanding with those who wish only to provide protection for your business and security for your family. We're as good as our word. We have one of your loved ones and will keep that individual until you relent and come to an agreement with us.
    Even though we know you have the bad habit of going to the police with your complaints, as if that would be of any use, we assume that this time, for your own good, you'll

be more discreet. It's in no one's interest for it to be known that we have this person, above all if you're interested in her not suffering as the result of another of your imprudent acts. This matter should remain between us and be resolved quietly and quickly.

Since you like to make use of the press, place a notice in *El Tiempo*, giving thanks to the Captive Lord of Ayabaca for performing the miracle you asked for. Then we'll know you've agreed to the conditions we proposed to you. And the person in question will immediately return safe and sound to her house. Otherwise, you may never hear from her again.

May God keep you.

Though he hadn't seen it, Lituma could guess at the spider signature on the letter.

"Who have they kidnapped, Señor Yanaqué?" Captain Silva asked.

"Mabel," the trucker said, choking. Lituma saw that the little man's eyes were wet and fat tears were running down his cheeks.

"Sit here, Don Felícito." The sergeant offered him his chair and helped him into it.

The trucker sat and covered his face with his hands. He wept slowly, silently. His weak body was shaken by sudden tremors. Lituma felt sorry for him. Poor man, now those sons of bitches had found the way to soften him up. It wasn't right, what an injustice.

"I can assure you of one thing, sir." The captain also seemed to be moved by what was happening to Felícito Yanaqué. "They're not going to touch a hair on your friend's head. They want to frighten you, that's all. They know it's not a good idea for them to harm Mabel in any way, that the person in their hands is untouchable."

"Poor girl," Felícito Yanaqué stammered, between hiccups. "It's my fault, I got her into this. What's going to happen to her? My God, I'll never forgive myself."

Lituma saw Captain Silva's plump face, with its shadow of a beard, moving from pity to anger and back to compassion. He watched him stretch out his arm, pat Don Felícito's shoulder, and, bringing his head forward, say firmly, "I swear to you by the thing I hold most holy, which is the memory of my mother, that nothing's going to happen to Mabel. She'll be returned to you safe and sound. By my blessed mother, I'm going to solve this case and those sons of bitches are going to pay dearly. I never make vows like this, Don Felícito. You're a man with serious balls, everybody in Piura says so. Don't go soft on us now, for the sake of all you hold dear."

Lituma was impressed. What the chief said was true: He never made vows like the one he'd just made. He felt his spirits rising: He'd do it, they'd do it. They'd catch them. Those shits would be sorry they'd done anything so low to this poor man.

"I won't weaken now or ever," the trucker stammered, wiping his eyes.

VIII

Miki and Escobita arrived right on time, at exactly eleven in the morning. Lucrecia opened the door for them herself, and they kissed her on the cheek. Then, when they were sitting in the living room, Justiniana came in to ask what they would like to drink. Miki asked for an espresso cut with milk and Escobita a glass of sparkling mineral water. It was a gray morning, and low clouds passed over the dark green, foam-flecked ocean in Lima bay. Out at sea some small fishing boats were visible. Ismael Carrera's sons wore dark suits, ties, handkerchiefs in their breast pockets, and glittering Rolex watches on their wrists. When they saw Rigoberto come in they rose to their feet: "Hello, uncle." "Damn stupid custom," thought the master of the house. He didn't know why, but he was exasperated by the fashion, widespread for some years among Lima's younger generation, of calling family acquaintances and older people "uncle" or "aunt," inventing a kinship that didn't exist. Miki and Escobita shook his hand and smiled, displaying cordiality too effusive to be true. "How well you're looking, Uncle Rigoberto," "Retirement agrees with you, uncle," "You look I don't know how many years younger than the last time we saw you."

"You have a nice view from here," Miki finally said, indicating the seawall and the Barranco ocean. "When it's clear you must be able to see all the way from La Punta to Chorrillos, isn't that right, uncle?"

"And I also see and am seen by all the hang gliders and paragliders who brush against the windows as they go by," Rigoberto agreed. "Any day now a gust of wind will blow one of those intrepid fliers right inside our house."

His "nephews" greeted the joke with exaggerated laughter. "They're more nervous than I am," Rigoberto told himself in surprise.

They were twins but looked nothing alike except for their height, athletic bodies, and bad habits. Did they spend hours in the gym of the Club de Villa or the Regatas Club, exercising and lifting weights? How to reconcile those muscles with their irregular lives, the alcohol, the cocaine, the wild parties? Miki had a round, self-satisfied face, a thick-lipped mouth full of carnivorous teeth, and a pair of pendulous ears. He was very white, almost a gringo with his light hair, and from time to time he would smile in a mechanical way, like a ventriloquist's dummy. Escobita, on the other hand, was very dark-skinned and had dark piercing eyes, a lipless mouth, and a thin, penetrating voice. He wore the long sideburns of a flamenco singer or a bullfighter. "Which one is stupider?" Rigoberto thought. "And which one more depraved?"

"Don't you miss the office now that all your time is free, uncle?" asked Miki.

"The truth is I don't, nephew. I read a great deal, listen to good music, lose myself for hours in my art books. I've always liked painting more than insurance, as Ismael must have told you. Now I can finally devote a great deal of my time to it."

"What a library you have here, uncle," Escobita exclaimed, indicating the orderly shelves in the adjacent study. "Damn, that's a lot of books! Have you read them all?"

"Well, not yet, not all of them." ("This one's stupider," he decided.) "Some are reference books, like the dictionaries and encyclopedias in this corner. But my theory is that there's more chance of reading a book if you have it at home than if it's in a bookstore."

The two brothers, disconcerted, kept looking at him, no doubt wondering whether he'd made a joke or was serious.

"With so many art books it's like you've brought to your study here all the museums in the world," declared Miki, putting on the face of an astute and learned man. "And this way you can visit them without bothering to leave your house. That's really convenient."

"When you're as imbecilic as this biped, you become intelligent," Rigoberto thought. It was impossible to know which he was: six of one, half a dozen of the other. A heavy, interminable silence had settled over the living room, and to hide the tension, the three of them looked toward the study. "The time has come," Rigoberto thought. He experienced a slight feeling of alarm but was curious to know what would happen. He felt absurdly protected because he was on his own territory, surrounded by his books and etchings.

"Well, uncle," Miki said, blinking very quickly, his finger in the air moving toward his mouth, "I think the moment has come for us to take the bull by the horns and move on to some sad topics."

With a gargling sound, Escobita continued to drink the mineral water in his half-empty glass. He scratched his forehead ceaselessly and his eyes darted from his brother to Rigoberto.

"Sad? Why sad, Miki?" Rigoberto assumed a surprised expression. "What's wrong, boys? Are we having some more little problems?"

"You know very well what's wrong, uncle," Escobita exclaimed, an offended tone in his voice. "Don't act dumb, please."

"Are you referring to Ismael?" Rigoberto played the fool. "Do you want to talk about him? About your father?"

"We're the laughingstock of Lima, the talk of the whole city." Miki assumed a melodramatic expression, zealously biting his little finger. He spoke without taking his finger out of his mouth and his voice sounded affected. "You must have known, because even the stones knew. No one talks about anything else in this city, maybe in all of Peru. I never imagined the family would be involved in a scandal like this."

"A scandal you could have avoided, Uncle Rigoberto," Escobita declared, almost pouting. Only now did he seem to notice that his glass was empty. He placed it on the table in the center of the room with exaggerated care.

"First melodrama, then threats," Rigoberto thought to himself. He was uneasy, naturally, but increasingly intrigued by what was happening. He observed the twins as if they were a pair of incompetent actors. His expression was attentive and courteous. He didn't know why, but he wanted to laugh.

"I?" He pretended to be baffled. "I don't know what you're trying to say, nephew."

"You're the person my papa always listened to," Escobita stated with great emphasis. "Maybe the only one he always listened to. You know that very well, uncle, so stop pretending. Please. We're not here to play guessing games. Please!"

"If you'd advised him, if you'd opposed him, if you'd made him see the great mistake he was about to make, the wedding would never have happened," Miki declared, slapping the table. Now he'd changed, and a small viper zigzagged at the back of his light-colored eyes. His voice had become heated.

Rigoberto heard some music down below, at the seawall: It was the knife grinder's penny whistle. He always heard it at the same time. The fellow was a punctual man. He'd have to see his face some time.

"A wedding, by the way, that's worthless because it's pure garbage," Escobita corrected his brother. "A travesty without the slightest legal standing. You know that too, uncle; you're not a lawyer for nothing. So let's talk turkey, if you don't mind, and call a spade a spade."

"What's this imbecile trying to say?" Don Rigoberto wondered. "They both use clichés however they choose, like wild cards, not knowing what they mean."

"If you'd let us know in time what my papa was planning, we'd have stopped it, even if it meant calling in the police," Miki insisted. He still spoke with a forced sadness that couldn't hide the trace of fury in his tone. Now his partially hooded eyes were threatening Rigoberto.

"But instead of warning us, you took part in that fraud and even signed as a witness, uncle." Escobita raised his hand and made an enraged gesture in the air. "You signed along with Narciso. The two of you even involved the driver, that poor illiterate, in your ugly, ugly intrigue. So cruel, to take advantage of an ignorant man like that. Frankly, we didn't expect anything like this from you, Uncle Rigoberto. I can't get it into my head that you'd go along with this pathetic farce."

"You've disappointed us, uncle," was Miki's finishing touch; he moved as if his clothes were too tight. "That's the simple truth: dis-ap-point-ed. Just as it sounds. It makes me sad to say this to you, but that's the way it is. I'm saying it to your face and as frankly as I can because it's the sad truth. You bear a huge responsibility for what's happened, uncle. And we're not the only ones who think so. Lawyers are saying it too. And to be perfectly frank, you don't know what you've let yourself in for. This could have very bad consequences in your private life and in your other one."

"What's the other one?" thought Don Rigoberto. Both of them kept raising their voices, and their initial affectionate courtesy had evaporated along with their smiles. The twins were very serious now, no longer hiding their resentment. "Will they offer me money? Threaten me with a hired killer? Pull out a revolver?" Everything was possible with a pair like this.

"We haven't come to reproach you." Escobita suddenly changed strategy, sweetening his voice again. He smiled, caressing one of his sideburns, but there was something twisted and belligerent in his smile.

"We love you very much, uncle," Miki agreed with a sigh. "We've known you since we were born, you're like our closest relative. Except . . ."

He couldn't finish the idea and was left with his mouth open and an indecisive, disheartened look in his eyes. He opted for nibbling furiously on his little finger again. "Yes, he's the stupider one," Don Rigoberto thought to himself.

"The feeling is mutual, nephews." He took advantage of the silence to get a sentence in. "Calm down, please. Let's talk like rational, civilized people."

"That's easier for you than for us," replied Miki, raising his voice.

"Of course," Don Rigoberto thought. "He doesn't know what he's saying, but sometimes he gets it right."

"It's not your father but ours who married his maid, an ignorant, lousy half-breed, a *chola*, and made us the laughingstock of all the decent families in Lima."

"A marriage that isn't worth a damn besides!" Escobita reminded him again, gesturing frenetically. "A farce with no legal basis at all. I suppose you're well aware of that, Uncle Rigoberto. So stop acting like a boob, it doesn't suit you at all."

"What should I be aware of, nephew?" he asked very serenely, with a curiosity that seemed genuine. "And I'd like you to explain the meaning of that word 'boob.' It's a synonym for imbecile, isn't it?"

"I mean you've gotten involved in a huge mess out of pure ignorance," Escobita exploded in anger. "A motherfucking mess, if you'll pardon my language. Maybe without meaning to, thinking you were helping your good friend. We grant your good intentions. But none of that matters, because the law is the law for everybody, in this case most of all."

"This could mean serious personal problems for you and your family." Miki's voice was filled with pity, and as he spoke, he put his little finger back in his mouth. "We don't want to scare you, but this is how things are. You never should have signed that paper. I tell you that objectively and impartially. And with all my love, of course."

"We're telling you this for your own good, Uncle Rigoberto," said his brother, adding nuance to their argument. "Thinking more of your own interest than of ours, though you may not believe it. I only hope you won't come to regret your mistake."

"Soon they'll be in a rage, and these animals are capable of hitting me," Rigoberto realized. The twins were letting themselves be carried away by anger, and their looks, gestures, and expressions were increasingly aggressive. "Will I have to defend myself against these two with my fists?" he wondered. He couldn't even remember the last time he'd been in a fight. In the Academy of La Recoleta, surely, during some recess.

"We've consulted the best lawyers in Lima. We know what we're talking about. That's why we can assure you that you're now involved in one huge goddamn mess. Forgive me for using such ugly words, but we men have to look truth in the face. It's better that you know."

"For complicity and concealment," Miki explained in a solemn tone, saying each word very slowly to emphasize its hostility. His thin voice kept breaking and his eyes were ablaze.

"The annulment of the marriage is under way and the judgment won't be long in coming," Escobita explained. "That's why the best thing you could do is help us, Uncle Rigoberto. The best thing for you, I mean."

"In other words, it's not us we want you to help but my papa, Uncle Rigoberto. Your lifelong friend, the person who's been like an older brother to you. And we want you to help yourself and get out of this fucking predicament that you've gotten yourself and us into. Do you understand?"

"Frankly, I don't, nephew. I don't understand anything except that the two of you are very upset." Rigoberto chided them with serenity, affection, and a smile. "Since you're both talking at the same time, I confess you have me a little confused. I really don't understand what this is about. Why don't you settle down and calmly explain what it is you want."

Did the twins believe they'd beaten him? Is that what they thought? Because their attitude became immediately more temperate. Now he saw that they were smiling, nodding, exchanging complicit, self-satisfied glances.

"Yes, yes, forgive us, we went a little too fast," Miki apologized. "You know we love you very much, uncle."

"His ears are as big as mine," thought Rigoberto. "But his flutter and mine don't."

"And forgive us above all for raising our voices to you," Escobita added, waving his hands in the air for no reason, like a frantic monkey. "But things being the way they are, it's just as well, you have to understand. This craziness of my doddering old papa has Miki and me running around in circles."

"It's very simple," Miki explained. "We understand perfectly that while my papa was your boss at the company, you couldn't refuse to sign that paper as a witness. Just like poor Narciso. The judge will take that into account, of course. As an extenuating circumstance. Nothing will happen to either of you. The lawyers guarantee it."

"In his mouth, the word 'lawyer' is like a magic wand," Rigoberto thought with amusement.

"You're wrong, Narciso and I didn't agree to be your papa's witnesses because we were his employees," he replied amiably. "I did it because Ismael, besides being my boss, is a lifelong friend. And Narciso did it because of the great affection he's always had for your father."

"Well, that wasn't much of a favor you did for your dear friend."
Escobita was angry again; his face turned red, as if he'd suffered
sudden sunstroke; his dark eyes were flashing. "The old man didn't
know what he was doing. He's been senile for some time: For some
time he hasn't known where he is, or who he is, and least of all
what he was doing when he let himself be bamboozled by that
damn worthless *chola* who he wanted to get his rocks off with, if
you'll excuse the expression."

"Get his rocks off with?" Don Rigoberto thought. "That must
be the ugliest expression in the Spanish language. A thorny, reeking
phrase."

"Do you believe that, if he was in full possession of his facul-
ties, my papa, who was always a gentleman, would marry a servant
who, to make matters even worse, must be forty years younger
than he is?" Miki backed up his brother, opening his mouth wide
and displaying his large teeth.

"Do you believe that?" Now Escobita's eyes were red and his
voice was breaking. "It's not possible, you're intelligent and well
educated, don't kid yourself or try to kid us. Because not you and
not anybody else can pull the wool over our eyes."

"If I'd believed that Ismael was not in full possession of his fac-
ulties, I wouldn't have agreed to be his witness, nephew. Please let
me speak. I understand that you're very concerned. It's to be expected, of course. But you should try to accept the facts as they
are. It's not what you think. Ismael's marriage surprised me a great
deal too. As it surprised everyone, naturally. But Ismael knew very
well what he was doing, of that I'm certain. He decided to get married with complete lucidity and absolute knowledge of what he was
about to do, and of what the consequences would be."

As he spoke he saw indignation and hatred intensify on the
twins' faces.

"I'm assuming you wouldn't dare repeat the bullshit you're
saying now in front of a judge."

Escobita got up from his seat, in a rage, and took a step toward
him. Now he wasn't red but ashen and trembling.

Don Rigoberto didn't move from his chair. He expected to be
shaken and perhaps hit, but Escobita controlled himself, turned,

and sat down again. His round face was covered with perspiration. "The threats have come. Will punches be next?"

"If you wanted to scare me, you've succeeded, Escobita," he acknowledged, as calmly as before. "You've both succeeded, I should say. Do you want to know the truth? I'm dying of fear, nephews. You're both young, strong, impulsive, and with credentials that would strike terror in the heart of the cleverest man. I know them very well because, as you recall, I've often helped you out of the situations and difficulties you've gotten yourselves into since you were very young. Like the time you raped that girl in Pucusana, remember? I even recall her name: Floralisa Roca. That was her name. And naturally I haven't forgotten either that I had to take fifty thousand dollars to her parents so you two wouldn't go to prison because of the charming thing you'd done. I know very well that if you wanted to, you could make mincemeat out of me. That's perfectly clear."

Disconcerted, the twins looked at each other, grew serious, tried to smile, but without success, became exasperated.

"Don't take it like that," Miki said at last, taking his little finger out of his mouth and patting him on the arm. "We're all gentlemen here, uncle."

"We'd never lay a hand on you," Escobita declared in alarm. "We love you, uncle, even though you don't believe it. In spite of how badly you've behaved with us by signing that filthy paper."

"Let me finish," Rigoberto said, pacifying them, moving his hands. "In spite of my fear, if the judge asks me to testify, I'll tell him the truth. That Ismael made the decision to marry knowing perfectly well what he was doing. That he isn't doddering, or demented, and didn't let himself be bamboozled by Armida or anyone else. Because your father is still more alert than the two of you put together. That's the absolute truth, nephew."

Another dense, thorny silence fell in the room. Outside, the clouds had turned black, and in the distance, on the ocean's horizon, there were electric shafts that might have been a ship's reflectors or the lightning bolts of a storm. Rigoberto felt the tumult in his chest. The twins were still ashen and looked at him in a way, he told himself, that meant they were making a great effort not to attack him and beat him to a pulp. "You did me no favor at all when you got me involved in this, Ismael," he thought.

Escobita was the first to speak. He lowered his voice, as if he were going to tell Rigoberto a secret, and stared into his eyes with a look that flashed with contempt.

"Did my papa pay you for this? How much did he pay you, uncle, if you don't mind my asking?"

The question took Rigoberto so much by surprise that he was left openmouthed.

"Don't take the question the wrong way," said Miki, trying to smooth things over, lowering his voice as well and gesturing to pacify him. "There's no reason to be embarrassed, everybody has his needs. Escobita asked you this since, if it's a question of money, we're also prepared to reward you. Because, to tell the truth, we need you, uncle."

"We need you to go before the judge and state that you signed as a witness under pressure and threats," Escobita explained. "If you and Narciso testify to that, everything will move much faster and the marriage will be annulled one two three. Obviously we're prepared to compensate you, uncle. And generously."

"Services are paid for and we know very well what kind of world we live in," Miki added. "With absolute discretion, of course."

"Besides, you'll be doing my papa a great favor, uncle. The poor man must be desperate now, not knowing how to escape the trap he fell into in a moment of weakness. We'll get him out of the mess and in the end he'll thank us, you'll see."

Rigoberto listened, not blinking or moving, petrified in his seat, as if lost in wise reflection. The twins waited anxiously for his answer. The silence lasted close to a minute. In the distance the knife grinder's penny whistle sounded faintly from time to time.

"I'm going to ask the two of you to leave this house and never set foot in here again," Don Rigoberto said at last, with the same serenity he had maintained throughout. "The truth is you're worse than I thought, boys. And if there's anyone who knows you well it's me, ever since you were in short pants."

"You're offending us," said Miki. "Don't make a mistake, uncle. We respect your gray hairs, but only so far."

"We won't let this stand," declared Escobita, banging the table. "You have everything to lose, just so you know. Even your retirement is on the table."

"Don't forget who's going to own the company as soon as the crazy old coot kicks the bucket," Miki threatened.

"I asked you to leave," said Rigoberto, standing and pointing at the door. "And above all, don't show up here again. I don't want to see you anymore."

"Do you think you're going to throw us out of your house just like that, you lousy hustler?" said Escobita, standing as well and clenching his fists.

"Shut up," his brother cut him off, holding him by the arm. "Things can't degenerate into a fight. Apologize to Uncle Rigoberto for insulting him, Escobita."

"It's not necessary. It's enough if the two of you leave and don't come back," said Rigoberto.

"He's the one who's offended us, Miki. He's throwing us out of his house like two mangy dogs. Or maybe you didn't hear him."

"Apologize, damn it," ordered Miki, getting to his feet as well. "Right now. Beg his pardon."

"All right." Escobita gave in, trembling like a leaf. "I beg your pardon for what I said to you, uncle."

"You're forgiven," Rigoberto agreed. "This conversation is over. Thank you for your visit, boys. Goodbye."

"We'll talk again when we're calmer," said Miki in farewell. "I'm sorry it ended this way, Uncle Rigoberto. We wanted to reach a friendly understanding with you. In view of your inflexibility, we'll have to take this to court."

"This won't end well for you, and I tell you that from the heart because you'll be sorry," said Escobita. "So you'd better think it over."

"Let's go, brother, and just shut up." Miki took his brother's arm and dragged him to the front door.

As soon as the twins left the house, Rigoberto saw Lucrecia and Justiniana come into the room, alarmed expressions on their faces. The maid held a rolling pin like a deadly weapon.

"We heard everything," said Lucrecia, grasping her husband's arm. "If they'd done anything, we were ready to burst in and attack those hyenas."

"Ah, is that what the rolling pin's for?" Rigoberto asked, and Justiniana nodded, very seriously, swinging her improvised cudgel in the air.

"I had the poker from the fireplace in my hand," said Lucrecia. "We would have scratched out those hoodlums' eyes, I swear it, love."

"I behaved rather well, didn't I?" Rigoberto threw out his chest. "I didn't let that pair of morons intimidate me for a moment."

"You behaved like a great man," said Lucrecia. "And this time, at least, intelligence defeated brute force."

"Like a real man, señor," Justiniana echoed Lucrecia.

"Not a word about any of this to Fonchito," Rigoberto ordered. "The boy has enough headaches already."

The women agreed and suddenly, at the same time, all three burst into laughter.

IX

Six days after *El Tiempo* published Don Felícito Yanaqué's second notice (anonymous, unlike his first), the kidnappers still hadn't given any signs of life. And Sergeant Lituma and Captain Silva, in spite of all their efforts, had found no trace of Mabel. The kidnapping hadn't yet reached the press, and Captain Silva said this kind of miracle couldn't last; given the interest that the case of the owner of Narihualá Transport had awakened all over Piura, it was impossible for an event this important not to soon be front-page news in the papers and all over radio and television. Any day now, everything would become public knowledge, and Colonel Rascachucha would have another extraordinary temper tantrum complete with violent shouting, cursing, and foot-stamping.

Lituma knew his boss well enough to know how upset the chief was, even though he didn't talk about it, simulated certainty, and continued to make his usual cynical, vulgar comments. No doubt he was wondering, as Lituma was, whether the spider gang hadn't gone too far and Don Felícito's mistress, that cute little brunette, wasn't dead and buried in some garbage dump on the outskirts of town. Each time they met with the trucker, who was being consumed by this misfortune, the sergeant and captain were affected by the dark circles under his eyes, the tremor in his hands, and how his voice would break off in the middle of a phrase; he'd sit there dazed and mute, looking in terror at nothing, his watery eyes subject to fits of frantic blinking. "He could have a heart attack at any time and we'd have a stiff on our hands," Lituma thought fearfully. His boss was smoking twice as many cigarettes as usual, clenching the butts between his teeth and biting them, something he did only in times of extreme stress.

"What do we do if Señora Mabel doesn't show up, Captain? I'm telling you, this mess keeps me awake every night."

"We kill ourselves, Lituma," said the chief, trying to joke. "We'll play Russian roulette and leave this world with our balls intact, like Seminario in your bet. But she'll show up, don't be so pessimistic. They know from the notice in *El Tiempo*, or they think they know, that they've finally broken Yanaqué. Now they're making him suffer a little more just to clinch the deal. That isn't what really worries me, Lituma. Do you know what does? That Don Felícito will lose his head and suddenly decide to publish another notice, do an about-face and ruin our plan."

It hadn't been easy to convince him. It had taken the captain several hours to make him give in, presenting every possible argument for his taking the notice to *El Tiempo* that same day. He spoke to him first in the police station and then in El Pie Ajeno, a bar he and Lituma had to all but drag him to. They watched him drink half a dozen carob-bean cocktails, one after the other, even though, as he repeated several times, he never drank. Alcohol wasn't good for him, it upset his stomach and gave him diarrhea. But now it was different. He'd suffered a terrible blow, the most painful of his life, and alcohol would control his longing to have another crying fit.

"I beg you to believe me, Don Felícito," said the chief, making a show of his patience. "Understand, I'm not asking you to surrender to the gang. I'd never think of advising you to pay the extortion they're demanding."

"That's something I'd never do," the trucker repeated, shaking and adamant. "Even if they kill Mabel and I had to kill myself so I wouldn't have to live with that remorse on my conscience."

"I'm only asking you to pretend, that's all. Make them think you accept their conditions," the captain insisted. "You won't have to cough up a penny for them, I swear on my mother. And on Josefita, that gorgeous woman. We need them to release the girl, that will put us right on their trail. I know what I'm talking about, believe me. This is my profession and I know for a fact how these shits act. Don't be stubborn, Don Felícito."

"I'm not doing this out of stubbornness, Captain." The trucker had calmed down and now his expression was tragicomic because a lock of hair had fallen over his forehead and covered part of his right eye; he didn't seem to notice. "I'm really fond of Mabel, I love her. It breaks my heart that someone like her, who has nothing to do with this, is the victim of those greedy, vicious criminals. But I can't give them the satisfaction. Understand, Captain, it's not for my own sake. I can't insult my father's memory."

He was silent for a while, staring into his empty cocktail glass, and Lituma thought he'd begin to whimper again. But he didn't. Instead, with his head down, not looking at them, as if speaking not to them but to himself, the small man in his close-fitting, ash-colored jacket and vest began to recall his father. Blue flies buzzed in circles around their heads, and in the distance they could hear a heated argument between two men over a traffic accident. Felícito spoke in a hesitant way, searching for the words that would give the story he was telling proper weight and allowing himself at times to be overcome by emotion. Lituma and Captain Silva soon realized that the tenant farmer Aliño Yanaqué, from the Hacienda Yapatera, in Chulucanas, was the person Felícito had loved most in his life. And not only because the same blood ran in their veins but because thanks to his father, he'd been able to lift himself out of poverty, or rather, out of the wretchedness in which he was born and spent his childhood—a wretchedness they couldn't even imagine—to become a businessman, the owner of a large fleet of cars, trucks, and buses, an accredited transport company that made his humble family name shine. He'd earned people's respect; those who knew him also knew he was trustworthy and honorable. He'd been able to give his children a good education, a decent life, a profession, and would leave them Narihualá Transport, a business both customers and competitors thought well of. All this was due more to the sacrifices of Aliño Yanaqué than to his own efforts. He'd been not only his father but also his mother and his family, because Felícito had never known the woman who brought him into the world or any other relative. He didn't even know why he'd been born in Yapatera, a village of blacks and mulattoes where the Yanaqués, being Europeans, that is *cholos*, seemed like foreigners. They led an isolated life, because the dark-skinned people of Yapatera didn't make friends with Aliño and his son. Either because they

had no family or because his father didn't want Felícito to know
who his aunts and uncles and cousins were or where they could be
found, they'd always lived alone. He didn't remember it, he was very
young when it happened, but he knew that soon after he was born
his mother ran off, who knows where or with whom. She never
came back. For as long as he could remember his father had worked
like a mule, on the tiny farm the boss gave him and on the boss's
hacienda, with no Sundays or holidays off, every day of the week
and every month of the year. Aliño Yanaqué spent everything he
earned, which wasn't much, so that Felícito could eat, go to school,
have shoes and clothes, notebooks and pencils. Sometimes he gave
him a toy for Christmas or a coin so he could buy a lollipop or
taffy. He wasn't one of those fathers always kissing and spoiling
their children. He was frugal, austere, and never gave him a kiss
or a hug or told him jokes to make him laugh. But he deprived
himself of everything so his son wouldn't be an illiterate tenant
farmer when he grew up. Back then Yapatera didn't even have a
school. Felícito had to go from his house to the public school in
Chulucanas, five kilometers each way, and he didn't always find a
kindly driver who'd let him climb into his truck and save him the
walk. He didn't recall ever missing a single day of school. He always got good grades. Since his father couldn't read, he had to read
his report card to him, and it made Felícito happy to see Aliño proud
as a peacock when he heard the teachers praise his son. Since there
was no room in the only secondary school in Chulucanas, they had
to move to Piura so that Felícito could continue his education. To
Aliño's great joy, Felícito was accepted to School Unit San Miguel
of Piura, the most prestigious national secondary school in the city.
Following his father's instructions, Felícito hid from his classmates
and teachers the fact that Aliño earned his living loading and un-
loading merchandise in the Central Market, near the slaughterhouse, and at night picked up garbage in municipal trucks. All that
effort so his son could study and grow up to be something more
than a tenant farmer or a porter or a garbage collector. The advice
Aliño gave before he died, "Never let anybody walk all over you,
my son," had been the motto of his life. And Felícito wasn't going
to let those goddamn son of a bitch thieves, arsonists, and kidnappers walk all over him now.

"My father never asked for charity or let anybody humiliate him," he concluded.

"Your father must have been a person as respectable as you are, Don Felícito," said the chief, flattering him. "I'd never ask you to betray him, I swear. I'm only asking you to feint, to play a trick, by putting the notice that they asked for in *El Tiempo.* They'll think they've broken you and let Mabel go. That's what matters most now. They'll show themselves, and we'll be able to catch them."

Finally Don Felícito agreed. Together he and the captain wrote the text that would be published in the paper the following day:

THANKS TO THE CAPTIVE LORD OF AYABACA
With all my heart I thank the divine Captive Lord of Aya-baca who, in his infinite kindness, performed the miracle I asked him for. I'll always be grateful and ready to take all the steps that in his great wisdom and mercy he may wish to point out to me.
A devoted follower

During this time, while they were waiting for some sign from the spider gangsters, Lituma received a message from the León brothers. They'd persuaded Rita, Mono's wife, to let him go out at night, so instead of lunch they'd have dinner on Saturday. They met in a Chinese restaurant near the convent of the nuns from the Lourdes Academy. Lituma left his uniform in the Calanchas' boardinghouse and went in civilian clothes, wearing the only suit he owned. He took it to a laundry beforehand to have it washed and ironed. He didn't put on a tie but bought a shirt at a store that auctioned off its stock. He had his shoes polished at a news-stand and showered at a public bath before he went to meet his cousins.

It was harder for him to recognize Mono than José. He'd re-ally changed. Not only physically—though he was much fatter than when he was young and had very little hair, purple bags under his eyes, and wrinkles around his sideburns and mouth and on his neck. He was dressed casually in elegant clothes and wore white loafers. He had a thin chain on his wrist and another around his neck. But the greatest change was in his manner: calm, serene, belonging

to someone very self-assured because he's discovered the secret to
life and how to get on well with everyone. There was no trace left
of the silly tricks and clownishness of his boyhood, which had
earned him his nickname: Mono, the Monkey.

He embraced Lituma very affectionately. "How terrific to see
you again, Lituma!"

"All that's missing is for us to sing the anthem of the Unconquerables," exclaimed José. And clapping his hands, he asked the
Chinese waiter to bring some ice-cold Cusqueña beers.

The reunion was a little strained and difficult at first, because
their catalogues of shared memories were followed by great parentheses of silence, punctuated by little forced laughs and nervous
glances. A good deal of time had gone by, each had lived his life,
it wasn't easy to revive the old camaraderie. Lituma shifted uncomfortably in his seat, telling himself that maybe he should have
avoided this meeting. He thought of Bonifacia, of Josefino, and
something in his stomach contracted. And yet, as they kept emp-
tying the bottles of beer that accompanied the platters of fried rice,
Chinese noodles, Peking duck, wonton soup, and crispy fried
prawns, their blood ties came to life and their tongues loosened.
They began to feel more relaxed and comfortable. José and Mono
told jokes and Lituma urged his cousin to do some of the imita-
tions that had been his strong suit when he was young—the sermons of Father García in the Church of the Virgen del Carmen
on Plaza Merino, for example. Mono held back at first, but soon
he grew more animated and began to preach and hurl biblical thun-
derbolts like the old Spanish priest, philatelist, and grouch. Legend had it that, backed up by a crowd of pious old women, he'd
burned down the first brothel in the history of Piura, the one in
the middle of the sandy tract on the way to Catacaos, run by the
father of La Chunga from the Green House. Poor Father García!
The Unconquerables had embittered his life, shouting at him in
the streets "Burner! Burner!" They'd made the old grouch's final
years a calvary. Each time he passed them on the street, he'd shout
insults at them: "Bums! Drunkards! Degenerates!" Oh, how funny.
What times those were—times, as the tango said, that had gone
and would never came back.

They'd finished off the meal with a dessert of Chinese apples but were still drinking; Lituma's head was a soft, agreeable whirlpool. Everything was spinning and from time to time he yawned uncontrollably, almost dislocating his jaw. Suddenly, in a kind of semi-lucid doze, he realized that Mono had started to talk about Felícito Yanaqué. He was asking him something. He felt his drunkenness beginning to evaporate and regained control of his consciousness.

"What's happening with poor Don Felícito, cousin?" Mono repeated. "You must know something. Is he still determined not to make the payments they're demanding? Miguelito and Tiburcio are very worried, this mess has really fucked the two of them up. He may have been really hard on them, but they love their old man. They're afraid the crooks will kill him."

"You know Don Felícito's sons?" Lituma asked.

"Didn't José tell you?" Mono replied. "We've known them for a while."

"They'd bring the vehicles from Narihualá Transport to the shop for repairs and tuning." José seemed annoyed at Mono's confidences. "They're both nice guys. We're not good friends. Just acquaintances."

"We've done a lot of gambling with them," Mono added. "Tiburcio's damn good at dice."

"Tell me more about them," Lituma insisted. "I only saw them a couple of times when they came to the station to make their statements."

"Very good people," Mono declared. "They're very upset over what's happening to their father. Even though the old man was really a tyrant with them, it seems. He made them do everything in the business, beginning from the very bottom. He still has them working as drivers, supposedly paying them what the others make. No preferential treatment even though they're his sons. He doesn't pay them a penny more, and doesn't give them more time off. You probably know he put Miguelito in the army, supposedly to straighten him out, because he stepped off the straight and narrow. What a tough old bird!"

"Don Felícito is one of those rare types who appear only once in a while in this life," declared Lituma. "The most upstanding man I've known. Any other businessman would be making his payments by now and have gotten this nightmare off his back."

"Well, whatever, Miguelito and Tiburcio will inherit Narihualá and won't be poor anymore." José tried to change the subject. "And how are you doing, cousin? I mean, with women, for example. Do you have a wife, a girlfriend, girlfriends? Or just whores?"

"Don't go too far, José," Mono said, gesticulating, exaggerating the way he used to. "Look how you've embarrassed our cousin with that evil-minded curiosity of yours."

"You don't still miss the girl Josefino turned into a whore, cousin?" José asked with a laugh. "They called her Jungle Girl, didn't they?"

"I don't even remember her now," Lituma said, looking at the ceiling.

"Hey, don't remind our cousin of sad things, José."

"Let's talk about Don Felícito instead," Lituma suggested. "Really, he's got character; he's got balls. He's impressed me."

"Who hasn't he impressed—he's the hero of Piura, almost as famous as Admiral Grau," said Mono. "Maybe, now that he's become so popular, the gangsters won't dare to hurt him."

"Just the opposite, they'll try to hurt him precisely because of how famous he is; he's made them look ridiculous and they can't allow that," declared José. "The gangsters' honor is at stake, brother. If Don Felícito gets away with it, all the businessmen who pay extortion will stop tomorrow and the gang will break apart. Do you think they'll put up with that?"

Had his cousin José become nervous? Lituma, between yawns, noticed that José had started to make lines again on the surface of the table with the tip of his nail. He didn't stare, to avoid fooling himself the way he had the other day when he thought he was drawing spiders.

"And why don't you people do something, cousin?" Mono protested. "The Civil Guard, I mean. Don't take offense, Lituma, but the police, here in Piura at least, are useless. They don't do anything; they only take bribes."

"Not just in Piura," said Lituma, following his lead. "We're useless all over Peru, cousin. But let me tell you that I, at least, in all the years I've been wearing this uniform, have never asked anybody for a single bribe. And that's why I'm poorer than a beggar. But with Don Felícito, the truth is that the case isn't moving forward because we're very short on technology. The handwriting expert who was supposed to help us is on leave because they operated on his hemorrhoids. Imagine, the whole investigation held up because of one gentleman's damaged ass."

"Do you mean you still don't have clues about the crooks?" insisted Mono. Lituma would have sworn that José was begging his brother with his eyes not to keep harping on the same subject.

"We have some clues, but nothing very certain," the sergeant answered. "But sooner or later they'll make a false move. The problem is that now, in Piura, it's not one gang operating but several. But they'll fall. They always do something wrong and end up giving themselves away. Unfortunately, so far they haven't made any mistakes."

He asked them again about Tiburcio and Miguelito, the trucker's sons, and again he thought that José didn't like the subject. At a certain point the brothers contradicted each other.

"We actually haven't known them for very long," José repeated from time to time.

"What do you mean not very long, it's been six years at least," Mono corrected him. "Don't you remember the time when Tiburcio drove us to Chiclayo in one of his trucks? How long ago was that? A long time. When we tried to go into that business but it didn't work out."

"What business was that, cousin?"

"Selling agricultural machinery to the communities and co-operatives in the north," said José. "The bastards never paid. They protested every bill of exchange. We lost almost everything we'd invested."

Lituma didn't insist. That night, after saying goodbye to Mono and José, thanking them for the meal, taking a jitney to his boardinghouse, and getting into bed, he lay awake for a long time thinking about his cousins. Especially José. Why did he have so many doubts about him? Was it just because he drew with his fingernail on the table? Or was there really something suspicious in his behavior? He'd started acting strangely, as if he were worried, every time Don Felícito's sons came up. Or was this nothing but his own qualms about how lost the investigation was? Should he tell Captain Silva about his misgivings? Better to wait until it was all less insubstantial and something took shape.

But the first thing he did the next morning was to tell his boss everything. Captain Silva listened attentively, not interrupting him, taking notes in a tiny notebook with a pencil so small it disappeared between his fingers. When Lituma had finished, the captain murmured, "I don't think there's anything serious here. No clue to follow, Lituma. Your León cousins seem clean." But he sat there brooding, silent, chewing on his pencil as if it were a cigarette. Suddenly, he made a decision. "You know what, Lituma? Let's talk to Don Felícito's sons again. From what you've told me, it seems we still haven't gotten all the juice from those two. We'll have to squeeze a little harder. Make an appointment with them for tomorrow, each one separately, of course."

At that moment the guard at the entrance knocked on the cubicle door and his young, beardless face appeared in the opening: Señor Felícito Yanaqué was on the phone for the captain. It was extremely urgent. Lituma watched the chief pick up the old telephone receiver, heard him murmur, "Good morning, sir." And he saw his face light up as if he'd just been told he'd won the lottery. "We'll be right there," he shouted and hung up.

"Mabel's turned up, Lituma. She's in her house in Castilla. Let's go, run. Didn't I tell you? They swallowed the story! They let her go!"

"I've come to see you because I need your help, it's that simple." Rigoberto dropped into the chair that creaked under his weight and exhaled, overwhelmed. Pepín was the only person who still called him by his school nickname: Ears. In his adolescence, it had made him self-conscious. Not now.

That morning in the cafeteria at the Universidad Católica, at the beginning of the second year of law school, when Pepín O'Donovan suddenly announced—as casually as if he were discussing a class in civil law and principles, or the last Clásico match between Alianza and the U—that they wouldn't see each other for a while because he was leaving that night for Santiago de Chile to begin his novitiate, Rigoberto thought his friend was joking. "Do you mean you're going to become a priest? Don't kid around, man." True, both had joined Acción Católica, but Pepín had never even hinted to Ears that he'd heard the call. What he was telling him now was no joke but a deeply considered decision made in solitude and silence, over many years. Rigoberto learned afterward that Pepín had faced many problems with his parents, that his family tried everything to dissuade him from entering the seminary.

"Yes, man, of course," said Father O'Donovan. "If I can give you a hand, I'd be happy to, Rigoberto, that goes without saying."

Pepín had never been one of those overly pious boys who took communion at every Mass at school, the ones the priests flattered and tried to convince that they had a vocation, that God had chosen them for the priesthood. He was the most normal boy in the world, athletic, fond of parties, mischievous, and for a time he'd even had a girlfriend, Julieta Mayer, a freckled volleyball player who studied at the Academy of Santa Úrsula. He fulfilled his obligations by going to Mass, like all the students at La Recoleta, and he'd been a fairly diligent member of Acción Católica, but as far as Rigoberto could recall, no more devout than the others and not especially interested in the talks dedicated to religious vocations. He didn't even attend the retreats the priests organized from time to time at a country house they had in Chosica. No, it wasn't a joke but an irreversible decision. He'd felt the call from the time he was a boy and had thought it over carefully, not telling anyone before deciding to take the big step. Now there was no going back.

That same night he left for Chile. The next time they saw each other, it was many years later: Pepín was already Father O'Donovan, dressed as a priest, wearing eyeglasses, prematurely bald, and beginning his career as a die-hard cyclist. He was still a simple, amiable person, so that every time they saw each other it had become a kind of running joke for Rigoberto to tell him: "Good to know you haven't changed, Pepín, just as well that even though you are one, you don't seem like a priest." To which Pepín always responded by teasing Rigoberto with the nickname of his youth: "And those donkey's accessories of yours are still growing, Ears. Why is that, I wonder?"

"It's not about me," Rigoberto explained, "it's Fonchito. Lucrecia and I don't know what to do with the boy, Pepín. He's turning our hair gray, honestly."

They'd continued to see each other with some frequency. Father O'Donovan married Rigoberto and Eloísa, his first wife, Fonchito's late mother, and after he was widowed, Father O'Donovan also married him and Lucrecia in a small ceremony with only a handful of friends attending. He'd baptized Fonchito and occasionally visited the Barranco apartment, where he was received with great affection, to have lunch and listen to music. Rigoberto had helped him a few times with donations (his own and from the insurance company) for charitable work in the parish. When they saw each other, they tended to speak for the most part about music, which Pepín O'Donovan had always liked a great deal. From time to time Rigoberto and Lucrecia invited him to the concerts sponsored by the Philharmonic Society of Lima in the Santa Úrsula auditorium.

"Don't worry, man, it's probably nothing," said Father O'Donovan. "At the age of fifteen, all the young people in the world have and make problems. And if they don't, they're fools. It's normal."

"The normal thing would be for him to get drunk, go out with easy girls, smoke some marijuana, do all the stupid things you and I did when we were teenagers," said Rigoberto, in distress. "No, old man, that isn't the route Fonchito's taken. Instead, well, I know you're going to laugh, but for some time now he's gotten it into his head that he sees the devil."

Father O'Donovan tried to control himself but couldn't and burst into resounding laughter.

"I'm not laughing at Fonchito but at you," he explained between gales of laughter. "At you, Ears, talking about the devil. That word sounds very strange in your mouth. It sounds dissonant."

"I don't know if he's the devil, I never told you he is, I never used that word, I don't know why you do, Papa," Fonchito protested in a voice so faint that his father, in order not to miss a word he was saying, had to bend forward and bring his head close to the boy's.

"All right, forgive me, son," he apologized. "Just tell me one thing. I'm speaking to you very seriously, Fonchito. Do you feel cold each time Edilberto Torres appears? As if he'd brought an icy gust?"

"What silly things you're saying, Papa." Fonchito opened his eyes very wide, not sure whether to laugh or remain serious. "Are you kidding me or what?"

"Does he appear to him as the devil appeared to the famous Father Urraca, in the shape of a naked woman?" Father O'Donovan started to laugh again. "I suppose you've read that story by Ricardo Palma, Ears, it's one of his most amusing."

"Okay, it's okay," Rigoberto apologized again. "You're right, you never told me this Edilberto Torres was the devil. I beg your pardon, I know I shouldn't joke about this. The thing about the cold comes from a novel by Thomas Mann, where the devil appears to the main character, a composer. Forget my question. It's just that I don't know what to call this person, son. Someone who appears to you and disappears, who materializes in the most unexpected places, can't be flesh and blood like you and me. Isn't that so? I swear I'm not making fun of you. I'm speaking to you from the bottom of my heart. If he isn't the devil, then he must be an angel."

"Of course you're making fun of me, Papa, don't you see?" Fonchito protested. "I didn't say he's the devil or an angel either. I think he's a person like you and me, flesh and blood, of course, and very normal. If you like, we can end this conversation now and never talk again about Señor Edilberto Torres."

"It's not a game, it doesn't seem to be one," said Rigoberto very seriously. Father O'Donovan had stopped laughing and now was listening attentively. "The boy, though he doesn't say so, is completely changed by this. He's another person, Pepín. He always had a healthy appetite, he was never a fussy eater, and now he barely takes a mouthful. He's stopped playing sports, his friends come by for him and he invents excuses. Lucrecia and I have to push him to go outside. He's become taciturn, introverted, reticent, and he was always so sociable and talkative. He's constantly withdrawn, as if a great worry were eating him up inside. I no longer recognize my son. We took him to a psychologist who did all kinds of tests. And the diagnosis was that nothing's wrong, that he's the most normal child in the world. I swear to you we don't know what else to do, Pepín."

"If I were to tell you the number of people who believe they see visions, Rigoberto, you'd be flabbergasted," said Father O'Donovan, attempting to reassure him. "Generally they're old women. It's more unusual among children. They have bad thoughts more than anything else."

"Couldn't you talk to him, old man?" Rigoberto was in no mood for jokes. "Counsel him? I mean, I don't know. It was Lucrecia's idea, not mine. She thinks maybe with you he could be more open than he is with us."

"The last time was at the Larcomar Cineplex, Papa." Fonchito had lowered his eyes and hesitated when he spoke. "Friday night, when Chato Pezzuolo and I went to see the new James Bond. I was caught up in the movie, having a terrific time, and suddenly, suddenly . . ."

"Suddenly what?" urged Don Rigoberto.

"Suddenly I saw him, sitting next to me," said Fonchito, his head lowered and breathing deeply. "It was him, no doubt about it. I swear, Papa, there he was. Señor Edilberto Torres. His eyes were shining, and then I saw tears running down his cheeks. It couldn't have been the movie, Papa, nothing sad was on the screen, everything was fighting, kissing, adventures. I mean, he was crying over something else. And then, I don't know how to tell you this, but it occurred to me that he was so sad because of me. I mean, that he was crying because of me."

"Because of you?" Rigoberto spoke with difficulty. "Why would that man cry for you, Fonchito? What in you could he feel sorry about?"

"I don't know, Papa, I'm just guessing. But otherwise, why do you think he'd cry, sitting there beside me?"

"And when the movie was over and the lights went on, was Edilberto Torres still in the seat next to yours?" Rigoberto asked, knowing perfectly well what the answer would be.

"No, Papa. He was gone. I don't know exactly when he got up and left. I didn't see."

"All right, fine, of course," said Father O'Donovan. "I'll talk to him as long as Fonchito wants to talk to me. But don't try to force him. Don't even think about obliging him to come here. Nothing like that. Let him come willingly, if he feels like it. So the two of us can talk like a couple of friends, present it to him like that. Don't take this too seriously, Rigoberto. I'll bet it's just some kid's nonsense."

"I didn't, at first," Rigoberto said. "Lucrecia and I thought that since he's a boy with a lot of imagination, he was inventing the story to make himself important, to keep us hanging on his words."

"But does this Edilberto Torres exist or is he an invention?" asked Father O'Donovan.

"That's what I'd like to know, Pepín, that's why I've come to see you. So far I haven't been able to find out. One day I think he does exist and the next day I think he doesn't. Sometimes I think the boy's telling me the truth, and other times I think he's playing with us, fooling us."

Rigoberto had never understood why Father O'Donovan, instead of pursuing teaching and an intellectual career as a scholar and theologian within the Church—he was erudite and sensitive, loved ideas and the arts, and read a great deal—had stubbornly confined himself to pastoral work in a very modest parish in Bajo el Puente, where the residents were uneducated as a rule, a world in which his talent seemed wasted. Once he had dared to ask him about it. "Why didn't you write or give lectures, Pepín? Why didn't you teach at the university, for example?" If there was anyone among his acquaintances who seemed to have a clear intellectual vocation, a passion for ideas, it was Pepín.

"Because I'm needed more in my parish in Bajo el Puente." Pepín O'Donovan only shrugged. "Pastors are needed; there are more than enough intellectuals, Ears. You're mistaken if you think it's difficult for me to do what I do. Parish work interests me a great deal, it plunges me headfirst into real life. In libraries, one sometimes becomes too isolated from the everyday world, from ordinary people. I don't believe in your spaces of civilization that set you apart from others and turn you into an anchorite, but we've already discussed this."

He didn't seem like a priest because he never touched on religious subjects with his old schoolmate; he knew that Rigoberto had stopped believing when he was in the university, but being friends with an agnostic didn't seem to discomfit him in the least. On the few occasions he had lunch in the house in Barranco, after getting up from the table, he and Rigoberto would usually go into the study and play a CD, generally something by Bach, whose organ music Pepín O'Donovan loved.

"I was convinced he was making up all those appearances," Rigoberto explained. "But this psychologist who saw Fonchito, Dr. Augusta Delmira Céspedes, you've heard of her, haven't you? It seems she's very well known. She made me doubt again. She told me and Lucrecia in no uncertain terms that Fonchito wasn't lying, that he was telling the truth. That Edilberto Torres exists. She left us very confused, as you can imagine."

Rigoberto told Father O'Donovan that after going back and forth about it for a long time, he and Lucrecia had decided to find a specialized agency ("One of those agencies that jealous husbands hire to spy on their erring spouses?" the priest asked mockingly, and Rigoberto nodded: "Exactly"). A detective would follow Fonchito whenever he left the house, alone or with friends. The report from the agency—"which, by the way, cost me a fortune"—had been eloquent and contradictory: At no time had the boy had the slightest contact anywhere with older men, not at the movies, or at the Argüelles family's party, or when he went to school or came home, or even in his fleeting visit to a discotheque in San Isidro with his friend Pezzuolo. And yet, in that discotheque, when Fonchito went to the bathroom to pee, he'd had an unexpected encounter: There was the aforementioned gentleman, washing his hands (of course there was nothing about this in the report from the agency).

"Hello, Fonchito," said Edilberto Torres.

"At the discotheque?" asked Rigoberto.

"In the bathroom at the discotheque, Papa," Fonchito specified. He spoke with confidence, but it seemed as if his tongue were heavy and each word required enormous effort.

"Are you having a good time here with your friend Pezzuolo?" The gentleman seemed disconsolate. He'd washed his hands and now was drying them with a paper towel he'd just pulled from the small box on the wall. He wore his usual purple sweater but his suit was blue, not gray.

"Why are you crying, señor?" Fonchito dared to ask him.

"Edilberto Torres was crying there too, in the bathroom of a discotheque?" Rigoberto gave a start. "Like on the day you saw him sitting beside you at the Larcomar Cineplex?"

"At the movies I saw him in the dark and I might have been wrong," Fonchito responded with no hesitation. "Not in the bathroom at the discotheque. There was enough light. He was crying. Tears came out of his eyes and ran down his face. It was . . . it was . . . I don't know how to say it, Papa, it was sad, really sad, I swear. Seeing him cry in silence, not saying anything, looking at me with so much sorrow. He seemed to be suffering so much and it made me feel bad."

"Excuse me, but I have to go, señor," Fonchito stammered. "My friend Chato Pezzuolo is waiting for me outside. I don't know how to tell you how it makes me feel to see you like this, señor."

"In other words, as you can see, Pepín, this isn't a joke," Rigoberto concluded. "Is he telling us the whole story? Is he delirious? Is he hallucinating? Except for this, the boy seems very normal when he talks about other things. This month his grades in school have been just as good as usual. Lucrecia and I don't know what to think anymore. Is he losing his mind? Is this an adolescent crisis of nerves, something that will pass? Does he just want to frighten us and have us worry about him? That's why I've come, old man, that's why we thought of you. I'd be so grateful if you could help us. It was Lucrecia's idea, as I said: 'Father O'Donovan might be the solution.' She's a believer, as you know."

"Yes, naturally, of course I will, Rigoberto," his friend reassured him again. "As long as he agrees to talk to me. That's my only condition. I can see him at your house, or he can come here to the church. Or I can meet him somewhere else. Any day this week. I realize now that this is very important to both of you. I promise to do everything I can. The only thing, really, is that you not force him. Suggest it to him and let him decide whether he wants to talk to me."

"If you get me out of this, I'll even convert, Pepín."

"Not on your life," said Father O'Donovan, making the sign of *vade retro*. "We don't want sinners as refined as you in the Church, Ears."

They didn't know how to bring up the subject with Fonchito. It was Lucrecia who had the courage to speak to him. The boy was somewhat unnerved at first and took it as a joke. "But what do you mean, Stepmother, isn't my papa an agnostic? Was it his idea for me to talk to a priest? Does he want me to confess?" She explained that Father O'Donovan was a very experienced man and a very wise person whether he was a clergyman or not. "And if he persuades me to enter a seminary and become a priest, what will you and my papa say then?" the boy continued to joke.

"Absolutely not, Fonchito, don't say that even to be funny. You, a priest? God save us!"

The boy agreed, as he'd agreed to see Dr. Delmira Céspedes, and said he preferred to go to the church in Bajo el Puente. Rigoberto drove him in his car. He dropped him off and went to pick him up a couple of hours later.

"He's a very nice guy, your friend," was all Fonchito would say.

"In other words, the conversation was worthwhile?" Rigoberto explored the terrain.

"It was very good, Papa. That was a great idea. I learned a lot of things talking to Father O'Donovan. He doesn't seem like a priest, he doesn't give advice, he listens. You were right."

But he refused to say any more either to him or to his stepmother in spite of their requests. He limited himself to generalities, like the smell of cat urine that filled the church ("Didn't you notice, Papa?") even though the priest assured him he didn't have and had never had a cat and, in fact, saw mice in the sacristy from time to time.

Rigoberto soon deduced that something strange, perhaps something serious, had occurred during the couple of hours that Pepín and Fonchito talked. Otherwise, why had Father O'Donovan been avoiding him for the past four days, making up all kinds of excuses, as if he were afraid to meet with him and tell him about his conversation with the boy?

"Are you looking for reasons not to tell me how your conversation with Fonchito went?" He confronted him on the fifth day, when the priest deigned to answer the telephone.

There was a silence of several seconds on the phone, and finally Rigoberto heard the priest say something that left him stupefied.

"Yes, Rigoberto. The truth is, I am. I've been avoiding you. What I have to tell you is something you're not expecting," Father O'Donovan said mysteriously. "But since it can't be helped, let's talk about it. I'll come to your house for lunch on Saturday or Sunday. Which day is better for you?"

"Saturday, Fonchito usually has lunch that day at his friend Pezzuolo's house," said Rigoberto. "What you've said will keep me awake until Saturday, Pepín. And it'll be even worse for Lucrecia."

"That's how I've been since you had the bright idea of having me talk to your son," the priest said drily. "Until Saturday then, Ears."

Father O'Donovan must have been the only cleric who traveled through greater Lima not by bus or jitney but on a bicycle. He said it was his only exercise, but he did it so regularly that it kept him in excellent physical condition. Besides, he liked to pedal. He would think as he rode, preparing his sermons, composing letters, scheduling the day's tasks. True, he had to be constantly on the alert, especially at intersections and at the traffic lights that no one in this city respected, and where motorists drove as if trying to knock down pedestrians and cyclists instead of bringing their vehicle safely home. Even so, he'd been lucky: In the more than twenty years that he'd been traveling all over the city on two wheels, he'd been hit only once, with no serious consequences, and only one bicycle had been stolen. An excellent record!

On Saturday, at about midday, Rigoberto and Lucrecia, who were watching the street from the terrace of the penthouse where they lived, saw Father O'Donovan pedaling furiously along the Paul Harris Seawalk in Barranco. They felt great relief. It had seemed so strange that the cleric put off telling them about his conversation with Fonchito for so long that they had even worried he'd invent a last-minute excuse to avoid coming. What could have been said in the conversation to make him so reluctant to tell them about it?

Justiniana went downstairs to tell the porter to allow Father O'Donovan to bring his bicycle into the building to keep it safe from thieves, and rode up with him in the elevator. Pepín embraced Rigoberto, kissed Lucrecia on the cheek, and asked permission to go to the bathroom to wash his hands and face because he was sweaty.

"How long did it take you to cycle from Bajo el Puente?" asked Lucrecia.

"Just under half an hour," he said. "With the traffic jams we have now in Lima, it's faster to go on a bicycle than in a car."

He asked for fruit juice as an aperitif and looked at both of them slowly, smiling.

"I know you must have been saying terrible things about me for not telling you what happened," he said.

"Yes, Pepín, exactly, terrible, awful, dreadful things. You know how upset we are about this. You're a sadist."

"How was it?" Doña Lucrecia asked anxiously. "Did he talk to you honestly? Did he tell you everything? What's your opinion?"

Father O'Donovan, very serious now, took a deep breath. He murmured that the half hour of pedaling had tired him more than he cared to admit. And he was silent for a long time.

"Shall I tell you something?" He looked at them with an expression that was partly distressed, partly defiant. "The truth is I'm not at all comfortable about the conversation we're about to have."

"Neither am I, Father," said Fonchito. "There's no reason to have it. I know very well that my papa's nerves are on edge because of me. If you like, you do whatever you have to do and give me a magazine to read, even if it's a religious one. Then we'll tell my papa and stepmother that we talked and you can make up something to reassure them. And that'll be that."

"Well, well," said Father O'Donovan. "The fruit doesn't fall far from the tree, Fonchito. Do you know that at your age, in La Recoleta, your father was a great bamboozler?"

"Did you get to talk to him about that man?" asked Rigoberto, not hiding his anxiety. "Did he open up to you?"

"The truth is, I don't know," said Father O'Donovan. "This boy is like quicksilver, he always seemed to be slipping away from me. But don't worry. I'm sure of one thing at least. He's not crazy, he's not delirious, and he's not kidding you. I thought he was the healthiest, most centered child in the world. The psychologist who saw him told you the absolute truth: He has no mental problems at all, as far as I can judge. Of course, I'm not a psychiatrist or a psychologist—"

"But then this man's appearances," Lucrecia interrupted. "Did you find out anything certain? Does Edilberto Torres exist or not?"

"Though it might not be entirely accurate to say he's normal." Father O'Donovan corrected himself, avoiding the question. "Because the boy has something exceptional, something that differentiates him from the rest. I'm not referring only to his being intelligent. He's that, certainly. I'm not exaggerating one bit, Rigoberto, and I'm not saying this just to please you. But besides that, the boy has in his mind, his spirit, something that draws one's attention. A very special, very personal kind of sensibility we ordinary mortals don't possess. Literally. As for the rest, I don't know if this is a reason to be glad or frightened. And I don't discount the possibility that he wanted to give me that impression and succeeded, as a consummate actor would. I really wasn't sure whether I should come and tell you this. But I thought it was better if I did."

"Can we get to the point, Pepín?" Don Rigoberto had become impatient. "Stop beating around the damn bush. I'll speak frankly: Cut the bullshit, and let's get to the meat of the problem. Speak clearly and please stop trying to save your own ass."

"What awful language, Rigoberto," said Lucrecia in reproof. "It's just that we're so terribly worried, Pepín. Forgive him. I think this is the first time I've heard your friend Ears swearing like a truck driver."

"All right, I'm sorry, Pepín, but tell me once and for all, old man," Rigoberto insisted. "Does the ubiquitous Edilberto Torres exist? Does he appear to him in movie theaters, in discotheque bathrooms, on school bleachers? Can all this nonsense be true?"

Father O'Donovan had begun to perspire again, copiously, and now it was not due to the bicycle, thought Rigoberto, but the stress of having to render a verdict on this subject. What in hell was it? What was going on?

"Let's put it this way, Rigoberto," said the priest, handling his words with extreme caution, as if they had thorns. "Fonchito believes he sees and talks to him. I think that's incontrovertible. Well, I believe he believes it absolutely, so that he believes he isn't lying to you when he says he's seen and talked to him. Even though these appearances and disappearances seem, and are, absurd. Do you understand what I'm trying to say to you?"

Rigoberto and Lucrecia looked at each other and then at Father O'Donovan in silence. The priest now seemed as confused as they were. He'd become sad and clearly wasn't happy with his answer either. But it was evident he had no other and couldn't give a better explanation. He didn't know how.

"I understand, of course I do, but what you're telling me doesn't mean anything, Pepín," Rigoberto complained. "That Fonchito isn't trying to deceive us was one of the hypotheses, naturally. That he might be deceiving himself through autosuggestion: Is that what you believe?"

"I know that what I'm telling you is a disappointment, that you were both hoping for something more definitive, more categorical," Father O'Donovan continued. "I'm sorry, but I can't be more concrete, Ears. I can't. This is all I could make of it. That the boy isn't lying. He believes he sees the man and perhaps . . . perhaps it's possible he does. That he's the only one who sees him and nobody else does is something I can't get past. It's simple conjecture. I repeat: I don't exclude the possibility that your son is stringing me along. In other words, that he's more astute and skilled than I am. Maybe he takes after you, Ears. Do you remember at La Recoleta when Father Lagnier called you a mythomaniac?"

"But, then, what you've learned is not at all clear but very obscure, Pepín," Rigoberto murmured.

"Is it a question of visions? Or hallucinations?" Lucrecia attempted to make things more explicit.

"You can call it that, but not if you associate those words with mental unbalance or disease," the priest declared. "My impression is that Fonchito has total control of his mind and emotions. He's a well-balanced boy and distinguishes clearly between the real and the imaginary. I can definitely assure you of that, I'd bet my life on his sanity. In other words, this isn't something that can be resolved by a psychiatrist."

"I assume you're not talking about miracles," said Rigoberto, irritated and mocking. "Because if Fonchito is the only person who sees Edilberto Torres and speaks to him, you're talking about miraculous powers. Have we fallen so low, Pepín?"

"Of course I'm not talking about miracles, Ears, and neither is Fonchito," said the priest, now irritated as well. "I'm simply talking about something I don't know what to call. The child is having a very special experience. I won't say a religious experience because you don't know and don't want to know what that is, but let's compromise and use the word 'spiritual.' Something to do with sensitivity, with extreme emotion. Something that only very indirectly has to do with the material, rational world we move through. For him, Edilberto Torres symbolizes all human suffering. I know you don't understand me. That's why I was so afraid to come and tell you about my talk with Fonchito."

"A spiritual experience?" Doña Lucrecia repeated. "What does that mean exactly? Can you explain, Pepín?"

"It means that the devil appears to him, that his name is Edilberto Torres, and that as it turns out, he's Peruvian," summarized a sarcastic and angry Rigoberto. "Basically that's what you're telling us, Pepín, in the inane prattle of a miracle-faking priest."

"Lunch is served," said Justiniana, just in time, from the doorway. "You can come to the table whenever you like."

"At first it didn't bother me, it only surprised me," said Fonchito. "But now it does. Though 'bother' isn't the right word, Father. It disturbs me, rather, makes me feel bad, makes me sad. Ever since I saw him cry, you know? The first few times he didn't cry, he only wanted to talk. And though he doesn't tell me why he's crying, I think he's crying for all the bad things that happen. And for me, too. That's what hurts me the most."

There was a long silence, and finally Father O'Donovan said the prawns were delicious and he could tell they came from the Majes River. Should he congratulate Lucrecia or Justiniana for this delicacy?

"Neither one, but the cook," replied Lucrecia. "Her name's Navidad and she's from Arequipa, of course."

"When was the last time you saw this gentleman?" asked the priest, who'd lost the confident, secure air he'd had until now and seemed somewhat nervous. He asked the question with great diffidence.

"Yesterday, crossing the Puente de los Suspiros, in Barranco, Father," Fonchito answered immediately. "I was walking across the bridge and there were maybe three other people. And suddenly there he was, sitting on the railing."

"Crying, as usual?" asked Father O'Donovan.

"I don't know, I saw him for just a moment as I walked past. I didn't stop, I kept walking, walking faster," the boy explained, and now he seemed frightened. "I don't know if he was crying. But his face looked really sad. I don't know how to say it, Father. I swear to you I've never seen anyone as sad as Señor Torres. It's contagious, I'm upset for a long time afterward, full of sorrow, and I don't know what to do. I'd like to know why he's crying. I'd like to know what he wants me to do. Sometimes I tell myself he's crying for all the people who suffer. For the sick, the blind, for those who beg in the streets. Well, I don't know, lots of things go through my head when I see him. But I don't know how to explain them, Father."

"You explain them very well, Fonchito," Father O'Donovan said. "Don't worry about that."

"But then, what should we do?" asked Lucrecia.

"Advise us, Pepín," Rigoberto added. "I'm completely paralyzed. If it's as you say, then the boy has a kind of gift, a hypersensibility, and sees what no one else sees. It's that, isn't it? Should I talk to him about it? Should I say nothing? It worries me, it frightens me. I don't know what to do."

"Love him and leave him in peace," said Father O'Donovan. "What's certain is that this individual, whether or not he exists, is no pervert and doesn't wish to hurt your son in the slightest. Whether or not he exists, he has more to do with Fonchito's soul, well, with his spirit, if you prefer, than with his body."

"Something mystical?" Lucrecia interjected. "Could that be it? But Fonchito was never very religious. Just the opposite, I'd say."

"I'd like to be more precise, but I can't," Father O'Donovan confessed again; he looked defeated. "Something's happening to the boy that has no rational explanation. We don't know everything that's in us, Ears. Human beings, each of us, are chasms filled with shadows. Some men, some women, are more intensely sensitive than others, they feel and perceive things that the rest of us don't. Could this be purely a product of his imagination? Yes, perhaps. But it could also be something else I don't dare give a name to, Rigoberto. Your son is experiencing this so powerfully, so authentically, that I resist thinking it's purely imaginary. And I don't want to and won't say more than that."

He fell silent and sat looking at the plate of corvina and rice with a kind of hybrid feeling that was both stupefaction and tenderness. Lucrecia and Rigoberto had not tasted a mouthful.

"I'm sorry I haven't been much help to you," the priest added sadly. "Instead of helping you out of this tangled situation, I've become entangled in it too."

He was silent for a long time and looked at them both with concern.

"I'm not exaggerating if I tell you that this is the first time in my life I've confronted something I wasn't prepared for," he murmured very seriously. "Something that, for me, has no rational explanation. I already told you I don't discount the possibility that the boy is exceptionally good at deception and has made me swallow a huge fabrication. It's not impossible. I've thought about that a great deal. But no, I don't believe it. I think he's very sincere."

"You're not going to leave us very reassured knowing my son has daily communication with the beyond," said Rigoberto with a shrug, "and that Fonchito is a bit like the little shepherdess of Lourdes. She was a shepherdess, wasn't she?"

"You're going to laugh, the two of you are going to laugh," said Father O'Donovan, toying with his fork and not touching the corvina. "But I haven't stopped thinking about the boy for a moment. Of all the people I've known in my life, and there are many, I believe that Fonchito is closest to what we believers call a pure being. And not only because of how beautiful he is."

"Now the priest is showing, Pepín." Rigoberto was indignant. "Are you suggesting my son might be an angel?"

"An angel without wings in any case," Lucrecia said with a laugh, openly happy now, her eyes burning with mischief.

"I'll say it and repeat it even though it makes you both laugh," declared Father O'Donovan, laughing as well. "Yes, Ears, yes, Lucrecia, I mean it literally. And even though it amuses you. A little angel, why not?"

XI

When they reached the house in Castilla where Mabel lived, on the other side of the river, Sergeant Lituma and Captain Silva were dripping with sweat. The sun beat down mercilessly from a cloudless sky where turkey buzzards were circling, and there wasn't the slightest breeze to alleviate the heat. During the trip from the station, Lituma had been asking himself questions. In what condition would they find the cute brunette? Had those bastards mistreated Felícito Yanaqué's mistress? Had they beaten her? Raped her? Very possibly. Given how good-looking she was, why wouldn't they take advantage of having her at their mercy day and night.

Felícito himself opened the door of Mabel's house. He was euphoric, relieved, happy. The grim face that Lituma had always seen had changed, his recent tragicomic expression had disappeared. Now he grinned from ear to ear and his eyes gleamed with happiness. He looked rejuvenated. He wasn't wearing a jacket, and his vest was unbuttoned. He was so skinny, his chest and back almost touched, and he was really a runt, he almost looked like a midget to Lituma. As soon as he saw the two policemen he did something unheard-of for a man so little given to emotional displays: He opened his arms and embraced Captain Silva.

"It happened just as you said, Captain," he said effusively, patting him on the back. "They let her go, they let her go. You were right, Chief. I don't have the words to thank you. I'm alive again, thanks to you. And to you too, Sergeant. Many thanks, many thanks to you both."

His eyes were wet with emotion. Mabel was showering, she'd be with them right away. He had them sit in the living room, beneath the image of the Sacred Heart of Jesus, facing the small table that held a papier-mâché llama and a Peruvian flag. The electric fan twanged rhythmically and the current of air made the plastic flowers sway. The trucker, effusive and happy, nodded to all of the officers' questions: Yes, yes, she was fine, it had been terrifying, of course, but luckily they hadn't hit or abused her, thank God. All that time they'd kept her blindfolded, with her hands tied, what heartless, cruel people. Mabel would give them all the details herself as soon as she came out. And from time to time, Felícito would lift his hands to heaven: "If anything had happened to her, I would never have forgiven myself. Poor thing! All this *via crucis* on my account. I've never been very devout, but I promised God that from now on I'd go to Mass every Sunday without fail."

"He's head over heels in love with her," thought Lituma. You could be sure he'd have a great fuck. This reminded him of his own solitude, how long it had been since he'd had a woman. He envied Don Felícito and was furious with himself.

Mabel came out to greet them in a flowered robe, sandals, and a towel wrapped like a turban around her head. Like this, without makeup, wan, her eyes still frightened, she seemed less attractive to Lituma than on the day she came to the station to make her statement. But he liked her turned-up nose and the way her nostrils quivered, her slim ankles, the curve of her instep. Her skin was lighter on her legs than on her hands and arms.

"I'm sorry I can't offer you anything," she said, indicating that they should sit down. And still she tried to make a joke: "As you can imagine, I haven't been shopping for a few days and there's not even a Coke in the fridge."

"We're very sorry for what happened to you, señora." A very formal Captain Silva made a slight bow. "Señor Yanaqué was saying they didn't mistreat you. Is that true?"

Mabel made a strange face, half smile and half pout.

"Well, up to a point. Luckily they didn't beat me or rape me. But I wouldn't say they didn't mistreat me. I've never been so terrified in my life, señor. I'd never slept so many nights on the floor with no mattress and no pillow. And blindfolded and with my hands tied up like an Ekeko doll. I think my bones will ache for the rest of my life. Isn't that mistreatment? All right, I'm alive at least, that's true."

Her voice trembled and at moments a profound fear could be seen in the depths of her black eyes, which she made an effort to control.

"Damn motherfuckers," Lituma thought. He felt sorry and angry about what Mabel had endured. "Shit, they'll pay for this."

"You have no idea how much we regret bothering you now when you must want to rest." Captain Silva apologized, toying with his kepi. "But I hope you understand. We can't lose any time, señora. Would you mind if we asked you a few questions? It's essential before the guilty parties get away."

"Of course, sure, I understand," Mabel agreed, putting on a good face but unable to completely hide her annoyance. "Ask your questions, señor."

Lituma was impressed with how affectionate Felícito Yanaqué was with his little woman. Gently he passed his hand along her face, as if she were his pampered lapdog, moved stray locks of hair from her forehead and tucked them under the towel, brushed away the blowflies that came near her. He looked at her tenderly; he couldn't take his eyes off her. He held one of her hands in both of his.

"Did you ever see their faces?" the captain asked. "Would you recognize them if you saw them again?"

"I don't think so." Mabel shook her head but didn't seem very sure of what she was saying. "I only saw one of them, and that was hardly at all. The one standing beside the tree, the poinciana with the red flowers, when I came home that night. I hardly noticed him. He was standing sideways, and it was dark. Just when he turned to say something to me and I was about to get a look at him, they threw a blanket over my head. I was choking. And I didn't see anything else until this morning, when—"

She stopped, her face agitated, and Lituma realized she was making a great effort not to burst into tears. She tried to go on talking but made no sound. Felícito implored them with his eyes to have compassion for Mabel.

"Easy, easy does it," Captain Silva consoled her. "You're very brave, señora. You've had a terrible experience and they haven't broken you. I'll just ask you for one last little effort, please. Of course we'd prefer not to talk about this, we'd prefer to help you bury those bad memories. But the thugs who kidnapped you have to be put behind bars, have to be punished for what they did to you. You're the only one who can help us get to them."

Mabel agreed, with a mournful smile. Pulling herself together, she continued. Lituma thought her account was coherent and fluent, though at times she was shaken by whiplashes of fear and had to be quiet for a few seconds, trembling, turning pale, her teeth chattering. Was she reliving the moments of the nightmare, the tremendous fear she must have felt day and night for an entire week while she was held by the gang? But then, she resumed her story again, interrupted occasionally by Captain Silva ("What refined manners," thought Lituma, surprised), who would ask for more details.

The kidnapping had taken place seven days earlier, after a concert by a Marist choir in the Church of San Francisco on Calle Lima, which Mabel attended with her friend Flora Díaz, who owned a clothing store on Calle Junín called Creaciones Florita. They'd been friends for a long time and sometimes went out together to the movies, to have lunch, and to go shopping. Friday afternoons they usually went to the Church of San Francisco, where the independence of Piura had been proclaimed, since it presented music programs, concerts, choirs, dance, and professional groups. That Friday the Marist choir sang religious hymns, many of them in Latin, or that's what it sounded like. Flora and Mabel were bored and left before the program was over. They said goodbye at the entrance to the Puente Colgante and Mabel walked back to her house since it was so close. She didn't notice anything unusual during her walk, no pedestrian or car following her, nothing at all. Just stray dogs, swarms of kids getting into trouble, people enjoying the cool air and chatting in chairs and rockers they'd brought out to the doorways of houses, the bars, shops, and restaurants already full of customers and their jukeboxes playing different pieces of music at top volume, which mixed and filled the air with a deafening noise. ("Was there a moon?" asked Captain Silva, and for a moment Mabel was disconcerted: "Was there? I'm sorry, I don't remember.")

Her street was deserted, she thought she remembered. She barely noticed the male figure half leaning against the poinciana. She had the key in her hand, and if he'd tried to approach her she'd have become alarmed, called for help, started to run. But she didn't notice him making the slightest movement. She put the key in the lock and had to force it slightly—"Felícito must have told you it always sticks a little"—when she sensed somebody approaching. She didn't have time to react. She felt a blanket thrown over her head and several arms grabbing her, all at the same time. ("How many arms?" "Four, six, who knows?") They lifted her up and covered her mouth to stifle her screams. It seemed to her that everything happened in a second, there was an earthquake and she was in the middle of it. In spite of her tremendous panic she tried to kick and move her arms, until she felt them throwing her into a van, a car, or a truck and immobilizing her, securing her feet, hands, and head. Then she heard the words that still resounded in her ears: "Nice and quiet if you want to keep on living." She felt them pass something cold across her face, maybe a knife, maybe the butt or barrel of a revolver. The vehicle took off, shaking and bouncing her against the floor. She curled up and was silent, thinking: "I'm going to die." She didn't even have the strength to pray. Without complaining or resisting, she let them blindfold her, put a hood over her head, and tie her hands. She didn't see their faces because they did everything in the dark, probably while they were driving on the highway. There were no electric lights and it was pitch-black outside. Then it must have been cloudy, with no moon. They kept driving for a time that seemed to her like hours, centuries, but might have only been a few minutes. With her face covered, her hands tied, and her fear, she lost all sense of time. From then on she could never tell what day it was, if it was night, if people were watching her or had left her alone in the room. The floor where she lay was very hard. Sometimes she felt insects walking along her legs, maybe those horrible cockroaches she detested more than spiders and rats. Holding her by the arms, they made her get out of the van, grope her way in the darkness, stumbling; they pushed her into a house where a radio was playing Peruvian music, made her go down some stairs. After putting her on the floor on a rush mat, they left. She lay in the dark, trembling. Now she could pray. She pleaded with the Virgin and all the saints she could think of, Santa Rosa de Lima and the Captive Lord of Ayabaca of course, to help her. Not to let her die like this, to end her torture.

During the seven days she was held captive she didn't have a single conversation with her kidnappers. They never took her out of that room. She never saw the light again because they never removed her blindfold. There was a container or bucket where she could take care of her needs, in the dark, twice a day. Somebody took it away and brought it back clean, never saying a word to her. Twice a day, the same person or somebody else, always mute, brought her a plate of rice and vegetables and some soup, a luke-warm soda or a small bottle of mineral water. They removed the hood and untied her hands so she could eat, but they never took off the blindfold. Each time Mabel begged them, implored them to tell her what they were going to do with her, why they had abducted her, the same strong, commanding voice always replied: "Be quiet! You're risking your life by asking questions." She wasn't allowed to bathe, or even wash herself. That's why the first thing she did when she was free was take a long shower and scrub herself with the sponge until she had welts. And then get rid of all the clothes, even the shoes, that she'd been wearing for those horrible seven days. She would make up a parcel and give it to the poor of San Juan de Dios.

This morning, without warning, several of them, to judge by their footsteps, had come into her room-prison. Without a word, they lifted her, made her walk, climb some steps, and lie down again in a vehicle that must have been the same van, car, or truck they'd used to kidnap her. They kept driving and driving for a very long time, and the shaking bruised all the bones in her body until the vehicle finally stopped. They untied her hands and ordered: "Count to a hundred before you take off the blindfold. If you take it off before then, we'll shoot you." When she removed the blindfold, she discovered that they'd left her in the middle of the sandy tract, near La Legua. She'd walked for more than an hour before reaching the first houses in Castilla, where she caught a taxi that took her home.

As Mabel recounted her odyssey, Lituma continued to pay careful attention to her story but couldn't ignore Don Felícito's demonstrations of affection to his mistress. There was something childish, adolescent, angelic in the way the trucker smoothed her forehead with his hand, looking at her with a religious devotion, murmuring, "Poor thing, poor thing, my love." At times the way he fawned over her made Lituma uncomfortable—it seemed exaggerated and a little ridiculous at the trucker's age. "He must be thirty years older than she is," he thought. "This girl could be his daughter." The old guy was head over heels in love. Was Mabelita one of the fiery ones or was she cold? Fiery, no doubt about it.

"I told her she should go away from here for a while," Felícito Yanaqué said to the policemen. "To Chiclayo, Trujillo, Lima, anywhere. Until this case is closed. I don't want anything to happen to her again. Don't you think that's a good idea, Captain?"

The officer shrugged. "I don't think anything will happen to her if she stays here," he said, mulling it over. "The bandits know she's protected now and wouldn't be crazy enough to come near her, knowing the chance they'd be taking. I'm very grateful for your statement, señora. It will be very useful to us, I assure you. Would you mind my asking you just a few more questions?"

"She's very tired," Don Felícito protested. "Why don't you leave her alone for now, Captain? Question her tomorrow, or the day after. I want to take her to the doctor and have her spend the day in the hospital so she can have a complete checkup."

"Don't worry, old man, I'll rest later," Mabel interjected. "Go ahead and ask me whatever you'd like, señor."

Ten minutes later, Lituma said to himself that his superior had gone too far. The trucker was right; the poor woman had suffered a terrible experience, had expected to die; those seven days had been a calvary for her. How could the captain expect Mabel to remember all the insignificant, stupid details he was harassing her with? He didn't understand. Why did his boss want to know whether from her prison she'd heard roosters crowing, hens cackling, cats meowing, or dogs barking? And how could Mabel estimate by their voices how many kidnappers there were and if they were all Piurans or whether one of them talked like he was from Lima, the sierra, or the jungle? Mabel did what she could, she wrung her hands, hesitated, it was only normal that sometimes she became confused or seemed astonished. She didn't remember that, señor, she hadn't paid attention to that, oh what a shame. And she apologized, shrugging, wringing her hands: "I was so stupid, I should have thought about those things, tried to be aware and remember. But I was so confused, señor."

"Don't worry, it's only natural that you weren't thinking straight, impossible to keep everything in your memory," Captain Silva said encouragingly. "But still, make one final little effort. Everything you can remember will be very useful to us, señora. Some of my questions may seem unnecessary, but believe me, sometimes the thread that leads us to our goal can come from one of those unimportant little trifles."

What seemed even stranger to Lituma was that Captain Silva was so insistent that Mabel recall the circumstances and details of the night she was kidnapped. Was she sure that none of her neighbors was out on the street, enjoying the cool air? Not a single woman leaning half out the window listening to a serenade or chatting with her boyfriend? Mabel didn't think so, but maybe there was; no, no, nobody was on that end of the street when she came home from the Marists' concert. Well, maybe there was somebody, it was possible, it's just that she didn't pay attention, didn't realize, how stupid. Lituma and the captain knew all too well there was no witness to the kidnapping because they'd questioned the entire neighborhood. No one saw anything, no one heard anything unusual that night. Maybe it was true or, perhaps, as the captain had said, nobody wanted to get involved. "Everybody's scared to death at the thought of the gangs. That's why they'd rather not see or know anything, that's how this useless scum is."

Finally the chief gave the trucker's girlfriend a breather and moved on to a trivial question.

"Señora, what do you think the kidnappers would have done to you if Don Felícito hadn't let them know he'd pay the ransom?"

Mabel opened her eyes very wide, and instead of answering the officer she turned to her lover.

"They asked you for a ransom for me? You didn't tell me, old man."

"They didn't ask for a ransom for you," he clarified, kissing her hand again. "They kidnapped you to force me to pay protection money for Narihualá Transport. They let you go because I made them think I agreed to their demands for money. I had to put a notice in *El Tiempo*, thanking the Captive Lord of Ayabaca for a miracle. It was the sign they were waiting for. That's why they let you go."

Lituma saw that Mabel turned very pale. She was trembling again and her teeth were chattering.

"Does this mean you're going to pay protection?" she stammered.

"Not on your life, baby," Don Felícito bellowed, emphatically shaking his head and hands. "Not that, not ever."

"They'll kill me, then," Mabel whispered. "And you too, old man. What's going to happen to us now, señor? Will they kill us both?" She sobbed and raised her hands to her face.

"Don't worry, señora. You'll have twenty-four-hour protection. But not for very long, it won't be necessary, you'll see. I swear to you, these thugs' days are numbered."

"Don't cry, don't cry, baby," Don Felícito comforted her, caressing and embracing her. "I swear nothing bad will happen to you again. Never again, I swear, dearest, you have to believe me. The best thing would be for you to leave the city for a little while like I've asked you to, please listen to me."

Captain Silva stood and Lituma followed his lead. "We'll give you round-the-clock protection," the chief assured them again as he was leaving. "Don't worry, señora." Mabel and Don Felícito didn't accompany them to the door; they remained in the living room, she whimpering and he consoling her.

Outside a torrid sun awaited them, along with the usual spectacle: ragged street kids kicking a ball, emaciated dogs barking, piles of trash on the corners, peddlers, and a line of cars, trucks, motorcycles, and bicycles competing for the road. Turkey buzzards weren't only in the sky; two of the hideous birds had landed and were picking through the garbage.

"What did you think, Captain?"

His boss took out a pack of black-tobacco cigarettes, offered one to the sergeant, took another for himself, and lit both with an old dark green lighter. He took a long drag and exhaled smoke rings. He had a very satisfied expression on his face.

"They fucked up, Lituma," he said, pretending to punch his subordinate. "Those assholes made their first mistake, just what I was waiting for. And they fucked up! Let's go to El Chalán, I'll buy you a nice fruit juice with lots of ice to celebrate."

He was grinning from ear to ear and rubbing his hands together the way he did when he won at poker, or dice, or checkers.

"That woman's confession is pure gold, Lituma," he added, inhaling and exhaling the smoke with delight. "You saw that, I suppose."

"I didn't see anything, Captain," a disconcerted Lituma confessed. "Are you serious or are you kidding me? I mean, the poor woman didn't even see their faces."

"Damn, what a bad cop you are, Lituma, and an even worse psychologist," the captain said mockingly, looking him up and down and laughing out loud. "Shit, I don't know how you ever got to be a sergeant. Not to mention my assistant, which is saying a lot."

Again he murmured to himself: "Pure gold, yes sir." They were crossing the Puente Colgante and Lituma saw that a group of street kids were swimming, splashing, and carrying on along the sandy banks of the river. He'd done the same things with his León cousins a million years ago.

"Don't tell me you didn't see that our smart Mabelita didn't say a single word that was true, Lituma," the captain added, becoming very serious. He puffed on the cigarette, exhaled the smoke as if defying heaven, with triumph in his voice and eyes. "All she did was contradict herself and tell us a damn pack of lies. She tried to stick it to us. And stick it up our asses too. As if you and I were a couple of real pricks, Lituma."

The sergeant stopped dead, stunned.

"What you're saying, are you serious, Captain, or are you putting one over on me?"

"Don't tell me you didn't see what was so obvious and so clear, Lituma." The sergeant realized that his boss was speaking very seriously, with absolute conviction. As he spoke he looked at the sky, blinking constantly because of the glare, exalted and happy. "Don't tell me you didn't see that sad-assed Mabelita was never kidnapped. That she's an accomplice of the extortionists and went along with the farce of the kidnapping to soften up poor Don Felícito, who she also wanted to fleece. Don't tell me you didn't see that thanks to the mistakes of those motherfuckers, the case is practically solved, Lituma. Rascachucha can rest easy and stop driving us fucking crazy. Their bed is made, and now all we have to do is lay hands on them and push them over the edge."

He threw the butt into the river and began to laugh out loud, scratching at his armpits.

Lituma had taken off his kepi and was smoothing down his hair.

"Either I'm dumber than I look or you're a genius, Captain," he declared, demoralized. "Or crazier than a coot, if you'll excuse me."

"Better believe I'm a genius, Lituma, and besides, I know all about people's psychology," the exultant captain assured him. "I'll make you a prediction, if you like. The day we arrest those thugs, which will happen very soon, as there's a God in heaven I'll fuck my darling Señora Josefita up the ass and break her cherry and keep her shrieking all night long. Hooray for life, damn it!"

XII

"Did you find poor Narciso?" asked Señora Lucrecia. "What happened to him?"

Don Rigoberto nodded and collapsed, exhausted, in a chair in the living room of his house.

"A real odyssey," he said, sighing. "Ismael did us no favor by involving us in his troubles in bed and with his children, my love."

The relatives of Narciso, Ismael Carrera's driver, had made an appointment to meet Rigoberto at the first gas station at the entrance to Chincha, and he drove on the highway for two hours to get there, but when he arrived no one was waiting for him. He spent a long time in the sun watching trucks and buses go by and swallowing the dust that a hot wind from the sierra blew into his face, and when he'd had enough and was tired and ready to go back to Lima, a little black boy appeared and said he was Narciso's nephew. Very dark-skinned and barefoot, he had large, effusive, conspiratorial eyes. He spoke in such a roundabout way that Don Rigoberto barely understood what he was trying to tell him. Finally, it became clear that there had been a change of plan: his uncle Narciso was waiting for Rigoberto in Grocio Prado, in the doorway of the same house where the Blessed Melchorita (the boy crossed himself when he said her name) had lived, performed miracles, and died. Another half hour of driving on a dusty road filled with potholes, which ran between vineyards and small farms that grew fruit for export. In the doorway of the house-museum-sanctuary of the Blessed One, on the Plaza de Grocio Prado, Ismael's driver finally appeared.

"Half in disguise, wearing a kind of poncho and a penitent's hood so that nobody would recognize him and, of course, dying of fear," Don Rigoberto recalled with a smile. "That black man was white with panic, Lucrecia. And really, it's no wonder. The hyenas hound him day and night, it's worse than I'd imagined."

First they'd sent a lawyer, that is, a fast-talking shyster, to try to bribe him. If he appeared before the judge and said he'd been coerced into being a witness at his employer's wedding and, in his opinion, Señor Ismael Carrera hadn't been in his right mind on the day he married, they'd give him a gratuity of twenty thousand soles. When he replied that he'd think about it but in principle preferred not to have dealings with the judiciary or anyone in the government, the police showed up at his family's house in Chincha with a summons. The twins had filed a complaint against him for complicity in several crimes, among them conspiracy and the abduction of his boss!

"All he could do was hide again," Rigoberto continued. "Fortunately, Narciso has friends and relatives all over Chincha. And it's lucky for Ismael that he's the most upright and loyal fellow in the world. In spite of how frightened he is, I doubt those two thugs are going to break him. I paid him his salary and gave him a little extra, just in case, for anything unforeseen. This business gets more complicated every day, my love."

Don Rigoberto stretched and yawned in the easy chair in the living room, and while Doña Lucrecia prepared lemonade, he stared at the ocean of Barranco for a long time. It was a windless afternoon and several hang gliders were in the air. One passed by so close he could clearly see his head encased in a helmet. Damn mess, happening now when he was supposed to begin a retirement he thought would be dedicated to rest, art, and travel—that is, to pure pleasure. Things never worked out as planned: It was a rule with no exceptions. "I never imagined my friendship with Ismael would turn out to be so onerous," he thought. "Much less that I'd have to sacrifice my small piece of civilization for it." If the sun had been out, this would have been Lima's magical time. A few minutes of absolute beauty. The fiery ball would sink into the sea on the horizon behind the islands of San Lorenzo and El Frontón, burning up the sky, turning the clouds pink, and for a few minutes putting on a show, both serene and apocalyptic, that signaled the onset of night.

"What did you say to him?" Doña Lucrecia asked, sitting beside him. "Poor Narciso, what he's gotten himself into for being so decent to his employer."

"I tried to reassure him," recounted Don Rigoberto, tasting the lemonade with pleasure. "I told him not to be frightened, that nothing would happen to him or me because we'd been witnesses, that there was absolutely no crime in what we did. And that Ismael would win this battle with the hyenas. That Escobita and Miki's campaign, the fuss they were making, didn't have the slightest basis in law. That if he wanted more reassurance, he should consult a lawyer in Chincha whom he trusted and send me the bill. In short, I did everything I could. He's a very honorable man and I repeat: Those thugs won't be able to control him. But they certainly are giving him a very hard time."

"And us too, aren't they?" Doña Lucrecia complained. "I tell you, ever since this joke began, I'm even afraid to go out. Everybody asks me about the couple, as if it were the only thing Limeños cared about. Everybody I see looks like a reporter. You can't imagine how much I hate them when I hear and read all the foolishness and lies they write."

"She's frightened too," thought Don Rigoberto. His wife smiled at him, but he could detect a fleeting glimmer in her eyes and saw the uneasy way she was constantly wringing her hands. Poor Lucrecia. Not only had the European trip she'd so looked forward to been canceled but, on top of everything else, there was this scandal. And old man Ismael was still on his honeymoon in Europe, staying out of touch, while in Lima his boys were making life impossible for Narciso, for him, and for Lucrecia; they had even thrown the insurance company into an uproar.

"What is it, Rigoberto?" Lucrecia asked with some surprise. "The man who laughs alone is thinking of his evil deeds."

"I'm laughing at Ismael," Rigoberto explained. "He's been on his honeymoon for a month. And he's over eighty! I've confirmed it, he's an octogenarian, not a septuagenarian. *Chapeau!* Do you see, Lucrecia? All that Viagra will eat up his brains, and the hyenas' accusation that he's soft in the head will turn out to be true. Armida must be a wild animal. She'll drain him dry!"

"Don't be vulgar, Rigoberto." His wife laughed and pretended to admonish him.

"She knows how to make the best of a bad time," Rigoberto thought tenderly. Over the past few days, while the twins' campaign of intimidation had filled their house with judicial and police citations and bad news—the worst: they'd managed to tie up his retirement process with some legal dirty tricks—Lucrecia hadn't shown the least sign of weakness. She'd supported him body and soul in his decision not to give in to the hyenas' extortion and remain loyal to his employer and friend.

"The one thing that bothers me," said Lucrecia, reading his mind, "is that Ismael hasn't even called or dropped us a line. Doesn't that seem strange to you? Can he really not know about the headaches he's giving us? Doesn't he realize what poor Narciso is going through?"

"He knows everything," Rigoberto assured her. "Arnillas is in touch with him and keeps him up to date. They speak every day, he told me."

Dr. Claudio Arnillas, Ismael Carrera's attorney for many years, was now Rigoberto's intermediary with his former employer. According to him, Ismael and Armida were traveling through Europe and would return to Lima very soon. He assured him that the plans of Ismael Carrera's sons to annul the marriage and have their father declared incompetent to head the insurance company on the grounds of incapacity and senile dementia were doomed to the most resounding failure. All Ismael had to do was appear and submit to the relevant medical and psychological tests, and their accusations would collapse.

"But then, I don't understand why he doesn't do that right now, Dr. Arnillas," exclaimed Don Rigoberto. "For Ismael this scandal has to be even more painful than it is for us."

"Do you know why?" explained Dr. Arnillas, adopting a Machiavellian expression and hooking his thumbs behind the psychedelic-colored suspenders holding up his trousers. "Because he wants the twins to keep spending what they don't have: the money they must be borrowing all over the place to pay their army of shyster lawyers and the bribes they're coughing up for the police and judges. It's more than likely they're being skinned alive, and he wants them completely ruined. Señor Carrera planned every-thing down to the smallest detail. Do you see?"

Don Rigoberto saw very clearly now that Ismael Carrera's rancor toward the hyenas, from the day he discovered that in their eagerness to inherit everything they were waiting impatiently for his death, was unhealthy and irreversible. He never would have imagined the peaceable Ismael capable of a vengeful hatred of this magnitude, least of all toward his own children. Would Fonchito ever desire his death? And by the way, where was that boy?

"He went out with his friend Pezzuolo, I think to the movies," Lucrecia said. "Haven't you noticed that for the past few days he's seemed better? As if he'd forgotten about Edilberto Torres."

Yes, he hadn't seen that mysterious character for more than a week. At least that's what he'd told them, and Don Rigoberto had never caught his son in a lie.

"All of this wrecked the trip we'd planned so carefully," Doña Lucrecia said with a sigh, suddenly becoming sad. "Spain, Italy, France. What a shame, Rigoberto. I'd been dreaming about it. And do you know why? It's your fault, you kept telling me about it in that detailed, obsessive way. The places we'd visit, the museums, the concerts, the theaters, the restaurants. Well, what can you do except be patient."

Rigoberto agreed. "We've only postponed it, my love," he re-assured her, kissing her hair. "Since we can't go in the spring, we'll go in the fall. A very nice time of year too, with the trees turning golden and the leaves carpeting the streets. For operas and con-certs, it's the best time of year."

"Do you think this mess with the hyenas will be over by October?"

"They don't have any money, and they're spending the little they have trying to annul the marriage and have their father declared incompetent," Rigoberto said. "They won't succeed and they'll be ruined. Do you know something? I never imagined that Ismael was capable of doing what he's doing. First, marrying Armida. And

second, planning so unforgiving a revenge against Miki and Escobita. It's true that it's impossible to know anyone else completely, people are unfathomable."

They spent a long time talking as it grew dark and the lights in
the city came on. They could no longer see the ocean, and the sky
and the night were filled with lights that seemed like fireflies. Lucrecia told Rigoberto she'd read an essay Fonchito had written for
school that had made an impression on her. She couldn't get it out
of her head.

"Did he show it to you himself?" Rigoberto asked pointedly.
"Or were you snooping through his desk?"

"Well, it was right there, in plain sight, and it made me curious. That's why I read it."

"It's not right for you to read his things without his permission and behind his back." Rigoberto seemed to be reprimanding
her.

"It left me thinking," she continued, ignoring him. "It's a half-
philosophical, half-religious text. About liberty and evil."

"Do you have it handy?" Rigoberto was interested. "I'd like to
take a look at it too."

"I made a copy for you, Mr. Nosy," said Lucrecia. "I left it in
your study."

Don Rigoberto shut himself in with his books, records, and
etchings to read Fonchito's composition. "Liberty and Evil" was
very short. It maintained that God, when He created man, probably had decided he wasn't an automaton like plants and animals,
whose lives were programmed from birth to death, but a creature
endowed with free will, capable of deciding his actions on his own.
This was how liberty was born. But this faculty with which man
was endowed allowed human beings to choose evil, even, perhaps,
to create it, doing things that contradicted all that emanated from
God, and this represented the devil's reason for being, the basis
of his existence. Therefore evil was the child of liberty, a human
creation. Which didn't mean that liberty was evil in and of itself;
no, it was a gift that had permitted great scientific and technical
discoveries, social progress, the elimination of slavery and colo-
nialism, the birth of human rights, etcetera. But it was also the

origin of the terrible, never-ending cruelties and suffering that accompanied progress like its shadow.

Don Rigoberto was concerned. It occurred to him that all the ideas in the essay were somehow associated with the appearances of Edilberto Torres and his fits of weeping. Or was the essay the result of Fonchito's conversation with Father O'Donovan? Had his son seen Pepín again? Just then Justiniana burst into his study, very excited. She'd come to tell him that the "newlywed" was on the phone.

"That's what he said I should tell you, Don Rigoberto," the girl explained. " 'Tell him the newlywed is calling, Justiniana.' "

"Ismael!" Don Rigoberto jumped up from his desk. "Hello? Hello? Is that you? Are you in Lima? When did you get back?"

"I haven't returned yet, Rigoberto," said a playful voice, which he recognized as belonging to his boss. "I'm calling from a place, but naturally I won't say where it is, because a little bird told me your phone is bugged by you know who. A very beautiful place, so eat your heart out with envy."

He burst into very joyful laughter and Rigoberto, alarmed, suddenly suspected that yes, his ex-boss and friend was in his dotage, hopelessly senile. Were the hyenas capable of paying one of those agencies to interfere with his phone? Impossible, the gray matter couldn't take that in. Or perhaps it could.

"Well, well, what more could you wish for," he replied. "Better for you, Ismael. I see that your honeymoon is going full speed ahead and you still have some wind left. I mean, at least you're still alive. I'm glad, old man."

"I'm in fine shape, Rigoberto. Let me tell you something: I've never felt better or happier than I have during this time. And that's the truth."

"Fantastic, then," Rigoberto repeated. "Well, I don't want to give you bad news, least of all by telephone. But I suppose you're aware of what you've caused here and the trouble that's raining down on us."

"Claudio Arnillas keeps me up to date with plenty of details and sends me newspaper clippings. I enjoy reading that I've been kidnapped and am suffering from senile dementia. It seems you and

Narciso have been complicit in my abduction, isn't that right?" He burst into laughter again—long, loud, and very sarcastic.

"How nice that you can take everything with so much good humor," Rigoberto grumbled. "Narciso and I aren't enjoying this as much, as you can imagine. The brothers have driven Narciso half crazy with their intrigues and threats. And us as well."

"I'm very sorry for the bother I'm causing you, brother." Ismael tried to smooth things over, and became very serious. "I'm sorry they've interfered with your retirement and that you've had to cancel your trip to Europe. I know everything, Rigoberto. A thousand apologies to you and Lucrecia for these problems. I swear to you it won't be for much longer."

"What do a retirement and a trip to Europe matter compared to the friendship of a grand fellow like you," Don Rigoberto said sarcastically. "I'd better not tell you about the judicial summonses that compel me to testify as a presumed accomplice in your concealment and abduction; I don't want to ruin that lovely honeymoon of yours. Well, I hope all this will soon be something we can laugh over and tell anecdotes about."

Ismael guffawed again, as if it all had little to do with him.

"You're the kind of friend that doesn't exist anymore, Rigoberto. I always knew it."

"Arnillas must have told you that your driver had to hide. The twins have set the police on him, and given how unstable they are, I wouldn't be surprised if they also send in a couple of hired killers to cut off his you-know-what."

"They're very capable of it," Ismael acknowledged. "That black man is worth his weight in gold. Reassure him, tell him he shouldn't worry, that his loyalty will have its reward, Rigoberto."

"Are you coming back soon or will you continue your honeymoon until your heart explodes and you drop dead?"

"I'm finishing up a little matter that will amaze you, Rigoberto. As soon as it's settled, I'll return to Lima and put things in order. You'll see, this mess will disappear in the blink of an eye. I'm really sorry for the headaches I've caused. That's why I called, no other reason. We'll see each other very soon. Kisses to Lucrecia and a big hug for you."

"Another one for you and kisses to Armida." Don Rigoberto said goodbye.

When he hung up, he sat staring at the phone. Venice? The Riviera? Capri? Where could the lovebirds be? Somewhere exotic like Indonesia or Thailand? Could Ismael be as happy as he said? Yes, no doubt, judging by his juvenile laughter. At eighty he'd discovered that life could be more than work—it could also mean doing mad things. Running off, savoring the pleasures of sex and revenge. Better for him. Just then an impatient Lucrecia came into his study.

"What happened? What did Ismael say? Tell me, tell me."

"He seems very happy. He's laughing at everything, believe it or not," he told her. And then he was struck again by the same suspicion. "Do you know something, Lucrecia? What if he really has become senile? What if he doesn't even realize the crazy things he's doing?"

"Are you serious or are you joking, Rigoberto?"

"Until now he'd seemed absolutely lucid and clearheaded to me," he said hesitantly. "But as I listened to him laughing on the phone, I started to think. Because he thought everything going on here was incredibly funny, as if he didn't care at all about the scandal or the mess he's gotten us into. Well, I don't know, maybe I'm a little touchy. Do you realize the situation we'll be in if it turns out that Ismael has been stricken overnight by senile dementia?"

"I wish you'd never put that idea into my head, Rigoberto. I'll be thinking about it all night. Too bad for you if I can't sleep, I'm warning you."

"It's sheer nonsense, don't pay any attention to me, it's a kind of magic charm so that what I say might happen, doesn't," Rigoberto reassured her. "But the truth is, I didn't expect to find him so unconcerned. As if this all had nothing to do with him. Sorry, I'm sorry. Now I know what's going on. He's happy. That's the key to everything. For the first time in his life Ismael knows what it means to have a real fuck, Lucrecia. What he had with Clotilde were conjugal diversions. With Armida there's a little sin in the middle and the thing works better."

"Again your dirty talk," his wife protested. "Besides, I don't know what you have against conjugal diversions. I think ours work wonderfully well."

"Of course, my love, they're marvelous," he said, kissing Lucrecia on her hand and her ear. "The best thing for us is to do what he's doing and not give the matter any importance. Load up on patience and wait for the storm to blow over."

"Don't you want to go out, Rigoberto? Let's go to the movies and eat out."

"Let's watch a movie here instead," her husband replied. "Just the thought that one of those people with their little tape recorders might show up to take photographs and ask me about Ismael and the twins upsets my stomach."

Ever since journalists had seized upon the news of Ismael's marriage to Armida, and his children's police and judicial actions to annul the marriage and declare him incompetent, nothing else was talked about in newspapers, on radio and television programs, on social networks and blogs. The facts disappeared under a frenetic spluttering of exaggerations, inventions, gossipmongering, libel, and general baseness, in which iniquity, coarseness, perversion, resentment, and rancor came to the surface. If he hadn't found himself dragged into the journalistic confusion, constantly hounded by hacks who compensated for their ignorance with morbid curiosity and insolence, Don Rigoberto told himself that this spectacle of Ismael Carrera and Armida transformed into the great entertainment in the city—dipped in print, radio, and television filth and unceasingly scorched in the bonfire that Miki and Escobita had lit and stirred up every day with statements, interviews, short articles, fantasies, and deliriums—would have been somewhat entertaining, as well as instructive and informative with respect to this country, this city, the human spirit in general, and the very evil that now concerned Fonchito, to judge by his essay. "Instructive and informative, yes," he thought again. With respect to many things. The function of journalism in our time, at least in this society, was not to inform but to make the line between the lie and the truth disappear, to replace reality with a fiction in which the oceanic mass of neuroses, frustrations, hatreds, and traumas of a public devoured by resentment and envy was made manifest. One more proof that the small spaces of civilization would never prevail against immeasurable barbarism.

The phone conversation with his former employer and friend had left him depressed. He didn't regret having lent him a hand by acting as a witness at his marriage. But the consequences of that signature were beginning to overwhelm him. It wasn't so much the judicial and police complications, or the delay in processing his retirement; he thought (knock on wood, anything could happen) that this, bad as it was, would be settled. And he and Lucrecia would be able to travel to Europe. The worst thing was the scandal he found himself drawn into: Almost every day he was dragged through a journalistic sewer, muddied by a pestilential sensationalism. Bitterly he asked himself, "What good has it done you, this small refuge of books, prints, records, all these beautiful, refined, subtle, intelligent things you collected so zealously, believing that in this tiny space of civilization you'd be protected against lack of culture, frivolity, stupidity, and emptiness?" His old idea that these islands or fortresses of culture had to be erected in the middle of the storm, invulnerable to the surrounding barbarism, wasn't working. The scandal provoked by his friend Ismael and the hyenas had leaked its acid, its pus, its poison into his study, this territory where for so many years—twenty, twenty-five, thirty?—he'd withdrawn to live his true life. The life that made up for the company's policies and contracts, the intrigues and pettiness of local politics, the mendacity and idiocy of the people he was obliged to deal with every day. Now, with the scandal, it did him no good to search out the solitude of his study. He'd done so the night before. He put a beautiful recording on the phonograph, Arthur Honegger's oratorio *King David*, recorded right in the Notre Dame Cathedral, which had always moved him a great deal. This time, he hadn't been able to concentrate on the music for an instant. He was distracted, his mind fixed on the images and concerns of the past few days, the shock, the bilious displeasure each time he discovered his name in the reports that, though he didn't buy those newspapers, friends had sent to him or commented on in an inflexible way, poisoning his life and Lucrecia's. He had to turn off the phonograph and sit still, his eyes closed, listening to the beating of his heart with a brackish taste in his mouth. "In this country not even a tiny space of civilization can be built," he concluded. "In the end, barbarism demolishes everything." And once again he told himself, as he always did whenever he felt depressed, how mistaken he'd been when, as a young man, he decided not to emigrate, to remain here, in Lima the Horrible, convinced he'd be able to organize his life in a way that, even though he'd have to spend many hours a day submerged in the mundane noise of upper-class Peruvians to earn his daily bread, he'd really live in the pure, beautiful, elevated enclave made of sublime things that he would create as an alternative to the everyday yoke. That was when he'd had the idea of saving spaces, the idea that civilization was not, had never been a movement, a general state of things, an environment that would embrace all of society, but rather was composed of tiny citadels raised throughout time and space, which resisted the ongoing assault of the instinctive, violent, obtuse, ugly, destructive, bestial force that dominated the world and now had come into his own home.

That night, after supper, he asked Fonchito if he was tired.

"No," his son replied. "Why, Papa?"

"I'd like to talk with you for a moment, if you don't mind."

"As long as it isn't about Edilberto Torres, I'd be happy to," Fonchito said mischievously. "I haven't seen him again, so don't worry."

"I promise we won't talk about him," replied Don Rigoberto. And as he used to do when he was a boy, he shaped a cross with two fingers and swore, kissing them: "I swear to God."

"Don't take God's name in vain—after all, I'm a believer," Doña Lucrecia admonished. "Go into the study. I'll tell Justiniana to bring you your ice cream there."

In the study, while they were enjoying the lucuma ice cream, Don Rigoberto, between mouthfuls, spied on Fonchito. Sitting across from him with his legs crossed, he ate his ice cream in slow spoonfuls and seemed absorbed in some distant thoughts. He was no longer a child. How long had he been shaving? His face was smooth and his hair was tousled; he didn't play a lot of sports but looked as if he did because his body was slim and athletic. He was a very good-looking boy, and the girls must be crazy about him.

Everyone said so. But his son didn't seem interested in those kinds of things; instead, he was interested in hallucinations and religious ideas. Was that a good or bad thing? Would he have preferred Fonchito to be a normal kid? "Normal," he thought, imagining his son speaking the syncopated, simian jargon of the young people of his generation, getting drunk on weekends, smoking marijuana, getting high on coke, taking Ecstasy in the discos along the Asia beach at kilometer 100 on the Pan-American, as so many of Lima's wealthy children did. A shudder ran through his body. A thousand times better for him to see phantoms or even the devil himself and write essays about evil.

"I read what you wrote about liberty and evil," he said. "It was right there, on your desk, and I was curious. I hope you don't mind. It impressed me a great deal, in fact. It's very well written and full of original ideas. Which course is it for?"

"Language," said Fonchito, not giving the subject much importance. "Professor Iturriaga asked for an essay on anything. That topic came to mind. But it's only a rough draft. I still have to correct it."

"I was surprised, because I didn't know you were so interested in religion."

"You thought it was religious?" Fonchito was surprised. "I think it's more like philosophy. Well, I don't know, philosophy and religion blend into each other, that's true. Weren't you ever interested in religion, Papa?"

"I studied at La Recoleta, a priests' academy," said Don Rigoberto. "After that, at the Universidad Católica. And for a time I was even a leader of Acción Católica, with Pepín O'Donovan. Of course it interested me a great deal when I was young. But one day I lost my faith and never got it back again. I think I lost it as soon as I began to think. To be a believer, you can't think too much."

"In other words, you're an atheist. You believe there isn't anything before or after this life. That's being an atheist, isn't it?"

"We're getting into deep waters," exclaimed Don Rigoberto. "I'm not an atheist, an atheist is also a believer. He believes that God doesn't exist, isn't that so? I'm more of an agnostic, if I'm anything. Someone who declares that he's perplexed, incapable of believing either that God exists or that God doesn't exist."

"Neither fish nor fowl," said Fonchito with a laugh. "It's a very convenient way to avoid the problem, Papa."

He had a fresh, healthy laugh, and Don Rigoberto thought he was a good kid. He was going through an adolescent crisis, suffering doubts and uncertainties regarding the afterlife and this life, which spoke well of him. How he would have liked to help him. But how, how could he?

"Something like that, though there's no need to make fun of me," he agreed. "Shall I tell you something, Fonchito? I envy believers. Not the fanatics, of course, who horrify me. Real believers. The ones who have a faith and try to organize their lives in accordance with their beliefs. Soberly, with no fuss and no foolishness. I don't know many, but I do know some. And they seem enviable to me. By the way, are you a believer?"

Fonchito became serious and reflected for a moment before answering.

"I'd like to know more about religion, because I was never taught." He avoided answering with a reproachful tone. "That's why Chato Pezzuolo and I have joined a Bible-study group. We meet on Fridays after classes."

"An excellent idea." Don Rigoberto was pleased. "The Bible's a marvelous book that everyone ought to read, believers and nonbelievers. First of all, for their general culture. But also to better understand the world we live in. Many things that happen around us come directly or indirectly from the Bible."

"Is that what you wanted us to talk about, Papa?"

"No, not really," said Don Rigoberto. "I wanted to talk to you about Ismael and the scandal we're caught up in. I'm sure it's all over your school too."

Fonchito laughed again. "I've been asked a thousand times if it was true you helped him to marry his cook, as the papers say. You're on all the blogs that cover that mess."

"Armida was never his cook," explained Don Rigoberto. "More like his housekeeper. She cleaned and managed the house, especially after Ismael lost his wife."

"I've been to his house two or three times and don't remember her at all," said Fonchito. "Is she pretty, at least?"

"Presentable, let's say," Don Rigoberto conceded in a Solomonic way. "Much younger than Ismael, of course. Don't believe all the nonsense in the press. That he was abducted, that he's senile, that he didn't know what he was doing. Ismael's in his right mind and that's why I agreed to be a witness. Of course I didn't suspect that the uproar would be so awful. Well, it'll pass. I wanted to tell you that they've held up my retirement in the company. The twins have accused me of alleged complicity in an abduction that never happened. And so for now I'm tied up here in Lima with summonses and lawyers. That's what it's about. We're going through a difficult period, and until this is resolved, we'll have to tighten our belts a little. Because it's not a good idea to liquidate all the savings our future depends on. Yours especially. I wanted to keep you up to date."

"Of course, Papa," said Fonchito, encouraging him. "Don't worry. If you have to you can suspend my allowance until this is over."

"That won't be necessary," Don Rigoberto said with a smile. "There's more than enough for your allowance. At school, the teachers and students, what do they say about all this?"

"Most are siding with the twins, naturally."

"The hyenas? It's obvious they don't know them."

"The thing is they're racists," Fonchito declared. "They can't forgive Señor Ismael for marrying a *chola*. They believe nobody in his right mind would do that, and that the only thing Armida wants is to keep his money. You don't know how many boys I've fought with defending your friend's marriage, Papa. Only Pezzuolo backs me up, but more out of friendship than because he thinks I'm right."

"You're defending a good cause, son." Don Rigoberto patted his knee. "Because even if nobody believes it, Ismael's marriage was for love."

"Can I ask you a question, Papa?" the boy said suddenly, just as it seemed he was about to leave the study.

"Of course, son. Whatever you like."

"It's just that there's something I don't understand," Fonchito ventured uncomfortably. "About you, Papa. You always liked art, painting, music, books. It's the only thing you seem passionate about. So, then, why did you become a lawyer? Why did you spend your whole life working in an insurance company? You should have been a painter, a musician, well, I don't know. Why didn't you follow your calling?"

Don Rigoberto nodded and reflected a moment before answering.

"Because I was a coward, son," he finally murmured. "Because I lacked faith in myself. I never believed I had the talent to be a real artist. But maybe that was an excuse for not trying. I decided not to be a creator but only a consumer of art, a dilettante of culture. Because I was a coward is the sad truth. So now you know. Don't follow my example. Whatever your calling is, follow it as far as you can and don't do what I did, don't betray it."

"I hope you're not annoyed, Papa. It was a question I'd been wanting to ask you for a long time."

"It's a question I've been asking myself for many years, Fonchito. You've forced me to answer and I thank you for that. Go on, that's enough, good night."

He went to bed in wonderful spirits after his conversation with Fonchito. He told Doña Lucrecia how much good it had done him to hear his son being so judicious after an entire afternoon sunk in bad humor and unpleasantness. But he didn't tell her about the last part of their conversation.

"It made me happy to see him so calm, so mature, Lucrecia. Involved in a Bible-study group, imagine. How many kids his age would do something like that? Very few. Have you read the Bible? I confess I've read only parts, and that was a long time ago. Wouldn't you like it if, as a kind of game, we started to read it too and talk about it? It's a very beautiful book."

"I'd be delighted. Perhaps this way you'll reconvert and come back to the Church," said Lucrecia, adding, after a few seconds' thought: "I hope reading the Bible won't be incompatible with making love, Ears."

She heard her husband's mischievous laugh, and almost at the same time, she felt his avid hands running up and down her body.

"The Bible is the most erotic book in the world," she heard him say eagerly. "You'll see, when we read the Song of Songs and the outrageous things Samson does with Delilah and Delilah does with Samson, you'll see."

XIII

"Even though we're in uniform, this isn't an official visit," said Captain Silva, making a courtly bow that swelled his belly and wrinkled the khaki shirt of his uniform. "It's a friendly visit, señora."

"Sure, all right," said Mabel, opening the door. She looked at the police in surprise and fear, blinking. "Come in, come in, please."

The captain and sergeant had arrived unexpectedly, just as she was thinking to herself once again that she had been moved by the old man's demonstrations of affection. She'd always been fond of Felícito Yanaqué or, at least, even though she'd been his mistress for eight years, she'd never felt an aversion toward him, the physical and moral dislike that in the past had led her to break off abruptly with transitory lovers and benefactors who gave her headaches because of their jealousies, demands, and whims, their resentment and spite. Some breakups had meant a serious economic loss for her. But the feeling was stronger than she was. When she became sick of a man, she couldn't keep sleeping with him. She'd get allergies, headaches, chills, she'd start thinking about her stepfather; she could barely control the urge to vomit each time she had to undress for him and cater to his desires in bed. That's why, she told herself, though she'd gone to bed with a lot of men since she was a kid—she ran away from home at the age of thirteen and went to live with an aunt and uncle after that thing happened with her stepfather—she wasn't and never would be what's called a whore. Because whores knew how to pretend when it was time to go to bed with their clients and she didn't. Mabel, in order to make love, had to feel at least some affection for the man, and also had to get the goods, as the vulgar Piuran saying went; he had to follow the particular forms—invitations, dates, little gifts, gestures, manners—that made their going to bed decent and gave it the appearance of a sentimental relationship.

"Thank you, señora," said Captain Silva, raising his hand to his visor in imitation of a military salute. "We'll do our best not to take up too much of your time."

"Thank you, señora," Sergeant Lituma echoed.

Mabel had them sit in the living room and brought in two cold bottles of Inca Kola. To hide her nervousness, she tried not to speak; she only smiled at them and waited. The police removed their kepis, settled into the armchairs, and Mabel noticed that their foreheads and hair were soaked in perspiration. She thought she ought to turn on the fan but didn't; she was afraid that if she got up from her seat, the captain and sergeant would notice the trembling that had begun in her legs and hands. What explanation would she give if her teeth began to chatter too? "I don't feel very well and have a little fever because, well because of that thing we women have, you know what I mean." Would they believe her?

"What we'd like, señora"—Captain Silva sweetened his voice a little—"is not to question you but to have a friendly conversation. They're very different things, you understand. I said friendly, and I'll repeat it."

In these eight years she'd never felt disgusted by Felícito. No doubt because the old man was so decent. If, on the day he visited, she didn't feel well because she had her period or simply because she didn't want to spread her legs for him, the owner of Narihualá Transport didn't insist. Just the opposite; he was concerned, wanted to take her to the doctor, go to the pharmacy to buy her medicine, hand her the thermometer. Was he really in love with her? Mabel had thought a thousand times that he was. In any case, the old man made the monthly payments on the house and gave her a few thousand soles a month just to go to bed with her once or twice a week. And in addition to all that, he always gave her presents, on her birthday and at Christmas, and also on the holidays when nobody gave anybody anything, like the national holidays or in October during Piura Week. Even in the way he went to bed with her, he always showed it wasn't only sex that mattered to him. He whispered a lover's words in her ear, kissed her tenderly, looked at her in ecstasy, as if he were a boy wet behind the ears. Wasn't that love? Mabel often thought that if she insisted, she could get Felícito to leave his wife, that shapeless *chola* who looked more like a bogeyman than a human being, and marry her. It would be very easy. All she had to do was get pregnant, for example, turn on the tears, and drive him to distraction: "You wouldn't want your child to be a bastard, right, old man?" But she'd never tried it, and wouldn't try it, because Mabel valued her freedom, her independence, too much. She wasn't going to sacrifice them in exchange for relative security; besides, she didn't particularly like the idea of becoming, in just a few years, a nurse and caretaker for a very old man whose dribble she'd have to wipe away and whose sheets she'd have to wash because he peed in his sleep.

"You have my word we won't take very long, señora," the captain repeated, procrastinating, unwilling to explain clearly the reason for this unexpected visit. He looked at her in a way that gave the lie to his good manners, Mabel thought. "Besides, as soon as you grow tired of us, just say the word and we'll clear out."

Why was the captain exaggerating his courtesy to such a ridiculous extent? What was he up to? He wanted to reassure her, of course, but his affectations and syrupy manners and false smiles increased Mabel's mistrust. What did this pair want? Unlike the captain, the sergeant, his assistant, couldn't hide the fact that he was jumpy. He was watching her in a strange way, uneasy and cautious, as if he were a little frightened of what might happen, and he couldn't stop kneading his double chin with fingers that seemed almost frantic.

"As you can see with your own eyes, we didn't bring a tape recorder," Captain Silva added, opening his hands and patting his pockets in a theatrical way. "Not even paper and pencil. So rest assured, there won't be any record at all of what we say here. It will be confidential. Between you and us. And nobody else."

After the week of her abduction, Felícito had been so incredibly affectionate and solicitous that Mabel felt overwhelmed. She'd received a large bouquet of red roses wrapped in cellophane with a card in his own hand that said: "With all my love and sorrow for the hard trial I've put you through, my dear Mabelita, the man who adores you sends you these flowers: your Felícito." It was the biggest bouquet she'd ever seen. When she read the card her eyes filled with tears that fell on her hands and wet them, something that happened only when she had nightmares. Would she accept the old man's offer that she leave Piura until all this was over? She wasn't sure. More than an offer, it was a demand. Felícito was frightened, he thought they could hurt her, and he pleaded with her to go to Trujillo, Chiclayo, Lima, even Cusco if she preferred, wherever she liked, as long as she got far away from the damn spider extortionists. He promised her the moon: She'd lack for nothing and enjoy every comfort for as long as her trip lasted. But she hadn't made up her mind. It's not that she wasn't afraid, nothing like that. Unlike the many fearful people she knew, Mabel had felt fear only once before, when she was a kid and her stepfather, taking advantage of the fact that her mother was at the market, came into her room, pushed her onto the bed, and tried to undress her. She had defended herself, scratched him, and ran out into the street, half undressed and screaming. That was when she learned what fear really was. She never experienced anything like it again. Until now. Because over the past days, fear, a great, deep, constant fear, was back in her life. Twenty-four hours a day. Night and day, afternoon and morning, asleep and awake. Mabel thought she'd never be rid of it until she died. When she went out, she had the unpleasant sensation of being watched; even in the house, with the doors and windows locked, she'd have sudden frights that chilled her body and took her breath away. Then she'd imagine that her blood had stopped circulating in her veins. In spite of knowing she was protected, and perhaps for that very reason. Was she protected? Felícito had assured her she was after he'd talked to Captain Silva. True, there was a guard in front of her house, and when she went out two plainclothes police, a man and a woman, followed her at a certain distance, discreetly. But it was precisely this twenty-four-hour-a-day vigilance that increased her nervousness, as did Captain Silva's assurance that the kidnappers wouldn't be imprudent or stupid enough to attempt another attack on her, knowing the police were guarding her day and night. In spite of that, the old man didn't think she was out of danger. According to him, when the kidnappers realized he'd lied to them, that he'd placed the notice in *El Tiempo* thanking the Captive Lord of Ayabaca for the miracle only so they'd free her, and that he didn't intend to pay protection, they'd be furious and would try to take their revenge on someone he loved. And since they knew so much about him, they'd also know that the person Felícito loved most in the world was Mabel. She had to leave Piura, disappear for a while, he'd never forgive himself if those bastards hurt her again.

Feeling her heart pound, Mabel remained silent. Above the heads of the two police and at the foot of the Sacred Heart of Jesus, she saw her face reflected in the mirror and was surprised at how pale she looked. She was as white as one of those phantoms in horror movies.

"I'm going to ask you to listen to me without getting nervous or scared," Captain Silva said after a long silence. He spoke softly, lowering his voice, as if he were going to tell her a secret. "Because even though it may not seem like it, this private arrangement we're going to make, I repeat, it's for your own good."

"Tell me once and for all what's going on. What is it that you want?" Mabel managed to say, choking. The captain's evasiveness and hypocritical circumspection were irritating her. "Say what you've come to say. I'm not a fool. Let's not waste any more time, señor."

"We'll get to the point then, Mabel," said the chief, transformed. Suddenly his good manners and respectful behavior disappeared. He raised his voice and looked at her now very seriously, with an impertinent, superior air. To make matters worse, he began to address her with the familiar *tú*. "I'm very sorry for you, but we know everything. Just what I said, Mabelita. Everything, every little thing, every last little thing. For example, we know that for a good long time you've not only had Don Felícito Yanaqué as a lover but someone else too. Better looking and younger than the old man in the hat and vest who pays for this house."

"How dare you!" Mabel protested, turning a violent red. "I won't permit it! What slander!"

"You'd better let me finish before you get so mouthy." Captain

Silva's emphatic voice and threatening manner stopped her dead. "Afterward you can say whatever you want and cry as much as you like and even stamp your feet, if the spirit moves you. Right now, just keep quiet. I have the floor and you button your lip. Understood, Mabelita?"

Maybe she'd have to leave Piura. But the idea of living alone in a strange city—she'd only left this city to go to Sullana, Lobitos, Paita, and Yacila, she'd never crossed the boundaries of the department either to the north or to the south, she'd never gone up to the sierra—demoralized her. What would she do all alone in a place without family or friends? She'd have less protection than she did here. Would she spend her time waiting for Felícito to come to visit her? She'd live in a hotel, be bored morning and night, watching television for hours on end, if there even was television, and waiting, waiting. And she didn't like feeling that a police officer, a man or a woman, was always watching her steps, taking notes on whom she talked to, whom she said hello to, who approached her. More than protected, she felt spied on, and the feeling, instead of reassuring her, made her tense and insecure.

Captain Silva stopped talking for a moment to calmly light a cigarette. Unhurriedly, he exhaled a large mouthful of smoke that hung in the air and saturated the room with the biting odor of tobacco.

"You'll probably say, Mabel, that the police aren't interested in your private life, and you'd be right," the chief continued, dropping his ash on the floor and adopting an air that was part philosophical, part bullying. "But what concerns us is not whether you have two or ten lovers, but that you've been crazy enough to conspire with one of them to extort Don Felícito Yanaqué, the poor old man who, besides everything else, really loves you. What an ungrateful girl you've turned out to be, Mabelita!"

"What a thing to say!" She was on her feet and now, quivering, indignant, she too raised her voice, as well as a fist. "I won't say another word without a lawyer. Let me tell you, I know my rights. I . . ."

How stubborn Felícito was! Mabel never would have imagined that the old man was prepared to die rather than give money to the extortionists. He seemed so meek, so understanding, and then suddenly he displayed an iron will to all of Piura. The day after she was freed, she and Felícito had a long conversation. At one point Mabel unexpectedly asked him, point-blank, "If the kidnappers had said they'd kill me if you didn't give them the money, would you have let them kill me?"

"Now you see it didn't happen that way, love," the trucker stammered, very uncomfortable.

"Answer me honestly, Felícito," she insisted. "Would you have let them kill me?"

"And afterward I would've killed myself," he conceded, his voice breaking and his expression so pathetic she took pity on him. "Forgive me, Mabel. But I'll never pay an extortionist. Not even if they kill me or the thing I love most in this world, which is you."

"But you told me yourself that all your colleagues in Piura do it," Mabel replied.

"And lots of businessmen and entrepreneurs too, it seems," Felícito acknowledged. "The truth is I learned that only now, through Vignolo. It's their business. I'm not criticizing them. Each man knows what he's doing and how to defend his interests. But I'm not like them, Mabel. I can't do it. I can't betray my father's memory."

And then the trucker, with tears in his eyes, began to talk about his father to a surprised Mabel. Never, in all the years they'd been together, had she heard him refer to his parent so emotionally. With feeling, with tenderness, just like when they were intimate in bed and he said sweet things to her as he caressed her. He'd been a very humble man, a sharecropper, a Chulucano from the countryside, and then, here in Piura, a porter, a municipal garbage collector. He never learned to read or write, he went barefoot most of his life, something you noticed when they left Chulucanas and came to the city so that Felícito could go to school. Then he had to wear shoes and you could see how strange it felt to him when he walked and how his feet hurt when he had them on. He wasn't a man who showed his love by hugging and kissing his son, or saying those affectionate things parents say to their kids. He was severe, hard, even ready with his fists when he got angry. But he'd shown him he loved him by making him study, by dressing him and feeding him, even when he had nothing to put on his own back or in his own mouth, by sending him to a school for drivers so that Felícito could learn to drive and get his license. Thanks to that illiterate sharecropper, Narihualá Transport existed. His father might have been poor but he was a great man because of his upstanding spirit, because he never harmed anyone, or broke the law, or felt rancor toward the woman who abandoned him, leaving him with a newborn to bring up. If all of that about sin and evil and the next life was true, he had to be in heaven now. He didn't even have time to do any evil, he spent his life working like a dog in the worst-paying jobs. Felícito remembered seeing him drop with fatigue at night. But even so, he never let anyone walk all over him. According to him, that was the difference between a man who was worth something and a man who was worth only a rag. That had been the advice he gave him before he died in a bed with no mattress in the Hospital Obrero: "Never let anybody walk all over you, son." Felícito had followed the advice of the father who, because they had no money, he couldn't even bury in a niche; he couldn't stop them from tossing him into a common grave.

"Do you see, Mabel? It's not the five hundred dollars the crooks are asking for. That's not the point. If I give it to them, they'd be walking all over me, turning me into a rag. Tell me you understand, honey."

Mabel hadn't really understood, but hearing him say those things made an impression on her. Only now, after being with him for so long, did she realize that behind his insignificant appearance—a little man, so thin, so small—Felícito had a cast-iron character and a bulletproof will. It was true, he'd let himself be killed before he gave in.

"Sit down and shut up," the officer ordered and Mabel shut up and dropped back into her seat, defeated. "You don't need a lawyer *yet*. You're not arrested *yet*. We're not questioning you *yet*. This is a friendly, confidential conversation, I already told you that. And it would be better for you to get that into your head once and for all. So let me talk, Mabelita, and listen to what I'm going to say very carefully."

But before he continued, he took another long drag of his cigarette and expelled the smoke slowly, making rings. "He wants to make me suffer, that's why he came," thought Mabel. She felt weak and exhausted, as if at any moment she might fall asleep. In the armchair, leaning forward slightly, as if he didn't want to miss a syllable of what his boss was saying, Sergeant Lituma didn't speak or move. And he didn't take his eyes off him for a second.

"There are various charges and they're serious," the captain went on, looking into her eyes as if he wanted to hypnotize her. "You tried to make us believe you'd been kidnapped but it was all a farce, cooked up by you and your pal to coerce Don Felícito, the gentleman who's dying of love for you. It didn't work out because you weren't counting on this man's determination to refuse to be extorted. To soften him up, you even set fire to Narihualá Transport on Avenida Sánchez Cerro. But that didn't work out either."

"I set fire to it? Is that what you're accusing me of? Being an arsonist too?" Mabel protested, trying in vain to stand again, but weakness or the captain's belligerent gaze and aggressive expression stopped her. She dropped back into the chair, shrinking into herself and crossing her arms. Now she was not only sleepy, she felt warm as well and began to perspire. She felt her hands begin to drip with sweat and fear. "So I was the one who set fire to Narihualá Transport?"

"We have some other details, but these are the most serious charges as far as you're concerned," said the captain, calmly turning to his subordinate. "Let's see, Sergeant, inform the señora of the crimes she could be tried for and the sentences she might receive."

Lituma became animated, shifted in his seat, wet his lips with his tongue, took a paper out of his shirt pocket, unfolded it, cleared his throat, and read like a pupil reciting a lesson for his teacher.

"Unlawful association for the purpose of committing a criminal act in a kidnapping scheme and sending anonymous letters and extortion threats. Unlawful association for the purpose of destroying a commercial site with explosives, with the aggravating circumstance of putting at risk the houses, businesses, and persons in the area. Active participation in a false kidnapping for the purpose of frightening and coercing a businessman into paying protection. Dissimulation, duplicity, and deception before the authorities during their investigation into the false kidnapping." He put the paper back in his pocket and added: "These would be the principal charges against the señora, Captain. The prosecutor might add other, less serious ones, like the clandestine practice of prostitution."

"And how high could the penalty go if the señora is convicted, Lituma?" the captain asked, his mocking eyes fixed on Mabel.

"Eight to ten years in prison," the sergeant replied. "It would depend on the aggravating and extenuating circumstances, naturally."

"You're trying to scare me, but you've made a mistake," murmured Mabel, making an enormous effort to get her tongue, as dry and harsh as an iguana's, to form words. "I won't answer any of those lies without a lawyer present."

"Nobody's asking you questions *yet*," Captain Silva said ironically. "For now, the only thing you're being asked to do is listen. Understood, Mabelita?"

He kept looking at her with a leer that forced her to lower her eyes. Disheartened, defeated, she nodded.

As a result of nerves, fear, and the idea that with every step she took she'd have an invisible pair of cops on her tail, she didn't leave the house for five days. She went out only to run to the Chinese store on the corner to buy a few things, to the laundry, and to the bank. She hurried back to close herself in with her worries and tortured thoughts. On the sixth day she couldn't stand any more. Living this way was like being in prison, and Mabel wasn't made for confinement. She needed to be out, see the sky, smell, hear, walk in the city, listen to the bustle of men and women, hear the donkeys braying and the dogs barking. She wasn't and would never be a cloistered nun. She called her friend Zoila and suggested they go to the movies, the late-afternoon show.

"And see what, honey?" asked Zoila.

"Anything, whatever they're showing," Mabel answered. "I need to see people, talk a little bit. I'm suffocating here."

They met in front of Los Portales, on the Plaza de Armas. They had lunch at El Chalán, and went into the multiplex at the Centro

Comercial Open Plaza, next to the Universidad de Piura. They saw a fairly graphic movie with nudity. Zoila, who pretended to be very proper, crossed herself when there were sex scenes. She was shameless; in her personal life she was a real libertine, changed partners every other day, and even bragged about it: "As long as your body holds out, you have to use it, baby." She wasn't especially pretty, but she had a good body and nice taste in clothes. Because of that and her uninhibited ways, she was successful with men. When they left the theater, she suggested they have something to eat at her house, but Mabel said no, she didn't want to go back to Castilla alone when it was late.

She took a taxi, and as the old jalopy plunged into the half-darkened neighborhood, Mabel told herself that, after all, it was lucky the police had kept the kidnapping from the press. They thought this would confuse the extortionists and make it easier to catch them. But she was convinced that at any moment the news would reach the papers, radio, and television. What would her life turn into if that scandal broke? Maybe the best thing would be to listen to Felícito and leave Piura for a while. Why not go to Trujillo? They said it was big, modern, lively, with a nice beach and colonial houses and parks. And that the Marinera Dance Competition held there every summer was worth seeing. Were those two cops in plain clothes following her in a car or on a motorcycle? She looked through the rear and side windows and didn't see any vehicles. Probably her protection was a lie. You had to be a half-wit to believe the cops' promises.

She got out of the taxi, paid, and walked the twenty-some paces from the corner to her house down the center of an empty street, even though at almost all the neighboring doors and windows the dim lights of the neighborhood flickered. She could make out the silhouettes of people inside. She had her door key ready. She opened the door, went in, and when she reached out her hand to the light switch, she felt another hand in the way, blocking her and covering her mouth, stifling her scream as a man's body pressed against hers and a well-known voice whispered in her ear, "It's me, don't be scared."

"What are you doing here?" Mabel protested, trembling. She

thought she'd collapse onto the floor if he weren't holding her up. "Have you gone crazy, you asshole? Have you gone crazy?"

"I needed to fuck you," said Miguel, and Mabel felt his feverish lips on her ear, her neck, eager, avid, his strong arms squeezing her and his hands touching her everywhere.

"Stupid pig, imbecile, vulgar filthy moron," she protested, defending herself, furious. She was dizzy with indignation and fear. "Don't you know the police are watching the house? Don't you know what can happen to us on account of you, you dirty idiot?"

"Nobody saw me come in, the cop is in the dive on the corner drinking coffee, nobody was on the street." Miguel kept embracing her, kissing her, pressing her body against his, rubbing against her. "Come on, let's go to bed, I'll fuck you and leave. Come on, baby."

"You dumb, miserable dog, how do you have the nerve to come here, you're out of your mind." They were in the dark and, furious and frightened, she was trying to resist and push him away, at the same time feeling that in spite of her rage, her body was beginning to give in. "Don't you realize that you're ruining my life, damn you? And ruining your own too, you bastard."

"I swear nobody saw me come in, I was very careful," he repeated, pulling at her clothes to try to undress her. "Come on, come on. I want you, I'm hungry for you, I want to make you cry out, I love you."

Finally she stopped defending herself. Still in the dark, fed up, exhausted, she allowed him to undress her and throw her down on the bed, and for a few minutes she abandoned herself to pleasure. Could that be called pleasure? It was, in any case, something very different from what she'd felt at other times. Tense, on edge, sad. Not even at the height of her excitement, when she was about to come, could she get the images of Felícito, the police who questioned her at the station house, the scandal that would explode if the news reached the press, out of her head.

"Now go, and don't set foot in this house again until all of this is over," she ordered when she felt Miguel release her and fall back onto the bed. "If your father finds out because of this crazy thing you did tonight, I'll get back at you. I swear it'll be bad. I swear you'll regret it the rest of your life, Miguel."

"I told you nobody saw me. I swear nobody did. At least tell me if you liked it."

"I didn't like anything and I hate you with all my heart, just so you know," Mabel said, slipping out of Miguel's hands and standing up. "Go on, leave right now and don't let anybody see you go out. Don't come back here, you idiot. You'll get us sent to prison, you son of a bitch, why can't you see that."

"All right, I'm going, don't be like that," said Miguel, sitting up. "I'm putting up with your insults because you're so stressed. Otherwise, I'd knock them down your throat, sweetie."

She could hear Miguel dressing in the semidarkness. Finally he bent over to kiss her and at the same time, with the vulgarity that erupted from all the pores of his body at intimate moments, he said, "For as long as I like you, I'll come here to fuck you every time my prick tells me to, baby."

"Eight to ten years in prison is a lot of years, Mabelita," said Captain Silva, changing his voice again; now he seemed sad and compassionate. "Especially if you're in the women's prison at Sullana. A hell, I can tell you, I know it like the back of my hand. There's no water or electricity most of the time. The inmates sleep in piles, two or three in each cot along with their kids, a lot of them on the floor, stinking of shit and piss because the bathrooms are almost always out of order, and they take care of their needs in buckets or plastic bags that are emptied only once a day. A body can't put up with that system for very long. Least of all a nice little woman like you, accustomed to a different kind of life."

Even though she wanted to shout and insult him, Mabel remained silent. She'd never been inside the women's prison at Sullana, but she'd seen it from the outside, passing by. She sensed that the captain wasn't exaggerating at all in his description.

"After a year or a year and a half of that kind of life, surrounded by prostitutes, murderers, thieves, drug traffickers, many of them driven crazy in prison, a young, beautiful woman like you gets old, ugly, and half nuts. I don't want that for you, Mabelita."

The captain sighed, filled with pity over the possible fate of the lady of the house.

"You might say that it's perverse to tell you these things and paint this kind of picture for you," the implacable chief continued. "You'd be wrong. The sergeant and I aren't sadists. We don't want to frighten you. What do you say, Lituma?"

"Of course not, just the opposite," the sergeant declared, shifting again in the armchair. "We've come with good intentions, señora."

"We want to spare you those horrors." Captain Silva grimaced, contorting his face, as if he'd had an awful hallucination, and raised his hands in alarm. "The scandal, the trial, the interrogations, the prison bars. Can you imagine it, Mabel? Instead of paying the penalty for complicity with those thugs, we want you to be free, no strings attached, living the good life you've been living for years. Do you see why I told you our visit was for your own good? It is, Mabelita, believe me."

Now she could sense what this was about. From panic she'd moved on to rage and from rage to profound dejection. Her eyelids were heavy, and again she felt a weariness that made her close her eyes for a few moments. How marvelous it would be to sleep, to lose consciousness and memory, to doze off right here, curled up in the chair. To forget, to feel that none of this had happened, that life was what it had always been.

Mabel brought her face close to the windowpane and after a little while saw Miguel go out and disappear a few meters farther on, swallowed up by the dark. She looked over the area carefully. She couldn't see anyone. But that didn't reassure her. The cop could be standing in the doorway of a nearby house and could have seen him from there. He'd report to his bosses and the police would inform Don Felícito Yanaqué: "Your son and employee, Miguel Yanaqué, visits your mistress's house at night." The scandal would explode. What would happen to her? As she bathed, changed the sheets, and then lay down, the lamp on the night table lit, trying to sleep, she asked herself again, as she had so often in the past two and a half years since she'd begun to see Miguel in secret, how Felícito would react if he ever found out. He wasn't the kind of man who pulled a knife or a revolver in defense of his honor, the kind who thinks that sexual affronts are washed away with blood. But he'd leave her. She'd be on the street. Her savings would last barely a few months, and only if she cut expenses drastically. At this point it wouldn't be so easy for her to establish another relationship as comfortable as the one she had with the owner of Narihualá Transport. She'd been stupid. An idiot. It was her own fault. She always knew that sooner or later she'd have to pay the price. She was so depressed that sleep eluded her. This would be another night of insomnia and nightmares.

She dozed off from time to time and had intermittent attacks of panic. She was a practical woman and never wasted time feeling sorry for herself or crying over her mistakes. What she regretted most in life was giving in to the insistent young man who had pursued her, caught up with her, courted her, and with whom she'd flirted without suspecting he was Felícito's son. It had begun two and a half years earlier, when in the streets, stores, restaurants, and cafeterias in the center of Piura, she realized she was often running into a white, athletic, good-looking, well-dressed boy who gave her suggestive looks and flirtatious smiles. She learned who he was when, after making him beg more than a little, and accepting fruit juice from him in a pastry shop, going out to eat with him, going dancing a couple of times in a discotheque along the river, she agreed to go to bed with him in a motel in Atarjea. She was never in love with Miguel. Well, Mabel hadn't been in love with anybody since she was a kid, maybe because that was who she was or maybe because of what happened with her stepfather when she was thirteen. She'd been so disappointed with her first loves as a girl that from then on she'd had affairs, some longer than others, some very brief, but they had never involved her heart, only her body and her reason. She thought that's how her affair with Miguel would be, that after two or three encounters it would dissolve on her own terms. But this time it didn't happen that way. The boy had fallen in love. He stuck to her like a leech. Mabel realized the relationship had become a problem and tried to break it off. She couldn't. The only time she hadn't been able to get rid of a lover. A lover? Not really, since because he was either very poor or a tightwad, he rarely gave her presents, didn't take her to nice places, and even warned her they'd never have a formal relationship because he wasn't one of those men who wants to be a father and have a family. In other words, his only interest in her was sex.

When she tried to force the break, he threatened to tell his father everything. From that moment on she knew the story would end badly, and that of the three, she'd suffer the most.

"Effective cooperation with the justice system," Captain Silva explained, smiling enthusiastically. "That's what it's called in legal jargon, Mabelita. The key word isn't 'cooperation,' it's 'effective.' It means that the cooperation has to be useful and productive. If you cooperate honestly and help us to put the crooks who got you involved in this mess behind bars, you're exempt from prison, even from being tried. And with good reason, because you're a victim too. No strings attached, Mabelita! Imagine what that means!"

The captain took a couple of drags on his cigarette, and she saw the little clouds of smoke thicken the rarefied atmosphere of the living room and then gradually disperse.

"You must be asking yourself what kind of cooperation we want from you. Why don't you explain, Lituma."

The sergeant agreed.

"For now, we want you to continue pretending, señora," he said, very respectfully. "Just like you've pretended all this time with Señor Yanaqué and with us. Exactly the same. Miguel doesn't know we know everything, and you, instead of telling him, will keep acting as if this conversation never took place."

"That's exactly what we want from you," Captain Silva agreed. "I'll be frank, give you more proof of our confidence. Your cooperation can be very useful to us. Not to nab Miguel Yanaqué. He's already fucked and can't make a move without our knowing about it. But we're not sure about his accomplices. We don't know who they are. With your help, we'll set a trap and send them to prison, where gangsters should be, instead of on the street, making life hard for decent people. You'd be doing us a great service. And we'll return it, pay you back with another great favor. I'm speaking for the National Police and the justice system. This deal has the prosecutor's approval. You heard right, Mabelita. The prosecutor himself, Dr. Hermando Símula! You won the lottery with me, girl."

From then on, she continued seeing Miguel only so he wouldn't carry out his threat to tell Felícito about their affair "even if the spiteful old man puts a bullet in you and another in me, sweetie." She knew the insane things a jealous man could do. Deep down, she hoped something would happen—an accident, an illness, anything to get her out of this. She did her best to keep Miguel at a distance, inventing excuses not to go out with him or have sex with him. But from time to time she couldn't help it, and though she was unwilling and frightened, they went out to eat in sleazy bars, to dance in shabby discotheques, and to have sex in small hotels that rented rooms by the hour on the road to Catacaos. Only rarely did she let him visit her in the house in Castilla. One afternoon, she and her friend Zoila went into El Chalán for tea and Mabel ran into Miguel face-to-face. He was with a very young, very pretty girl, and they were lovey-dovey, holding hands. She watched as the boy became confused, blushed, and turned his head to avoid greeting her. Instead of jealousy, she felt relief. Now the break would be easier. But the next time they saw each other, Miguel whimpered, begged her to forgive him, swore he'd repented, Mabel was the love of his life, etcetera. And she, stupid, so stupid, forgave him.

That morning, after not closing her eyes all night, a more and more common occurrence recently, Mabel was depressed, her head filled with premonitions. She also felt sorry for the old man. She hadn't wanted to hurt him. She never would've gotten involved with Miguel if she'd known he was Felícito's son. How strange that he had a son so white and so good-looking. Felícito wasn't the type a woman falls in love with, but he did have the qualities that make a woman feel affection for a man. She'd grown used to him. She didn't think of him as a lover but as a close friend. He gave her security, made her think that as long as he was nearby, he'd get her out of any situation. He was a decent person, with good intentions, one of those men you can trust. She'd be very sorry to embitter him, or hurt him, or offend him. Because he'd suffer so much if he found out she'd gone to bed with Miguel.

At about midday, when the police knocked at the door, she had the feeling that the threat she'd sensed since the previous night was about to materialize. She opened the door and saw Captain Silva and Sergeant Lituma in the doorway. My God, my God, what was going to happen?

"Now you know what the deal is, Mabelita," said Captain Silva. He looked at his watch and stood up, as if he were remembering something. "You don't have to answer me now, of course. I'll give you till tomorrow, at this time. Think about it. If that lunatic Miguel comes to visit you again, don't even think about telling him about our conversation. Because that would mean you'd sided with the gangsters against us. An aggravating circumstance in your file, Mabelita. Isn't that right, Lituma?"

As the captain and the sergeant were walking toward the door, she asked them, "Does Felícito know you've come here to make me this offer?"

"Señor Yanaqué doesn't know anything about it, and even less that the spider extortionist is his son Miguel and you're his accomplice," the captain replied. "When he finds out, he'll have a fit. But that's life, as you know better than anybody. When you play with fire, somebody gets burned. Think about our proposition, sleep on it, and you'll see it's the best thing for you to do. We'll talk tomorrow, Mabelita."

When the police left, she closed the door and leaned her back against the wall. Her heart was pounding. "I'm fucked, I'm fucked. You did it to yourself, Mabel." Leaning against the wall, she dragged herself into the living room—her legs were trembling and sleep was still irresistible—and let herself drop into the nearest armchair. She closed her eyes and immediately fell asleep, or passed out. She had a nightmare she'd had before. She'd fallen into quicksand and was sinking through that gritty surface; both legs were already entangled in viscous filaments. Making a great effort, she was able to move toward the closest shore, but it wasn't her salvation: Instead, crouching there, waiting, was a shaggy beast, a dragon from the movies, with sharp tusks and piercing eyes, watching and waiting for her.

When she woke her neck, head, and back hurt, and she was soaked in sweat. She went to the kitchen and sipped a glass of water. "You've got to calm down, have a cool head. You've got to think calmly about what you're going to do." She went to lie down in the bed, taking off only her shoes. She didn't feel like thinking. She would have liked to take a car, a bus, a plane, get as far as possible from Piura, go to a city where nobody knew her. Start a new life from the beginning. But it was impossible, wherever she went the police would find her, and running away would only make her guilt worse. Wasn't she a victim too? The captain had said so and it was absolutely true. Maybe it had been her idea? Not at all. She'd discussed it with that imbecile Miguel when she found out what he was planning. She agreed to take part in the farce of the kidnapping only when he threatened her—again—with telling the old man about their affair. "He'll throw you out like a dog, sweetie. And then how will you live as well as you're living now?"

He'd forced her, and she had no reason to be loyal to a son of a bitch like him. Maybe all she could do was cooperate with the police and the prosecutor. Her life wouldn't be easy, of course. There'd be revenge, she'd become a target, they'd put a bullet or a knife in her. What was better? That or prison?

She didn't leave the house again that day or night, devoured by doubts, her head a madhouse. The only thing that was clear was that she was fucked and would keep being fucked because of the mistake she'd made when she got involved with Miguel and agreed to this charade.

She ate nothing that night; she fixed a ham and cheese sandwich but she couldn't even taste it. She went to bed thinking that in the morning the two cops would be back to ask what her answer was. She spent the whole night worrying, making plans and then changing them. Sometimes she was overcome by sleep, but as soon as she dozed off she would wake in a fright. When the first light of the new day came into the house in Castilla, she felt herself growing calmer. She began to see things clearly. A short time later, she'd made her decision.

XIV

The winter Tuesday in Lima, which Don Rigoberto and Doña Lucrecia would consider the worst day of their lives, dawned, paradoxically, with a cloudless sky and the promise of sun. After two weeks of persistent fog and damp and an intermittent drizzle that barely wet anything but penetrated down to one's bones, this kind of beginning seemed a good omen.

Rigoberto's appointment in the office of the examining magistrate was for ten that morning. Dr. Claudio Arnillas, with his invariable gaudy suspenders and crooked-leg walk, picked him up at nine, as previously arranged. Rigoberto thought this new proceeding before the judge would, like the earlier ones, be a sheer waste of time—stupid questions about his duties and responsibilities as manager of the insurance company, to which he would reply with obvious explanations and equivalent foolishness. But this time he discovered that the twins had escalated their judicial harassment; in addition to paralyzing his retirement process under the pretext of examining his responsibilities and personal income during his years of service at the company, they'd opened a new judicial investigation into an alleged fraudulent action to the detriment of the insurance company in which he had supposedly been an accessory after the fact, a beneficiary, and an accomplice.

Don Rigoberto barely remembered the episode, which had occurred three years before. The client, a Mexican residing in Lima, owner of a small farm and a factory that produced dairy products in the Chillón valley, had been the victim of a fire that destroyed his property. Following the police investigation and the judge's decision, he was compensated according to his policy for the losses he'd suffered. When, after a partner's accusations, he was charged with contriving to set the fire himself in order to fraudulently collect the insurance, the individual had already left the country, leaving no trace of his new location, and the company had been unable to recoup its losses from the swindle. Now the twins said they had proof that Rigoberto, manager of the company, had acted negligently and suspiciously throughout the entire affair. The proof consisted of the testimony of a former employee of the company who'd been fired for incompetence and who claimed he could prove the manager had been in cahoots with the swindler. It was a preposterous situation, and Dr. Arnillas, who'd already filed a judicial rejoinder against the twins and their false witness for libel and slander, assured him the accusation would collapse like a house of cards; Miki and Escobita would have to pay fines for offenses to his honor, false testimony, and intent to defraud justice.

The process took the entire morning. The narrow, suffocating office was simmering with heat and flies, and the walls were marred by tacked-up forms. Sitting in a small, rickety chair that barely held half his buttocks and, to make matters even worse, that rocked back and forth, Rigoberto was constantly balancing to avoid falling to the floor as he responded to the judge's questions, which were so arbitrary and absurd that, he said to himself, they had no purpose other than to waste his time and make him lose his temper and his patience. Had this judge also been bribed by Ismael's sons? Every day that dissolute pair piled on another annoyance intended to force him into testifying that their father wasn't in his right mind when he married his servant. Not only holding up his retirement but now this. The twins knew very well that this accusation might be counterproductive for them. Why were they making it? Was it simply blind hatred, a desire for bullheaded revenge because of his complicity in that marriage? A Freudian transference, perhaps. They were furious, out for his blood because they couldn't do anything to Ismael and Armida, who were having the time of their lives in Europe. They were wrong. He wouldn't give in. We'd see who laughed last in the war they'd declared on him.

The judge was a small, thin, badly dressed man who spoke without looking into the eyes of his interlocutor in a voice so low and indecisive that Don Rigoberto's irritation increased by the minute. Was anyone recording the interrogation? Apparently not. A secretary sat hunched between the judge and the wall, his head buried in an enormous file, but there was no tape recorder visible. For his part, the magistrate had a small notebook in which, from time to time, he scrawled something so rapidly it couldn't have been even a very brief synthesis of his statement. Which meant this entire interrogation was a farce intended only to harass him. Rigoberto was so annoyed that he had to make a huge effort to take part in the ridiculous pantomime and not explode in a fit of rage. When they left, Dr. Arnillas said he ought to be happy: By showing so little enthusiasm, the investigative magistrate had made it clear he didn't take the hyenas' accusation seriously. He'd declare it null and void, Dr. Arnillas was absolutely certain of that.

Rigoberto returned home tired, in a bad mood, and with no desire for lunch. It was enough for him to see Doña Lucrecia's contorted face to realize that more bad news was waiting for him.

"What's wrong?" he asked as he took off his jacket and hung it in the bedroom closet. Since his wife didn't answer right away, he turned to look at her. "What's the bad news, my love?"

Agitated, her voice trembling, Doña Lucrecia murmured, "Edilberto Torres, imagine." Half a moan escaped her, and she added: "He appeared in a jitney. Again, Rigoberto, my God, again!"

"Where? When?"

"On the Lima–Chorrillos jitney, Stepmother," Fonchito said, very calm, his eyes begging her not to give the matter any importance. "I got on at the Paseo de la República, near Plaza Grau. He got on at the next stop, on the Zanjón."

"He did? Was it really him? Was it?" she exclaimed, bringing her face close, examining him. "Are you sure about what you're telling me, Fonchito?"

"Hello, young friend," Señor Edilberto Torres greeted him, making one of his customary bows. "What a coincidence, look where we've met. I'm happy to see you, Fonchito."

"Dressed in gray, with a jacket and tie and his garnet-colored sweater," the boy explained. "Nicely combed and shaved, very pleasant. Of course it was him, Stepmother. And this time, fortunately, he didn't cry."

"Since the last time we saw each other, I think you've grown a little," said Edilberto Torres, looking him over from head to toe. "Not only physically. Now you have a more serene, a more definite gaze. Almost the gaze of an adult, Fonchito."

"My papa has forbidden me to talk to you, señor. I'm sorry, but I have to obey him."

"Has he told you the reason for this prohibition?" Señor Torres asked, not at all perturbed. He observed him with curiosity, smiling slightly.

"My papa and stepmother think you're the devil, señor."

Edilberto Torres didn't seem very surprised, but the jitney driver was. He stepped lightly on the brakes and turned to look at the two passengers in the backseat. When he saw their faces, he calmed down. Señor Torres's smile broadened, but he didn't laugh out loud. He nodded, taking the matter as a joke.

"In our day everything's possible," he remarked in his perfect announcer's diction, and shrugged. "The devil even wanders the streets of Lima and mobilizes his recruits on jitneys. Speaking of the devil, I've learned that you've become friends with Father O'Donovan, Fonchito. Yes, the one with a Bajo el Puente parish, who else. Do you get on well with him?"

"He was kidding you, don't you see that, Lucrecia?" stated Don Rigoberto. "It's a joke that he'd appear again in a jitney. And more than impossible that he'd mention Pepín. He was simply deceiving you. He's been deceiving us from the very beginning, and that's the truth."

"You wouldn't say that if you'd seen his face, Rigoberto. I think I know him well enough to know when he's lying and when he's not."

"Do you know Father O'Donovan, señor?"

"On some Sundays I go to hear his Mass, even though his parish is fairly far from where I live," replied Edilberto Torres. "I walk there because I like his sermons. They're those of an educated, intelligent man who speaks to everybody, not just to believers. Didn't he give you that impression when you chatted with him?"

"I've never heard his sermons," Fonchito explained. "But yes, he seemed very intelligent. Experienced in life and especially in religion."

"You ought to hear him when he speaks from the pulpit," advised Edilberto Torres. "Especially now that you're interested in spiritual matters. He's eloquent, elegant, and his words are full of wisdom. He must be one of the last good orators the Church has. Because sacred oratory, so important in the past, entered its decadence a long time ago."

"But he doesn't know you, señor," Fonchito dared to say. "I spoke about you to Father O'Donovan, and he didn't even know who you were."

"For him I'm just another face among the faithful in his church," replied Edilberto Torres, very calmly. "A face lost among many others. How good that you're interested in religion now, Fonchito. I've heard that you're part of a group that meets once a week to read the Bible. Do you enjoy doing that?"

"You're lying to me, darling," Señora Lucrecia reprimanded him lovingly, trying to conceal her surprise. "He couldn't have said that to you. It isn't possible for Señor Torres to know about your study group."

"He even knew that last week we finished reading Genesis and began Exodus." Now the boy's face was very worried. He too seemed disturbed. "He even knew that detail, I swear. It surprised me so much I told him it did, Stepmother."

"There's no reason for you to be surprised, Fonchito," Edilberto Torres replied with a smile. "I think very highly of you, and I'm interested in knowing how things are going for you in school, in your family, in life. That's why I do my best to find out what you're doing and whom you see. It's an expression of affection for you, nothing more. Don't make a mountain out of a molehill. Do you know that saying?"

"He'll hear from me when he gets home from school," said Don Rigoberto, suddenly enraged. "Fonchito can't keep toying with us this way. I'm sick and tired of his trying to make us swallow so many lies."

In a bad mood, he went to the bathroom and washed his face

with cold water. He sensed something unsettling, had a premoni-tion of new unpleasantness. He'd never believed that human des-tiny was written, that life was a script that human beings acted in without knowing it, but ever since Ismael's ill-fated marriage and the alleged appearances of Edilberto Torres, he'd had the feeling he'd glimpsed predestination. Could his days be a sequence pre-determined by a supernatural power, as the Calvinists believed? The worst thing on that ominous Tuesday was that the family's head-aches had only just begun.

They sat down at the table. Rigoberto and Lucrecia were silent; they wore funereal faces, and reluctantly picked at a salad, totally without appetite. Then Justiniana burst into the dining room with-out knocking.

"You're wanted on the phone, señor." She was very excited, her eyes sparkling as they did on important occasions. "It's Señor Ismael Carrera, no less!"

Rigoberto jumped up. Almost stumbling, he went to take the call in his study.

"Ismael?" he asked eagerly. "Is that you, Ismael? Where are you calling from?"

"From here, Lima, where else," his friend and former boss re-plied in the same unconcerned, jovial tone he'd used in his last call. "We arrived last night and are impatient to see you both, Rigo-berto. But since you and I have so much to talk about, why don't just the two of us get together right away. Have you had lunch? All right, then come and have coffee with me. Yes, right now, I'll expect you here at my house."

"I'll be right there." Rigoberto said goodbye like an automa-ton. "What a day, what a day."

He didn't taste another mouthful and rushed out, promising Lucrecia he'd come back immediately and tell her all about his con-versation with Ismael. The arrival of his friend, the source of all the conflicts in which he found himself entangled with the twins, made him forget about his interview with the investigating mag-istrate and the reappearance of Edilberto Torres on a Lima–Chorrillos jitney.

The silly old man and his brand-new wife had finally returned

from their honeymoon. Had he been kept up to date by Claudio
Arnillas about all the problems the hyenas' persecution was causing him? He'd speak to Ismael frankly, tell him enough was enough,
that ever since he'd agreed to be his witness, his life had turned
into a judicial and police nightmare, that he had to do something
immediately to make his sons stop their harassment.

But when he reached the neocolonial mansion in San Isidro,
almost squashed by the buildings around it, Ismael and Armida
received him with so many demonstrations of friendship that his
intention to speak clearly and forcefully collapsed. He marveled at
how serene, happy, and elegant the couple looked. Ismael was in
casual clothes, a silk ascot around his neck, and sandals that must
have felt like gloves on his feet; his leather jacket matched the soft-
collared shirt, from which rose his smiling face, recently shaved and
scented with a delicate anise fragrance. Even more extraordinary
was the transformation in Armida. She seemed to have recently
emerged from the hands of expert hairdressers, makeup artists, and
manicurists. Her formerly black tresses were now chestnut, and a
charming wave had replaced her straight hair. She wore a light print
dress, with a lilac shawl over her shoulders, and medium-heeled
shoes of the same color. Everything about her, her cared-for hands,
the pale red nails, her earrings, her fine gold chain, the brooch on
her chest, even her confident manner—she greeted Rigoberto, offering her cheek for him to kiss—was that of a lady who'd spent
her life among well-mannered, rich, worldly people and was devoted to caring for her body and wardrobe. To the naked eye, there
was no trace left in her of the former domestic employee. Had she
dedicated the months of her European honeymoon to receiving
lessons in deportment?

As soon as the greetings were concluded they led him into the
room next to the dining room. Through the large window one
could see the garden filled with crotons, bougainvillea, geraniums,
and floripondios. Rigoberto noticed that beside the table, where
the cups, coffeepot, and a serving dish of cookies and pastries were
arranged, were several packages, large and small boxes beautifully
wrapped in fancy paper and ribbons. Were they gifts? Yes. Ismael
and Armida had brought them for Rigoberto, Lucrecia, Fonchito,

and even Justiniana in gratitude for the kindness they'd shown the bride and groom: shirts and silk pajamas for Rigoberto, blouses and shawls for Lucrecia, athletic clothes and sneakers for Fonchito, a dustcoat and sandals for Justiniana, in addition to sashes, belts, cuff links, datebooks, handmade notebooks, engravings, chocolates, art books, and an erotic drawing to hang in the bathroom in the privacy of one's own home.

They looked rejuvenated, sure of themselves, happy, and so supremely peaceful that Rigoberto felt infected by the newlyweds' serenity and good humor. Ismael must have been very sure of what he was doing, perfectly safe from the machinations of his children. Just as he'd predicted at that lunch at La Rosa Náutica, he was probably spending more than they were to undo their plots. He probably had everything under control. Just as well. Why was Rigoberto worrying, then? With Ismael in Lima, the trouble caused by the hyenas would be resolved, perhaps with a reconciliation if his ex-boss could resign himself to letting the fools have a little more money. All the traps that had overwhelmed him would be undone in a few days and he'd recover his secret life, his civilized space. "My sovereignty and my freedom," he thought.

After coffee, Rigoberto listened to a few anecdotes of the couple's travels through Italy. Armida, whose voice he barely remembered having heard before, had recovered the gift of speech. She expressed herself with assurance, few mistakes in syntax, and excellent humor. After a while she withdrew, "so that the two gentlemen can discuss important matters." She explained that she'd never taken a siesta in her life, but now Ismael had taught her to lie down for fifteen minutes with her eyes closed after lunch, and in fact, in the evening she felt very well thanks to that short rest.

"Don't worry about anything, my dear Rigoberto," said Ismael, patting him on the back, as soon as they were alone. "Another cup of coffee? A glass of cognac?"

"I'm delighted to see you so happy and looking so well, Ismael," Rigoberto answered, shaking his head. "I'm delighted to see both of you so well. The truth is, you and Armida are radiant. Clear proof that the marriage is going wonderfully. I'm very glad, naturally. But, but—"

"But those two devils are driving you crazy, I'm well aware of that," Ismael finished the sentence, patting him on the back again, still smiling at him and at life. "Don't worry, Rigoberto, listen to me. I'm here now and I'll take care of everything. I know how to confront these problems and resolve them. A thousand pardons for all the trouble your generosity toward me has brought you. I'll work on this matter all day tomorrow with Claudio Arnillas and the other lawyers in his firm. I'll get the judgments and all these difficulties off your back. Now, sit down and listen. I have news that concerns you. Shall we have that cognac now, old man?"

He quickly poured two drinks and raised his glass. They toasted and wet their lips and tongues; the drink shone with bright red reflections at the bottom of the crystal and had an aroma reminiscent of oak casks. Rigoberto noticed that Ismael was watching him roguishly. A mischievous, mocking smile animated his wrinkled eyes. Did he have his denture adjusted on his honeymoon? It had moved around before, but now it seemed to rest very firmly on his gums.

"Rigoberto, I've sold all my shares in the company to Assicurazioni Generali, the best and biggest underwriter in Italy," he exclaimed, spreading his arms and laughing out loud. "You're very familiar with them, aren't you? We've worked with them quite often. Their headquarters are in Trieste but they're all over the world. They've wanted to expand into Peru for some time and I took advantage of the opportunity. An excellent deal. You see, my honeymoon wasn't only a pleasure trip. It was for work too."

He was enjoying himself, as amused and happy as a child opening presents from Santa Claus. Don Rigoberto hadn't really taken in the news. He vaguely recalled reading in *The Economist* a few weeks ago that Assicurazioni Generali had plans to venture into South America.

"You've sold the company your father founded and where you've worked your whole life?" he finally asked, disconcerted. "To an Italian transnational? How long have you been negotiating with them, Ismael?"

"Just about six months," his friend explained, slowly moving his glass of cognac back and forth. "It was a quick negotiation,

there weren't any complications. And, I repeat, a very good deal.
I've made an excellent deal. Make yourself comfortable and listen.
For obvious reasons, before it was successfully concluded, this had
to be confidential. That was the reason for the audit I authorized
them to make and that surprised you so much last year. Now you
know what was behind it: They wanted to examine the state of the
company with a magnifying glass. I wasn't in charge of it and didn't
pay for it; Assicurazioni Generali did. Now that the transfer is a
fact, I can tell you everything."

Ismael Carrera spoke for close to an hour; Rigoberto interrupted
him only a handful of times to request a few explanations. He listened to his friend, amazed at his memory, for without the slightest hesitation he was unfolding for him, as if they were the layers
of a palimpsest, months of offers and counteroffers. Rigoberto was
stunned. It seemed incredible that so delicate a negotiation could
have been carried out so secretly that not even he, the general manager of the company, knew anything about it. The negotiators'
meetings had taken place in Lima, Trieste, New York, and Milan;
those who took part were lawyers, principal shareholders, authorized personnel, advisers, and bankers from several countries, but
practically all of Ismael Carreras's Peruvian employees had been ex-
cluded, as were Miki and Escobita, of course. Those two, who'd
received their inheritance in advance when Don Ismael removed
them from the company, had already sold a good part of their
shares, and only now did Rigoberto learn that the person who'd
bought them through intermediaries was Ismael himself. The hyenas still held a small parcel of shares and would become minor
(the smallest, in fact) partners in the Peruvian branch of Assicurazioni Generali. How would they react? A disdainful Ismael
shrugged. "Badly, of course. And so what?" Let them holler. The
sale had been made in compliance with all national and foreign reg-
ulations. The administrative entities of Italy, Peru, and the United
States had given the transaction their approval. They'd paid all relevant taxes to the last penny and complied with every rule and law.

"What do you think, Rigoberto?" Ismael Carrera concluded his
exposition. He opened his arms again like an actor greeting the
audience and waiting for applause. "Am I still sharp, still acting
like a businessman?"

Rigoberto nodded. He was disoriented and didn't know what to think. His friend looked at him, smiling and pleased with himself.

"The truth is, you never cease to amaze me, Ismael," he finally said. "You're enjoying a second youth, I can see that. Has Armida rejuvenated you? I still can't wrap my mind around your having let go so easily of the business your father created and that you built up, investing blood, sweat, and tears in it for half a century. You'll think it's absurd, but I feel sad, as if I'd lost something of mine. And you're as happy as a drunken sailor."

"It wasn't all that easy," Ismael corrected him, serious now. "I had plenty of doubts at first. It made me sad, too. But given the situation, it was the only solution. If I'd had different heirs—but then, why talk about depressing things. You and I know very well what would happen if my children had control of the company. They'd sink it in the blink of an eye. Best-case scenario, they'd sell it at a loss. In the hands of the Italians, it will continue to exist and prosper. You can collect your retirement without any kind of cuts and with a bonus besides, old man. It's all arranged."

It seemed to Rigoberto that his friend's smile had become melancholy. Ismael sighed, and a shadow crossed his eyes.

"What are you going to do with so much money, Ismael?"

"Spend my final years calm and happy," he replied immediately. "And I hope healthy too. Enjoying life a little, with my wife at my side. Better late than never, Rigoberto. You know better than anyone that until now I lived only to work."

"Hedonism's a good philosophy, Ismael," Rigoberto agreed. "Aside from everything else, it's mine, too. Until now I've been able to follow it only in part. But I hope to imitate you when the twins leave me in peace and Lucrecia and I can set off on the trip to Europe we organized. She was very disappointed when we had to cancel our plans because of your sons' demands."

"I've already told you, I'll take care of that tomorrow. It's at the top of my agenda, Rigoberto," said Ismael, standing up. "I'll call you after our meeting in Arnillas's office. And let's set a date to have lunch or dinner together, with Armida and Lucrecia."

As he returned home, leaning on the steering wheel of his car, all kinds of ideas whirled around in Don Rigoberto's head like the water in a fountain. How much money could Ismael have gotten from the sale of his shares? Many millions. A fortune, in any case. Even though Ismael's company had been doing only so-so recently, it was a solid institution with a magnificent portfolio and a first-rate reputation in Peru and abroad. True, an octogenarian like Ismael could no longer keep up with managerial responsibilities. He must have put his capital into safe investments, debenture bonds, pension funds, businesses in the safest fiscal paradises: Lichtenstein, Guernsey, or Jersey, or perhaps Singapore or Dubai. The interest alone would allow him and Armida to live like royalty anywhere in the world. What would the twins do? Fight with the new owners? They were such idiots that this couldn't be discounted. They'd be squashed like cockroaches. It couldn't happen too soon. No, probably they'd try to nibble away at some of the money from the sale. Ismael probably had it safely tucked away. No doubt they'd resign themselves if their father softened and threw them a few crumbs to get them to stop fucking around. Then everything would settle down. If only it would happen soon. Then his plans for a joyful retirement rich in material, intellectual, and artistic pleasures could finally materialize.

But in his heart of hearts he couldn't convince himself that everything would work out so well for Ismael. He was haunted by the suspicion that instead of being settled, matters would become even more complicated, and instead of escaping the legal and judicial tangle in which Miki and Escobita had caught him, he'd find himself even more thoroughly trapped until the end of his days. Or was that pessimism due to the abrupt reappearance of Edilberto Torres?

As soon as he reached his house in Barranco, he gave his wife a detailed account of the latest events. She shouldn't worry about the sale of the company to an Italian insurer, because as far as the two of them were concerned, the transfer would probably help to resolve things if Ismael, along with the new owners, would agree to placate the twins with some money so they'd leave them alone. What made the greatest impression on Lucrecia was that Armida had returned from her honeymoon transformed into an elegant, sociable, and worldly lady. "I'll call her to welcome her home and arrange that lunch or dinner very soon, my love. I'm dying to see her transformation into a respectable matron."

Rigoberto went into his study and on the computer looked up everything he could about Assicurazioni Generali S.p.A. The largest insurer in Italy. He'd been in touch with the company and its subsidiaries on several occasions. Recently, it had expanded significantly into Eastern Europe, the Middle and Far East, and in a more limited way, Latin America, where it had centralized its operations in Panama. This was a good opportunity for the company to move into South America, using Peru as a springboard. The country was doing well, its laws were stable, and investments were growing.

He was still immersed in research when he heard Fonchito come home from school. He closed the computer and waited impatiently for his son to come in and say hello. When the boy entered the study and approached to kiss him, still with his Markham Academy backpack on his shoulders, Rigoberto decided to bring up the subject immediately.

"So it seems Edilberto Torres has appeared again," he said sadly. "I thought we'd gotten rid of him forever, Fonchito."

"So did I, Papa," his son replied with disarming sincerity. He removed the backpack, placed it on the floor, and sat down facing his father's desk. "We had a very brief conversation. Didn't my stepmother tell you about it? Just until the jitney reached Miraflores. He got off at the Diagonal, near the park. Didn't she tell you?"

"Of course she told me, but I'd like it if you told me too." He noticed that Fonchito had ink stains on his fingers and that his tie was unknotted. "What did he say to you? What did you talk about?"

"The devil," Fonchito said with a laugh. "Yes, yes, don't laugh. It's true, Papa. And this time he didn't cry, fortunately. I told him you and my stepmother thought he was the devil incarnate."

He spoke with such evident naturalness, there was something so fresh and authentic in him, Rigoberto thought, how could he not believe him.

"They still believe in the devil?" Edilberto was surprised. He spoke to him in a whisper. "It seems there aren't many people in our day who believe in that gentleman. Have your parents told you why they have so low an opinion of me?"

"Because of how you appear and disappear so mysteriously, señor," explained Fonchito, lowering his voice too, because the subject seemed to interest the other passengers on the jitney, who'd started to look at them sideways. "I shouldn't be talking to you. I already told you I've been forbidden to."

"You tell them I told you that they can forget their fears and rest easy," Edilberto Torres assured him in a barely audible voice. "I'm not the devil or anything like it, just a normal, ordinary person like you and like them. And like all the people on this jitney. Besides, you're wrong, I don't appear and disappear in a miraculous way. Our meetings are the result of chance. Sheer coincidence."

"I'm going to speak to you frankly, Fonchito." Rigoberto continued looking into the boy's eyes for a long time, and he looked back without blinking. "I want to believe you. I know you're not a liar and never have been. I know very well you've always told me the truth, even when it might have gone against your own interests. But in this case, I mean, the damned case of Edilberto Torres—"

"Why 'damned,' Papa?" Fonchito interrupted. "What has that man done to you to make you use such a terrible word about him?"

"What has he done to me?" Don Rigoberto exclaimed. "He's made me doubt my son for the first time in my life, made me incapable of believing you're still telling the truth. Do you understand, Fonchito? It's a fact. Each time I hear you telling me about your meetings with Edilberto Torres, no matter how hard I try I can't believe that what you're saying is true. I'm not reprimanding you, try to understand. What's happening to me now because of you makes me sad, it depresses me very much. Wait, wait, let me finish. I'm not saying that you want to lie to me or deceive me. I know you'd never do that. No, at least not in a deliberate, intentional way. But I'm begging you to think a moment about what I'm going to say, with all the love I feel for you. Reflect on it. Isn't it possible that what you're telling me and Lucrecia about Edilberto Torres is only a fantasy, a kind of waking dream, Fonchito? These kinds of things happen to people sometimes."

He stopped speaking because he saw that his son had turned pale. His face had become filled with an invincible sadness. Rigoberto regretted speaking.

"You mean I've gone crazy and see visions, things that don't exist. Is that what you're telling me, Papa?"

"I didn't say you were crazy, of course not," Rigoberto apologized. "I didn't even think it. But Fonchito, it isn't impossible that this individual is an obsession, a fixed idea, a waking nightmare. Don't look at me so incredulously. It could be true, trust me. I'm going to tell you why. In real life, in the world we live in, it's impossible for a person to appear this way, suddenly, in the most unlikely places—on the soccer field at school, in the bathroom of a discotheque, on a Lima–Chorrillos jitney. And for that person to know everything about you, your family, what you do and don't do. It just isn't possible, do you see?"

"What will I do if you don't believe me, Papa," said the boy, crestfallen. "I don't want to make you sad either. But how can I agree with you that I'm hallucinating when I'm certain that Señor Torres is flesh and blood and not a phantom. Maybe the best thing would be for me not to tell you about him anymore."

"No, no, Fonchito, I want you always to tell me about these meetings," Rigoberto insisted. "Though it's hard for me to accept what you're saying about him, I'm sure you believe you're telling me the truth. You can be certain about that. If you're lying to me, you're doing it without meaning to or realizing it. Well, you must have homework to do, don't you? Go ahead then, if you want to. We'll talk more later."

Fonchito picked up his backpack from the floor and took a couple of steps toward the study door. But before opening it, as if he'd just remembered something, he turned to his father.

"You dislike him so much, yet Señor Torres thinks very highly of you, Papa."

"Why do you say that, Fonchito?"

"Because I think I know your papa has problems with the police, with the law, you must know about it already," said Edilberto Torres in farewell, after he'd already signaled the driver that he was getting off at the next stop. "It's obvious to me that Rigoberto is an irreproachable man and I'm sure what's happening to him is very unjust. If I can do anything for him, I'd be delighted to lend a hand. Tell him that for me, Fonchito."

Don Rigoberto didn't know what to say. In silence he contemplated the boy, who remained where he stood, looking at him calmly, waiting for his response.

"He said that to you?" he stammered after a moment. "In other words, he sent me a message. He knows about my legal problems and wants to help me. Is that it?"

"Exactly, Papa. You see, he has a very high opinion of you."

"Tell him I accept with pleasure." Rigoberto finally regained control of himself. "Of course. The next time he shows up, thank him and tell him I'd be delighted to talk to him. Wherever he likes. Have him call me. Maybe he can help me out, let's hope so. What I want most in the world, son, is to see and talk to Edilberto Torres in person."

"Okay, Papa, I'll tell him if I see him again. I promise. You'll see he isn't a spirit but flesh and blood. I'm going to do my homework. I have a lot to get through."

When Fonchito left the study, Rigoberto tried to open the computer again but closed it almost immediately. He'd lost all interest in Assicurazioni Generali S.p.A. and in Ismael's serpentine financial dealings. Was it possible that Edilberto Torres had said that to Fonchito? Was it possible he knew about his legal troubles? Of course not. Once again the boy had set a trap for him and he'd fallen into it like a simpleton. And if Edilberto Torres scheduled a meeting with him? "Then," he thought, "I'll return to religion, I'll reconvert and live out the rest of my days in a Carthusian monastery." He laughed and mumbled, "How infinitely boring. So many oceans of stupidity in the world."

He stood and went to look at the nearest shelves where he kept his favorite art books and catalogues. As he examined them, he recalled the shows where he'd bought them. New York, Paris, Madrid, Milan, Mexico City. How painful to be seeing lawyers and judges, thinking about the twins, those functional illiterates, instead of losing himself morning, noon, and night in these volumes, prints, and designs, listening to good music, fantasizing, traveling in time, experiencing extraordinary adventures, getting emotional, growing sad, enjoying, crying, becoming exalted and excited. He thought: "Thanks to Delacroix I was present at the death of Sardanapalus surrounded by naked women, and thanks to the young Grosz I beheaded them in Berlin while at the same time, with an enormous phallus, I sodomized them. Thanks to Botticelli I was a Renaissance Madonna, and thanks to Goya a lascivious monster who devoured his children, beginning with their calves. Thanks to Aubrey Beardsley, a faggot with a rose up my ass, and to Piet Mondrian, an isosceles triangle."

He was beginning to enjoy himself and, almost unconsciously, his hands had already found what he'd been looking for since he'd begun his examination of the shelves: the catalogue of the 2004 retrospective that the Royal Academy dedicated to Tamara de Lempicka that had run from May to August, which he had visited in person the last time he was in England. There, in the crotch of his trousers, he felt the outline of an encouraging tickle in the intimacy of his testicles, while at the same time he felt himself becoming emotional and filling with nostalgia and gratitude. Now, along with the tickle he felt a light burning at the tip of his cock. With the book in his hands he went to sit in his reading armchair and lit the lamp whose light would allow him to enjoy the reproductions in full detail. The magnifying glass was within reach. Was it true that, according to her final wishes, the ashes of the Polish-Russian artist Tamara de Lempicka were dropped from a helicopter by her daughter Kizette into the crater of the Mexican volcano Popocatépetl? What an Olympian, cataclysmic, magnificent way for the woman to say goodbye to this world, a woman who, as her paintings testified, knew not only how to paint but how to enjoy herself, an artist whose fingers imparted an exalted and at the same time icy lasciviousness to these supple, slithering, rounded, opulent nudes who paraded before his eyes: *Rhythm, La Belle Rafaela, Myrto, The Model, The Slave.* His five favorites. Who said that art deco and eroticism were incompatible? In the 1920s and 1930s, this Polish-Russian woman with the tweezed eyebrows, burning, voracious eyes, sensual mouth, and crude hands populated her canvases with an intense lechery, icy only in appearance, because in

the imagination and sensibility of an attentive spectator the sculp-
tural immobility of the canvas disappeared and the figures became
animated, intertwined, they assailed, caressed, united with, loved,
and enjoyed one another with complete shamelessness. A beautiful, marvelous, exciting spectacle: those women portrayed or
invented by Tamara de Lempicka in Paris, Milan, New York,
Hollywood, and in her final seclusion in Cuernavaca. Inflated,
fleshy, exuberant, elegant, they proudly displayed the triangular na-
vels for which Tamara must have felt a particular predilection, as
great as the one inspired by the abundant, succulent thighs of im-
modest aristocrats whom she stripped only to clothe them in lechery and carnal insolence. "She gave dignity and good press to
lesbianism and the *garçon* style, made them acceptable and worldly,
exhibiting them in Parisian and New York salons," he thought.
"It doesn't surprise me at all that, inflamed by her, Gabriele
D'Annunzio's mad cock tried to violate her in his house, the Vit-
toriale, on Lake Garda, where he took her under the pretext of having her paint his portrait, though in fact he was crazed with the
desire to possess her. Did she escape through a window?" He slowly
turned the pages of the book, barely stopping at the mannered aris-
tocratic men, with blue tubercular circles under their eyes, pausing at the splendid, languid female figures with shifting eyes, hair
as flat as helmets, scarlet nails, upright breasts, majestic hips, who
almost always seemed to be writhing like cats in heat. He spent a
long time lost in his illusion, feeling sure he'd be filled once again
with the desire that had been extinguished so many days and weeks
ago, ever since his pedestrian problems with the hyenas had begun. He was ecstatic over these beautiful damsels decked out in
low-cut, transparent dresses, gleaming jewels, all of them possessed
by a profound desire that struggled to become manifest in their
enormous eyes. "To go from art deco to abstraction, what mad-
ness, Tamara," he thought. Though even the abstract paintings of
Tamara de Lempicka exuded a mysterious sensuality. Moved and
happy, he noticed in his lower belly a small tumult, the dawning
of an erection.

And at that moment, returning to ordinary reality, he noticed
that Doña Lucrecia had come into the study without his having

heard her open the door. What was wrong? She stood next to him, her eyes wet and dilated and her lips half open, trembling. She struggled to speak but her tongue didn't obey, instead of words, an incomprehensible stammering emerged.

"More bad news, Lucrecia?" he asked in terror, thinking about Edilberto Torres, about Fonchito. "Bad news again?"

"Armida called crying like a madwoman," Doña Lucrecia sobbed. "Right after he said goodbye to you, Ismael collapsed in the garden. They took him to the American Clinic. And he just passed, Rigoberto! Yes, yes, he just died!"

XV

"What's wrong, Felícito?" the holy woman repeated, bending toward him and fanning him with the old straw fan riddled with holes that she held in her hand. "Don't you feel well?"

The trucker saw the concern in Adelaida's large eyes, and in the fog that filled his head it occurred to him that since she could prophesy, she must know what was wrong. But he didn't have the strength to answer her; he was dizzy and certain that at any moment he'd faint. He didn't care. Sinking into a deep sleep, forgetting everything, not thinking: how wonderful. He thought vaguely of asking the Captive Lord of Ayabaca for help; Gertrudis was especially devoted to him. But he didn't know how.

"Do you want a nice glass of cool water right from the filter, Felícito?"

Why was Adelaida talking so loud, as if he were going deaf? He nodded and, still in a fog, saw the mulatta wrapped in her rough mud-colored tunic running in her bare feet toward the back of the herbs and saints shop. He closed his eyes and thought: "You have to be strong, Felícito. You can't die yet, Felícito Yanaqué. Balls, man! Where are your balls?" He felt his dry mouth and his heart struggling to grow larger among the ligaments, bones, and muscles of his chest. He thought: "It's coming right out of my mouth." At that moment he realized how precise that expression was. Not impossible, hey waddya think. That organ was thundering so energetically and so uncontrollably inside his rib cage that it could suddenly leap free, escape the prison of his body, climb up his larynx, and be ejected in a great spewing of bile and blood. He'd see his heart at his feet, flattened on the dirt floor of the holy woman's house, deflated now, quiet now, perhaps surrounded by scurrying, chocolate-colored cockroaches. That would be the last thing in this life he'd remember. When he opened the eyes of his soul, he'd be before God. Or maybe the devil, Felícito.

"What's going on?" he asked uneasily. Because as soon as he saw their faces, he knew something very serious had happened, which explained the urgency of their summons to the station, their uncomfortable expressions, the evasive eyes and false half smiles of Captain Silva and Sergeant Lituma. The two policemen had become mute and petrified as soon as they'd seen him walk into the narrow cubicle.

"Here you go, Felícito, nice and cool. Open your mouth and drink it slow, in little sips, baby. It'll do you good, you'll see."

He nodded, and without opening his eyes he parted his lips and felt with relief the cool liquid Adelaida brought to his mouth, as if he were a baby. The water seemed to douse the flames on his palate and tongue, and even though he couldn't speak and didn't want to, he thought: "Thanks, Adelaida." The tranquil semidarkness in which the holy woman's shop was always submerged calmed his nerves a little.

"Important business, my friend," the captain said at last, becoming serious and standing to shake his hand with unusual effusiveness. "Come, let's have a coffee somewhere cooler on the avenue, where we can talk better than in here. It's hotter than hell in this cave, don't you agree, Don Felícito?"

And before he had time to respond, the chief took his kepi from the hook and, followed like a robot by Lituma, who avoided looking him in the eye, headed for the door. What was wrong with them? What important business? What was going on? What fly had bitten this pair of cops?

"Do you feel better, Felícito?" the holy woman asked.

"Yes," he managed to stammer with difficulty. His tongue, palate, and teeth hurt. But the glass of cool water had done him good and returned some of the energy that had been draining from his body. "Thanks, Adelaida."

"That's good, thank God for that," the mulatta exclaimed, crossing herself and smiling at him. "That was some scare you gave me, Felícito. You were so pale! Oh, hey waddya think! When I saw you come in and drop into the rocker like a sack of potatoes, you looked like a corpse. What happened, baby, who died?"

"With all this mystery you have me on pins and needles, Captain," Felícito insisted, beginning to be alarmed. "What is this business, if you don't mind my asking?"

"A good, strong coffee for me," Captain Silva told the waiter. "An espresso cut with milk for the sergeant. What'll you have, Don Felícito?"

"A soda, Coca-Cola, Inca Kola, whatever." He was impatient now, tapping on the table. "Okay, let's get to the point. I'm a man who knows how to hear bad news, with all that's happened I'm getting used to it. Let's have it, no more beating around the bush."

"The matter's resolved," said the captain, looking him in the eye. But he looked at him not with joy but with sorrow, even compassion. Surprisingly, instead of continuing, he fell silent.

"Resolved?" Felícito exclaimed. "Do you mean you caught them?"

He saw the captain and sergeant nod, still very serious and displaying a ridiculous solemnity. Why were they looking at him in that strange way, as if they felt sorry for him? On Avenida Sánchez Cerro there was infernal noise, people going and coming, car horns, shouts, barking, braying. A band was playing a waltz, but the singer didn't have Cecilia Barraza's sweet voice, how could he when he was an old man reeking of aguardiente?

"Do you remember the last time I was here, Adelaida?" Felícito spoke very quietly, searching for the words, afraid he'd lose his voice. To breathe more easily he'd unbuttoned his vest and loosened his tie. "When I read the first spider letter to you."

"Yes, Felícito, sure I remember." The holy woman's enormous, worried eyes drilled into him.

"And do you remember that when I was saying goodbye, you had a sudden inspiration and told me to do what they wanted and give them the money they asked for? Do you remember that too, Adelaida?"

"Sure I do, Felícito, sure, how could I not remember. Are you ever going to tell me what's wrong? Why are you so pale and dizzy?"

"You were right, Adelaida. Like always, you were right. I should've listened to you. Because, because . . ."

He couldn't go on. His voice broke in the middle of a sob and he began to cry. Something he hadn't done for a very long time, not since the day his father died in that dark, dingy corner of the emergency room of the Hospital Obrero de Piura. Or maybe not since the night he had sex with Mabel for the first time. But that didn't count as crying because that had been for happiness. And now tears came all the time.

"Everything's resolved and now we'll explain it to you, Don Felícito." The captain finally came back to life, repeating what he'd already told him. "I'm really afraid you won't like what you're going to hear."

He sat up straight in his seat and waited, every sense alert. He had the impression that the people in the small bar had disappeared, that the street noises had become muted. Something made him suspect that what was coming would be the worst misfortune he'd suffered in a good long time. His legs began to tremble.

"Adelaida, Adelaida," he moaned as he wiped his eyes. "I had to let this out somehow. I couldn't control myself. I'm sorry, I swear I don't usually cry."

"Don't worry about it, Felícito." The holy woman smiled, patting him affectionately on his hand. "It does us all good to let the tears flow once in a while. I start wailing too sometimes."

"Go ahead and talk, Captain, I'm ready," the trucker declared. "Loud and clear, please."

"Let's take it slow," Captain Silva said hoarsely, playing for time. He raised the cup of coffee to his mouth, took a sip, and continued: "The best thing is for you to hear about the plot the way we did, from the beginning. Lituma, what's the name of the officer who was guarding Señora Mabel?"

Candelario Velando, twenty-three years old, from Tumbes. Two years on the force, and this was the first time his superiors had him in plain clothes for a job. They stationed him across from the señora's house on that dead-end street in the Castilla district, near the river and the Salesian fathers' Don Juan Bosco Academy, and ordered him to make sure nothing happened to the lady who lived there. He was supposed to come to her aid if necessary, write down who came to visit her, follow her without being seen, take notes on whom she met, whom she visited, what she did or stopped do-ing. They gave him a service weapon with ammunition for twenty shots, a camera, a notebook, a pencil, and a cell phone to use only in case of an emergency, never for personal calls.

"Mabel?" The holy woman's half-mad eyes opened very wide. "Your girlfriend? It was her?"

Felícito nodded. The glass of water was empty, but he didn't seem to realize it, because from time to time he brought it up to his mouth and moved his lips and throat as if he were taking a sip.

"It was her, Adelaida." He moved his head several times. "Yes, Mabel. I still can't believe it."

He was a good policeman, reliable and punctual. He liked the profession and so far had refused to take bribes. But that night he was very tired, he'd been following the señora on the street and guarding her house for fourteen hours, and as soon as he sat down in that corner where there was no light and leaned his back against the wall, he fell asleep. He didn't know for how long; it must have been a while, because when he woke with a start, the street was quiet, the kids spinning tops had disappeared, and in the houses the lights had been turned off and the doors locked. Even the dogs had stopped running around and barking. The entire neighbor-hood seemed to be asleep. He stood up in a daze, and, keeping to the shadows, approached the señora's house. He heard voices. He put his ear to one of the windows. It seemed to be an argument. He couldn't hear a word of what they were saying but he had no doubt it was a man and a woman, and they were fighting. He ran to crouch at another window and from there he could hear better. They were insulting each other and cursing but there were no blows, not yet. Only long silences, and then voices again, quieter. She seemed to be consenting. She'd had a visitor, and apparently the visitor was fucking her. Candelario Velando knew right away it wasn't Señor Felícito Yanaqué. Did the señora have another lover, then? Finally, the house was completely silent.

Candelario went back to the corner where he'd fallen asleep. He sat down again, lit a cigarette, and waited, leaning his back against the wall. This time he didn't nod off or become distracted. He was sure the visitor would reappear at some point. And in fact, he did reappear after a long time, taking the precautions that gave him away: barely opening the door, putting only his head out, looking to the right and the left, and only when he was sure no one would see him, beginning to walk. Candelario saw the full length of his body, and his silhouette and movements confirmed it couldn't be the very short old man who owned Narihualá Transport. This was a young man. Candelario couldn't make out his face, it was too dark. When he saw him heading toward the Puente Colgante, he went after him, walking slowly, trying not to be seen, keeping a fair distance without losing sight of him. He moved a little closer as they crossed the Puente Colgante because night owls were on the bridge and he could hide among them. Candelario saw him take one of the paths on the Plaza de Armas and disappear into the bar of the Hotel Los Portales. He waited a moment and then went in too. He was at the bar—young, white, good-looking, with an Elvis Presley pompadour—gulping down what must have been a small bottle of pisco. Then Candelario recognized him. He'd seen him when he came to the station on Avenida Sánchez Cerro to make his statement.

"Are you sure it was him, Candelario?" Sergeant Lituma asked, looking doubtful.

"It was Miguel, absolutely, positively, definitely," Captain Silva said drily, bringing the cup of coffee up to his lips again. He seemed very uncomfortable saying what he was saying. "Yes, Señor Yana-qué. I'm very sorry. But it was Miguel."

"My son Miguel?" the trucker repeated very rapidly, blinking constantly, waving one of his hands; he'd suddenly turned pale. "At midnight? At Mabel's?"

"They were having an argument, Sergeant," the guard Cande-lario Velando explained to Lituma. "They were really fighting, using curse words like 'whore,' 'motherfucker,' and worse. After that it was quiet for a long time. I imagined then what you must be imagining now: They made up and went to bed. And why else but to fuck, though I didn't hear or see any of that. That's only a guess."

"You shouldn't tell me those things," Adelaida said, uncomfortable and lowering her eyes. Her lashes were long and silky and she was upset. She gave the trucker an affectionate pat on the knee. "Unless you think it will help you to tell me about them. Whatever you like, Felícito. Whatever you say. That's what friends are for, hey waddya think."

"A guess that reveals what a filthy mind you have, Candelario." Lituma smiled at him. "Okay, boy. You passed. Since there are asses involved, the captain will like your story."

"Finally, the end of the thread. We began to pull on it and undo the knot. I already suspected something when I questioned her after the kidnapping. There were too many contradictions, she didn't know how to lie. That's how it was, Señor Yanaqué," the chief added. "Don't think this is easy for us. I mean, giving you this awful news. I know it feels like a knife in the back. But it's our duty, I hope you'll forgive us."

"No chance there's been a mistake?" he murmured in a voice that was hollow now, and somewhat pleading. "No chance at all?"

"None at all," stated Captain Silva pitilessly. "It's been proved ad nauseam. Señora Mabel and your son Miguel have been pulling the wool over your eyes for a long time now. That's where the spider story begins. We're really sorry, Señor Yanaqué."

"It's more your son Miguel's fault than Señora Mabel's," Lituma said, then immediately apologized for adding his two cents: "I'm sorry, I didn't mean to interrupt."

Felícito Yanaqué no longer seemed to be listening to the two police officers. His pallor had intensified; he looked at empty space as if a ghost had just materialized. His chin trembled.

"I really know what you're feeling and my heart goes out to you, Felícito." The holy woman had placed a hand on her chest. "Well, yes, you're right. It'll do you good to get it off your chest. Nothing you tell me will leave here, baby, you know that."

She hit her chest and Felícito thought, "How strange, it sounded hollow." Ashamed, he felt his eyes filling with tears again.

"He's the spider," Captain Silva declared categorically. "Your son, the white-skinned one. Miguel. It seems he didn't do it just for the money; his motives are more twisted. And maybe, maybe, that's why he went to bed with Mabel. He has something personal against you. A grudge, resentment, those bitter things that poison a person's soul."

"Because you forced him to do military service, it seems," Lituma intervened again. And this time too he apologized: "Excuse me. At least, that's what he led us to believe."

"Are you listening to what we're telling you, Don Felícito?" the captain asked, leaning toward the trucker and grasping his arm. "Do you feel sick?"

"I feel great." The trucker forced a smile. His lips and nostrils were trembling, as were the hands holding the empty bottle of Inca Kola. A yellow ring encircled the whites of his eyes, and his voice was like a thread. "Just go on, Captain. But excuse me, I'd like to know one thing, if I can. Was Tiburcio, my other son, also involved?"

"No, it was just Miguel." The captain tried to be encouraging. "I can assure you of that definitively. You can rest easy as far as that's concerned, Señor Yanaqué. Tiburcio wasn't involved and didn't know anything about it. When he finds out, he'll be as shocked as you are now."

"This terrible story has a good side, Adelaida," the trucker grunted, after a long pause. "Even if you don't believe it, it does."

"I believe it, Felícito," said the holy woman, opening her mouth wide, showing her tongue. "Life's always like that. Good things always have their bad side and bad things their good side. So, what's the good side here?"

"I've resolved a doubt that's been eating at my heart ever since I got married, Adelaida," Felícito Yanaqué murmured. At that moment he seemed to recover: He regained his voice, his color, a certain sureness in his speech. "Miguel isn't my son. He never was. Gertrudis and her mother made me marry her by telling me she was pregnant. Sure she was pregnant, but not by me, by another man. I was her dumb *cholito*. They stuck me with a stepson, passing him off as mine, and Gertrudis was saved from the shame of being a single mother. I mean, tell me how that white kid with blue eyes could be my son? I always suspected something fishy there. Now I finally have the proof, though it's a little late. He isn't mine, my blood doesn't run in his veins. A son of mine, a son of my blood, would never have done what he did to me. Do you see, do you get the picture, Adelaida?"

"I see, baby, I get it," the holy woman agreed. "Give me your glass, I'll fill it again with cool water from the distilling stone. I can't tell you how it makes me feel to see you drink water from an empty glass, hey waddya think."

"And Mabel?" the trucker mumbled, his eyes lowered. "Was she involved in the spider plot from the beginning? Was she?"

"Unwillingly, but yes." Captain Silva was modulating his words, as if reluctant to speak. "She was. She never liked the idea, and according to her, at first she tried to talk Miguel out of it, which is possible. But your son is strong-willed, and—"

"He isn't my son," Felícito Yanaqué interrupted, looking him in the eye. "Excuse me, I know what I'm saying. Go on, what else, Captain."

"She was fed up with Miguel and wanted to break it off, but he didn't let her and threatened to tell you about their affair," Lituma interjected again. "And she began to hate him for dragging her into this mess."

"Does this mean you've talked to Mabel?" asked the trucker, disconcerted. "What did she confess to?"

"She's cooperating with us, Señor Yanaqué." Captain Silva nodded. "Her testimony was instrumental in our learning about the entire spider plot. What the sergeant told you is correct. At first, when she became involved with Miguel, she didn't know he was your son. When she found out, she tried to break it off, but it was too late. She couldn't because Miguel blackmailed her."

"He threatened to tell you everything, Señor Yanaqué, so you'd kill her or at least give her a good beating," Sergeant Lituma interjected again.

"And leave her in the street without a cent, which is the main thing," the captain continued. "It's what I told you before, Don Felícito. Miguel hates you, he feels a great deal of rancor toward you. He says it's because you forced him and not his brother Tiburcio to do military service. But it looks to me like there's something else. Maybe his hatred goes all the way back to when he was a kid. You'd know."

"He also must have suspected he wasn't my son, Adelaida," the trucker added. He sipped at the fresh glass of water the holy woman had just brought him. "All he had to do was look at his face in the mirror to realize he didn't have, couldn't have my blood. And that's how he must have begun to hate me, what else could it be. What's strange is that he always hid it, never showed it to me. Do you see?"

"What do you want me to see, Felícito?" exclaimed the holy woman. "Everything's very clear, even a blind person could see it. She's a girl and you're an old man. Did you think Mabel would be faithful to you until she died? Especially with you having a wife and family and her knowing she'd never be anything but your girl-friend. Life is what it is, Felícito, you must've known that. You come from poor people, you know what suffering means, like me and all the poor Piurans."

"Of course, the kidnapping never was a kidnapping, it was a joke," said the captain. "To put pressure on you, on your feelings, Don Felícito."

"I knew it, Adelaida. I never had any illusions. Why do you think I always chose to look the other way and never asked what else Mabel was up to? But I never imagined she'd get involved with my own son!"

"So now maybe he's your son?" the holy woman chided him mockingly. "What difference does it make who she got involved with, Felícito. How can that matter to you now? Don't think about it anymore, compadre. Turn the page, forget about it, it's over. It's for the best, believe me."

"Do you know what I think about now with real sorrow, Adelaida?" His glass was empty again. Felícito was shuddering. "The scandal. You must think that's silly, but it's what tortures me most. It'll be in tomorrow's papers, on radio and television. Then the reporters will come after me. My life will be a circus again. Reporters persecuting me, curious people on the street, in the office. I don't have the patience or energy to go through all that again, Adelaida. Not anymore."

"He fell asleep, Captain," whispered Lituma, pointing to the trucker whose eyes were closed, his head bent.

"I think he has," the captain agreed. "The news crushed him.

His son, his girlfriend. From bad to worse. No surprise there, damn it."

Felícito heard them without hearing them. He didn't want to open his eyes, not even for a moment. He dozed, hearing the noise and hubbub on Avenida Sánchez Cerro. If all this hadn't happened, he'd be at Narihualá Transport, reviewing the morning's movement of buses, trucks, and cars, studying today's total number of passengers and comparing it to yesterday's, dictating letters to Señora Josefita, settling accounts or cashing checks at the bank, getting ready to go home for lunch. He felt so much sadness that he began to tremble from head to foot, as if he had tertian fever. Never again would his life have the tranquil rhythm it once had, never again would he be an anonymous face in the crowd. Now he'd always be recognized on the street; when he went into a movie theater or a restaurant the gossiping would begin, rude glances, whispers, fingers pointing him out. This very night or tomorrow at the latest, the news would become public, all of Piura would know about it. And his life would be hell again.

"Do you feel better after that little snooze, Don Felícito?" asked Captain Silva, giving him an affectionate pat on the arm.

"I nodded off for a minute, I'm sorry," he said, opening his eyes. "Forgive me. So many emotions at the same time."

"Sure, of course," the officer reassured him. "Do you want to keep going or leave the rest for later, Don Felícito?"

He nodded, murmuring: "Let's go on." During the few minutes he'd had his eyes closed, the bar had filled with people, most of them men. They smoked, ordered sandwiches, sodas, beers, cups of coffee. The captain lowered his voice so he wouldn't be overheard at the next table.

"Miguel and Mabel have been detained since last night and the investigating judge is up to date on everything. We have a meeting with the press at the station at six tonight. I don't think you want to be present for that, do you, Don Felícito?"

"No way," exclaimed the trucker, horrified. "Of course not!"

"You don't have to come," the captain assured him. "But prepare yourself. The reporters are going to drive you crazy."

"Miguel confessed to all the charges?" Felícito asked.

"At first he denied them, but when he found out that Mabel had turned on him and would testify at the hearing, he had to accept reality. As I said, her testimony is devastating."

"Thanks to Señora Mabel, in the end he confessed to everything," Sergeant Lituma added. "She's made our work easier. We're writing up the report. It'll be in the hands of the investigating judge tomorrow at the latest."

"Will I have to see him?" Felícito spoke so quietly, the policemen had to lean their heads in to hear him. "Miguel, I mean."

"At the trial, absolutely," the captain said. "You'll be the star witness. You're the victim, remember."

"And before the trial?" the trucker insisted.

"The investigating judge or the prosecutor may ask for a face-to-face meeting," the captain explained. "In that case, yes. We don't need to do that because, as Lituma said, Miguel confessed to all the charges. His lawyer may decide on another strategy and deny everything, claim that his confession is invalid because it was forced out of him through illegal means. You know, the usual story. But I don't think he has any out. As long as Mabel cooperates, he's a goner."

"How much time will they give him?" the trucker asked.

"That will depend on the lawyer who represents him and how much he can spend on his defense," said the chief, looking somewhat skeptical. "It won't be much. The only act of violence was the small fire at your office. Extortion, false abduction, and conspiracy to commit a crime aren't all that serious under the circumstances. Because they didn't result in anything, they were all faked. Two or three years at most, I doubt he'll get any longer. And since he's a first-time offender and has no record, he might even avoid jail altogether."

"What about her?" the trucker asked, wetting his lips with his tongue.

"Since she's cooperating with the law, the sentence will be very light, Don Felícito. Maybe nothing will happen to her. After all, she was the white guy's victim too. That's what her lawyer might argue, and he wouldn't be wrong."

"Do you see, Adelaida?" Felícito Yanaqué said with a sigh. "They

put me through weeks of torture, they burned my place on Avenida Sánchez Cerro—the losses have been big: A lot of customers
left because they were afraid the extortionists would throw a bomb
at my buses. And those two crooks will probably go home free and
live the good life. Do you see what justice is in this country?"

He stopped talking because he saw that something had changed
in the holy woman's eyes. She was staring at him, her eyes wide,
very serious and concentrated, as if she saw something unsettling
inside or through him. She grasped one of his hands between her
large, calloused hands with their dirty nails. She squeezed it with
great strength. Felícito shuddered, dying of fear.

"An inspiration, Adelaida?" he stammered, trying to free his
hand. "What do you see, what's going on? Please, dear friend."

"Something's about to happen to you, Felícito," she said, squeezing his hand even harder, staring at him insistently with her deep,
now feverish eyes. "I don't know what, maybe what happened to
you this morning with the cops, maybe something else. Worse or
better, I don't know. Something tremendous, very strong, a jolt
that will change your whole life."

"Do you mean, something different from everything that's already happening to me? Even worse things, Adelaida? Isn't my cross
heavy enough?"

She moved her head like a madwoman and didn't seem to hear
him. She raised her voice.

"I don't know if it'll be better or worse, Felícito," she shouted,
terrified. "But I do know it's more important than anything that's
happened to you so far. A revolution in your life, that's what I see."

"Even worse?" he repeated. "Can't you tell me anything concrete, Adelaida?"

"No, no I can't." The holy woman freed his hand and slowly
began to recover her usual appearance and manner. He saw her
sigh and pass her hand over her face as if she were brushing away
an insect. "I only tell you what I feel, what the inspiration makes
me feel. I know it's confusing. For me too, Felícito. It's not my
fault, it's what God wants me to feel. He's the one in charge. That's
all I can tell you. Be prepared, something's going to happen. Something that will surprise you. I only hope it isn't for the worse, baby."

"For the worse?" the trucker exclaimed. "The only thing worse that could happen to me now would be to die, run over by a car, bitten by a rabid dog. Maybe that would be the best thing for me, Adelaida. Dying."

"You're not going to die yet, I can promise you that. Your death isn't something the inspiration told me about."

The holy woman looked exhausted. She was still on the floor, sitting on her heels and rubbing her hands and arms slowly, as if brushing away dust. Felícito decided to leave. Half the afternoon was over. He hadn't eaten a thing at midday but wasn't hungry. The mere idea of sitting down to eat filled him with disgust. With an effort he got up from the rocker and took out his wallet.

"You don't need to give me anything," said the holy woman from the floor. "Not today, Felícito."

"Yes, I do," said the trucker, leaving fifty soles on the nearest counter. "Not for that confused inspiration but for having comforted and advised me with so much kindness. You're my best friend, Adelaida. That's why I've always trusted you."

He went out, buttoning his vest, adjusting his tie, his hat. He felt very hot again. The presence of so many people crowding the streets in the center of Piura oppressed him. Some recognized and greeted him with nods and bows while others were more secretive, merely pointing him out. Still others took pictures of him with their cell phones. He decided to stop by Narihualá Transport in case there were new developments. He looked at his watch: five o'clock. The press conference at the police station was at six. An hour until the news went off like gunpowder. It would explode on the radio and the Internet, to be spread by blogs and televised reports. He'd be the most popular man in Piura again. "Deceived by son and mistress," "Son and mistress tried to extort him," "The spiders were his son and his girlfriend, and on top of everything, they were lovers too!" He felt nauseated imagining the headlines, the caricatures that would show him in embarrassing poses, wearing horns that stretched to the clouds. What dogs they were! Ungrateful, thankless dogs! What Miguel had done angered him less. Because, thanks to the spider extortion, he'd confirmed his suspicion that Miguel wasn't his son. Who could his real father be? Did

Gertrudis even know? Back then, any patron at the inn fucked her, so there were plenty of candidates. Should he leave her? Get a divorce? He'd never loved her, but now, after so long, he couldn't even feel rancor toward her. She hadn't been a bad wife; in all these years her conduct had been exemplary, she'd lived only for her home and her religion. The news would shake her, naturally. A photograph of Miguel in handcuffs, behind bars for having tried to extort his father, the father he shared a mistress with, wasn't something a mother would easily accept. She'd cry and hurry to the cathedral so the priests could console her.

What Mabel had done was worse. He thought about her and a hollow opened in his stomach. She was the only woman he'd ever really loved. He'd given her everything: house, allowance, gifts. A freedom no other man would have granted to the woman he kept. So she'd go to bed with his son! So she'd extort him in cahoots with that hateful wretch! He wasn't going to kill her, or even punch her in her lying mouth. He wouldn't see her again. Let her make her living whoring. Let's see if she could find another lover as considerate as him.

Instead of walking down Calle Lima, at the Puente Colgante he turned toward the Eguiguren Seawalk. There were fewer people there and he could walk more calmly, free of the feeling of knowing that people were looking at him and pointing him out. He thought of the old mansions that had lined this seawalk when he was a kid. They'd fallen into disrepair one after the other because of the havoc caused by El Niño: the rains, the river overflowing its banks and flooding the neighborhood. Instead of rebuilding, the whites had made their new homes in El Chipe, far from the center of town.

What would he do now? Go on with his work at Narihualá Transport as if nothing had happened? Poor Tiburcio. He'd suffer a terrible blow. His brother, Miguel, whom he'd always been so close to, suddenly a criminal who tried to rob his father with the help of his father's mistress. Tiburcio was a very good man. Maybe not very intelligent but decent, reliable, incapable of anything as low as what his brother had done. He'd be destroyed by the news.

The Piura River was very high, carrying away branches, small shrubs, papers, bottles, plastic. It looked muddy, as if there'd been landslides in the mountains. Nobody was swimming in it.

As he went up the seawalk to Avenida Sánchez Cerro, he decided not to go to the office. It was a quarter to six, and the reporters would swarm like flies around Narihualá Transport as soon as they learned the news. Better to shut himself up in his house, lock the door to the street, and not go out for a few days until the storm had calmed down. Thinking about the scandal sent chills up and down his spine.

He walked up Calle Arequipa toward his house, feeling anxiety pooling again in his chest and making it difficult to breathe. So Miguelito had a grudge against him, had hated him even before he forced him to do military service. The feeling was mutual. No, not true, he'd never hated his bastard son. That was different from never having loved him because he sensed they didn't have the same blood. But he didn't remember showing a preference for Tiburcio. He'd been a fair father, careful to treat them both identically. It's true he'd made Miguel spend a year in the barracks. It was for his own good. So that he'd get on track. He was an awful student, he only liked to have fun, kick around soccer balls, drink in the chicha bars. He'd caught him guzzling drinks in seedy bars and restaurants with evil-looking friends, spending his allowance in brothels. Things would go very badly for him if he continued down that path. "If you keep this up, I'll put you in the army," he'd warned him. He kept it up, and he put him in. Felícito laughed. Well, it hadn't really straightened him out if he ended up doing what he'd done. Let him go to jail, let him find out what that meant. Let's see who'd give him work after that, with that kind of record. He'd come out more of a bandit than when he went in, just like everyone else who passed through the prisons, those universities of crime.

He was in front of his house. Before opening the large studded door, he walked over to the corner and tossed some coins into the blind man's jar.

"Good afternoon, Lucindo."

"Good afternoon, Don Felícito. God bless you."

He went back, feeling the tightness in his chest, breathing with difficulty. He opened the door and closed it behind him. From the vestibule he heard voices in the living room. Just what he needed. Visitors! It was strange, Gertrudis didn't have women friends who dropped in unannounced, she never gave teas. He stood uncertainly in the vestibule until he saw his wife's broad shape appear in the doorway to the living room. He saw her come toward him, enclosed in one of those dresses that looked like a habit, speeding up that laborious walk of hers. What was with that expression on her face? Well, she must have heard the news by now.

"So now you know everything," he murmured.

But she didn't let him finish. She pointed toward the living room and spoke hurriedly.

"I'm sorry, I'm very sorry, Felícito. I've had to put her up here in the house. There was nothing else I could do. It'll only be for a few days. She's running away. It seems they might kill her. An incredible story. Come on, she'll tell you yourself."

Felícito Yanaqué's chest was a drum. He looked at Gertrudis, not really understanding what she was saying, but instead of his wife's face he saw Adelaida's, transformed by the visions of her inspiration.

XVI

Why was Lucrecia taking so long? Don Rigoberto paced back and forth like a caged animal in front of the door of his Barranco apartment. His wife still hadn't come out of the bedroom. He was dressed in mourning and didn't want to be late for Ismael's funeral, but because of Lucrecia and her incorrigible dawdling, her ability to find the most absurd pretexts to delay their departure, they'd get to the church after the funeral party had already left for the cemetery. He didn't want to attract attention by showing up at Los Jardines de la Paz after the burial service had already begun, drawing the glances of everyone there. No doubt there'd be many people, as there had been the night before at the vigil, not only out of friendship for the deceased but because of the unhealthy Limeño curiosity to finally see in person the widow in the scandal.

But Don Rigoberto knew there was nothing he could do but resign himself and wait. Probably the only fights he'd had with his wife in all the years they'd been married had been due to Lucrecia's tardiness whenever they went out, regardless of whether it was to a movie, a meal, an art show, the bank, or on a trip. At first, when they were newlyweds, when they had just started living together, he believed his wife was late because of a simple dislike or contempt for punctuality. Because of it they argued, lost their tempers, quarreled. Gradually, by observing her and reflecting, Don Rigoberto realized that his wife's dallying when it was time to leave for any engagement wasn't something superficial, the negligence of a pampered woman. It was a response to something deeper, an ontological state of mind, because without her being conscious of what was happening to her, each time she had to leave a place (her own house, the house of a friend she was visiting, the restaurant where she'd just had dinner) she was seized by a hidden anxiety, an insecurity, a dark, primitive fear of having to leave, go away, change where she was, and so she invented all kinds of excuses (getting a handkerchief, changing her handbag, finding her keys, making sure the windows were locked, the television or the stove turned off, or the telephone not off the receiver), anything that would delay for a few minutes or seconds the terrifying act of leaving.

Had she always been like this? Even as a girl? He didn't dare ask. But he'd confirmed that as the years went by, this urge, mania, or calamity became more pronounced, to the point where Rigoberto sometimes thought with a shudder that the day might come when Lucrecia, with the same mildness as Melville's character, might contract Bartleby's metaphysical lethargy or indolence and decide never again to move from her house, perhaps her room, even her bed. "Fear of leaving behind her being, losing her being, being left without her being," he told himself again. It was the diagnosis he'd made of his wife's delays. The seconds passed and Lucrecia still didn't appear. He'd already called to her three times, reminding her that it was getting late. Undoubtedly, given her distress and nervous upset since receiving the call from Armida announcing Ismael's sudden death, her panic at losing her being, forgetting it like an umbrella or a raincoat if she went out, had gotten worse. She'd keep delaying and they'd be late for the funeral.

Finally Lucrecia came out of the bedroom. She too was dressed in black and wearing dark glasses. Rigoberto hurried to open the door for her. His wife's face was still contorted by grief and uncertainty. What would happen to them now? The night before, during the vigil in the Church of Santa María Reina, Rigoberto saw her sob as she embraced Armida beside the open coffin where Ismael lay with a handkerchief tied around his head to keep his jaw from hanging open. At that moment Rigoberto himself had to make a great effort to control his desire to cry. To die just when he thought he'd won all his battles and felt like the happiest man in creation. Had his happiness killed him, perhaps? Ismael Carrera wasn't used to it.

They went down in the elevator directly to the garage, and with Rigoberto at the wheel, drove quickly toward the Church of Santa María Reina, in San Isidro; the funeral party would leave from there for the cemetery, Los Jardines de la Paz, in La Molina.

"Did you notice last night that Miki and Escobita didn't go up to Armida even once during the vigil?" Lucrecia remarked. "Not once. How inconsiderate. Those two are really mean-spirited."

Rigoberto had noticed and, of course, so had most of the crowd who, over the course of several hours, until close to midnight, had filed past the funeral chapel covered in flowers. The wreaths, arrangements, bouquets, crosses, and cards filled the area and spread into the courtyard and then all the way to the street. Many people loved and respected Ismael, and there was the proof: hundreds saying goodbye to him. There would be as many or more this morning at the burial. But last night there had been, and would be now as well, people who viciously condemned him for marrying his servant, and even those who sided with Miki and Escobita in the lawsuit they'd brought to have the marriage annulled. Like Lucrecia's and his own, people's eyes at the vigil had been focused on the hyenas and Armida. The twins, dressed in mourning and in dark glasses they hadn't removed, looked like two movie gangsters. The dead man's widow and his sons were separated by a few meters that the twins never attempted to cross. It was almost comical. Armida, in mourning from head to toe and wearing a dark hat and veil, sat close to the coffin, holding a handkerchief and a rosary and telling the beads slowly as she moved her lips in silent prayer. Now and then she wiped away tears. Now and again, helped by the two large men with the faces of outlaws directly behind her, she stood, approached the coffin, and bent over the glass to pray or weep. Then she would receive condolences from recent arrivals. After that the hyenas would move, approach the coffin, and remain for a moment or two, crossing themselves, in distress, not turning their heads, not even once, back toward the widow.

"Are you sure those two brawny men who looked like boxers and were beside Armida all night were bodyguards?" asked Lucrecia.

"They could have been relatives. Don't drive so fast, please. One dead body is enough for now."

"Absolutely sure," said Rigoberto. "Claudio Arnillas confirmed it, because Ismael's lawyer is her lawyer now. They were bodyguards."

"Don't you think that's a little ridiculous?" remarked Lucrecia. "Why the devil does Armida need bodyguards, I'd like to know."

"She needs them now more than ever," replied Don Rigoberto, slowing down. "The hyenas could hire a killer and have her murdered. That kind of thing happens now in Lima. I'm afraid those two degenerates will destroy that woman. You can't imagine the fortune the brand-new widow has inherited, Lucrecia."

"If you keep driving like this, I'm getting out," his wife warned him. "Ah, so that was the reason. I thought she was putting on airs and had hired those giants just to show off."

When they reached the Church of Santa María Reina, on the Gutiérrez de San Isidro Oval, the cortege was already leaving, so they joined the caravan without getting out of the car. The line of automobiles was endless. Don Rigoberto saw, as the hearse passed, many pedestrians making the sign of the cross. "Fear of dying," he thought. As far as he could recall, he'd never been afraid of death. "At least, not yet," he corrected himself. "All of Lima must be here."

And in fact, all of Lima was there. The Lima of big businesses, owners of banks, insurance, mining, fishing, and construction companies, television stations, newspapers, country estates, and ranches, as well as many of the employees of the company Ismael had led until a few weeks ago, and even some humble people who must have worked for him or owed him favors. There was a military man wearing a dress uniform with gold braid, probably an aide-de-camp to the president, and the ministers of finance and foreign trade. A minor incident occurred when the coffin was taken out of the hearse and Miki and Escobita attempted to go to the head of the retinue. They succeeded for only a few seconds, because when Armida emerged from her car on the arm of Dr. Arnillas and surrounded now not by two but four bodyguards, the four immediately opened a path for her to the front of the cortege, firmly moving the twins out of the way. Miki and Escobita, after a moment's confusion, chose to cede to the widow and fell back to either side of the coffin. They grasped the straps and followed the cortege with lowered heads. Most of those attending were men, but there were also a good number of elegant women who, during the priest's prayer for the dead, kept staring insolently at Armida. They couldn't see very much. Dressed all in black, she wore a hat and large sunglasses that hid a good part of her face. Claudio Arnillas—he wore his usual multicolored suspenders under a gray jacket—remained at her side, and the four security men formed a wall at her back that no one attempted to breach.

When the ceremony was over and the coffin finally hoisted into one of the recesses that was closed with a marble tablet bearing the name of Ismael Carrera and the dates of his birth and death in golden letters—he had died three weeks before his eighty-second birthday—Dr. Arnillas, his stride more unruly than usual because of his fast pace, and the four bodyguards took Armida to the exit, preventing anyone from approaching her. Rigoberto noted that once the widow had left, Miki and Escobita stood together at the tomb and many people came up to embrace them. He and Lucrecia withdrew without greeting them. (The previous night, at the vigil, they'd approached the twins to offer their condolences, and the handshake had been glacial.)

"Let's stop by Ismael's house," Doña Lucrecia suggested to her husband. "Even if it's only a moment, to see if we can talk to Armida."

"All right, let's try it."

When they arrived at the house in San Isidro, they were surprised not to see a crowd of cars parked near the door. Rigoberto got out, announced himself, and after a wait of several minutes, they were shown into the garden, where they were received by Dr. Arnillas. With an air appropriate to the circumstances, he seemed to have taken control of the situation, though perhaps not completely. He seemed uncertain.

"A thousand pardons on Armida's behalf," he said. "She was awake all night at the vigil, and we've made her lie down. The doctor has ordered her to rest for a while. But come in, let's go to the room by the garden and have something to drink."

Rigoberto's heart contracted a little when he saw the lawyer leading them to the room where two days earlier he'd seen his friend for the last time.

"Armida is very grateful to you both," said Claudio Arnillas. He looked worried and very serious, pausing as he spoke. His gaudy suspenders gleamed each time his jacket opened. "According to her, you're the only friends of Ismael she trusts. As you can imagine, the poor woman feels very helpless now. She's going to need your support—"

"Excuse me, Doctor, I know this isn't the right time," Rigoberto interrupted. "But you know better than anybody everything that's been left hanging with Ismael's death. Do you have any idea of what's going to happen now?"

Arnillas nodded. He'd asked for coffee and held the cup to his mouth. He blew on it slowly. In his lean, bony face, his steely, astute eyes looked doubtful.

"It all depends on those two gentlemen," he said with a sigh, expanding his chest. "Tomorrow the will is opened at Nuñez Notary. I more or less know its contents. We'll see how the hyenas react. Their lawyer is a shyster who advises them to threaten and make war. I don't know how far they'll want to take this. Señor Carrera has left practically his entire fortune to Armida, so we'll have to be prepared for the worst."

He shrugged, resigning himself to the inevitable. Rigoberto assumed that the inevitable was the twins screaming bloody murder. And he thought about the extraordinary paradoxes in life: one of the humblest women in Peru transformed overnight into one of the richest.

"But didn't Ismael give them their inheritance in advance?" he recalled. "He did that when he had to throw them out of the company because of all the trouble they were making, I remember that very clearly. He gave them each a large amount of money."

"But he did it informally, with a simple letter." Dr. Arnillas shrugged again and frowned as he adjusted his glasses. "There was no public document of any kind, and no formal acceptance on their part. The matter can be legally contested, and undoubtedly will be. I doubt very much that the twins will give up so easily. I'm afraid the battle will go on for some time."

"Let Armida settle and give them something so they'll leave her in peace," Don Rigoberto suggested. "The worst thing for her would be a prolonged lawsuit. It would last for years and the lawyers would keep three-quarters of the money. Oh, I'm sorry, Doctor, I didn't mean you, it was a joke."

"Thanks for my share," Dr. Arnillas said with a laugh and stood up. "I certainly agree. A settlement is always best. We'll soon see where this is heading. I'll keep you informed, of course."

"Will I still be involved in this?" Rigoberto asked, standing up as well.

"Naturally we'll try to prevent that," the lawyer halfheartedly reassured him. "Judicial action against you now makes no sense since Don Ismael has died. But you never know with our judges. I'll call you immediately as soon as I have any news."

For the three days following the burial of Ismael Carrera, Rigoberto was paralyzed by uncertainty. Lucrecia called Armida several times, but she never came to the phone. A woman's voice would answer, someone who sounded more like a secretary than a domestic servant. Señora Carrera was resting, and for the moment, for obvious reasons, she preferred not to receive visitors; she'd give her the message, naturally. Rigoberto couldn't communicate with Dr. Arnillas either. He was never in his office or his house; he'd just gone out or hadn't returned yet, he had urgent meetings, he'd return the call as soon as he had a free moment.

What was going on? What could be going on? Had the will already been opened? What would the twins' reaction be when they learned that Ismael had declared Armida his sole heir? They'd contest the will and argue it was null and void because it violated Peruvian laws that stipulated an obligatory third for the children. The law wouldn't recognize the advance payment of their inheritance that Ismael had made to the twins. Would Rigoberto still be implicated in the hyenas' lawsuit? Would they persist? Would he be summoned again to appear before that horrible judge in that claustrophobic office? Would he be obliged to stay in Peru until the suit was settled?

He devoured the papers and listened to all the radio and television reports, but the matter wasn't news yet, it was still confined
to the offices of executors, notaries, and lawyers. In his study, Rigoberto racked his brains trying to guess what was happening in those
stuffy offices. He had no desire to listen to music—even his beloved Mahler got on his nerves—or concentrate on a book, or look
at his prints, losing himself in fantasy. He could barely eat. He
hadn't said much more than good morning and good night to
Fonchito and Doña Lucrecia. He didn't go out for fear he'd be surrounded by reporters and not know how to answer their questions.
In spite of all his prejudices, he had to use the sleeping pills he hated.

Finally, very early on the fourth day, when Fonchito had just
left for school and Rigoberto and Lucrecia, still in their bathrobes,
were sitting down to breakfast, Dr. Claudio Arnillas came to the
penthouse in Barranco. He looked as if he'd survived a disaster. The
dark circles under his eyes indicated sleepless nights, the stubble on
his face made it seem as if he'd forgotten to shave for the past
three days, and his clothing—a crooked tie, very wrinkled shirt
collar, one of the psychedelic suspenders unfastened, his shoes
unpolished—displayed a carelessness that was surprising, for he always was very well dressed and groomed. He shook their hands,
apologized for showing up unexpectedly and so early, and accepted
a cup of coffee. Immediately after sitting down at the table, he
explained what had brought him.

"Have you seen Armida? Have you spoken to her? Do you know
where she is? I need you to be very frank with me. For her sake
and your own."

Don Rigoberto and Doña Lucrecia shook their heads and looked
at him, mouths agape. Dr. Arnillas realized his questions had
stunned them and seemed to become even more depressed.

"I can see you have no clue, like me," he said. "Yes, Armida's
disappeared."

"The hyenas . . ." murmured Rigoberto, who'd turned pale. He
imagined the poor widow abducted and perhaps murdered, her
corpse thrown to the sharks in the ocean or onto some garbage
dump outside the city for the turkey buzzards and stray dogs to
finish off.

"Nobody knows where she is." Dr. Arnillas, despondent, slumped in his chair. "The two of you were my last hope."

Armida had disappeared twenty-four hours earlier in a very strange way, after spending the entire morning at Nuñez Notary, summoned there along with Miki and Escobita, their shyster lawyer, Arnillas, and two or three attorneys from his office. The meeting was interrupted at one, for lunch, and was supposed to reconvene at four. Armida, with her chauffeur and four bodyguards, returned to her house in San Isidro. She said she had no desire to eat and would take a short nap in order to be rested for the afternoon appearance. She went to her room, and at a quarter to four, when the maid knocked on her door and went in, the bedroom was empty. No one had seen her leave the room or the house. The bedroom was in perfect order—the bed was made—and there was no indication of violence. The bodyguards, the butler, the chauffeur, the two maids who were in the house—no one had seen her or noticed any stranger lurking outside. Dr. Arnillas immediately called the twins, convinced they were responsible for her disappearance. But Miki and Escobita, terrified by what had happened, raised a huge fuss and in turn accused Arnillas of trying to ambush them. Finally, all three went together to file a complaint with the police. The minister of the interior had intervened, giving instructions to everyone to say nothing about it for the moment. No information was to be given to the press until the kidnappers contacted the family. There had been a general mobilization but so far no trace of either Armida or her abductors.

"It was them, the hyenas," Doña Lucrecia declared. "They bought off the bodyguards, the chauffeur, and the servants. Of course it was them."

"That's what I thought at first, señora, though now I'm not so sure," Dr. Arnillas explained. "Armida's disappearance isn't to their advantage at all, especially right now. The talks at Nuñez Notary were heading in the right direction. An agreement was being worked out so they could receive a little more money. It all depends on Armida. Ismael didn't leave any loose ends. The bulk of the inheritance is sheltered in offshore foundations in the safest fiscal paradises on earth. If the widow disappears, nobody will receive a penny of the fortune. Not the hyenas, not the servants, not any-body. I wouldn't even be able to collect my fees. So things are look-ing pretty bleak."

His sad, helpless expression was so ridiculous that Rigoberto couldn't control his laughter.

"May I ask what you're laughing at, Rigoberto?" Doña Lucrecia looked at him in annoyance. "Do you think there's something funny in this tragedy?"

"I know why you're laughing, Rigoberto," said Dr. Arnillas. "Because now you feel free. In fact, the lawsuit over Ismael's mar-riage isn't going forward. It'll be dismissed. In any case, it wouldn't have had the slightest effect on the inheritance, which, as I told you, is beyond the reach of Peruvian law. Nothing can be done. The money belongs to Armida. She and the kidnappers will divide it up. Do you realize that? Of course it's laughable."

"You mean the Swiss and Singaporean bankers will have it," added Rigoberto, serious again. "I'm laughing at what a stupid end-ing to this story that would be if it really happens, Dr. Arnillas."

"In other words, we, at least, are free of the nightmare?" asked Doña Lucrecia.

"In principle, yes," Arnillas concurred. "Unless you're the ones who have kidnapped or killed the multimillionaire widow."

And suddenly he laughed too, hysterical, noisy laughter, laugh-ter devoid of any joy. He removed his glasses, wiped them with a flannel cloth, tried to straighten out his clothes, and becoming very serious again murmured, "Laughing to keep from crying, as the saying goes." He stood and took his leave, promising to keep them informed. If they heard any news—he didn't discount the possi-bility that the kidnappers might call them—they could reach him on his cell phone any time, day or night. Control Risk, a specialized firm in New York, would be negotiating the ransom.

As soon as Dr. Arnillas left, a disconsolate Lucrecia began to cry. Rigoberto tried in vain to comfort her. She was shaken by sobs, and tears rolled down her cheeks. "Poor thing, poor thing," she whispered. "They've killed her, it was those dogs, who else could it be. Or they had her abducted to rob her of everything Ismael left her." Justiniana brought her a glass of water with a few drops of paregoric, which finally calmed her down. She stayed in the living room, quiet and dejected. Rigoberto was moved, seeing his wife so despondent. Lucrecia was right. It was very possible the twins were behind this; they had the most to lose and must be going crazy at the idea that the entire inheritance would slip away from them. My God, what stories ordinary life devised; not masterpieces to be sure, they were doubtless closer to Venezuelan, Brazilian, Colombian, and Mexican soap operas than to Cervantes and Tolstoy. But then again not so far from Alexandre Dumas, Émile Zola, Charles Dickens, or Benito Pérez Galdós.

He felt confused and demoralized. Of course, it was good to have shaken off that damn lawsuit. As soon as it was confirmed, he'd update the tickets to Europe. Right. Put an ocean between them and this melodrama. Paintings, museums, operas, concerts, first-rate theater, exquisite restaurants. Right. Poor Armida, she got out of hell, had a taste of heaven, and was right back in the flames again. Kidnapped or murdered. Which was worse?

Justiniana came into the dining room, her expression very serious. She looked disconcerted.

"What is it now?" asked Rigoberto, and Lucrecia, as if emerging from a centuries-long sleep, opened her eyes, still wet from crying, very wide.

"I think Narciso's lost his mind," said Justiniana, putting a finger to her temple. "He's acting very strange. He wouldn't give his name, but I recognized his voice right away. He seems very frightened. He wants to talk to you, señor."

"I'll take the call in my study, Justiniana."

He hurried out of the dining room, heading for his study. He was sure this call would bring bad news.

"Hello, hello," he said into the receiver, prepared for the worst.

"You know who you're talking to, don't you?" answered a voice he recognized right away. "Please don't say my name."

"All right, agreed," said Rigoberto. "Will you tell me what's wrong?"

"It's urgent I see you," said a frightened and perturbed Narciso. "I'm sorry to bother you, but it's very important, señor."

"Yes, of course, certainly." He tried to think where they could meet. "Do you remember where we had lunch the last time with your employer?"

"I remember it very well," said the driver after a brief pause.

"Wait for me there in exactly an hour. I'll pick you up in the car. See you soon."

When he returned to the dining room to tell Lucrecia about Narciso's call, Rigoberto found his wife and Justiniana glued to the television set. They were hypnotized by Raúl Vargas, the star reporter for news channel RPP, who was giving details and speculating about the mysterious disappearance yesterday of Doña Armida de Carrera, the widow of the well-known businessman Don Ismael Carrera, recently deceased. The orders of the minister of the interior not to divulge the news had been useless. Now all Peru, like them, would be aware of this new development. Limeños would have their entertainment for a while, listening to Raúl Vargas. He said more or less what they already knew: She'd disappeared yesterday, early in the afternoon, after an appearance at Nuñez Notary related to the opening of the deceased's will. The meeting was scheduled to resume in the afternoon. The disappearance occurred during the break. The police had detained all the servants in the house, as well as the widow's four bodyguards, for questioning. There was no confirmation of an abduction, but that was the assumption. The police had announced a number to call if anyone had seen her or knew of her whereabouts. He showed photographs of Armida and of Ismael's burial, recalled the scandal of the marriage of the wealthy entrepreneur to his former maid. And he announced that the dead man's two sons had issued a communiqué expressing their sorrow at what had happened and their hope that the señora would reappear safe and sound. They offered a reward to anyone helping to find her.

"The whole pack of reporters will want to interview me now," Rigoberto said, cursing.

"They've already begun," Justiniana said, administering the final blow. "So far two radio stations and a newspaper have called."

"The best thing is to disconnect the phone," Rigoberto ordered.

"Right away," said Justiniana.

"What did Narciso want?" asked Doña Lucrecia.

"I don't know, but he was very frightened," he explained. "The hyenas must have done something to him. I'm going to see him now. We made a plan like they do in the movies, without saying where. Probably we'll never find each other."

He showered and went straight down to the garage. As he was leaving, he saw reporters with cameras at the entrance to his building. Before driving to La Rosa Náutica, where he'd had lunch for the last time with Ismael Carrera, he drove around the streets of Miraflores to make certain no one was following him. Narciso probably had money problems, but that was no reason to take so many precautions and hide his identity. Or maybe it was. Well, he'd find out soon enough what was wrong. He drove into the parking lot of La Rosa Náutica and saw Narciso emerge from between the cars. He opened the door for him, and the black man climbed in and sat down beside him.

"Hello, Don Rigoberto. Please excuse me for bothering you."

"Don't worry about it, Narciso. Let's take a ride and we'll be able to talk quietly."

The driver wore a blue cap pulled down to his eyes and seemed thinner than the last time they'd seen each other. Rigoberto drove along the Costa Verde toward Barranco and Chorrillos, joining an already dense line of vehicles.

"You've probably seen that Ismael's problems don't end even after he's dead," Rigoberto finally remarked. "You must know by now that Armida's disappeared, don't you? It seems she's been kidnapped."

Since he received no answer and heard only the driver's anxious breathing, he glanced over at him. Narciso was looking straight ahead, his lips pursed and an alarmed look in his eyes. His hands were interlaced and he was squeezing them hard.

"That's just what I wanted to talk to you about, Don Rigoberto," he mumbled, turning to look at him and then immediately looking away.

"Do you mean Armida's disappearance?" Don Rigoberto turned toward him again.

Ismael's driver kept looking straight ahead, but he nodded with conviction two or three times.

"I'm going to turn into the Regatas and park there so we can talk in peace. Otherwise, I'll have an accident."

He drove into the Club Regatas lot and parked in the first row facing the ocean. It was a gray, cloudy morning, and many gulls, cormorants, and pelicans were flying around and screeching. A very thin girl in a blue sweat suit was doing yoga on the deserted beach.

"Don't tell me you know who kidnapped Armida, Narciso."

This time, the driver turned to look him in the eye and smiled, opening his mouth. His white teeth gleamed.

"Nobody's kidnapped her, Don Rigoberto," he said, becoming very serious. "That's exactly what I wanted to talk to you about, because it's making me a little nervous. I just wanted to do Armida—I mean, Señora Armida—a favor. She and I were good friends when she was only Don Ismael's servant. I always got along with her better than with the other employees. She didn't put on airs and was very unaffected. And if she asked me for a favor for the sake of our old friendship, how could I say no? Wouldn't you have done the same thing?"

"I'm going to ask you for one thing, Narciso," Rigoberto interrupted. "Just tell me everything from the beginning. Don't leave out the smallest detail. Please. But first tell me, is she alive?"

"As alive as you and me, Don Rigoberto. At least she was yesterday."

In spite of Rigoberto's request, Narciso didn't get directly to the point. He liked, or couldn't avoid, preambles, interpolations, uncontrolled digressions, circumlocutions, long parentheses. And it wasn't always easy to lead him back to the chronological order that was the backbone of the narrative. Narciso quickly became lost in extraneous clarifications and comments. And yet, in a complicated and convoluted way, Rigoberto did learn that on the afternoon of the day he'd seen Ismael for the last time in his house in San Isidro, as it was growing dark, Narciso had been there too, called by Ismael Carrera himself. Both he and Armida thanked him profusely for his help and loyalty and tipped him very generously. That was why, when he learned a day later of the sudden death of his former employer, he hurried to offer his condolences to the señora. He also brought along a note, since he was sure she wouldn't receive him. But Armida had him come in and exchanged a few words with him. The poor woman was shattered by the misfortune God had just sent to test her fortitude. As he was leaving, she asked to his surprise whether he had a cell phone where she could call him. He gave her the number, wondering in astonishment why she'd ever want to contact him.

And two days later, that is, the day before yesterday, Señora Armida called him late at night, when Narciso was about to get into bed after watching Magaly's program on TV.

"What a surprise, what a surprise," the driver said when he recognized her voice.

"Before, I always used the familiar *tú* with her," Narciso explained to Don Rigoberto. "But after she married Don Ismael, I couldn't anymore. Except I couldn't say *usted* either. So I tried to talk to her in an impersonal way, if you know what I mean."

"I understand perfectly, Narciso," Rigoberto said, trying to get him to focus. "Go on, go on. What did Armida want?"

"I want you to do me a big favor, Narciso. Another favor, a huge one. I'm asking again for the sake of our old friendship."

"Of course, sure, happy to," said the driver. "And what is the favor exactly?"

"I want you to take me to a certain place tomorrow afternoon. Without anybody knowing. Could you do that?"

"And where did she want you to take her?" Don Rigoberto urged him along.

"It was the most mysterious thing," Narciso digressed once again. "I don't know if you remember, but behind the indoor garden, near the servants' room, in Don Ismael's house there's a little service door that's almost never used. It goes to the alley where they pick up the trash at night."

"I'd be grateful if you wouldn't get sidetracked, Narciso," Rigoberto insisted. "Could you just tell me what Armida wanted?"

"For me to wait for her there, in my old jalopy, all afternoon. Until she came out. And without anybody seeing me. Isn't that strange?"

It had seemed very strange to Narciso. But he did what she asked without any more questions. Early yesterday afternoon, he parked his car in the alley across from the service door of Don Ismael's house. He waited close to two hours, dying of boredom, dozing sometimes, sometimes listening to funny remarks on the radio, watching stray dogs rooting through the garbage bags, asking himself over and over again what it all meant. Why was Armida taking so many precautions to leave her house? Why didn't she go through the main door, in her Mercedes-Benz, with her new uniformed chauffeur and muscle-bound bodyguards? Why in secret and in Narciso's old car? Finally the small door opened and Armida appeared, holding an overnight bag.

"Well, well, I was beginning to lose it," said Narciso in greeting, opening the car door for her.

"Drive away fast, Narciso, before anybody sees us," she ordered. "I mean fly."

"She was really in a hurry, Don Rigoberto," the driver explained. "That's when I began to worry."

"Why so many secrets, Armida, if you don't mind my asking?"

"Good, you're calling me Armida again and using *tú*," she said with a laugh. "Seems like old times. Good call, Narciso."

"A thousand pardons," said the driver. "I know I have to use *usted* now that you're a great señora."

"Cut the bullshit and just call me *tú*, because I'm the same person I always was," she said. "You're not my driver, you're my friend and my pal. Do you know what Ismael said about you? 'That man is worth his weight in gold.' That's the truth, Narciso. You are."

"At least tell me where you want me to take you," he said.

"To the Cruz de Chalpón Terminal?" Don Rigoberto was amazed. "She was taking a trip? Armida was going to take a bus, Narciso?"

"I don't know if she actually did it, but that's where I drove her," the driver agreed. "To that terminal. I told you she had an overnight bag. I guess she was taking a trip. She told me not to ask any questions and I didn't."

"The best thing would be for you to forget all about this, Narciso," Armida repeated, shaking his hand. "For my sake and yours. There are bad people who want to hurt me. You know who they are. And all my friends too. You haven't seen me, or brought me here, you don't know anything about me. I'll never be able to repay all I owe you, Narciso."

"I couldn't sleep all night," the driver added. "The hours went by and I got more and more scared, I'll tell you. More and more. First the scare the twins gave me, now this. That's why I called you, Don Rigoberto. And right after we spoke, I heard on RPP that Señora Armida had disappeared, that she'd been kidnapped. That's why I'm still shaking."

Don Rigoberto patted his shoulder.

"You're too good a person, Narciso, that's why you get scared so often. And now you're involved again in a fine mess. You'll have to go to the police and tell them this story, I'm afraid."

"No way, Don Rigoberto," replied the driver with determination. "I don't know where Armida has gone or why. If something's happened to her, they'll look for a fall guy. You should realize that I'm the perfect fall guy. Don Ismael's ex-driver, the señora's pal. And to top it all off, I'm black. I'd have to be crazy to go to the police."

"He's right," thought Don Rigoberto. "If Armida doesn't show up, Narciso will end up paying the piper."

"Okay, you're probably right," he said. "Don't tell anybody what you've told me. Let me think. Then we'll see what advice I can give you, after I mull it over. Besides, Armida may turn up at any moment. Call me tomorrow like you did today, at breakfast time."

He dropped Narciso off in the parking lot of La Rosa Náutica and returned to his house in Barranco. He drove directly into the garage to avoid the reporters who were still crowded around the entrance to the building. Twice as many as before.

Doña Lucrecia and Justiniana were still glued to the television, watching the news with a look of astonishment. They listened to his story openmouthed.

"The richest woman in Peru running away with a small bag in a rundown bus, like some pauper heading for nowhere," Don Rigoberto concluded. "The soap opera isn't over, it goes on and on and gets harder to understand every day."

"I understand very well," exclaimed Doña Lucrecia. "She was

sick of everything: lawyers, reporters, hyenas, gossips. She wanted to disappear. But where?"

"Where else but Piura," said Justiniana, very sure of what she was saying. "She's Piuran and even has a sister there, named Gertrudis, I think."

XVII

"She hasn't even cried once," thought Felícito Yanaqué. And in fact, she hadn't. But Gertrudis did stop speaking. She hadn't opened her mouth, at least not with him or Saturnina, the servant. Maybe she spoke to her sister Armida, who, ever since her unannounced arrival in Piura, had been sleeping in the room where Tiburcio and Miguel slept when they were boys, before they left home to live on their own.

Gertrudis and Armida spent long hours there, behind closed doors, and it was impossible that in all that time they hadn't exchanged a single word. But since the previous afternoon, when Felícito returned from Adelaida's place and told his wife the police had discovered that the spider extortionist was Miguel, and that their son had already been arrested and confessed to everything, Gertrudis had stopped speaking. She didn't open her mouth again in front of him (Felícito, of course, hadn't mentioned Mabel at all). But Gertrudis's eyes had flared and filled with anguish, and she'd clasped her hands as if praying. Felícito had seen her in that posture all the times they'd been together in the last twenty-four hours. As he summarized the story the police had told him, leaving out Mabel's name, his wife didn't ask him anything or comment at all or respond to the few questions he asked her. She continued to sit in the semidarkness of the television room, mute, turned in on herself like a piece of furniture, looking at him with those brilliant, suspicious eyes, her hands crossed, as immobile as a pagan idol. Then, when Felícito warned her that the news would be made public very soon, reporters would swarm around the house like flies, and she shouldn't open the door or answer a call from any newspaper, radio, or television reporter, she stood, still without a word, and went to her sister's room. It surprised Felícito that Gertrudis hadn't attempted to see Miguel immediately at the police station or in prison. Like her silence, was her mute strike only for him? She must have spoken to Armida, because that night at dinner, when Felícito greeted his sister-in-law, she seemed to know what had happened.

"I'm very sorry to be a bother just when the two of you are having such a difficult time," she said, shaking his hand, an elegant lady whom he resisted calling sister-in-law. "It's just that I had nowhere else to go. It'll be for only a few days, I promise. Please forgive my invading your home like this, Felícito."

He couldn't believe his eyes. This lady, so attractive, so well dressed, wearing such beautiful jewelry, was Gertrudis's sister? She looked much younger, and her clothes, shoes, rings, earrings, and watch were those of a rich woman who lived in a big house with gardens and a swimming pool in El Chipe, not someone who'd come out of El Algarrobo, that seedy boardinghouse in a Piuran slum.

That night at dinner, Gertrudis didn't touch a mouthful and didn't say a word. Saturnina removed her plates of angel-hair broth and chicken and rice, untasted. All afternoon and well into the night there was endless knocking at the door, and the telephone didn't stop ringing, even though no one opened the door or picked up the receiver. From time to time Felícito peeked through the curtains: Those crows hungry for carrion were still there with their cameras, crowded together on the sidewalk and in the roadway of Calle Arequipa, waiting for someone to come out so they could attack. Saturnina, who didn't live in, was the only one who came out, rather late at night, and Felícito saw her defend herself against the assault, raising her arms, shielding her face from the lightning bolts of the flashbulbs, and starting to run.

Alone in the living room, he watched the local news on television and listened to news reports on the radio. Miguel appeared on the screen, looking serious, his hair uncombed, in handcuffs, dressed in a tracksuit and basketball sneakers; and then Mabel, without cuffs, looking in fear at the bursts of light from the cameras. In his heart Felícito was grateful that Gertrudis had taken refuge in her bedroom and wasn't beside him, watching the news programs that morbidly emphasized that his mistress, named Mabel, whom he'd set up in a house in the Castilla district, had deceived him with his own son and conspired to commit extortion, sending the famous spider letters and setting fire to Narihualá Transport.

He saw and heard it all with a sinking heart and perspiring hands, feeling the warning signs of another attack of vertigo like the one that had made him pass out at Adelaida's, yet at the same time he had the curious sensation that this was very distant and strange and had nothing to do with him. He didn't even feel involved when his own image appeared on the screen while the announcer spoke of his dear Mabel (calling her his "paramour"), his son Miguel, and his transport company. It was as if he'd been separated from himself; the Felícito Yanaqué of the television images and radio news was someone else who had usurped his name and face.

After he was already in bed, unable to sleep, he heard Gertrudis's footsteps in the adjoining bedroom. He looked at the clock: almost one. As far as he could recall, his wife never stayed up so late. He couldn't sleep, he was awake all night, sometimes thinking, but most of the time his mind was a blank, attentive to his heartbeat. At breakfast, Gertrudis continued her silence; all she had was a cup of tea. Not long afterward, Josefita, called by Felícito, came to report what was happening at the office, to receive instructions, and to take down the letters he dictated. She brought a message from Tiburcio, who was in Tumbes. When he heard the news, he'd called the house several times but no one answered. He drove the bus on that route, and as soon as he reached Piura he would come straight to see his parents. Felícito's secretary seemed so disturbed by the news that he almost didn't recognize her; she avoided looking him in the eye, and the only comment she made was how annoying the reporters were, they'd driven her crazy the night before at the office, and now they'd surrounded her when she came to the house and wouldn't let her near the door for a long time, though she shouted at them that she had nothing to say, didn't

know anything, was only Señor Yanaqué's secretary. They asked
the most impertinent questions, but of course she hadn't said a
word. When Josefita left, Felícito saw through the window how
she was assaulted again by the men and women with tape recorders
and cameras crowded on the sidewalks of Calle Arequipa.

At lunch, Gertrudis sat at the table with him and Armida, but
again she didn't taste a mouthful or say a word. Her eyes were
like glowing embers, and she kept her hands clasped. What was
going on in her stupefied mind? It occurred to him that she
was asleep, that the news about Miguel had turned her into a
sleepwalker.

"How awful, Felícito, what's happening to you both," a crestfallen Armida apologized once again. "If I'd known about this, I
never would have dropped in on you so unexpectedly. But as I told
you yesterday, I had nowhere else to go. I'm in a very difficult situation and need to hide. I'll explain it all whenever you like. I know
you have other, more important things on your mind now. At least
believe me when I say I won't stay much longer."

"Yes, you can tell me all about it, but not now," he agreed.
"When this storm dies down a little. What bad luck, Armida, to
come to hide here, where all the reporters in Piura have congre-
gated on account of this scandal. Those cameras and tape recorders
make me feel like a prisoner in my own house."

Gertrudis's sister nodded with an understanding half smile.

"I've already gone through that and know what it means," he
heard her say. He didn't understand what she was referring to but
didn't ask her to explain.

Finally, at dusk, after a good amount of brooding, Felícito decided the moment had come. He asked Gertrudis to come into the
television room. "You and I have to talk alone," he said. Armida
withdrew immediately to her bedroom. Gertrudis docilely followed
her husband into the next room. Now she was in an armchair facing
him in the semidarkness, unmoving, shapeless, silent. She looked
at him but didn't seem to see him.

"I didn't think the time would ever come when we'd talk about
what we're going to talk about now," Felícito began, very quietly.
He noticed in surprise that his voice was trembling.

Gertrudis didn't move. She wore the colorless dress that resembled a cross between a robe and a tunic, and looked at him as if he weren't there, her eyes flashing with a tranquil fire in her plump-cheeked face with its large but inexpressive mouth. Her hands were on her lap, tightly clasped, as if she were suffering from a terrible stomachache.

"I suspected something from the beginning," the trucker continued, making an effort to control the nervousness that had taken possession of him, "but I didn't say anything so as not to embarrass you. I would've carried it to the grave if this thing that happened hadn't happened."

He took a breath, sighing deeply. His wife hadn't moved a millimeter and hadn't blinked even once. She seemed petrified. An invisible fly began to buzz somewhere in the room, flying into the ceiling and walls. Saturnina was watering the garden and he could hear the spatter of water on the plants from the watering can.

"I mean," he continued, stressing each syllable, "that you and your mother deceived me. That time, in El Algarrobo. Now, it doesn't matter anymore. A lot of years have gone by, and I promise you that today it doesn't matter if I discover that you and the Boss Lady told me a fairy tale. The only thing I need to die easy is for you to confirm it, Gertrudis."

He stopped speaking and waited. She remained in the same posture, unyielding, but Felícito noticed that one of the bedroom slippers his wife was wearing had moved slightly to the side. There was some life there, at least. After a while, Gertrudis parted her lips and uttered a phrase that resembled a growl: "To confirm what, Felícito?"

"That Miguel isn't and never was my son," he said, raising his voice a little. "That you were pregnant by some other man when you and the Boss Lady came to talk to me one morning in El Algarrobo and made me believe I was the father. After denouncing me to the police to force me to marry you."

When he finished he felt troubled and upset, as if he'd eaten something indigestible or drunk a glass of overly fermented chicha.

"I thought you were the father," said Gertrudis, with absolute serenity. She spoke without getting angry, reluctantly, as she always spoke about everything except religious matters. And after a long pause, she added in the same neutral, disinterested manner: "My mama and I had no intention to deceive you. I was sure then that you were the father of the baby I had in my belly."

"And when did you realize he wasn't mine?" Felícito asked with an energy that was becoming rage.

"Only when Miguelito was born," Gertrudis acknowledged, without her voice changing in the least. "When I saw how white he was, with those light eyes and that dark blond hair. He couldn't be the son of a Chulucanas *cholo* like you."

She fell silent and continued looking into her husband's eyes with the same impassivity. Gertrudis seemed to be talking to him from under water, Felícito thought, or from inside an urn of thick glass. He felt as if something insurmountable and invisible divided them, even though she was only a meter away.

"A real son of a whore, it isn't surprising you did what you did to me," he muttered. "And did you find out then who Miguel's real father was?"

His wife sighed and shrugged with a gesture that might have been lack of interest or weariness. She shook her head two or three times as she raised her shoulders.

"So how many men at El Algarrobo did you go to bed with, hey waddya think?" Felícito felt a lump in his throat and wanted this to be over immediately.

"All the ones my mama brought to my bed," Gertrudis growled, slowly and concisely. And sighing again with an air of infinite fatigue, she clarified: "A lot. Not all of them from the boardinghouse. Sometimes guys from the street too."

"The Boss Lady brought them all to you?" It was hard for him to speak, and his head was buzzing.

Gertrudis remained motionless, indistinct, a silhouette with no edges, her hands clasped. She looked at him with an absent, luminous, tranquil fixity that troubled Felícito more and more.

"She picked them and charged them, I didn't," his wife added with a slight change in the color of her voice. Now she seemed not only to inform but to defy him too. "Who was Miguel's father? I don't know. Some white guy, one of those gringos who came through El Algarrobo. Maybe one of the Yugoslavs who came to work on the Chira River irrigation. They came to Piura on weekends to get drunk and stayed at the boardinghouse."

Felícito regretted their conversation. Had he made a mistake by bringing up the subject that had followed him like a shadow all his life? Now it was there, between them, and he didn't know how to get rid of it. He felt it as a tremendous obstacle, an intruder who'd never leave this house again.

"How many did the Boss Lady bring to your bed?" he bellowed. He was sure at any moment he'd faint again or vomit. "All of Piura?"

"I didn't count them," said Gertrudis, calmly, making a deprecatory face. "But, since you're interested in knowing, I'll say it again: a lot. I took care of myself the best I could. I didn't know much about it, back then. The douches I had every day helped, I thought, that's what my mama told me. Something happened with Miguel. Maybe I got careless. I wanted to have an abortion with a midwife in the neighborhood who was part witch. They called her Mariposa, maybe you knew her. But the Boss Lady wouldn't let me. She came up with the idea of getting married. I didn't want to marry you either, Felícito. I always knew I'd never be happy with you. It was my mama who forced me to."

The trucker didn't know what to say. He sat motionless across from his wife, thinking. What a ridiculous situation, sitting there facing each other, paralyzed, silenced by a past so ugly it suddenly revived dishonor, shame, pain, and sorrow, bitter truths that added to the misfortune they were already suffering because of his false son and Mabel.

"I've been paying for my faults all these years, Felícito," he heard Gertrudis say, almost without moving her full lips or taking her eyes off him for a second, though she didn't appear to see him and spoke as if he weren't there. "Bearing my cross in silence. Knowing very well that the sins one commits have to be paid for. Not only in the next life, in this one too. I've accepted it. I've repented for myself and for the Boss Lady. I've paid for myself and my mama. I don't feel the rancor toward her that I did when I was young. I keep paying and hope that with so much suffering, Our Lord Jesus Christ will forgive so many sins."

Felícito wanted her to be quiet right now and leave. But he didn't have the strength to stand and walk out of the room. His legs were trembling. "I wish I were that buzzing fly and not me," he thought.

"You helped me pay for them, Felícito," his wife continued, lowering her voice a little. "And I'm grateful. That's why I never said anything. That's why I never made a jealous scene or asked questions that might have bothered you. That's why I never let on that I knew you'd fallen in love with another woman, that you had a mistress who wasn't old and ugly like me, but young and pretty. That's why I never complained about Mabel and never blamed you. Because Mabel also helped me pay for my sins."

She fell silent, waiting for the trucker to say something, but since he didn't open his mouth, she added: "I never thought we'd have this conversation either, Felícito. You wanted it, not me."

Again she paused for a long time and murmured, making the sign of the cross in the air with her gnarled fingers. "Now this thing Miguel did to you is the penance you have to pay for yourself. And for me too."

After her last words, Gertrudis stood with an agility Felícito didn't remember her possessing and shuffled out of the room. He remained seated in the television room, not hearing the noises, the voices, the horns, the bustle of Calle Arequipa, or the mototaxi engines, sunk in a dense lethargy, a despair and sadness that didn't let him think and deprived him of even the energy needed to get to his feet. He wanted to, he wanted to leave this house even though as soon as he walked outside the reporters would be all over him with their relentless questions, each one stupider than the last, he wanted to go to the Eguiguren Seawalk and sit down to watch the brown-and-gray river water, watch the clouds in the sky, breathe in the warm afternoon, listen to the birds calling. But he didn't try to move because his legs weren't going to obey him, or vertigo would knock him to the carpet. It horrified him to think that his father, from the next life, might have heard the conversation he'd just had with his wife.

He didn't know how long he was in that state of viscous somnolence, feeling time pass, ashamed and sorry for himself, Gertrudis, Mabel, Miguel, everybody. From time to time, like a ray of clear light, his father's face would appear in his mind, and that fleeting image would relieve him for an instant. "If you'd been alive and found out about all this, you'd have died again," he thought.

Suddenly he realized that Tiburcio had come into the room without his having noticed. He was kneeling beside him, holding his arms, looking at him in fright.

"I'm fine, don't worry," he reassured his son. "I just dozed off for a minute."

"Do you want me to call a doctor?" He was in the blue coveralls and cap that were the company's drivers' uniform; on the visor was written "Narihualá Transport." In one hand he held the untanned leather gloves he wore to drive the buses. "You look very pale, Father."

"Did you just get back from Tumbes?" he replied. "A good trip?"

"Almost full and a lot of cargo," Tiburcio said. His face still looked frightened, and he was studying Felícito, as if trying to pull out a secret. He clearly would have liked to ask endless questions but didn't dare. Felícito pitied him too.

"I heard the news about Miguel on the radio in Tumbes," said Tiburcio, clearly confused. "I couldn't believe it. I called the house a thousand times but nobody answered the phone. I don't know how I managed to drive here. Do you think what the police say about my brother is true?"

Felícito was about to interrupt to say, "He isn't your brother," but stopped himself. Weren't Miguel and Tiburcio brothers? Half brothers, maybe, but brothers.

"It might be a lie, I think they're lies," Tiburcio was saying now, upset, still on the floor, still holding his father's arms. "The police might have forced a false confession out of him, beat him, tortured him. Everybody knows they do those things."

"No, Tiburcio. It's true," said Felícito. "He was the spider. He planned all of it. He confessed because that woman, his accomplice, accused him. Now I'm going to ask you for a big favor, son. Let's not talk about it anymore. Not ever again. Not about Miguel or the spider. For me, it's as if your brother has ceased to exist. I mean, as if he'd never existed. I don't want him mentioned in this house. Never again. You can do whatever you like. Go to see him, if you want. Bring him food, find him a lawyer, whatever. I don't care. I don't know what your mother will want to do. Just don't tell me anything. I don't want to know. He'll never be mentioned in my presence. I curse his name and that's it. Now, help me up, Tiburcio. I don't know why, but it's as if my legs were suddenly rebelling."

Tiburcio stood, and holding him by both arms, lifted him effortlessly.

"I'm going to ask you to come with me to the office," said Felícito. "Life must go on. We have to get back to work and straighten out the company: It's been through a rough time. The family's not the only one suffering over this, son. Narihualá Transport is too. We have to get it moving again."

"The street's full of reporters," Tiburcio cautioned him. "They were all over me when I arrived and wouldn't let me pass. I almost got into a fight with one of them."

"You'll help keep those savages away from me, Tiburcio." He looked into his son's eyes and, giving his face a clumsy caress, sweetened his voice: "I'm grateful to you for not mentioning Mabel, son, or asking about that woman. You're a good son, you know."

He grasped the boy's arm and walked with him toward the door. A clamor broke out as soon as he opened it, and the flashbulbs made him blink. "I have nothing to say, gentlemen, thank you very much," he repeated two, three, ten times while, clutching Tiburcio's arm, he struggled to make his way along Calle Arequipa, pursued, shoved, jostled by the swarm of reporters who kept interrupting one another and pushing microphones, cameras, notebooks, and pencils in his face. They asked questions he couldn't understand. He kept repeating periodically, as if it were a refrain: "I have nothing to say, ladies, gentlemen, thank you very much." They followed him to Narihualá Transport but couldn't go in because the watchman slammed the heavy door in their faces. When he sat down at the board placed over two barrels that still served as his desk, Tiburcio handed him a glass of water.

"And that elegant lady named Armida, did you know her,

Father?" his son asked. "Did you know my mama had a sister in Lima? She never told us about her."

He shook his head and lifted a finger to his mouth. "A big mystery, Tiburcio. She came to hide here because it seems they're hounding her in Lima and even want to kill her. You'd better forget about her and not tell anybody you saw her. We have enough problems without inheriting my sister-in-law's too."

It required a huge effort, but he began to work. To look over accounts, drafts, due dates, current expenditures, income, bills, payments to providers, collections. At the same time, at the back of his mind, he was formulating a plan of action for the days that followed. And after a while he began to feel better, to suspect that it was possible to win this extremely difficult battle. Suddenly he felt a powerful desire to listen to the warm, tender voice of Cecilia Barraza. Too bad he didn't have any of her CDs at the office—songs like "Thistle or Ash," "Innocent Love," "Sweet Affection," or "The Bull Kills"—or a machine to play them on. As soon as things improved, he'd buy one. After the fire damage had been repaired, on afternoons or nights when he stayed to work in the office, he'd put on a series of CDs by his favorite singer. He'd forget about everything and feel happy, or sad, always moved by the voice that could bring out in waltzes, handkerchief dances, polkas, vendors' cries, all Peruvian music, the most delicate feelings hidden deep inside him.

When he left Narihualá Transport, it was late at night. No reporters were on the avenue; the watchman told him they'd grown tired of waiting and left a while back. Tiburcio had gone too, at Felícito's insistence, more than an hour ago. He walked up Calle Arequipa; there were few people now, and he couldn't look at anyone, keeping to the shadows so he wouldn't be recognized. Fortunately, no one stopped him or started a conversation with him on the way. In the house, Armida and Gertrudis were already asleep, or at least he didn't hear them. He went to the television room and put on some CDs, keeping the volume very low. And he stayed there for a couple of hours, sitting in the dark, distracted and moved; his worries didn't leave him, but certainly they were somewhat alleviated by the songs intimately interpreted for him by Cecilia

Barraza. Her voice was a balm, cool, limpid water into which he sank, body and soul, became clean and calm, felt joy; something sound, sweet, and optimistic rose from the deepest part of him. He tried not to think about Mabel, not to remember the intense, happy moments he'd spent with her over the past eight years, tried to recall only that she'd betrayed him, gone to bed with Miguel and conspired with him, sending the spider letters, faking a kidnapping, setting fire to his office. That was what he had to remember so the idea of never seeing her again wouldn't be so bitter.

He got up very early next day, did qigong exercises, thinking of Lau the storekeeper as he usually did during this obligatory morning routine, ate breakfast, and left for the office before the late-rising reporters had arrived at the door of his house to continue the hunt. Josefita was already there and very happy to see him.

"It's so good that you've come back to the office, Don Felícito," she said, flattering him. "We were missing you around here."

"I couldn't keep taking a vacation," he replied, removing his hat and jacket and sitting down at the board. "I've had enough scandals and foolishness, Josefita. Starting today, it's back to work. That's what I like, it's what I've done all my life, and it's what I'll do from now on."

He guessed that his secretary wanted to tell him something but hadn't quite decided to yet. What had happened to Josefita? She looked different. More fixed up and made-up than usual, wearing eye-catching, flirtatious clothes. Little smiles and suspicious blushes passed over her face from time to time, and he thought she moved her hips a little more now when she walked.

"If you want to tell me a secret, I promise you I'm like the tomb, Josefita. And if it's a romantic problem, you know you can cry on my shoulder."

"It's just that I don't know what to do, Don Felícito." She lowered her voice and blushed from head to toe. She brought her face close to her employer's and whispered, her eyes as wide as an innocent girl's, "You know, that police captain keeps calling me. Can you guess why? To ask me out, of course!"

"Captain Silva?" The trucker pretended to be surprised. "I suspected he was one of your conquests. Hey waddya think, Josefita!"

"So it seems, Don Felícito," his secretary continued, affecting extreme modesty. "He pays me all kinds of compliments whenever he calls, you can't imagine the things he says. That man is so fresh! You don't know how embarrassed it makes me. Yes, yes, he wants to take me out. I don't know what to do. What advice would you give me?"

"Well, I don't know what to say, Josefita. Of course, I'm not surprised that you've made this conquest. You're a very attractive woman."

"But a little fat, Don Felícito," she complained, pretending to pout. "Though according to what he said, that isn't a problem for Captain Silva. He claimed he doesn't like the starving girls in ads but does like well-padded women, like me."

Felícito Yanaqué burst into laughter and she joined in. It was the first time the trucker had laughed like this since he'd heard the bad news.

"Have you found out at least if the captain's married, Josefita?"

"He promised me he's single and has no commitments. But who knows, men spend their whole lives telling women that story."

"I'll try to find out, leave it to me," offered Felícito. "Meanwhile have a good time and enjoy life, you deserve it. Be happy, Josefita."

He inspected the departure of the jitneys, buses, and vans, and the delivery of packages, and midmorning he left for the appointment he had with Dr. Hildebrando Castro Pozo in his tiny, crowded office on Calle Lima. He was the lawyer for his transport business and had taken care of all Felícito Yanaqué's legal affairs for several years. He explained in detail what he had in mind, and Dr. Castro Pozo took notes on everything he said in his usual diminutive notebook, writing with a pencil as little as it was. He was a small, elegant man in his sixties, wearing a vest and tie, lively, energetic, amiable, concise, a modest but effective professional, not at all high-priced. His father had been a well-known fighter for social causes, a defender of peasants, who suffered through prison and exile and was the author of a book about indigenous communities that had made him famous. He'd been a deputy in Congress. When Felícito finished explaining what he wanted, Dr. Castro Pozo regarded him with satisfaction.

"Of course it's feasible, Don Felícito," he exclaimed, toying with his tiny pencil. "But let me study the matter calmly and give you all the legal twists and turns so we can move forward without taking any risks. I'll need a couple of days at most. Do you know something? What you want to do fully confirms what I've always thought about you."

"And what have you thought about me, Dr. Castro Pozo?"

"That you're an ethical man, Don Felícito. Ethical down to the soles of your feet. One of the few I've known, in fact."

What could that mean, "an ethical man"? Intrigued, Felícito told himself he'd have to buy a dictionary one of these days. He was always hearing words whose meaning he didn't know. And it embarrassed him to go around asking people what they meant. He went to his house for lunch. Even though he found the reporters stationed there, he didn't even stop to tell them he wouldn't give any interviews. He walked around them, greeting them with a nod, not answering the questions they asked him, moving quickly.

After lunch, Armida asked to talk to him alone for a moment. But to Felícito's surprise, when he and his sister-in-law withdrew to the television room, Gertrudis, once again cloistered in stubborn silence, followed them. She sat down in one of the armchairs and remained there for the duration of the long conversation Armida and the trucker had, listening, not interrupting them even once.

"It must seem strange to you that since I arrived, I've been wearing the same dress," his sister-in-law began in the most trivial way.

"If you want me to be frank, Armida, everything about this seems strange to me, let alone that you haven't changed your dress. To begin with, your showing up this way, out of the blue. Gertrudis and I have been married for I don't know how many years, and until a few days ago I don't think she ever told me you even existed. Can you think of anything stranger than that?"

"I haven't changed my clothes because I don't have anything else to wear," his sister-in-law continued as if she hadn't heard him.

"I left Lima with what I had on my back. I tried one of Gertrudis's dresses, but I was swimming in it. Well, I ought to begin this story at the beginning."

"Explain at least one thing to me," Felícito asked her. "Because Gertrudis, as you must have seen, has become mute and will never explain it to me. Are you full sisters?"

Armida shifted in her seat, disconcerted, not knowing how to answer. She looked for help to Gertrudis, who remained silent, folded in on herself, like one of those mollusks with odd names sold in the Central Market by fishwives. Her expression was one of total apathy, as if nothing she heard had anything to do with her, but she didn't take her eyes off either one of them.

"We don't know," Armida said finally, gesturing toward her sister with her chin. "We've talked a lot about it these past three days."

"Ah, in other words, Gertrudis talks to you. You're luckier than I am."

"We have the same mother, that's the only thing we know for sure," Armida declared, slowly regaining her self-control. "She's a few years older than me. But neither one of us remembers our father. Maybe he was the same man. Maybe not. There's nobody left to ask, Felícito. As far back as we can remember, the Boss Lady—that's what they called my mama, do you remember?—didn't have a husband."

"Did you live in El Algarrobo too?"

"Until I was fifteen," Armida said. "It wasn't a boardinghouse yet, just a wayside inn for mule drivers in the middle of the sandy tract. When I was fifteen I went to Lima to find a job. It wasn't easy. I went through some hard times, worse than you can imagine. But Gertrudis and I never lost touch. I wrote to her sometimes, though she answered only once in a blue moon. She never liked writing letters. The fact is, Gertrudis only spent two or three years in school. I was luckier and finished elementary school. The Boss Lady made sure I went to school, but she put Gertrudis to work in the boardinghouse very early."

Felícito turned to his wife.

"I don't understand why you didn't tell me you had a sister," he said.

But she kept looking at him as if she were looking through water and didn't respond.

"I'll tell you why, Felícito," Armida intervened. "Gertrudis was ashamed, she didn't want you to find out her sister was working in Lima as a maid. Especially after she married you and became respectable."

"You were a domestic servant?" the trucker said in surprise, looking at his sister-in-law's dress.

"All my life, Felícito. Except for a time when I worked in a textile factory in Vitarte." She smiled. "I can see you think it's strange for me to have a fine dress and shoes, and a watch like this. They're Italian, just imagine."

"That's right, Armida, I think it's very strange," Felícito concurred. "You look like anything but a servant."

"It's just that I married the man who owned the house where I worked," Armida explained, blushing. "An important man, and prosperous."

"Ah, *caramba*, I get it, a marriage that changed your life," said Felícito. "In other words, you won the lottery."

"In a certain sense I did, but in another way, no," Armida corrected him. "Because Señor Carrera, I mean Ismael, my husband, was a widower. He had two sons from his first marriage. They've hated me since I married their father. They tried to annul the marriage, they filed a complaint against me with the police, they went before a judge and accused their father of being a demented old man. They said I'd tricked him, given him cocaine, and used all other kinds of witchcraft."

Felícito saw that Armida's face had changed. It wasn't serene anymore. Now there was sadness and anger in her expression.

"Ismael took me to Italy for our honeymoon," she added, sweetening her voice and smiling. "They were very nice weeks. I never imagined I'd see such pretty things, such different things. We even saw the pope on his balcony, from St. Peter's Square. That trip was like a fairy tale. My husband always had business meetings, and I spent a lot of time alone, being a tourist."

"That's how she got the dress, those jewels, that watch, those shoes," thought Felícito. "A honeymoon in Italy! She married a rich man! A gold digger!"

"Over there in Italy, my husband sold an insurance company he had in Lima," Armida continued. "So it wouldn't fall into the hands of his sons, who couldn't wait to inherit it, even though he'd already given them an advance on their inheritance. They're big spenders and the worst kind of bums. Ismael suffered a lot because of them and that's why he sold the company. I tried to understand the whole complicated situation but couldn't follow his legal explanations. Well, we went back to Lima, and as soon as we got there, my husband had a heart attack that killed him."

"I'm very sorry," Felícito stammered. Armida had fallen silent, and her eyes were lowered. Gertrudis was motionless, implacable.

"Or they killed him," added Armida. "I don't know. He used to say his sons wanted him to die so much so they could get his money that they would even hire somebody to kill him. He died so suddenly, I can't help thinking that the twins—his sons are twins—somehow caused the heart attack that killed him. If it was a heart attack and not poison. I don't know."

"Now I'm beginning to understand your escaping to Piura and hiding here, not even going outside," said Felícito. "Do you really think your husband's sons might—"

"I don't know if it's even occurred to them or not, but Ismael used to say they were capable of anything, even having him killed." Armida was agitated now and talking quickly. "I began to feel unsafe and very scared, Felícito. There was a meeting with them at the lawyers' offices. They talked to me and looked at me in a way that made me think they might have me killed too. My husband used to say that nowadays in Lima you can hire a killer to murder anybody for a few soles. Why wouldn't they do that if it meant keeping all of Señor Carrera's inheritance?"

She paused and looked into Felícito's eyes.

"That's why I decided to escape. It occurred to me that nobody would come to look for me here, in Piura. That's pretty much the story I wanted to tell you, Felícito."

"Well, well," he said. "I understand, I do. The thing is, what bad luck. Fate delivered you straight into the lion's den. The thing is, it's called jumping from the frying pan into the fire, Armida."

"I told you I'd stay only two or three days, and I promise you

I'll keep my word," said Armida. "I need to talk to a person who lives in Lima. The only one my husband trusted completely. He was a witness at our wedding. Would you help me contact him? I have his phone number. Would you do me that huge favor?"

"But call him yourself, from here," said the trucker.

"It wouldn't be smart." Armida hesitated, pointing at the telephone. "What if the line's bugged? My husband thought the twins had tapped all our phones. Better to call outside, from your office, and use your cell phone, it seems cell phones are harder to bug. I can't leave this house. That's why I've turned to you."

"Give me the number and the message I should give him," said Felícito. "I'll do it from the office this afternoon. Very happy to, Armida."

That afternoon, when he'd shoved his way past the roadblock of reporters and was walking to his office along Calle Arequipa, Felícito Yanaqué told himself that Armida's story seemed straight out of one of the adventure films he liked to see on the rare occasions he went to the movies. And he'd thought that kind of brutal action had nothing to do with real life. But Armida's story and his own, ever since he received the first spider letter, were nothing more or less than action movies.

At Narihualá Transport he went to a quiet corner to make the call without Josefita hearing. A man's voice answered immediately and seemed disconcerted when Felícito asked for Señor Don Rigoberto.

"Who's calling?" the man asked, after a silence.

"I'm calling for a woman friend," replied Felícito.

"Yes, yes, that's me. What friend are you talking about?"

"A friend of yours who prefers not to say her name, for reasons you understand," said Felícito. "I imagine you know who I mean."

"Yes, I think so," said Señor Rigoberto in a hoarse voice. "Is she all right?"

"Yes, she's fine, and sends you her regards. She'd like to talk to you, in person, if that's possible."

"Yes, of course, naturally," the man said right away, without hesitating. "Very happy to. How should we do this?"

"Can you travel to the place she comes from?" asked Felícito.

There was a long silence, and another forced clearing of the throat.

"I could, if necessary," he said finally. "When?"

"Whenever you like," replied Felícito. "The sooner the better, of course."

"I understand," said Señor Rigoberto. "I'll get tickets immediately. This afternoon."

"I'll reserve a hotel room for you," said Felícito. "Could you call me on this cell when you've decided on the date you'll be traveling? I'm the only one who uses it."

"Very good, we're agreed, then." Señor Rigoberto said goodbye. "Happy to meet you and see you soon, sir."

Felícito Yanaqué worked all afternoon at Narihualá Transport. From time to time he thought about Armida's story, and wondered how much of it was true and how much was exaggerated. Was it possible that a rich man, owner of a large company, would marry his maid? He could barely wrap his mind around it. But was it much more unbelievable than a son stealing his father's mistress and then the two of them trying to extort him? Greed drove men crazy, it was a known fact. As night was falling, Dr. Hildebrando Castro Pozo appeared in his office with a large sheaf of papers in a lime-green folder.

"As you can see it didn't take much time, Don Felícito," he said, handing him the folder. "These are the documents that have to be signed, there where I've written an X. Unless he's an imbecile, he'll be delighted to do it."

Felícito reviewed them carefully, asked some questions that the attorney answered, and was satisfied. He thought he'd made a good decision, and even if this didn't resolve all the problems plaguing him, at least it would lift a great weight from his shoulders. And the uncertainty that had followed him for so many years would evaporate forever.

When he left the office, instead of going straight to his house he made a detour and stopped at the police station on Avenida Sánchez Cerro. Captain Silva wasn't there, but Sergeant Lituma received him. He was a little surprised at the sergeant's solicitude.

"I want to talk to Miguel right away," Felícito Yanaqué repeated. "I don't care if you or Captain Silva are present at the interview."

"That's fine, Don Felícito, I imagine there won't be any problem," said the sergeant. "I'll talk to the captain first thing tomorrow."

"Thank you," said Felícito as he took his leave. "Give my best to Captain Silva and tell him that my secretary, Señora Josefita, sends her regards."

XVIII

Don Rigoberto, Doña Lucrecia, and Fonchito arrived in Piura at midmorning on the LAN Perú flight, and took a taxi to Hotel Los Portales on the Plaza de Armas. The reservations made by Felícito Yanaqué—a double room and an adjacent single—suited them perfectly. As soon as they'd settled in, the three of them went out for a walk. They took a turn around the Plaza de Armas, shaded by tall old tamarinds and colored at intervals by the bright red blossoms of poincianas.

It wasn't very hot. They stopped for a while to look at the central monument, La Pola, a bold marble woman who represented liberty, a gift from President José Balta in 1870, and had a glance at the dreary cathedral. Then they sat down in a pastry shop, El Chalán, to have a cold drink. Rigoberto and Lucrecia, intrigued and somewhat skeptical, observed their environs and people they didn't know. Would they really have the secret meeting with Armida as planned? They wanted to intensely, of course, but all the mystery surrounding this trip made it difficult for them to take any of it too seriously. At times they thought they were playing one of those games old people play in order to feel young.

"No, it can't be a joke or a trap," Don Rigoberto declared one more time, trying to convince himself. "The gentleman I spoke to on the phone made a good impression on me, as I've said. Undoubtedly humble, provincial, somewhat timid, but well intentioned. A good person, I'm certain. I have no doubt he was speaking for Armida."

"Doesn't it seem as if the whole situation is kind of unreal?"

Doña Lucrecia replied with a nervous little laugh. She held a mother-of-pearl fan and fanned her face constantly. "It's hard to believe the things that are happening to us, Rigoberto. Coming to Piura, telling everybody we needed a rest. Nobody believed it, of course."

Fonchito didn't seem to be listening. He sipped his eggfruit frappe from time to time, his eyes fixed on the table, totally indifferent to what his father and stepmother were saying, as if absorbed by a secret worry. He'd been this way since his last encounter with Edilberto Torres, which was why Don Rigoberto had decided to bring him to Piura, though he would miss a few days of school because of the trip.

"Edilberto Torres?" Don Rigoberto gave a start in his desk chair. "Him again? Talking about Bibles?"

"In the flesh, Fonchito," said Edilberto Torres. "Don't tell me you've forgotten me. I don't believe you're so ungrateful."

"I've just confessed and am doing the penance the priest gave me," stammered Fonchito, more surprised than frightened. "I can't talk to you now, señor, I'm very sorry."

"In Fátima Church?" repeated Don Rigoberto, incredulous, swinging around as if suddenly possessed by Saint Vitus's dance and dropping the book on Tantric art he was reading. "He was there? Inside the church?"

"I understand and beg your pardon," said Edilberto Torres, lowering his voice, pointing at the altar with his index finger. "Pray, pray, Fonchito, it helps. We'll talk afterward. I'm going to pray too."

"Yes, in Fátima Church," Fonchito confirmed, pale, his eyes a little wild. "My friends and I, the ones from the Bible group, went there for confession. The others had finished, and I was the last to go into the confessional. There weren't many people left in the church. And suddenly I realized he was there, I don't know for how long. Yes, right there, sitting next to me. I was really frightened, Papa. I know you don't believe me, I know you'll say I invented our meeting this time too. Talking about the Bible, yes."

"All right, fine," Don Rigoberto decided. "Now we should go back to the hotel. We'll have lunch there. Señor Yanaqué said he'd get in touch with me some time this afternoon. If that's really his name. An odd name, it sounds like the stage name of one of those rock singers covered with tattoos, doesn't it?"

"It seems like a very Piuran last name to me," Doña Lucrecia offered. "Maybe it's Tallan."

He paid the check and the three of them left the pastry shop. When they crossed the Plaza de Armas, Rigoberto had to push aside the shoeshine boys and lottery-ticket sellers who kept offering their services. Now it was definitely hotter. The sun was white in a cloudless sky, and all around them trees, benches, flagstones, people, dogs, cars seemed to be burning.

"I'm sorry, Papa," murmured Fonchito, pierced by sorrow. "I know I'm giving you bad news, I know this is a difficult time for you, with the death of Señor Carrera and the disappearance of Armida. I know it's rotten for me to do this. But you asked me to tell you everything, to tell you the truth. Isn't that what you want, Papa?"

"I've had some financial problems, like everyone else these days, and my health is none too good," said Señor Edilberto Torres, downcast and sad. "I've gone out very little recently. That's the reason you haven't seen me in so many weeks, Fonchito."

"Did you come to this church because you knew I'd be here with my friends from the Bible-study group?"

"I came here to meditate, to ease my mind and see things more calmly, with greater perspective," explained Edilberto Torres, but he didn't look serene. He was trembling, as if suffering great anguish. "I do this frequently. I know half the churches in Lima, perhaps even more. This atmosphere of withdrawal, silence, and prayer does me good. I even like the pious old women and the smell of incense and antiquity that permeates the small chapels. Maybe I'm old-fashioned, and proud of it. I also pray and read the Bible, Fonchito, even though that surprises you. More proof that I'm not the devil, as your papa believes."

"He's going to be sad when he finds out I've seen you," the boy said. "He thinks you don't exist, that I invented you. And my stepmother does too. They really believe it. That's why my papa was so enthusiastic when you said you could help him with the legal problems he had. He wanted to see you, meet with you. But you disappeared."

"It's never too late," declared Señor Torres. "I'd be delighted to meet with Rigoberto and ease any concerns he has about me. I'd like to be his friend. I'd guess we're about the same age. The truth is I don't have friends, only acquaintances. I'm certain he and I would get along very well."

"I'll have a dried-beef stew," Don Rigoberto told the waiter. "It's a typical Piuran dish, isn't it?"

Doña Lucrecia ordered grilled sea bass with a mixed salad, and Fonchito only a ceviche. The dining room at the Hotel Los Portales was almost empty, and some slow-moving fans kept the air cool. They drank lemonade with lots of ice.

"I want to believe you, I know you don't lie to me, that you're an honest kid with decent feelings," Don Rigoberto concurred, his expression exasperated. "But this individual has become a burden in my life and in Lucrecia's. It's clear we'll never be free of him, that he'll pursue us to the grave. What did he want this time?"

"For us to have a conversation about profound things, a dialogue between friends," said Edilberto Torres. "God, the afterlife, the world of the spirit, transcendence. Since you're reading the Bible, I know those topics interest you, Fonchito, and I know too that you're somewhat disappointed by your readings in the Old Testament. That you were expecting something else."

"And how do you know that, señor?"

"A little bird told me," Edilberto Torres said with a smile, but there was no joy at all in his smile, only the usual hidden anxiety. "Pay no attention to me, I'm joking. All I wanted to say is that the same thing happens to everybody who begins reading the Old Testament. Keep it up, keep it up, don't be discouraged, and you'll see that very soon your impression will change."

Don Rigoberto gave another start behind his desk. "How did he know you're disappointed by your biblical reading? Is that true, Fonchito? Are you?"

"I don't know if I'm disappointed," Fonchito admitted, somewhat sharply. "It's just that everything's so violent. Beginning with

God, with Yahweh. I never would have imagined He was so fierce, hurling so many curses, commanding adulterous women to be stoned, ordering those who failed to perform the rituals to be killed. That He'd have the foreskins of the enemies of the Hebrews cut off. I didn't even know what foreskin meant until I read the Bible, Papa."

"Those were barbarous times, Fonchito," Edilberto Torres reassured him, pausing frequently as he spoke without changing his taciturn expression. "All that happened thousands of years ago, in the days of idolatry and cannibalism. A world where tyranny and fanaticism reigned. Besides, you shouldn't take what the Bible says literally. A good deal that appears there is symbolic, poetic, exaggerated. When fearsome Yahweh disappears and Jesus Christ appears, God will become gentle, pitying, and compassionate, you'll see. But for that you have to get to the New Testament. Patience and perseverance, Fonchito."

"He told me again that he wants to see you, Papa. Anyplace, anytime. He'd like to be friends with you, since you're the same age."

"I heard that story the last time that ghost materialized next to you, on the jitney," Don Rigoberto said mockingly. "Wasn't he going to help me with my legal problems? And what happened? He vanished into thin air! It'll be the same thing this time. Well, son, I don't understand you. Do you or don't you like the Bible readings you're doing now?"

"I don't know if we're doing it the right way." The boy avoided answering. "Because, though sometimes we like it a lot, other times everything gets very complicated with all the nations the Jews fight in the desert. It's impossible to remember so many exotic names. We're more interested in the stories. They're not like religious stories, more like adventures from *Arabian Nights*. Pecas Sheridan, one of my friends, said the other day that this wasn't a good way to read the Bible, that we weren't taking full advantage of it. That it would be better to have a guide. A priest, for example. What do you think, señor?"

"This tastes pretty good," said Don Rigoberto, chewing a mouthful of his dried-beef stew. "I like the *chifles* a lot, that's what they call fried plantain slices here. But I'm afraid with all this heat it'll be a little hard to digest."

After they finished their dishes they ordered ice cream and were just beginning their dessert when they saw a woman come into the restaurant. Standing in the doorway, she scrutinized the place, looking for someone. She was no longer young, but there was something fresh and bright about her, the youthful traces in her plump, smiling face, her bulging eyes and wide, heavily painted mouth. Her false, fluttering lashes were charming, her round, gaily colored earrings danced, and she had on a very tight white dress with a flower print; her generous hips did not keep her from moving with agility. After looking over the three or four occupied tables, she headed resolutely for the one where the three of them were sitting. "Señor Rigoberto, right?" she asked, smiling. She shook hands with each one and sat down in the empty chair.

"My name's Josefita and I'm Señor Felícito Yanaqué's secretary," she introduced herself. "Welcome to the land of the *tondero* dance and the 'hey waddya think.' Is this your first time in Piura?"

She spoke not only with her mouth but also with her expressive, darting green eyes, moving her hands constantly.

"The first, but it won't be the last," Don Rigoberto replied pleasantly. "Señor Yanaqué couldn't come?"

"He preferred not to, because, as you probably know, Don Felícito can't set foot on the streets of Piura without a swarm of reporters following him."

"Reporters?" Don Rigoberto was amazed, opening his eyes very wide. "And may I ask why they're following him, Señora Josefita?"

"Señorita," she corrected him, and added with a blush: "Though now I have an admirer who's a captain in the Civil Guard."

"A thousand pardons, Señorita Josefita," Rigoberto apologized, bowing his head. "Can you tell me why reporters are chasing Señor Yanaqué?"

Josefita stopped smiling. She looked at them with surprise and even a little pity. Fonchito had emerged from his lethargy and seemed suddenly attentive to what the newcomer was saying.

"Don't you know that at this moment Don Felícito Yanaqué is more famous than the president of the republic?" she exclaimed, dumbfounded, showing the tip of her tongue. "For some time now he's been talked about on radio and television, and in the papers. But sad to say, it's for bad reasons."

Don Rigoberto and his wife were clearly so astonished that Josefita had to explain how the owner of Narihualá Transport had passed from anonymity to popularity. It was obvious that these Limeños were in the dark about the spider story and the subsequent scandals.

"It's a magnificent idea, Fonchito," Señor Edilberto Torres agreed. "To sail with confidence on the ocean of the Bible, one needs an experienced navigator. It could be a cleric like Father O'Donovan, of course. But also a layman, someone who's devoted many years to studying the Old and New Testaments. Myself, for example. Don't think I'm bragging, but the truth is I've spent a good part of my life studying Scripture. I can see in your eyes you don't believe me."

"Now the pedophile is passing himself off as a theologian and an expert in biblical studies," Don Rigoberto said indignantly. "I can't tell you how much I want to see his face, Fonchito. Any time now he'll tell you he's a priest—"

"He already told me that, Papa," Fonchito interrupted. "I mean, he's not a priest now but he was one. He hung up his seminarian's habit before being ordained. He couldn't endure chastity, that's what he told me."

"I shouldn't talk to you about these things, you're still too young," added Señor Edilberto Torres, turning pale, his voice trembling. "But that's what happened. I masturbated all the time, sometimes several times a day. It grieves and troubles me, because believe me, my vocation to serve God was very strong. Since the time I was a boy, like you. Except I never could defeat the damned demon of sex. The time came when I thought I'd go mad because of the temptations that pursued me day and night. And then, what could I do, I had to leave the seminary."

"He talked to you about that?" Don Rigoberto was shocked. "About masturbation, about jerking off?"

"And then did you get married, señor?" the boy asked timidly.

"No, no, I'm still a bachelor." Señor Torres gave a somewhat forced laugh. "You don't need to be married to have a sex life, Fonchito."

"According to the Catholic religion you do," declared the boy.

"Certainly, because the Catholic religion is very intransigent and puritanical in sexual matters," the man explained. "Other religions are more tolerant. Besides, in our permissive time, even Rome will modernize, no matter how difficult it may be."

"Yes, yes, now I remember," Señora Lucrecia interrupted Josefita. "Of course, I read it somewhere or saw it on television. Señor Yanaqué is that man: His son and mistress wanted to kidnap him and steal all his money?"

"Well, well, this is unbelievable." Don Rigoberto was completely disheartened by what he was hearing. "It means we've walked right into the lion's den. If I understand you correctly, your employer's office and house are surrounded by reporters day and night. Is that right?"

"No, not at night." With a triumphant smile Josefita tried to cheer up this big-eared man, who not only turned pale but also began to grimace and contort his face. "When the scandal first broke, yes, those early days were unbearable. Reporters circling his house and office twenty-four hours a day. But then they got tired; now, at night, they go to sleep or to get drunk, because here all the reporters are bohemians and romantics. Señor Yanaqué's plan will work very well, don't worry."

"And what is his plan?" asked Rigoberto. He hadn't finished his ice cream and still held the glass of lemonade he'd just emptied in a single swallow.

Very simple. They should stay in the hotel or, at the most, if they preferred, go to a movie; there were several modern theaters now in the new malls, she recommended the Centro Comercial Open Plaza in Castilla, not very far, right next to the Puente Andrés Avelino Cáceres. It wasn't a good idea for them to appear on the streets of the city. When night came, when all the reporters had left Calle Arequipa, Josefita herself would come for them and take them to Señor Yanaqué's house. It was near the theater, just a couple of blocks away.

"What bad luck for poor Armida," lamented Doña Lucrecia as

soon as Josefita had left. "She really fell into a trap worse than the one she wanted to escape. I don't understand how the reporters or the police haven't found her yet."

"I wouldn't want you to be scandalized by my confidences, Fonchito." A remorseful Edilberto Torres apologized, lowering his eyes and his voice. "But tormented by that damned demon of sex, I went to brothels and paid prostitutes. Horrible things that made me feel disgusted with myself. God willing you'll never succumb to those repugnant temptations, the way I did."

"I know very well where that degenerate wanted to lead you by talking about touching yourself and hookers," Don Rigoberto said in a hoarse, choking voice. "You should have left immediately and not encouraged him. Didn't you realize that his supposed confidences were a strategy designed to make you fall into his net, Fonchito?"

"You're wrong, Papa," he replied. "I assure you Señor Torres was sincere, he had no hidden motives. He looked very sad, full of grief for having done those things. Suddenly his eyes grew red, his voice broke, and he began to cry again. It broke my heart to see him like that."

"It's just as well I've brought something good to read," remarked Don Rigoberto. "We have a long time to wait until nightfall. I'm guessing you won't want to go to a movie in this heat."

"Why not, Papa?" Fonchito protested. "Josefita said they had air-conditioning and were very modern."

"We could see something of their progress. Don't they say that Piura is one of the Peruvian cities that's developing the fastest?" Doña Lucrecia agreed. "Fonchito's right. Let's take a little walk around that shopping center, there's probably something good playing. We never go to the movies as a family in Lima. Come on, Rigoberto."

"I'm so ashamed of doing those bad, dirty things that I impose my own penance. And sometimes, as punishment, I flog myself until I bleed, Fonchito," confessed Edilberto Torres, his voice breaking and his eyes red.

"And didn't he ask you then to do the flogging?" Don Rigoberto exploded. "I'll search heaven and earth for that pervert and won't stop until I find him and put the screws to him, I'm warning you. He'll go to prison or I'll put a bullet in him if he tries to do anything to you. If he shows up again, tell him that for me."

"And then he began crying even harder and couldn't go on talking, Papa," Fonchito reassured him. "It isn't what you think, I swear it isn't. Because listen, in the middle of crying, suddenly he stopped and ran out of the church, without saying goodbye or anything. He seemed desperate, like someone who's going to kill himself. He isn't a pervert but a man in a lot of pain. He's more to be pitied than feared, I swear."

Then a nervous knocking on the study door interrupted them. One of the panels opened and Justiniana's worried face peered in.

"Why do you think I closed the door?" Rigoberto stopped her, raising an admonishing hand, not letting her speak. "Don't you see that Fonchito and I are busy?"

"But they're here, señor," the maid said. "They've planted themselves at the door, and even though I told them you're busy, they want to come in."

"They?" Don Rigoberto gave a start. "The twins?"

"I didn't know what else to tell them or what to do," Justiniana said, very upset, speaking quietly and gesticulating. "I'm really sorry. They say it's very urgent and will take only a few minutes of your time. What should I tell them, señor?"

"All right, show them into the living room," Rigoberto said in a resigned voice. "You and Lucrecia stay alert in case something happens and you have to call the police."

When Justiniana withdrew, Don Rigoberto grasped Fonchito's arms and looked deep into his eyes. He regarded him with affection but also with an anxiety that was apparent in his uncertain, imploring speech.

"Foncho, Fonchito, my dear son, I beg you, I implore you for the sake of all you hold dear. Tell me that everything you've told me isn't true. That you made it up. That it hasn't happened. Tell me Edilberto Torres doesn't exist, and you'll make me the happiest creature on earth."

He saw the boy's face become demoralized as he bit his lips until they turned purple.

"Okay, Papa," he heard him say, with an intonation no longer that of a child but of an adult. "Edilberto Torres doesn't exist. I invented him. I'll never talk about him to you again. Can I go now?"

Rigoberto agreed. He watched Fonchito leave the study and noted that his hands were trembling. Rigoberto's heart was icy. He loved his son very much but, he thought, in spite of all his efforts, he'd never understand him, Fonchito would always be an unfathomable mystery to him. Before facing the hyenas, he went to the bathroom and splashed cold water on his face. He'd never get out of this labyrinth, more and more passageways, basement chambers, turns, and switchbacks. Is this what life was, a labyrinth that, no matter what you did, brought you ineluctably into the clutches of Polyphemus?

In the living room, Ismael Carrera's sons stood waiting for him. Both were dressed in suits and ties, as usual, but contrary to his expectations, they hadn't come to do battle. Was the defeated, victimized attitude they displayed authentic or merely a new tactic? What were they up to? Both greeted him with affection, patting him on the shoulder and making an effort to display contrition. Escobita was the first to apologize.

"I behaved very badly the last time we were here, uncle," he whispered, downcast, wringing his hands. "I lost my temper, I said stupid things and insulted you. I was upset, half crazy. I beg your pardon. I'm in a state of confusion, I haven't slept for weeks, I take pills for my nerves. My life's become a calamity, Uncle Rigoberto. I swear we'll never disrespect you again."

"All of us are confused, and no wonder," Don Rigoberto acknowledged. "The things that are happening make us all lose our tempers. I feel no rancor toward you. Sit down and let's talk. To what do I owe this visit?"

"We can't stand any more, uncle." Miki came forward. He'd always seemed the more serious and judicious of the two, at least when it came time to speak. "Life has become unbearable for us. I suppose you know that. The police think we've kidnapped or killed Armida. They interrogate us and ask the most offensive questions. Snitches follow us day and night. They ask for bribes, and if we don't give them something they come in and search our apartments at any hour. As if we were common criminals, what do you think of that?"

"And the papers and the television, uncle!" Escobita interjected. "Have you seen the filth they throw at us? Every day and every night on all the newscasts. We're rapists, we're drug addicts, and given that background we're probably responsible for the disappearance of that damn *chola*. It's so unfair, uncle!"

"If you begin by insulting Armida, who's now your stepmother whether you like it or not, you're off to a bad start, Escobita," Don Rigoberto reprimanded him.

"You're right, I'm sorry, but I'm already half crazed," Escobita apologized. Miki was again obsessively biting his nails; he did it finger by finger, unceasingly, unmercifully. "You don't know how awful it's become to read the paper, or listen to the radio, or watch television. They slander you day and night, call you a degenerate, a bum, a cocaine addict, and I don't know how many other vile things. What a country we live in, uncle!"

"And it's no use filing lawsuits or appeals for legal protection, they say those are attacks on freedom of the press," Miki complained. He smiled for absolutely no reason, then became serious again. "Well, we already know that journalism survives on scandals. Worst of all is the police. Doesn't it seem monstrous to you that on top of what Papa did to us, now they're trying to make us responsible for the disappearance of that woman? We're under a travel ban during the investigation. We can't even leave the country, right when the Open is starting in Miami."

"What's the Open?" Don Rigoberto asked, intrigued.

"The tennis championships, the Sony Ericsson Open," Escobita explained. "Didn't you know that Miki is a wizard with the racket, uncle? He's won a pile of prizes. We've offered a reward to whoever helps locate Armida. And just between us, we can't even pay it. We don't have the money, uncle. We're flat broke. Miki and I don't have a goddamn penny left. Just debts. And since we've become contagious, no bank, no moneylender, no friend is willing to cough up a cent."

"We don't have anything left to sell or pawn, Uncle Rigoberto," said Miki. His voice trembled so much that he spoke with long pauses and blinked constantly. "Not a cent, no credit, and as if that wasn't enough, we're suspected of kidnapping or murder. That's why we've come to see you."

"You're our last hope." Escobita grasped his hand and squeezed it firmly, nodding, with tears in his eyes. "Don't fail us, please, uncle."

Don Rigoberto couldn't believe what he was seeing and hearing. The twins had lost the haughtiness and certainty that had characterized them, they seemed defenseless, frightened, pleading for his compassion. How things had changed in so short a time!

"I'm very sorry for everything that's happening to you, nephews," he said, using that word sincerely for the first time. "I know somebody else's suffering is no consolation, but at least think about this: With all the bad things happening to you, it must be much worse for poor Armida. Don't you agree? Whether they've killed or kidnapped her, what a terrible thing for her, don't you think? Then too, I believe I've also been the victim of a good number of injustices—your accusations, for example, of my complicity in the supposed deception that led to Ismael marrying Armida. Do you know how many times I've had to go to make a statement to the police and the investigating judge? Do you know how much lawyers are costing me? Do you know that months ago I had to cancel the trip with Lucrecia to Europe that we'd already paid for? I still can't start collecting my pension from the insurance company because you two stalled the process. In short, if it's a question of counting misfortunes, the three of us are neck and neck."

They listened to him with heads lowered, silent, dejected, confused. Don Rigoberto heard strange music outside on the Barranco Seawalk. Was it the old knife grinder's penny whistle again? These two seemed to summon him. Miki chewed his nails and Escobita swung his left foot in a slow, symmetrical motion. Yes, it was the knife grinder's tune. It made him happy to hear it.

"We filed that complaint because we were desperate, uncle, Papa's marriage drove us crazy," said Escobita. "I swear we're very sorry for all the trouble we've caused you. The matter of your pension will be resolved very quickly now, I imagine. As you know, we don't have anything to do with the company anymore. Papa sold it to an Italian firm. Without even telling us."

"We'll withdraw the complaint whenever you say, uncle," Miki added. "As a matter of fact, it's one of the things we wanted to talk to you about."

"Thanks very much, but it's a little late now," said Rigoberto. "Dr. Arnillas explained that when Ismael died, the suit you filed, at least as far as I'm concerned, was dismissed."

"There's nobody else like you, uncle," said Escobita, displaying, Don Rigoberto thought, even more stupidity than it was reasonable to expect from him in everything he did and said. "By the way, Dr. Claudio Arnillas, that wimp in a clown's suspenders, is the worst traitor ever born in Peru. He lived by sucking on Papa's teats his whole life, and now he's our sworn enemy. A servant sold body and soul to Armida and those Italian mafiosi who bought Papa's company at bargain prices—"

"We came to straighten things out and you're complicating them," his brother cut him short. A contrite Miki turned to Don Rigoberto. "We want to hear you, uncle. Though it still saddens us that you helped Papa with that marriage, we trust you. Give us a hand, give us some advice. You've heard the disastrous situation we're in, we don't know what to do. What do you think we should do? You have a lot of experience."

"This is much nicer than I expected," exclaimed Doña Lucrecia. "Saga Falabella, Tottus, Passarela, Dejavu, so on and so forth. Well, well, nothing less than the best stores in the capital."

"And six movie theaters! All of them air-conditioned," Fonchito applauded. "You can't complain, Papa."

"All right," Don Rigoberto gave in. "You two choose the least bad movie and let's go into a theater right away."

Since it was still early in the afternoon and the heat outside was intense, there were almost no people in the elegant installations of the Centro Comercial Open Plaza. But the air-conditioning was a blessing, and while Doña Lucrecia looked in some shopwindows and Fonchito studied the films on the billboard, Don Rigoberto amused himself by looking at the yellow tracts of sand that surrounded the enormous expanse of the Universidad Nacional de

Piura and the sparse carob trees scattered among those tongues of golden earth where, though he didn't see them, he imagined fast-moving lizards peering all around with their triangular heads and gummy eyes, searching for insects. Armida's story was incredible! She ran away from scandal, lawyers, and her irate stepsons, only to seek refuge in the house of a man who was at the center of yet another monstrous scandal, complete with the tastiest ingredients of yellow journalism: adultery, extortion, anonymous letters signed with spiders, abductions, false abductions, and apparently even incest. Now he really was impatient to meet Felícito Yanaqué, to listen to Armida, to tell her about his last conversation with Miki and Escobita.

Then Doña Lucrecia and Fonchito came up to him. They had two suggestions: *Pirates of the Caribbean II* (his son's choice) and *A Fatal Passion* (his wife's). He opted for the pirates, thinking they would lull him better than the tearful melodrama the other title foretold and that he might manage to take a nap. How many months had it been since he'd set foot in a movie theater?

"When we come out, we could go to this tearoom," said Fonchito, pointing. "What delicious-looking pastries!"

"He seems happy and excited about this trip," Don Rigoberto thought. He hadn't seen his son so cheerful and lively for a long time. Ever since the appearance of the wretched Edilberto Torres, Fonchito had become reserved, melancholy, absentminded. Now, in Piura, he once again seemed the good-humored, curious, enthusiastic boy he used to be. There were barely half a dozen people inside the brand-new movie theater.

Don Rigoberto inhaled, exhaled, and began his speech.

"I have only one piece of advice to give you." He spoke solemnly. "Make peace with Armida. Accept her marriage to Ismael, accept her as your stepmother. Forget about the foolishness of trying to have the marriage annulled. Negotiate a financial compensation. Don't deceive yourselves, you'll never be able to seize everything she's inherited. Your father knew what he was doing and tied things up very nicely. If you insist on this legal action, you'll burn all your bridges and won't get a cent. Negotiate in a friendly way, agree on an amount that may not be what you wanted but could be enough

so you can live well without working, having a good time and playing tennis for the rest of your lives."

"And suppose the kidnappers have killed her, uncle?" Escobita's expression was so pathetic that Don Rigoberto shuddered.
In fact, what if they had killed her? What would happen to that fortune? Would it remain in the hands of bankers, managers, accoun-
tants, and international law firms, which now kept it beyond the
reach not only of these two poor devils but of tax collectors all
over the world?

"It's easy for you to ask us to be friends with the woman who
stole Papa from us, uncle," said Miki, with more grief than anger.
"And who has kept everything the family had, even the furniture,
my mother's dresses and jewelry. We loved our papa. It hurts us
very much that in his old age he became the victim of such a filthy
conspiracy."

Don Rigoberto looked him in the eye and Miki didn't look
away. This little scoundrel who'd embittered Ismael's last years, and
for months had kept him and Lucrecia on a tightrope, stuck in Lima
and smothered in judicial appearances, allowed himself the luxury
of a good conscience.

"There was no conspiracy, Miki," he said slowly, trying not to
let his rage show through his words. "Your papa married because
he cared for Armida. Maybe it wasn't love, but he cared for her
very much. She was good to him and comforted him when your
mother died, a very difficult time when Ismael felt very alone."

"And how well she comforted him, getting the poor old man
into bed," said Escobita. He stopped talking when Miki lifted an
energetic hand, indicating that he should shut his mouth.

"But above all, Ismael married her because of how terribly disappointed he was with the two of you," Don Rigoberto continued as if, unintentionally, his tongue had been unleashed all by
itself. "Yes, yes, I know very well what I'm saying, nephews. I know
what I'm talking about. And now you're going to know it too, if
you listen without further interruptions."

He'd been raising his voice, and now the twins were quiet and
attentive, surprised by the gravity with which he spoke to them.

"Do you want me to tell you why he was so disappointed in

you? Not because you're bums, playboys, drunkards who smoke marijuana and snort cocaine as if it were candy. No, no, all this he could understand and even excuse. Though, of course, he would have preferred his sons to be very different."

"We didn't come here for you to insult us, uncle," protested Miki, turning red.

"He was disappointed because he found out you were impatient for him to die so you could inherit his money. How do I know? Because he told me so himself. I can tell you where, what day, what time. And even the exact words he used."

And for several minutes, with absolute calm, Rigoberto reported the conversation of several months earlier at lunch in La Rosa Náutica, when his employer and friend told him he'd decided to marry Armida and asked him to be a witness at his wedding.

"He heard you talking in the San Felipe Clinic, saying stupid, immoral things beside his deathbed," Rigoberto concluded. "You precipitated the marriage of Ismael and Armida because you're insensitive and cruel. Or rather, because you're fools. You should have hidden your feelings at least for those few moments and let your father die in peace, believing his sons were sorry about what was happening to him, and had not begun to celebrate his death when he was still alive and listening to you. Ismael told me that hearing the two of you say those awful things gave him the strength to survive, to fight. You were the ones who revived him, not the doctors. Well, you know that already. It's the reason your father married Armida. And so that you'd never inherit his fortune."

"We never said what you say he said we said," was Escobita's confusing reply, and his words turned into a tongue twister. "My papa must have dreamed that on account of the strong medications they gave him to get him out of the coma. If you're really telling us the truth and haven't invented that whole story to fuck us over even more than we're fucked already."

He looked as if he were going to say something else but thought better of it. Miki said nothing and continued to bite his nails tenaciously. His expression had soured and he seemed dejected. His face had turned even redder.

"We probably said it and he heard us," Miki corrected his brother abruptly. "We said it often, that's true, uncle. We didn't love him because he never loved us. To the best of my memory, I never heard him say an affectionate word. He never played with us or took us to the movies or the circus the way our friends' fathers did. I don't think he ever sat down to talk to us. He barely spoke to us. He didn't love anybody except his company and his work. Do you know something? I'm not sorry at all that he found out we hated him. Because it was absolutely true."

"Shut up, Miki, anger is making you say damn fool things," Escobita protested. "I don't know why you told us that, uncle."

"For a very simple reason, nephew. So that once and for all you'll get rid of the ridiculous idea that your papa married Armida because he was doddering and had senile dementia, or because he was given potions or was the victim of black magic. He married because he found out that the two of you wanted him to die as soon as possible so you could have his fortune and squander it. That's the absolute, sad truth."

"We'd better leave, Miki," said Escobita, getting up from his chair. "Now do you see why I didn't want to pay this visit? I told you that instead of helping us he'd end up insulting us, like last time. We'd better go before I get angry again and punch this dirty slanderer in the face."

"I don't know about you two, but I loved the movie," said Señora Lucrecia. "It was a little silly, but I had a good time."

"More than an adventure movie, it's a fantasy," Fonchito agreed. "I thought the best things were the monsters, the skulls. And don't say you didn't like it, Papa. I watched you and you were totally absorbed by the screen."

"Well, it's true I wasn't bored at all," Don Rigoberto admitted. "Let's take a taxi back to the hotel. It's getting dark and the big moment's approaching."

They returned to Hotel Los Portales, and Don Rigoberto took a long shower. Now that it was almost time for their meeting with Armida, it seemed to him that everything he was experiencing was, in effect, as Lucrecia had said, a fantasy as amusing and silly as the movie they'd just seen, with no bearing on lived reality. But suddenly a shudder chilled his spine. Perhaps at this very moment, a gang of killers, international criminals, aware of the huge fortune left by Ismael Carrera, were torturing Armida, pulling out her nails, cutting off a finger or an ear, gouging out an eye, to force her to give them the millions they demanded. Or perhaps they'd gone too far and she was already dead and buried. Lucrecia showered too, dressed, and they went down to the bar to have a drink. Fonchito stayed in his room watching television. He said he didn't want to eat; he'd order up a sandwich and go to bed.

The bar was fairly crowded, but no one seemed to pay them any attention. They sat at the most isolated table and ordered two whiskeys with soda and ice.

"I still can't believe we're going to see Armida," said Doña Lucrecia. "Can it be true?"

"It's a strange feeling," replied Don Rigoberto. "As if we were living a fantasy, a dream that may turn into a nightmare."

"Josefita, what a common name, and what about her appearance," she remarked. "To tell you the truth, my nerves are on edge. Suppose all of this is a trick by some crooks to get money out of you, Rigoberto?"

"They'll be very disappointed," he said with a laugh. "Because my wallet's empty. But this Josefita hardly looked like a gangster, don't you agree? And by the same token, on the phone Señor Yanaqué seemed the most inoffensive creature in the world."

They finished their whiskeys, ordered two more, and finally walked into the restaurant. But neither of them felt like eating, so instead of sitting at a table, they went into the lounge near the entrance. They were there for close to an hour, consumed by impatience, never taking their eyes off the people entering and leaving the hotel.

At last Josefita arrived, with her bulging eyes, big earrings, and ample hips. She was dressed as she had been that morning. Her expression was very serious and her gestures conspiratorial. She came up to them only after checking behind her with darting eyes, and didn't even open her mouth to say good evening, indicating with a gesture that they should go with her. They followed her to the Plaza de Armas. Don Rigoberto, who almost never drank, was slightly dizzy after the two whiskeys, and the light breeze on the street made him a little dizzier. Josefita had them walk around the square, pass close to the cathedral, and then turn onto Calle Arequipa. The stores were already closed, the display windows lit and gated, and there weren't many pedestrians on the sidewalks. When they reached the second block, Josefita pointed at the entrance to an old house, its windows covered by curtains, and, still not saying a word, waved goodbye. They watched her walk away quickly, swinging her hips, not looking back. Don Rigoberto and Doña Lucrecia approached the large studded door, but before they could knock it opened, and a quiet, very respectful man's voice murmured, "Come in, come in please."

They went in. In a dimly lit vestibule, its one light moving in the breeze from the street, they were received by a small, sickly-looking man wearing a fitted jacket and vest. He bowed deeply as he extended a childlike hand.

"I'm happy to meet you, welcome to this house. Felícito Yanaqué, at your service. Come in, come in."

He closed the street door and led them through the shadowy vestibule into a living room, also dimly lit, with a television and a small bookcase that held CDs. Don Rigoberto saw a feminine silhouette emerging from one of the armchairs and recognized Armida. Before he could greet her, Doña Lucrecia stepped forward and he saw his wife enfold Ismael Carrera's widow in a close embrace. Both women began to cry, like two close friends meeting again after many years of being apart. When it was his turn to greet her, Armida offered Don Rigoberto her cheek for him to kiss. He did, murmuring, "How glad I am to see you safe and sound, Armida." She thanked them for coming, God would reward them, and Ismael also thanked them from wherever he was.

"What an adventure, Armida," said Rigoberto. "I suppose you know you're the most searched-for woman in Peru. The most famous too. You're on television morning, noon, and night, and everybody thinks you've been kidnapped."

"I don't have the words to thank you for taking the trouble to come to Piura." She wiped away her tears. "I need you to help me. I couldn't stay in Lima any longer. Appointments with lawyers and notaries and meetings with Ismael's sons were driving me crazy. I needed a little calm to think. I don't know what I would have done without Gertrudis and Felícito. This is my sister, and Felícito is my brother-in-law."

A slightly misshapen figure emerged from the shadows in the room. The woman, wearing a tunic, extended a thick, sweaty hand and greeted them silently, with a slight nod. Beside her, the small man, who apparently was her husband, seemed even tinier, almost a gnome. She held a tray with glasses and bottles of soft drinks.

"I've prepared some refreshments for you. Help yourselves."

"We have so much to talk about, Armida," said Don Rigoberto, "I don't know where to begin."

"The best place would be the beginning," said Armida. "But sit down, sit down. You must be hungry. Gertrudis and I have also prepared something for you to eat."

XIX

When Felícito Yanaqué opened his eyes, dawn was breaking, and the birds hadn't begun to sing yet. "Today's the day," he thought. The appointment was at ten; he had some five hours ahead of him. He didn't feel nervous; he'd know how to maintain his self-control, he wouldn't let himself be overwhelmed by anger, he'd speak calmly. The matter that had tormented him his whole life would be laid to rest forever; its memory would gradually fade until it disappeared from his recollection.

He got up, opened the curtains, and barefoot, wearing his child's pajamas, spent half an hour doing qigong exercises with the slowness and concentration taught to him by Lau, the Chinese. He allowed the effort to achieve perfection in each of his movements to take possession of his consciousness. "I almost lost the center and still haven't managed to get it back," he thought. He struggled to keep demoralization from invading again. But of course he'd lost the center, considering the stress he'd been under since receiving the first spider letter. Of all the explanations the storekeeper Lau had given him about qigong, the art, gymnastics, religion, or whatever it was he'd taught him, and which Felícito had since incorporated into his life, the only one he'd fully understood had to do with "finding the center." Lau repeated it each time he moved his hands to his head or stomach. At last Felícito understood: "the center" it was absolutely essential to find, the center he had to warm with a circular motion of his palms on his belly until he felt an invisible force that gave him the sensation of floating. It was the center not only of his body but of something more complex, a symbol of order and serenity, a navel of the spirit which, if he located and controlled it, marked his life with clear meaning and harmonious organization. Recently he'd had the feeling—the certainty—that his center had become unsettled and that his life was beginning to sink into chaos.

Poor Lau. They hadn't exactly been friends, because to establish a friendship you had to understand each other, and Lau never learned to speak Spanish, though he understood almost everything. Instead he spoke a simulated language that made it necessary to guess three-fourths of what he said. Not to mention the Chinese woman who lived with him and helped him in the grocery. She seemed to understand the customers but rarely dared to say a word to them, aware that what she spoke was gibberish, which they understood even less than they understood Lau. For a long time Felícito thought they were husband and wife, but one day, when because of qigong they'd established the relationship that resembled friendship, Lau told him that in fact she was his sister.

Lau's general store was on the edge of Piura back then, where the city and the sand tracts touched on the El Chipe side. It couldn't have been poorer: a hut with poles made of carob wood and a corrugated metal roof held down by rocks, divided into two spaces, one for the shop, with a counter and some rough cupboards, and another where brother and sister lived, ate, and slept. They had a few chickens and goats, and at one time they also had a pig, but it was stolen. They survived because of the truck drivers who passed by on their way to Sullana or Paita and stopped to buy cigarettes, sodas, and crackers, or to drink a beer. Felícito had lived nearby, in a boardinghouse run by a widow, years before he moved to El Algarrobo. The first time he went to Lau's store—it was very early in the morning—he'd seen him standing in the middle of the sand wearing only his trousers, his skeletal torso bare, doing strange exercises in slow motion. His curiosity aroused, he asked him questions, and Lau, in his cartoon Spanish, attempted to explain what he was doing as he moved his arms slowly and at times stayed as still as a statue, eyes closed, and, one might say, holding his breath. From then on, in his free time, the truck driver would stop in the grocery to talk with Lau, if you could call what they did a conversation, communicating with gestures and grimaces that attempted

to complement the words and sometimes, when there was a mis-
understanding, made them burst into laughter.

Why didn't Lau and his sister associate with the other Chinese
in Piura? There were a good number, owners of restaurants, gro-
ceries, and other businesses, some very prosperous. Perhaps because
all of them were in much better circumstances than Lau and they
didn't want to lose prestige by mixing with a pauper who lived like
a primitive savage, never changing his greasy, ragged trousers;
he had only two shirts that he generally wore open, displaying the
bones of his chest. His sister was also a silent skeleton, though very
active, for she was the one who fed the animals and went out to
buy water and provisions from distributors in the vicinity. Felícito
never could find out anything about their lives, about how and why
they'd come to Piura from their distant country or why, unlike the
other Chinese in the city, they hadn't been able to get ahead, had
remained, instead, in absolute poverty.

Their truest form of communication was qigong. At first Felícito began to imitate the movements as if he were playing, but Lau
didn't take it as a joke, encouraged him to persevere, and became
his teacher—a patient, amiable, understanding teacher, who accompanied each of his movements and postures with explanations in
rudimentary Spanish that Felícito could barely understand. But
gradually he let himself be infected by Lau's example and began
to do sessions of qigong not only when he visited the grocery but
also in the widow's boardinghouse and during the stops he made
on his trips. He liked it. It did him good. It calmed him when
he was nervous and gave him the energy and control to undertake
the challenges of the day. It helped him find his center.

One night, the widow woke Felícito saying that the half-crazy
Chinese woman from Lau's general store was shouting at the door
and nobody understood what she was saying. Felícito went out in
his underwear. Lau's sister, her hair uncombed, was gesticulating,
pointing toward the store and shrieking hysterically. He ran after
her and found the grocer naked, writhing in pain on a mat, his
fever soaring. It required tremendous effort to get a vehicle to take
Lau to the closest Public Assistance. The nurse on duty there said
they ought to move him to the hospital, at Assistance they han-

dled only minor cases and this looked serious. It took close to half an hour to find a taxi to take Lau to the emergency room at the Hospital Obrero, where they left him lying on a bench until the next morning because there were no free beds. The next day, when a doctor finally saw him, Lau was moribund and died a few hours later. Nobody had money to pay for a funeral—Felícito earned just enough to eat—and they buried him in a common grave after receiving a certificate explaining that the cause of death was an intestinal infection.

The curious thing about the case is that Lau's sister disappeared on the same night the storekeeper died. Felícito never saw her again or heard anything about her. The store was looted that same morning, and a short while later the sheets of corrugated metal and the poles were stolen, so that within a few weeks there was no trace left of the brother and sister. When time and the desert had swallowed up the last remnants of the hut, a cockpit was set up there, without much success. Now that part of El Chipe has been developed, and there are streets, electricity, water, sewers, and the houses of families entering the middle class.

The memory of the storekeeper Lau remained vivid for Felícito. After thirty years it was made real every morning, each time he did qigong exercises. After so much time he still wondered about the story of Lau and his sister, why they'd left China, what vicissitudes they'd suffered before they washed up in Piura, condemned to their sad, solitary existence. Lau repeated frequently that one always had to find the center, something he, apparently, had never achieved. Felícito told himself that perhaps today, when he did what he was going to do, he'd recover his lost center.

He felt somewhat tired when he finished, his heart beating a little faster. He showered calmly, polished his shoes, put on a clean shirt, and went to the kitchen to prepare his usual breakfast of goat's milk, coffee, and a slice of black bread that he toasted and spread with butter and dark honey. It was six thirty in the morning when he went out to Calle Arequipa. Lucindo was already on his corner, as if waiting for him. He dropped a sol in his tin can, and the blind man immediately acknowledged him.

"Good morning, Don Felícito. You're leaving earlier today."

"It's an important day for me and I have a lot to do. Wish me luck, Lucindo."

There weren't many people on the street. It was pleasant to walk along the sidewalk and not be pursued by reporters. And even more pleasant to know that in principle he'd inflicted a necessary defeat on those journalists, poor devils, who never found out that Armida, the supposed kidnapping victim, the person most sought after by the Peruvian press, had spent an entire week—seven days and nights!—hidden in his house, right under their noses, without their suspecting. What a shame they'd never know they'd missed the scoop of the century. Because Armida, at the packed press conference she gave in Lima, flanked by the minister of the interior and the chief of police, didn't reveal to the press that she'd taken refuge in Piura with her sister, Gertrudis. She only indicated vaguely that she'd stayed with friends to escape the siege by the press that had brought her close to a nervous breakdown. Felícito and his wife watched the conference—crowded with reporters, flashbulbs, and cameras—on television. He was impressed by the confidence his sister-in-law showed responding to questions, never revealing confusion, never whimpering, speaking calmly, engagingly. Her humility and simplicity, everyone said afterward, had found favor with the public, which from then on was less likely to believe the image of a greedy, gold-digging opportunist that had been circulated by the sons of Don Ismael Carrera.

Armida's secret departure from the city of Piura at midnight, in a Narihualá Transport car with his son Tiburcio at the wheel, was a perfectly planned and executed operation that no one, beginning with the police and ending with the reporters, found out about. At first Armida wanted to bring in from Lima someone named Narciso, her late husband's driver, in whom she had a great deal of confidence, but Felícito and Gertrudis convinced her that Tiburcio, in whom they had blind faith, should drive the car. He was a magnificent driver, a discreet person, and after all, her nephew. Señor Rigoberto, who encouraged Armida to return to Lima immediately and appear in public, eventually convinced her.

Everything worked out as planned. Don Rigoberto, his wife, and his son returned to Lima by plane. A couple of days later, after midnight, Tiburcio, who was happy to collaborate, appeared at the house on Calle Arequipa at the agreed-upon hour. Armida took her leave with kisses, tears, and thanks. After twelve hours of uneventful driving she arrived at her house in San Isidro, in Lima, where her lawyer, bodyguards, and the authorities were waiting for her, happy to announce that the widow of Don Ismael Carrera had reappeared safe and sound after her weeklong mysterious disappearance.

When Felícito reached his office on Avenida Sánchez Cerro, the first buses, vans, and jitneys of the day were preparing to leave for all the provinces of Piura and the neighboring departments of Tumbes and Lambayeque. Narihualá Transport was gradually recovering its old customers. People who had avoided the company because of the spider episode, afraid they would fall victim to some kind of violence by the supposed kidnappers, were now forgetting about the matter and trusting once again in the good service offered by its drivers. He finally had settled with the insurance company, which had agreed to pay half the cost of reconstruction following the damage caused by the fire. Repair work would begin soon. Though it would be with an eyedropper, the banks would give him credit again. Day by day normalcy was being restored. He breathed with relief: Today he'd bring to an end that unfortunate matter.

He worked all morning on ordinary problems, spoke to mechanics and drivers, paid some bills, made a deposit, dictated letters to Josefita, had two cups of coffee, and at nine thirty, taking the portfolio prepared by Dr. Hildebrando Castro Pozo, went to the police station to pick up Sergeant Lituma, who was waiting for him at the entrance. A taxi took them to the men's prison in Río Seco, outside the city.

"Are you nervous about this meeting, Don Felícito?" the sergeant asking during the trip.

"I don't think I am," he replied, hesitating. "We'll see when I have him in front of me. You never know."

In the prison, they had to go to the checkpoint, where guards searched Felícito's clothes to verify that he wasn't carrying weapons. The warden himself, a stooped, lugubrious man in shirtsleeves

who dragged both his voice and his feet, led them to a small room
that was protected by metal grating as well as a heavy wooden door.
The walls were covered by scrawls, obscene drawings, vulgarities.
As soon as he crossed the threshold, Felícito recognized Miguel
standing in the center of the room.

Only a few weeks had passed since he'd last seen him, but the
boy had undergone a remarkable transformation. He not only
seemed thinner and older, perhaps because his blond hair was long
and uncombed and a beard now dirtied his face, but his expression had changed too; previously juvenile and smiling, it was now
taciturn, exhausted, the expression of someone who's lost the drive
and even the desire to live because he knows he's defeated. But perhaps the greatest change was in his clothing. He used to be well-
dressed and smart with the flashy coquetry of a neighborhood Don
Juan, unlike Tiburcio who always wore the jeans and guayabera of
the drivers and mechanics, but now his shirt, open over his chest,
had no buttons, his trousers were wrinkled and stained, and his
shoes were muddy and had no laces. He wasn't wearing socks.

Felícito stared into his eyes and Miguel held his glance for only
a few seconds; then he began to blink, lowered his eyes, and kept
them focused on the floor. Felícito thought that only now had he
realized he barely reached Miguel's shoulder, that his son was more
than a head taller than him. Sergeant Lituma remained leaning
against the wall, very still, tense, as if he wished he could become
invisible. There were two metal chairs in the room, but all three
men remained standing. Cobwebs hung from the ceiling among
the "shit"s written on the walls and coarse drawings of cunts and
pricks. The room smelled of urine. The prisoner wasn't handcuffed.

"I haven't come to ask if you're sorry for what you've done,"
Felícito said at last, looking at the tangle of dirty blond hair a
meter away, satisfied that he was speaking firmly, not revealing the
rage that overwhelmed him. "You can take care of that up there,
when you die."

He paused and took a deep breath. He'd spoken very quietly,
and when he continued, he raised his voice.

"I've come about a matter that's much more important to me.
More than the spider letters, more than your attempt to extort

money from me, more than the fake kidnapping you planned with Mabel, more than the fire at my office." Miguel remained motionless, his head down, and Sergeant Lituma didn't move either. "I've come to tell you that I'm glad about what happened, glad you did what you did. Because thanks to that, I've been able to clear up a doubt I've had my whole life. You know what it is, don't you? You must have thought about it every time you saw your face in the mirror and wondered why you had a white mug when your mother and I are *cholos*. I spent my life asking myself that question too. Until now I swallowed it and didn't try to find out, for fear of hurting your feelings or Gertrudis's. But now there's no reason for me to worry about you. I solved the mystery. That's why I came. To tell you something that will make you as happy as it makes me. You're not my son, Miguel. You never were. Your mother and the Boss Lady—your mother's mother, your grandmother—when they found out Gertrudis was pregnant, made me believe I was the father to force me to marry her. They tricked me. I wasn't the father. I married Gertrudis out of the goodness of my heart. My doubts are cleared up now. Your mother came clean and confessed everything to me. A great joy, Miguel. I would have died of sadness if a son of mine, with my blood in his veins, had done what you did to me. Now I'm calm and even happy. It wasn't a son of mine, it was some bastard. What a relief to know it isn't my blood, my father's clean blood, in your veins. Another thing, Miguel. Not even your mother knows who got her pregnant with you. She says it was probably one of the Yugoslavs who came for the Chira irrigation. Though she isn't sure. Or maybe it was another of the hungry white men who'd fall into El Algarrobo boardinghouse and pass through her bed too. Make a note of that, Miguel. I'm not your father and not even your own mother knows whose jizzum made you. So you're one of the many bastards in Piura, one of those kids born to washerwomen or sheepherders after gangs of drunken soldiers shoot their loads. A bastard with lots of fathers, Miguel, that's what you are. I'm not surprised you did what you did with such a mix of blood in your veins."

He stopped speaking because the head with unkempt blond hair came up, violently. He saw the blue eyes bloodshot and filled with hatred. "He's going to attack me, he'll try to strangle me," he thought. Sergeant Lituma must have thought the same thing because he took a step forward, and with his hand on his holster, stood next to the trucker to protect him. But Miguel seemed crushed, incapable of reacting or moving. Tears ran down his cheeks and his hands and mouth trembled. He was ashen. He wanted to say something, but the words wouldn't come out, and at times his body made an abdominal noise, like a belch or retching.

Felícito Yanaqué started to speak again with the same contained coldness he'd used in his long statement.

"I haven't finished. A little patience. This is the last time we'll see each other, happily for you and for me. I'm going to leave you this portfolio. Read each of the papers carefully that my lawyer has prepared for you. Dr. Hildebrando Castro Pozo, you know him very well. If you agree, sign each of the pages where there's an X. He'll have the papers picked up tomorrow and will take care of procedures before the judge. It's something very simple. It's called a change of identity. You're going to give up the name Yanaqué, which doesn't belong to you anyway. You can keep your mother's surname or invent anything you like. In exchange, I won't press charges against the author of the spider letters, the man responsible for the fire at Narihualá Transport, and for the false abduction of Mabel. It's possible that because of this, you'll escape the years in prison you'd have faced otherwise and walk out of here. But, as soon as you're free, you're going to leave Piura. You won't set foot again in this place, where everybody knows you're a criminal. Besides, nobody would give you a decent job here. I don't want to run into you again. You have until tomorrow to think it over. If you don't want to sign those papers, so be it. The trial will follow and I'll move heaven and earth to make sure your sentence is a long one. It's your decision. One last thing. Your mother hasn't come to visit you because she doesn't want to see you again either. I didn't ask her, it was her own decision. That's it. We can leave, Sergeant. May God forgive you, Miguel. I never will."

He tossed the portfolio of papers at Miguel's feet and turned toward the door, followed by Sergeant Lituma. Miguel remained motionless, the green portfolio on the floor in front of him, his eyes filled with hatred and tears, silently moving his mouth, as if he'd been hit by a lightning bolt that had deprived him of movement, speech, and reason. "This will be the last image of him that I'll remember," thought Felícito. They walked silently to the prison exit. The taxi was waiting for them. As the rattling jalopy jounced its way through the outskirts of Piura on the way to the police station on Avenida Sánchez Cerro to drop off Lituma, he and the trucker were silent. When they were already in the city, the sergeant was the first to speak.

"May I say something, Don Felícito?"

"Go on, Sergeant."

"I never imagined anyone could say those awful things you said to your son in the prison. My blood ran cold, I swear."

"He isn't my son," said the trucker, raising his hand.

"I'm really sorry, I know that," the sergeant apologized. "Of course I agree with you, what Miguel did is unforgivable. But even so. Don't get angry, but those were the cruelest things I've ever heard anybody say, Don Felícito. I'd never have believed it of a person as good-hearted as you. I don't understand why the boy didn't attack you. I thought he would, which is why I opened my holster. I was ready to pull out the revolver, I tell you."

"He didn't dare to because I won the moral battle," replied Felícito. "What I said might have been harsh, but did I lie or exaggerate, Sergeant? I might have been cruel, but I only told him the absolute truth."

"A terrible truth that I swear I won't repeat to anybody. Not even Captain Silva. My word of honor, Don Felícito. On the other hand, you've been very generous. If you drop all charges against him, he'll go free. One other thing, changing the subject. That expression, 'shoot their load.' I heard it as a kid but had forgotten it. I don't think anybody says it nowadays in Piura."

"There aren't so many gangs of men shooting their load as there used to be," the taxi driver interposed, laughing with some nostalgia. "When I was a kid there were a lot. Soldiers don't go down to the river anymore or to the farms to fuck the *cholas*. Now things are stricter in the barracks and they're punished if they shoot their load. They even force them to get married, hey waddya think."

They said goodbye at the entrance to the police station, and the trucker ordered the taxi to take him to his office, but when the car was about to stop outside Narihualá Transport, he suddenly changed his mind. He told the driver to go back to Castilla and leave him as close as possible to the Puente Colgante. As they drove through the Plaza de Armas, he saw Joaquín Ramos, the reciter of poetry, dressed in black, wearing his monocle and dreamy expression, walking undaunted in the middle of the road, pulling his she-goat along. Cars swerved, and instead of insulting him, the drivers waved a hand in greeting.

The narrow street that led to Mabel's house was, as usual, full of ragged barefoot kids, emaciated mangy dogs, and you could hear, through the music and commercials on the radios played at top volume, barking and cackling and a shrieking parrot that kept repeating "cockatoo, cockatoo." Clouds of dust obscured the air. And now, after being so confident during his meeting with Miguel, Felícito felt vulnerable and unmanned as he thought about the encounter he was about to have with Mabel. He'd been postponing it since she left prison, provisionally free. At times he thought that perhaps it would be preferable to avoid it, to use Dr. Castro Pozo to conclude final details with her. But he'd just decided that nobody could replace him in this task. If he wanted to begin a new life, it was necessary, as he'd just done with Miguel, to settle accounts with Mabel. His hands were perspiring when he rang the bell. No one responded. After waiting a few seconds, he took out his key and opened the door. He felt his blood and breath quicken when he recognized the objects, the photographs, the llama, the flag, the pictures, the wax flowers, the Sacred Heart of Jesus that presided over the room. Everything as bright, orderly, and clean as it had been before. He sat down in the living room to wait for Mabel without removing his jacket or vest, only his hat. He shivered. What would he do if she came back to the house accompanied by a man who held her arm or had his hand at her waist?

But Mabel came in alone a short while later, when Felícito Yanaqué, because of the nervous tension of waiting, was yawning and beginning to feel an invading fatigue. He gave a start when he heard the street door. His mouth was very dry, like sandpaper, as if he'd been drinking chicha. He saw her frightened face and Mabel exclaimed ("Oh my God!") when she found him in the living room. He saw her turn as if to run out.

"Don't be frightened, Mabel." He reassured her with a serenity he didn't feel. "I've come in peace."

She stopped and turned. She stood looking at him, her mouth open, her eyes uneasy, not saying anything. She looked thinner. Wearing no makeup, with a simple kerchief holding back her hair, dressed in a plain housedress and old sandals, she seemed much less attractive than the Mabel in his memory.

"Sit down and let's talk awhile." He indicated one of the easy chairs. "I haven't come to reproach you or demand an explanation. I won't take much of your time. As you know, we have some matters to settle."

She was pale. Her mouth was closed so tightly that her face looked contorted. He saw her nod and sit on the edge of the chair, her arms crossed over her belly, as if for protection. Uncertainty and alarm were in her eyes.

"Practical things that only you and I can deal with directly," the trucker added. "Let's begin with the most important thing. This house. The agreement with the owner is to pay the rent to her every six months. It's paid through December. Starting in January, it'll be up to you. The contract's in your name, so you'll see what you want to do. You can renew it or cancel it and move. You'll decide."

"All right," she whispered, her voice barely audible. "I understand."

"Your account at the Banco de Crédito," he continued, feeling more confident when he saw Mabel's fragility and fear. "It's in your name, though it has my guarantee. For obvious reasons, I can't continue my endorsement. I'm going to withdraw it, but I don't think they'll close the account because of that."

"They already did," she said. She fell silent, and after a pause explained: "I found the notice here when I got out of prison. It said that under the circumstances, they had to cancel it. The bank only accepts honorable clients with no police record. I have to stop by and withdraw the balance."

"Have you done that yet?"

Mabel shook her head.

"I'm embarrassed," she confessed, looking at the floor. "Everybody knows me at that branch. I'll have to go one of these days, when I run out of money. For daily expenses there's still something left in the drawer of the night table."

"They'll open an account for you at any other bank, with or without a record," Felícito said drily. "I don't think you'll have any problem with that."

"All right," she said. "I understand perfectly. What else?"

"I just visited Miguel," he said, more on edge, gruffer, and Mabel went rigid. "I made him a proposition. If he agrees to change the name Yanaqué before a notary, I'll withdraw all legal charges and won't testify for the prosecution."

"Does that mean he'll go free?" she asked. She wasn't afraid now, she was terrified.

"If he accepts the deal I'm offering, yes. You will both be free, if there's no civil charge. Or the sentence will be very light. At least that's what my lawyer told me."

Mabel had raised her hand to her mouth. "He'll want revenge, he'll never forgive me for betraying him to the police," she murmured. "He'll kill me."

"I don't think he'll want to go back to prison for murder," Felícito said brusquely. "Besides, my other condition is that when he gets out of prison he must leave Piura and never set foot here again. So I doubt he'll do anything to you. Anyway, you can ask the police for protection. Since you cooperated with the cops, they'll give it to you."

Mabel had begun to cry. Tears wet her eyes and the effort she made to hold back her sobs gave her face a distorted, somewhat absurd expression. She'd shrunk into herself, as if she were cold.

"Even though you don't believe me, I hate that man with all my heart," he heard her say after a time. "Because he ruined my life forever."

She let out a sob and covered her face with both hands. It made no impression on Felícito. "Is she sincere or is this nothing but an act?" he wondered. It didn't really matter, either way, it was all the same to him. Ever since everything had happened, in spite of his rancor and anger, he'd had moments when he thought of Mabel with affection, even longing. But at this moment he felt none of that, not even desire; if he'd had her naked in his arms, he wouldn't have been able to make love to her. It was as if the eight years of accumulated feelings Mabel had inspired in him had at last been eclipsed.

"None of this would have happened if you'd told me when Miguel started hanging around." Again he had the strange sensation that none of this was occurring, he wasn't in this house, Mabel wasn't there beside him, crying or pretending to cry, and he wasn't saying what he was saying. "We both would've saved ourselves a lot of headaches, Mabel."

"I know, I know, I was a coward and a fool," he heard her say. "Do you think I haven't regretted it? I was afraid of him and didn't know how to get rid of him. Aren't I paying for it? You don't know what the women's prison in Sullana was like. Even though I was there for just a few days. And I know I'll keep dragging this behind me for the rest of my life."

"The rest of your life is a very long time," Felícito said sarcastically, still speaking calmly. "You're very young and have plenty of time to start your life over. That's not true for me, of course."

"I never stopped loving you, Felícito," he heard her say. "Though you won't believe me."

He let out a mocking little laugh. "If you did what you did loving me, what would you have done if you'd hated me, Mabel."

And hearing himself say this, he thought those words might be the lyrics of one of the songs by Cecilia Barraza that he liked so much.

"I'd like to explain it to you, Felícito," she begged, her face still hidden by her hands. "Not so you'll forgive me, not so everything can go back to the way it was before, but just so you'd know that things weren't what you think, they were very different."

"You don't have to explain anything to me, Mabel," he said, speaking now in a resigned, almost friendly way. "What had to happen happened. I always knew it would, sooner or later. That you'd get tired of a man so much older than you and fall in love with someone younger. That's a law of life."

She shifted in her seat.

"I swear on my mother that it isn't what you think," she whimpered. "Let me explain, tell you at least how everything was."

"What I couldn't imagine was that the young man would be Miguel," the trucker added in a hoarse voice. "Not to mention the spider letters, of course. But it's over now, and the best thing is for me to leave. We've settled all the practical things and there's nothing left hanging. I don't want this to end with an argument. Here's the key to the house."

He placed it on the table in the living room next to the wooden llama and the Peruvian flag, and stood up. She still had her face buried in her hands, and she was crying.

"At least, let's still be friends," he heard her say.

"You know very well you and I can't be friends," he answered, not turning around to look at her. "Good luck, Mabel."

He went to the door, opened it, went out, and closed it slowly behind him. The brightness of the sun made him blink. He walked through whirlwinds of dust, the noise of radios, the ragged children and mangy dogs, thinking he'd never again walk along this dusty street in Castilla and no doubt wouldn't see Mabel again either. If they happened to run into each other on a street in the center of town, he'd pretend he hadn't seen her and she'd do the same. They'd pass each other like two strangers. He thought too, without sadness or bitterness, that though he wasn't a useless old man yet, he probably wouldn't make love to a woman again. He wasn't about to look for another girlfriend, or visit a brothel at night and go to bed with whores. And the idea of making love to Gertrudis after so many years didn't even enter his mind. Maybe he'd have to jerk off occasionally, like a boy. Whatever the course of his future, one thing was certain: There wouldn't be a place in it for pleasure or for love. He didn't regret that, and he didn't despair. That's the way life was, and ever since he was a kid without shoes in Chulucanas and Yapatera, he'd learned to accept it just as it came.

Without his being aware of it, his steps had been leading him to his friend Adelaida's shop filled with herbs, sewing articles, saints, Christs, and Virgins. There was the holy woman, short, thickset, barefoot, wearing the tunic of unbleached linen that hung down to her ankles, watching him from the door of her house with her enormous, piercing eyes.

"Hello, Felícito, long time no see," she said in greeting, waving. "I was beginning to think you'd forgotten me."

"Adelaida, you know very well you're my best friend and I'll never forget you." He gave her his hand and patted her back affectionately. "I've had a lot of problems recently, you must know all about it. But here I am. Will you bring me a glass of that distilled water you have, it's so clean and cool. I'm dying of thirst."

"Come in, come in and sit down, Felícito. I'll bring you a glass right this minute, sure I will."

Compared to how hot it was outside, it was cool inside Adelaida's shop, submerged in its customary half-light and stillness. Sitting in the rocker of woven straw, he contemplated the cobwebs, the shelves, the tables with boxes of nails, buttons, screws, seeds, stalks of herbs, needles, religious cards, rosaries, Virgins and Christs of plaster and wood in every size, large and small candles, while he waited for the holy woman's return. Did Adelaida have any customers? As far as he could remember, all the times he'd come here, and he'd been here plenty of times, he'd never seen anyone buying anything. More than a shop, this place resembled a chapel. All that was missing was the altar. Every time he came here he had a feeling of peace that once, long ago, he used to have in churches when, during the early years of their marriage, Gertrudis would drag him to Mass on Sundays.

Adelaida handed him water from the distilling stone and he drank it with great pleasure.

"That's some mess you got yourself into, Felícito," said the holy woman, commiserating with a kind look. "Your girlfriend and your son hooked up to fleece you. My God, the ugly things you can see in this world. Just as well they put those two in jail."

"All that's over now, and do you know something, Adelaida? I don't care anymore." He shrugged and made a disdainful face. "That's all behind me, and now I'll start to forget about it. I don't want it to poison my life. Now I'm going to put my heart and soul into moving Narihualá Transport ahead. On account of these scandals, I haven't been paying attention to the company that puts food on my table. And if I don't take care of it, it'll be ruined."

"That's what I like, Felícito, the past dead and gone," the holy woman said approvingly. "And now to work! You've always been a man who doesn't give up, who keeps fighting till the end—"

"Do you know something, Adelaida?" Felícito interrupted her. "That inspiration you had the last time I came to see you, it came true. An extraordinary thing happened just like you said. I can't tell you more about it right now, but as soon as I can, I will."

"I don't want you to tell me anything." The fortune-teller became very serious and a shadow veiled her large eyes for an instant. "I'm not interested, Felícito. You know I don't like it when those inspirations come to me. Sad to say, it always happens with you. It's like you provoke them, hey waddya think."

"I hope I don't inspire any more, Adelaida," Felícito said with a smile. "I don't want any more surprises. From now on I want a peaceful, quiet life dedicated to my work."

They were silent for a long time, listening to the noise from the street. The horns and motors of cars and trucks, the shouts of the peddlers, the voices and bustling of the passersby reached them, somehow softened by the tranquility of the place. Felícito thought that in spite of knowing Adelaida for so many years, she was still a great mystery to him. Did she have a family? Had she ever had a husband? Probably she'd come from an orphanage, one of those abandoned babies taken in and brought up on public charity, and then had always lived alone, like a mushroom, without parents, brothers and sisters, husband or children. He'd never heard Adelaida talk about any relatives, or even any friends. Maybe Felícito was the only person in Piura the fortune-teller could call a friend.

"Tell me something, Adelaida," he asked. "Did you ever live in Huancabamba? Did you happen to grow up there?"

Instead of answering, the mulatta gave a loud laugh, her thick-lipped mouth opening wide, revealing her large, even teeth.

"I know why you asked me that, Felícito," she exclaimed through her laughter. "Because of the witches of Las Huaringas, isn't that right?"

"Don't think that I believe you're a witch or anything like it," he assured her. "It's just that you have, well, I don't know what to call it, this faculty, this gift, whatever it is, for seeing the things that are going to happen, and it's always amazed me. It's incredible, hey waddya think. Every time you get an inspiration, things happen just the way you say. We've known each other for a lot of years, haven't we? And whenever you've predicted something, it's happened exactly the way you say. You're not like everybody else, like simple mortals, you have something that nobody else has but you, Adelaida. If you wanted to, you could've been rich if you'd become a professional fortune-teller."

While he spoke, she had become very serious.

"More than a gift, it's a great burden that God put on my shoulders, Felícito," she said with a sigh. "I've said it so many times. I don't like it when those inspirations come to me all of a sudden. I don't know where they come from, or why it happens only with certain people, like you. It's a mystery to me too. For example, I never have inspirations about myself. I've never known what's going to happen to me tomorrow or the next day. Well, to answer your question: Yes, I was in Huancabamba, just one time. Let me tell you something. It makes me very sad that people go all the way up there, spending what they have and what they don't have, going into debt to get a cure from the masters, that's what they're called. They're liars, most of them at least. The ones who use a guinea pig, the ones who bathe sick people in the icy lake water. Instead of curing them, sometimes they kill them with pneumonia—"

Smiling, Felícito interrupted her, gesturing with both hands. "It's not always like that, Adelaida. A friend of mine, a driver for Narihualá Transport, his name was Andrés Novoa, had undulant fever and the doctors at the Hospital Obrero didn't know how to cure him. They said it was hopeless. He went to Huancabamba half dead, and one of the witches took him to Las Huaringas, made him bathe in the lake, and gave him I don't know what to drink. And he came back cured. I saw it with my own eyes, I swear, Adelaida."

"Maybe there are some exceptions," she admitted. "But for each real healer, there are ten crooks, Felícito."

They talked for a long time. The conversation moved from the witches, masters, healers, and shamans of Huancabamba, so famous that people from all over Peru came to consult them about their illnesses, to the praying women and holy women of Piura, generally humble old women dressed as nuns who went from house to house to pray beside the beds of the sick. They were satisfied with a tip of a few pennies or even just a plate of food for their prayers, which, many believed, completed the work of the doctors by helping to cure patients. To Felícito's surprise, Adelaida didn't believe in any of that either. She thought the praying women and healers were liars too. It was curious that someone with her gifts, who could anticipate the future of certain men and women, believed so little in the healing powers of others. Maybe she was right and there were lots of frauds, male and female, among those who claimed to have the power to heal the sick. Felícito was surprised to hear Adelaida say that not so long ago in Piura there had even been certain dark women, the consolers, called on by some families to help the dying pass, something they did in the midst of prayers, cutting the jugular with an extremely long nail they let grow on their index finger for just that purpose.

On the other hand, Felícito was amazed to learn that Adelaida was a steadfast believer in the legend that the image of the Captive Lord in the Church of Ayabaca had been sculpted by Ecuadoran carvers who really were angels.

"You believe in that superstition, Adelaida?"

"I believe it because I've heard the story told by the people who live there. It's been passed from parents to children ever since it happened, and if it's lasted this long, it must be true."

Felícito had often heard about that miracle but never took it seriously. It was said that many years ago now, a committee of important people from Ayabaca had taken up a collection to commission a sculpture of Christ. They crossed into Ecuador and found three men dressed in white who turned out to be carvers. They hired them immediately to come to Ayabaca and sculpt the image. They did but disappeared before they were paid their fee. The same committee went back to Ecuador to look for them, but nobody there knew them or anything about them. In other words, they were angels. It was something Gertrudis believed in, but it surprised him that Adelaida would swallow that miracle too.

They chatted for a long time, and Felícito felt much better than when he'd arrived. He hadn't forgotten his conversations with Miguel and Mabel—maybe he'd never forget them—but the hour he'd spent with Adelaida had helped to cool the memory of the encounters so they no longer weighed on him like a cross.

He thanked Adelaida for the distilled water and the conversation, and though she resisted, he obliged her to accept the fifty soles he put in her hand when he said goodbye.

When he went out, the sun seemed even stronger. He walked slowly toward his house, and on the way only two strangers approached to greet him. He thought, with some relief, that gradually he'd stop being famous and well known. People would forget about the spider, and soon they'd stop pointing him out and coming up to him. Perhaps the day wasn't distant when he'd be able to walk down the streets of the city again like an anonymous pedestrian.

When he reached his house on Calle Arequipa, lunch was ready. Saturnina had prepared a vegetable broth, the typical tuber-and-dried-beef dish of *olluquitos con charqui*, and rice. Gertrudis had a pitcher of lemonade with lots of ice ready. They sat down to eat in silence, and only when he'd finished his last spoonful of broth did Felícito tell his wife that he'd seen Miguel that morning and had proposed withdrawing the charges if Miguel agreed to drop his last name. She listened to him in silence, and when he stopped speaking she said nothing.

"I'm sure he'll accept and then go free," he added. "And he'll leave Piura, as I demanded. He'd never find work here with his record."

She nodded, not saying a word.

"Aren't you going to visit him?" Felícito asked.

Gertrudis shook her head. "I don't ever want to see him again either," she declared, eating the broth in slow spoonfuls. "After what he did to you, I couldn't."

They continued eating in silence, and only much later, when Saturnina had cleared the dishes, Felícito murmured, "I was in

XX

When Don Rigoberto awoke, it was still dark; he heard the murmur of the ocean and thought, "The day has finally come." He was engulfed by a sensation of relief and excitement. Was this happiness? Lucrecia slept peacefully beside him. She must be extremely tired, the day before she'd stayed up very late packing. He listened to the movement of the ocean for a while—a music never heard in Barranco during the day, only at night and at dawn, when the street noise subsided—and then he got up and went to the study in his pajamas and slippers. He searched the poetry shelves and found the book of works by Fray Luis de León. In the light of the lamp, he read the poem dedicated to the blind musician Francisco de Salinas. He'd been thinking about it the night before as he was dozing off and then had dreamed about it. He'd read it often and now, after reading it one more time, slowly, barely moving his lips, he confirmed it yet again: This was the most beautiful homage to music he knew, a poem that as it explained the inexplicable reality of music, was itself music. Music with ideas and metaphors, an intelligent allegory by a man of faith, which, filling the reader with an ineffable sensation, revealed the secret, transcendent, superior essence that dwells in some corner of the human animal and begins to rise to consciousness only through the perfect harmony of a beautiful symphony, an intense poem, a great opera, an outstanding exposition of art. A sensation that for Fray Luis, a believer, became confused with grace and the mystic trance. What was the music like, the creation of the blind organist to whom Fray Luis de León wrote this superb eulogy? He'd never heard it. So he had a job to do during his stay in Madrid: obtain a CD with the

compositions of Francisco de Salinas. One of the groups dedicated to ancient music—Jordi Savall's, for instance—must have
devoted a record to the man who inspired this marvel of a poem.

Closing his eyes, he thought that in a few hours he, Lucrecia,
and Fonchito would be crossing the skies, leaving behind the thick
clouds of Lima, beginning their postponed trip to Europe. At last!
They'd arrive in the middle of autumn. He imagined golden trees
and cobblestone streets decorated with leaves loosened by the cold.
He couldn't believe it. Four weeks, one in Madrid, another in Paris,
another in London, and the last divided between Florence and
Rome. He'd planned the thirty-one days so that their pleasure
would not be spoiled by fatigue, avoiding as much as possible those
unpleasant surprises that can ruin a trip. Reserved flights, tickets
to concerts, operas, and museum exhibitions already purchased,
hotels and pensions paid for in advance. It would be the first time
Fonchito had set foot on the continent of Rimbaud, the Europe
aux anciens parapets. It would be especially satisfying to show
his son the Prado, the Louvre, the National Gallery, the Uffizi,
St. Peter's, the Sistine Chapel on this trip. Surrounded by so many
beautiful things, would he forget this recent dark period and the
spectral appearances of Edilberto Torres, the incubus or succubus
(what was the difference?) who had so embittered Lucrecia's life
and his? He hoped so. This month would be a purifying bath: The
family would put behind them the worst period of their lives.
All three would return to Lima rejuvenated, reborn.

He recalled his last conversation with Fonchito in his study, two
days earlier, and his sudden impertinence.

"If you like Europe so much, if you dream about it day and
night, why have you spent your whole life in Peru, Papa?"

The question disconcerted him, and for a moment he didn't
know how to respond. He felt guilty about something but didn't
know what.

"Well, I think if I'd gone there to live, I would never have enjoyed the beautiful things on the old continent as much." He tried
to elude the danger. "I would have grown so accustomed to them
that eventually I wouldn't even notice them, which is what happens to millions of Europeans. In short, it never occurred to me

to move there, I always thought I had to live here. Accept my fate, if you like."

"All the books you read are by European writers," his son insisted. "And I think most of the CDs, drawings, and etchings are by Europeans too. By Italians, Englishmen, Frenchmen, Spaniards, Germans, and a couple of North Americans. Is there anything Peruvian that you like, Papa?"

Don Rigoberto was going to protest, to say there were many things, but he chose to assume a doubtful expression and make an exaggeratedly skeptical gesture.

"Three things, Fonchito," he said, pretending to speak with the pomposity of a learned pedant. "The paintings of Fernando de Szyszlo. César Moro's poetry in French. And prawns from Majes, of course."

"There's no way to talk to you seriously about anything, Papa," his son protested. "I think you've taken my question as a joke because you don't dare tell me the truth."

"The little snot-nose is sharper than a tack and loves to give his father a hard time," he thought. "Was I the same way when I was a kid?" He couldn't remember.

He was going over papers, taking a last look in his carry-on bag to make sure he hadn't forgotten anything. A short while later dawn broke, and he heard activity in the kitchen. Preparing breakfast already? When he went back to the bedroom, he saw the three suitcases in the hall, packed and tagged by Lucrecia. He went to the bathroom, shaved and showered, and when he returned to his bedroom, Lucrecia had gotten up and was waking Fonchito. Justiniana announced that breakfast was waiting for them in the dining room.

"I can't believe the day is here," he said to Lucrecia while he enjoyed his orange juice, café con leche, and toast with butter and marmalade. "During the past few months I'd begun to think we'd be trapped for years and years in the legal tangle the hyenas got me into, and would never set foot in Europe again."

"If I tell you what I'm most curious about on this trip, you're going to laugh," replied Lucrecia, who took only a cup of plain tea for breakfast. "Do you know what it is? Armida's invitation.

What will that dinner be like? Whom did she invite? I still can't believe that Ismael's old servant is going to give us a banquet in her house in Rome. I'm dying of curiosity, Rigoberto. About how she lives, how she entertains, who her friends are. Has she learned Italian? She has an elegant house, I imagine."

"Well, yes, certainly," said Rigoberto, somewhat disappointed. "She has enough money to live like a queen, of course. I hope she also has the taste and sensitivity to use that kind of fortune in the best way. After all, why shouldn't she? She's shown herself to be smarter than all of us put together. She got what she wanted, and now there she is, living in Italy with Ismael's entire inheritance in her pocket. And the twins defeated up and down the line. I'm happy for her, really."

"Don't speak badly of Armida, don't make jokes about her," said Lucrecia, putting a hand to her mouth. "She isn't and never was what people believe."

"Yes, yes, I know the conversation you had with her in Piura left you convinced," Rigoberto said with a smile. "What if she told you a fairy tale, Lucrecia?"

"She told me the truth," Lucrecia declared categorically. "I have complete confidence that she told me what happened, without adding or taking away anything. I have an infallible instinct for these things."

"I don't believe you. Was it really like that?"

"Really." Armida lowered her eyes, a little intimidated. "He never looked at me or paid me a compliment. Not even one of those nice things employers sometimes say to their maids just to make conversation. I swear by everything holy, Señora Lucrecia."

"How many times do I have to tell you to use the familiar *tú* with me, Armida?" Lucrecia reproached her. "It's hard for me to believe what you're saying is true. You really never noticed before that Ismael liked you, not even a little?"

"I swear by everything holy," said Armida, kissing her fingers in the shape of a cross. "Never, not ever, and may God punish me forever if I'm lying. Never. Never. That's why I was so shocked I almost fainted. 'But what are you saying! Have you gone crazy, Don Ismael? Am I losing my mind? What's going on here?'"

"Neither one of us is crazy, Armida," Señor Carrera said, smiling, speaking to her with a kindness she'd never heard from him, but he didn't go near her. "Of course you've heard what I said perfectly well. I'll ask you again. Do you want to marry me? I'm very serious. I'm too old now to court you, to make you fall in love the old-fashioned way. I offer you my affection and respect. I'm sure love will come too, later. Mine for you and yours for me."

"He told me he felt lonely, that he thought I was a good person, that I knew his habits, what he liked, what he disliked, and besides, he was sure I'd know how to take care of him. He made my head spin, Señora Lucrecia. I couldn't believe he was saying what I was hearing. But that's what happened, just like I'm telling it to you. Suddenly and without beating around the bush, just like that. That and only that is the truth. I swear."

"You amaze me, Armida." Lucrecia scrutinized her, a look of astonishment on her face. "But yes, after all why not. He simply told you the truth. He felt alone, he needed company, and you knew him better than anybody else. And did you accept right then and there?"

"You don't need to answer me now, Armida," he added, not taking a step toward her, not making the slightest move to touch her, take her hand, her arm. "Think about it. My proposal is very serious. We'll get married and go to Europe for our honeymoon. I'll try to make you happy. Think about it, please."

"I had a fiancé, Señora Lucrecia. Panchito. A good person. He worked for the City of Lince, in the registry office. I had to break it off with him. The truth is, I didn't have to think about it too long. It seemed like the story of Cinderella. Up to the last moment I wondered if Señor Carrera had been serious. But yes, yes, he was very serious, and now you see everything that's happened since."

"It makes me feel strange to ask you this, Armida," said Lucrecia, lowering her voice a great deal. "But I can't help myself, curiosity is killing me. Do you mean that before you got married there was nothing going on between you?"

Armida burst into laughter, raising her hands to her face.

"After I said yes, there was," she said, blushing and laughing.

"Of course there was. Señor Ismael was still a real man in spite of his age."

Lucrecia started to laugh too.

"I don't need you to tell me anything else, Armida," she said hugging her. "Oh, how funny it is that things happened like this. What a shame he died."

"I still don't buy that the hyenas have lost their fangs," said Rigoberto. "That they've become so tame."

"I don't believe that either. They're not fighting because they're probably plotting something awful," replied Lucrecia. "Did Dr. Arnillas tell you what Armida's arrangement with them is?"

Rigoberto shook his head.

"I didn't ask him," he answered, shrugging. "But there's no doubt they surrendered. If not, they wouldn't have withdrawn all their demands. She must have given them a good amount to subdue them like this. Or maybe not. Maybe that pair of idiots finally were convinced that if they continued fighting, they'd die old men without seeing a cent of the inheritance. The truth is, I don't give a damn. I don't want us to talk about those two villains for the next month, Lucrecia. During these four weeks let everything be clean, beautiful, pleasing, stimulating. The hyenas have no place in any of that."

"I promise I won't mention them again," Lucrecia said with a laugh. "Just one last question. Do you know what happened to them?"

"They must have gone to Miami to spend the money they got out of Armida on one long binge, where else," said Rigoberto. "Ah, but that's right, they can't go there because Miki was involved in that hit-and-run. Though maybe the statute of limitations is up on that. And now yes, the twins have vanished, disappeared, never existed. Let's not talk about them again. Hello, Fonchito!"

The boy was already dressed for the trip, he even had his suit jacket on.

"How elegant, my God," Doña Lucrecia welcomed him, giving him a kiss. "Your breakfast is all ready. I'll leave you two, it's getting late, I'd better hurry if you want to leave at nine sharp."

"Are you looking forward to our trip?" Don Rigoberto asked his son when they were alone.

"Yes, a lot, Papa. I've heard you talk so much about Europe for as long as I can remember that I've dreamed about going there for years."

"It'll be a nice experience, you'll see," said Don Rigoberto. "I've planned everything very carefully so you'll see the best things in old Europe and avoid everything ugly. In a sense, this trip will be my masterpiece. The one I didn't paint, or compose, or write, Fonchito, but that you'll live."

"It's never too late for that," the boy replied. "You have plenty of time, you can do what you really like. You're retired now and have all the freedom in the world."

Another uncomfortable observation he didn't know how to elude. He stood up, saying he was going to give his carry-on one final check.

Narciso appeared at nine on the dot, just as Don Rigoberto had asked. The station wagon he was driving, a late-model Toyota, was navy blue, and Ismael Carrera's old driver had hung a colored picture of the Blessed Melchorita from the rearview mirror. Of course, they had to wait some time for Doña Lucrecia to come out. When she said goodbye to Justiniana it was with unending embraces and kisses, and Don Rigoberto saw with a start that their lips were brushing. But Fonchito and Narciso didn't notice. When the station wagon drove down Quebrada de Armendáriz and took Costa Verde in the direction of the airport, Don Rigoberto asked Narciso how things were going in his new job at the insurance company.

"Terrific," said Narciso, showing white teeth as he smiled from ear to ear. "I thought Señora Armida's recommendation wouldn't mean much to the new owners, but I was wrong. They've been treating me very well. The manager met me in person, can you imagine. A very perfumed Italian gentleman. But I can't tell you how I felt when I saw him in the office that had been yours, Don Rigoberto."

"Better him than Escobita or Miki, don't you think?" Don Rigoberto guffawed.

"That's right, no doubt about it. You bet!"

"And what's your job, Narciso? The manager's driver?"

"Mainly. When he doesn't need me, I drive people from all over the company, I mean, the bosses." He looked happy, sure of himself. "Sometimes he also sends me to customs, to the post office, to banks. Hard work, but I can't complain, they pay me good money. And thanks to Señora Armida, now I have my own car. The truth is, that's something I never thought I'd have."

"She gave you a nice present, Narciso," remarked Doña Lucrecia. "Your station wagon is beautiful."

"Armida always had a heart of gold," the driver agreed. "I mean, Señora Armida."

"It was the least she could do for you," declared Don Rigoberto. "You behaved very well with her and Ismael. You agreed to be a witness to their marriage, knowing what you were exposing yourself to, and above all, you didn't let yourself be bought or intimidated by the hyenas. It's only right that she gave you this gift."

"This station wagon isn't a gift, it's a gift and a half, señor."

The Jorge Chávez Airport was crowded and the line at Iberia very long. But Rigoberto didn't become impatient. He'd gone through so much anguish these last few months, what with police and judicial appointments, the blocking of his retirement, the headaches Fonchito had given them with Edilberto Torres, how could he care about waiting in a line for a quarter of an hour, half an hour, or however long it took, if it was all behind him and tomorrow afternoon he'd be in Madrid with his wife and son. Impulsively he put his arms over the shoulders of Lucrecia and Fonchito and announced, brimming over with enthusiasm, "Tomorrow night we'll eat at the best and nicest restaurant in Madrid. Casa Lucio! Their ham and eggs with fried potatoes is an incomparable delicacy."

"Eggs and fried potatoes, a delicacy, Papa?" Fonchito said mockingly.

"Go ahead and laugh, but I assure you that no matter how simple it may seem, at Casa Lucio they've turned the dish into a work of art, something exquisite that makes your mouth water."

And at that very moment he saw, a few meters away, a curious couple he thought he knew. They couldn't have been more mismatched or anomalous. She, a stout, tall woman, with very plump cheeks, submerged in a kind of unbleached tunic that hung down to her ankles, and wrapped in a bulky green sweater. But the strangest thing was the absurd, flat little hat and veil that gave her a cartoonish air. The man, on the other hand, slim, small, feeble-looking, seemed packed into a very tight pearl-gray suit and gaudy, bright blue vest. He too wore a hat, pulled down to the middle of his forehead. They had a provincial air, appeared lost and disconcerted in the midst of the crowd at the airport, and looked at everything with apprehension and suspicion. They seemed to have escaped from an expressionist work painted by Otto Dix or George Grosz of bizarre, mismatched people in 1920s Berlin.

"Ah, you've seen them too," he heard Lucrecia say, indicating the couple. "It seems they're also traveling to Spain. And in first class, imagine that!"

"I think I know them, though I don't know from where," said Rigoberto. "Who are they?"

"But my boy," replied Lucrecia, "they're the couple from Piura, how could you not recognize them."

"Armida's sister and brother-in-law, of course," Rigoberto said, identifying them. "You're right, they're traveling to Spain too. What a coincidence."

He felt a strange, incomprehensible uneasiness, a disquiet, as if running into this Piuran couple on the Iberia flight to Madrid might constitute a threat to the program of activities he'd planned so carefully for their European month. "How silly," he thought. "What a persecution complex." How could this odd-looking couple spoil their trip? He observed them for some time as they went through procedures at the Iberia counter and weighed the very large suitcase with thick straps around it that they declared as their luggage. They looked lost and frightened, as if this were the first time they'd ever taken a plane. When they finally understood the instructions of the Iberia attendant, they linked arms as if to defend themselves against anything unforeseen and walked toward customs. What were Felícito Yanaqué and his wife, Gertrudis, going to do in Spain? Ah, of course, they were going to forget the scandal they'd lived through in Piura, complete with abductions, adulteries, and whores. They were probably taking a tour, spending their life savings. It didn't matter. These past few months he'd

become too susceptible, too sensitive, almost paranoid. That couple couldn't possibly harm their marvelous vacation in any way.

"Do you know, Rigoberto, I don't know why but it makes me
suspicious running into those two Piurans," he heard Lucrecia say,
and he shuddered. There was a certain anguish in his wife's voice.

"Suspicious?" He dissembled. "What nonsense, Lucrecia, there's
no reason for that. The trip will be even better than our honeymoon, I promise you."

When they finished checking in at the counter, they went up
to the second level of the airport, where there was another long
line, so the police could stamp their passports. And yet, when they
finally got to the boarding lounge, they still had a long time to
wait. Doña Lucrecia decided to take a look at the duty-free shops
and Fonchito went with her. Since he detested shopping, Rigoberto
said he'd wait for them in the café. He bought *The Economist* on
the way and discovered that all the tables in the small restaurant
were taken. He was about to sit at the entrance to the boarding
lounge when he saw Señor Yanaqué and his wife at one of the
tables. Very serious and very still, they had soft drinks and a plate of
biscuits in front of them. Following a sudden impulse, Rigoberto
approached them.

"I don't know if you remember me," he greeted them, extending his hand. "I was in your house in Piura a few months ago. What
a surprise to find you here. So you're going on a trip."

The two Piurans had stood, at first surprised, then smiling. They
shook hands effusively.

"What a surprise, Don Rigoberto, seeing you here. How could
we not remember our secret plotting."

"Have a seat, señor," said Señora Gertrudis. "It would be our
pleasure."

"Well, all right, delighted," Don Rigoberto thanked her. "My
wife and son are looking at the shops. We're traveling to Madrid."

"To Madrid?" Felícito Yanaqué's eyes opened wide. "So are we,
what a coincidence."

"What would you like to have, señor?" a very solicitous Señora
Gertrudis asked.

She seemed changed, she'd become more talkative and pleasant and was smiling now. He remembered her, during his days in Piura, as always severe and incapable of uttering a word.

"An espresso cut with milk," he told the waiter. "So you're going to Madrid. We'll be traveling companions."

They sat, smiled, exchanged impressions about the flight—would the plane leave on time or would it be late—and Señora Gertrudis, whose voice Rigoberto was sure he'd never heard during their meetings in Piura, talked now without stopping. She hoped this plane wouldn't pitch as much as the LAN plane that brought them from Piura the night before. It had bounced so much that tears came to her eyes because she thought they would crash. And she hoped Iberia wouldn't lose their suitcase, because if it was lost, what would they wear there in Madrid, where they'd be for three days and three nights and where it seemed the weather was very cold.

"Fall is the best season of the year all over Europe," Rigoberto reassured her. "And the prettiest, I promise you. It isn't cold, it's pleasantly cool. Are you just passing through Madrid?"

"In fact we're going to Rome," said Felícito Yanaqué. "But Armida insisted that we spend a few days in Madrid simply to see it."

"My sister wanted us to go to Andalucía too," said Gertrudis. "But that would mean being away a long time and Felícito has a lot of work in Piura with the company's buses and jitneys. He's reorganizing it from top to bottom."

"Narihualá Transport is moving forward, though it always gives me some headaches," Señor Yanaqué said, smiling. "My son Tiburcio has been taking over for me. He knows the business very well, he's worked there since he was a boy. He'll do a good job, I'm certain. But, you know, you have to be on top of everything yourself, because otherwise, things start to go wrong."

"Armida invited us on this trip," said Señora Gertrudis, a touch of pride in her voice. "She's paying for everything, it's so generous. Fares, hotels, everything. And in Rome she'll put us up in her house."

"She's been so nice we couldn't turn her down over a thing like this," explained Señor Yanaqué. "Imagine what this invitation must be costing her. A fortune! Armida says she's very grateful for our putting her up. As if it was any trouble at all for us. More like a great honor."

"Well, you were very good to her during those difficult days," remarked Don Rigoberto. "You gave her affection, moral support; she needed to feel close to her family. Now she's in a magnificent situation, so she's done very well to invite you. You'll love Rome, you'll see."

Señora Gertrudis got up to go to the ladies' room. Felícito Yanaqué pointed at his wife and, lowering his voice, confessed to Don Rigoberto, "My wife is dying to see the pope. It's the dream of her life, because Gertrudis is very caught up in religion. Armida promised to take her to St. Peter's Square when the pope comes out on the balcony. And maybe she can manage to find her a place among the pilgrims the Holy Father gives an audience to on certain days. Seeing the pope and visiting the Vatican will be the greatest happiness of her life. She became very Catholic after we got married, you know. Before that she really wasn't. That's why I decided to accept this invitation. For her sake. She's always been a very good woman. Very self-sacrificing at difficult times. If it hadn't been for Gertrudis, I wouldn't have made this trip. Do you know something? I've never taken a vacation before in my life. I don't feel good if I'm not doing something. Because what I like is working."

And suddenly, with no transition, Felícito Yanaqué began telling Don Rigoberto about his father. A sharecropper in Yapatera, a humble Chulucano with no education, no shoes, whose wife left him and who, breaking his back, brought up Felícito, making him study, learn a trade, so he could move up in the world. A man who was always rectitude personified.

"Well, how lucky to have had a father like that, Don Felícito," said Don Rigoberto, getting to his feet. "You won't regret this trip, I assure you. Madrid and Rome are cities full of interesting things, you'll see."

"Yes, I wish you the best," the other man said, standing up as well. "My regards to your wife."

But it seemed to Rigoberto that he wasn't at all convinced, that he wasn't at all hopeful about the trip, that he was sacrificing him-

self for his wife. He asked Felícito if his problems had been resolved and then immediately regretted it when he saw a strand of
worry or sadness cross the face of the small man in front of him.

"Luckily everything's resolved," he murmured. "I hope this trip
at least makes the Piurans forget about me. You don't know how
horrible it is to become well known, to appear in the papers and
on television, to have people point you out on the street."

"I believe it, I believe it," said Don Rigoberto, patting him on
the shoulder. He called over the waiter and insisted on paying the
entire bill. "All right, we'll see each other on the plane. My wife
and son are over there looking for me. So long."

They went to the departure gate but boarding hadn't begun
yet. Rigoberto told Lucrecia and Fonchito that the Yanaqués were
traveling to Europe as Armida's guests. His wife was moved by the
generosity of Ismael Carrera's widow.

"You don't see things like that these days," she said. "I'll say
hello to them on the plane. They put her up for a few days in their
house and didn't suspect they'd win the lottery because of that good
deed."

In the duty-free shop she'd bought several chains of Peruvian
silver to give as mementos to nice people they met on the trip, and
Fonchito had bought a DVD of Justin Bieber, a Canadian singer
who was driving young people wild all over the world. He'd watch
it on the plane on his computer. Rigoberto began to leaf through
The Economist but then remembered that he'd better carry in his
hand the book he'd chosen to read on the trip. He opened his
carry-on and took out his old copy, bought at a bouquiniste on
the banks of the Seine, of André Malraux's essay on Goya: *Saturn*.
For many years he'd selected carefully what he read on the plane.
Experience had shown him that during a flight, he couldn't read
just anything. It had to be exciting, something that would concentrate his attention enough to cancel out completely the subliminal
preoccupation that arose in him whenever he flew, remembering he
was ten thousand meters high—ten kilometers—moving at a speed
of nine hundred or a thousand kilometers an hour, and outside the
temperature was fifty or sixty degrees below zero. It wasn't exactly
fear he felt when he flew but something even more intense, the

certainty that any moment might be the end, the disintegration of his body in a fraction of a second and, perhaps, the revelation of the great mystery: knowing what, if anything, lay beyond death, a possibility that from the point of view of his old agnosticism, scarcely attenuated by the years, he tended to reject. But a certain kind of reading managed to put a stop to that ominous sensation, reading that could absorb him so much he forgot everything else. It had happened to him with a novel by Dashiell Hammett, Italo Calvino's *Six Memos for the Next Millennium*, Claudio Magris's *Danube*, and while rereading Henry James's *The Turn of the Screw*. This time he'd chosen Malraux's essay because he remembered the emotion he felt the first time he read it, the longing it awoke in him to see in real life, not in reproductions in books, the frescoes at the Quinta del Sordo and the etchings *The Disasters of War* and *Los Caprichos*. Every time he'd been in the Prado he spent time in the rooms with the Goyas. Rereading Malraux's essay would be a nice anticipation of that pleasure.

It was wonderful that the unpleasant story had finally been settled. He was firmly resolved not to allow anything to ruin these weeks. Everything had to be pleasant, beautiful, pleasing. He wouldn't see anyone or anything that might turn out to be depressing, irritating, or ugly; he would organize all their moves so that for an entire month he'd have the permanent feeling that happiness was possible, and everything he did, heard, saw, and even smelled (this last not so easy, obviously) would contribute to it.

He was deep in this lucid daydream when he felt Lucrecia's elbow indicating that boarding had begun. In the distance they saw that Don Felícito and Doña Gertrudis were boarding in business class. The line for economy passengers was very long, of course, which meant that the plane was full. In any event, Rigoberto felt calm; he'd asked the travel agency to reserve the three seats in the tenth row, next to the emergency door, which had more leg room and made the discomforts of the flight easier to bear.

When she walked onto the plane, Lucrecia shook hands with the Piurans, and the couple greeted her with a great deal of affection. Rigoberto and his family were in fact placed in the row next to the emergency door, with ample room for their legs. He sat beside the window, Lucrecia on the aisle, and Fonchito in the middle.

Don Rigoberto sighed. He heard without listening the instructions someone from the crew was giving about the flight. When the plane began to taxi along the runway toward the point of take-off, he'd managed to become interested in an editorial in *The Economist* about whether the euro, the common currency, would survive the crisis shaking Europe, and whether the European Union would survive the disappearance of the euro. When, with the four engines roaring, the plane pulled away at a speed that increased by the second, he suddenly felt Fonchito's hand pressing his right arm. He looked away from the magazine and turned to his son: The boy was looking at him in astonishment, with an indescribable expression on his face.

"Don't be afraid, son," he said in surprise, but then he stopped talking because Fonchito was shaking his head, as if to say, "It's not that, it's not that."

The plane had just left the ground and the boy's hand clutched at his arm as if he wanted to hurt him.

"What is it, Fonchito?" he asked, glancing at Lucrecia in alarm, but she didn't hear them over the noise of the engines. His wife had her eyes closed and seemed to be dozing or praying.

Fonchito was trying to tell him something but though his mouth moved, no words passed his lips. He was very pale.

An awful premonition made Don Rigoberto lean toward his son and murmur in his ear, "We're not going to allow Edilberto Torres to fuck up this trip, are we, Fonchito?"

Now the boy did manage to speak, and what Don Rigoberto heard froze his blood.

"He's here, Papa, here on the plane, sitting right behind you. Yes, yes, Señor Edilberto Torres."

Rigoberto felt a tug at his neck and it seemed to be bruised and injured. He couldn't move his head, turn around to look at the seat behind him. His neck hurt horribly and his head had begun to boil. He had the stupid idea that his hair was smoking like a bonfire. Could it be possible that the son of a bitch was here, on this plane, traveling with them to Madrid? Fury rose in his body like irresistible lava, a savage desire to stand and attack Edilberto Torres, hit and insult him without pity until he was exhausted. In spite of the sharp pain in his neck, he finally managed to turn his upper body. But in the row behind him there was no man at all, only two older women and a little girl with a lollipop. Disconcerted, he turned to look at Fonchito, and he was greeted by a surprise: His son's eyes were sending out sparks of mockery and joy. And at that instant he burst into laughter.

"You fell for it, Papa," he said, choking on his healthy, mischievous, clean, childish laughter. "Isn't it true you fell for it? If you could have seen your face, Papa!"

Now Rigoberto, relieved, moving his head, smiled, and then he laughed too, reconciled with his son, with life. They had risen above the cloud cover and a radiant sun lit the interior of the plane.